BLOODSPOOR

2

'She's well-known?'

Liddell nodded. 'At home she's almost a celebrity.'

Schlietvan studied the photograph again. Distantly, fifteen floors below his penthouse office, the midday Johannesburg traffic rumbled up Eloff Street, the noise muffled by the sealed glass and mingling with the hum of the air-conditioner.

'Why do they do it, Mr Liddell?' He looked up shaking his head. 'You tell me that then, why do they do it?'

Liddell smiled. 'Don't I remember something about long and thick and black, Colonel?'

Schlietvan leant back in his chair, stretched out his legs and laughed.

Even after only ten minutes he liked this Britisher, but then he liked all Britishers – the real ones. Not the whining politicians with their hypocritical rantings about Apartheid. They didn't represent the true Britain. The Britain he knew was made up of the Special Branch officers from Scotland Yard who worked with his own agents in London, the people from naval intelligence who visited him on their way down to the Simonstown base, the others like this one who came from what they called the 'Foreign Office' and laughed when they used the phrase to introduce themselves.

Solid competent men, all of them. Professionals like himself who realized it was the same battle whether it was being fought in London or Johannesburg. Against communism and common vicious criminals – and who knew the two were synonymous. That's why they worked together so well: it was a freemasonry of shared conviction, one of the last that stood between the free world and the corrupt dictatorships of the Soviet bloc.

'Long and thick and black,' Schlietvan chuckled.

He tucked his legs back under the desk and hunched himself

The leopard threw no reflection at all — only the same unbroken black shadow that had enfolded the springbok before it died.

pan. The springbok herd whirled, stampeded and galloped terrified back across the grass. Beyond them a column of wildebeeste broke into a lumbering anxious trot. Some zebra cantered in wild aimless circles, three trotting jackals stopped, fore-feet frozen in mid-stride, a spotted hyena changed direction and came forwards barking uncertainly.

The leopard growled, a deep challenging snarl. Then to seal its claim to the territory and the prey, it urinated carefully round the buck's body. Afterwards, it picked up the buck by the shoulder, shook it grunting until the carcass hung easily towards the ground, climbed with it back into the tree and settled down to eat.

Twenty minutes later, belly full after forty-eight hours without food, the leopard dropped back to the earth and set off north-west through the bush. Most of the pan beyond the thicket of scrub and thorn was level grassy plain. But on the far side there was a bare sandy depression, grey-white in the starlight, with a bowl of rainwater at its centre.

The leopard padded over the crusted sand to the edge of the water. Then before drinking it gazed across the surface at the upward slope beyond.

Two small fires glowed there in the darkness. The fires had been burning in the same place for six nights, the period since the leopard had last moved its hunting territory north. Well before then, it had become used to their presence. Ever since it had started to travel restlessly across the desert the mounds of flame had never been more than a few miles from the kills.

The fires were no longer a threat – nor was the woman who sat between them on the grass bank looking down. The leopard growled in her direction, a token gesture of challenge and territorial right now. Then it began to drink.

For an instant as its head went down to the pool the woman stiffened and caught her breath. She'd been observing the animal for three months but each time she saw it again she felt the same shock of awe and disbelief as when she'd seen it first.

There was no moon but in the brilliance of the Kalahari stars the animal's reflection should have shown clear, roseate, white-dappled in the water.

1

The leopard lay utterly still on the branch.

Before, when the herd of springbok had come into the range of its vision, its tail had stiffened and the tip had flicked backwards and forwards, slowly, silently, delicately. Now there was no movement at all, not even the lift of the breast muscles as it breathed.

The herd, fanning out as they grazed, drifted in a crescent across the pan. They reached the low scrub rimming the trees, separated into groups and moved forwards.

One young buck, foraging ahead of the rest, skittered nervously as an eagle owl planed down the night air and then soared effortlessly towards the stars. The buck stood for a moment tense, nostrils flared, leg tendons quivering for flight. Then, the owl's shadow gone, it lowered its head and moved into the cone of darkness below the thorn-tree where the grass, sheltered from the Kalahari sun, was thicker and sweeter than the dry turf beyond.

An instant later the buck registered another shadow against the starlit gaps between the branches, a shadow like the owl's but vast and black and travelling so fast that this time the buck wasn't even able to lift its head. There was no sound, merely a ruffle in the air. Then two hundred pounds of bone, muscle, claw and tooth came smashing down through the leaves.

The leopard's front talons ripped deep into the buck's haunches, its jaws searched for, caught and savaged the pale slender throat, and the antelope collapsed, dead instantly with spine, thigh bones and neck shattered.

The kill did raise noises. Small muted noises – the thud of the leopard's weight crushing the buck against the hard winter earth, the rustle of grass, the pumping of blood from the open neck artery – but loud enough to alert every other animal in the

1

BLOODSPOOR

Published by
The Dial Press/James Wade
1 Dag Hammarskjold Plaza
New York, New York 10017

Originally published in Great Britain by Raven Books, London,
in association with Macdonald and Jane's Publishers.

Manufactured in the United States of America

First U.S.A. printing

Library of Congress Cataloging in Publication Data

McVean, James.
Bloodspoor.

I. Title.
PZ4.M1768B   1978   [PR6063.A284]   823'.9'14
ISBN 0-8037-0863-7   78-2653

James McVean

BLOODSPOOR

The Dial Press / James Wade
New York

last book.

'She's published two works, or rather she was a contributor to one and wrote the second under her own name. The first was an analysis of prey taken by a pride of lions in the Kruger National Park, she did that with a group of Americans. The second, the one that made her "famous", so to speak, was about cheetahs in East Africa. A television documentary went with it, she appeared on various chat shows, I gather she comes over as a bit of a character and, well, it more or less turned her into a household name —'

Schlietvan nodded. The effect of her television appearances was news to him, but the rest he knew. He'd also read her publisher's biography – a copy of her book had been on his desk that morning.

'Just after Christmas,' Liddell went on, 'she came out to Botswana. She told our High Commission people there she was going to spend six months in the bush looking at leopards. She also gave them a contact, a charter pilot she'd hired to fly supplies to her camp once a month. The idea was that if she had any problems or anyone wanted to get in touch with her, the pilot would act as a courier.'

'Which is exactly what he did, right?'

Schlietvan tapped the pages lying by the photograph. Five of them. Not the originals, of course – they were still at the British High Commission in Gaborone – but copies of a telex transcription, identical to the ones which had reached Liddell in London early the previous day.

Five pages of rhetoric. Rambling, incoherent, misspelt, but chilling too in its bitter impassioned rage. A fluttering white bundle anchored to a stone cairn which had been all that was left of Alison Welborough-Smith's camp when the charter pilot arrived there on his monthly flight.

Liddell nodded. 'He read the first few lines, flew straight back and handed them in to the High Commissioner. I got the alert and the full text yesterday. The only other thing that's reached me is the pilot's report about the camp site. He didn't stay long, he didn't know if the group was still around. But he thought it hadn't been stripped recently; it could have

7

happened two or three weeks ago. So, God knows where they've got her now.'

They. *The Army of the Wind before the Storm* as they'd grandiloquently signed themselves at the foot of the final page. A group of black terrorists who'd seized Miss Welborough-Smith, destroyed her camp and were holding her hostage against a ransom to be paid by the British government in weapons – the list was typed out in clumsy painstaking detail – within thirty days of the pilot's flight, with the threat that if it wasn't she would be killed.

'Whoever the hell they are, we've never heard of them before,' Liddell added: 'And I imagine you haven't either.'

Schlietvan shook his head. 'Not as such, no. But then of course there's this strange coincidence, this business of the Mlanda connection. Maybe that gets us somewhere —'

He paused and Liddell sat back and waited.

George Mlanda. A brilliant, daring and ruthless black independence leader. A man who'd been born in South Africa, fled the country as a youth to join the Zimbabwe nationalist movement, and made himself a legend to the local Rhodesian population with a series of raids against the white forces from across the Mozambique border.

Yet for Mlanda the 'liberation' of Rhodesia was only a first step, the snapping of the weakest link in the chain of white dominance. His real aim, the final goal, was the overthrow of the white regime in his homeland, South Africa itself. For Schlietvan that made the guerrilla commander one of the most wanted men in the southern half of the continent.

Liddell knew all of that from the files. He also knew that there was a link between Mlanda and Alison Welborough-Smith.

'It was last Monday,' Schlietvan continued. 'One of our patrols up on the Caprivi strip ran into a group crossing it from the Angolan side in the darkness. There was the usual quick fire-fight, the usual panic and the *munds* ran. But they left three behind, two dead, one lightly wounded. The patrol called in a helicopter, the wounded man was brought down here and he talked —'

8

The South African's voice was flat, quiet, making a statement of the obvious in his harsh nasal accent. When people were handed over to the Bureau of State Security they talked – there was no other possibility.

'He didn't know much, he was a young trainee learning to tell one end of a rifle from the other. But he said one thing of interest. His training camp was in southern Angola. Two months ago Mlanda paid it a visit. The boy was excited, impressed like they all were. After the usual morale speech he stayed near the fire while Mlanda ate with the camp commandant. Mlanda was talking and laughing and boasting. The boy heard him say he'd screwed this white woman in Tanzania a couple of years before, and now she was in Botswana watching leopards and she was going to be very valuable. That was all, but it was enough. We made a check — '

Schlietvan smiled. 'You will forgive us, I'm sure, our own sources in your High Commission, Mr Liddell.'

'Doubt we could stop you even if we didn't,' Liddell laughed back.

'Well, we checked and there was no other possibility. It had to be this Welborough-Smith woman. That was Wednesday. We sent you the standard notification right away in case something was planned for her. Twenty-four hours later I get your telex and I know it's not just planned – it's happened. And today, just to complete everything, you arrive. Like I say, it's a coincidence, no?'

Liddell nodded in agreement as Schlietvan chuckled once more.

Two years earlier, while she was working on her cheetah book in Tanzania, Mlanda had met Miss Welborough-Smith. Naïve, perhaps lonely, probably sexually frustrated, maybe idealistic and overwhelmed by his reported charisma, she'd had a brief affair with him.

Well, she was paying a savage price now for whatever pleasure she'd had then. Mlanda had used her, moved on, then decided she could be of further use to him – far greater use than a conquest he could boast about round a camp fire. She must have told him about her plan to study leopards in the Kalahari when she'd finished with the cheetahs. He'd remembered that, possibly learned of her new-found fame as a naturalist and sent one of his guerrilla units into Botswana to seize her and hold her to ransom – a ransom that could not be paid under any circumstances whatsoever.

'I assume you won't meet any of these demands, Mr Liddell?'

Schlietvan had obviously realized what he was thinking. Liddell shook his head firmly.

'There's no possibility even of negotiation,' he said, 'An unequivocal directive was issued to all our embassies several years ago. Whoever the hostage, whatever was at stake, our government would never treat on ransom terms with any kidnapper. That holds good today – in this case or in any other.'

'But if this woman was killed,' Schlietvan folded his powerful arms on the table-top, 'it would create a difficult and unpleasant situation?'

'It would be a bloody nightmare,' Liddell said crisply.

That, if anything, was an understatement. When the directive went out the assumption was that future victims would continue to be employees of commercial concerns – and the ransoms demanded levelled against those concerns. Until now the assumption had proved correct. But it had also had to take into account the virtually unthinkable, that one day the government itself might be held to ransom.

With Alison Welborough-Smith the unthinkable had become fact. Not only that but in the worst possible way. The hostage a woman and a publicly-known wildlife expert. The reason for her plight a salacious and headline-grabbing sexual relationship. The country where she was held a former British protectorate. And the choice offered the most provocative of all – either a surrender to terrorist blackmail or its rejection which would be taken as tacit support for the policies of Apartheid.

Liddell looked at the South African security chief, grim, angry, blank-faced.

In one sense the decision had already been made by the outstanding directive; there could be no surrender to blackmail.

10

But even if it hadn't the result of the alternative would be identical – as he'd said, a nightmare.

'Do you know the Kalahari, Mr Liddell?'

Liddell shook his head again.

'Please look at this — '

Schlietvan stood up, walked to the far end of the large thickly-carpeted room and pressed a button below a Perspex frame on the wall. Instantly, the frame was backlit by a strong yellow-white glow.

'My new toy — '

He laughed happily as Liddell joined him in front of the screen, and tapped the button several times. Each time the image on the screen changed, showing successively larger-scale sections of a relief map.

'Within half a minute I can be looking at any part of Africa south of the equator on a scale as big as one inch to the mile. But let's start with an overall view — '

He pressed the button again and the southern half of the continent came into focus.

'This, of course, is the general area we're concerned with. Your former colony, Bechuanaland, and now our neighbour Botswana — '

Schlietvan touched the Perspex to the north of the South African border.

The independent black republic of Botswana – the name had been changed with independence eleven years before. Huge, impoverished, land-locked. A country the size of France with barely three-quarters of a million inhabitants and only fifty miles of paved road. The population lived mainly in a string of little towns and villages to the east of the capital, Gaborone. Apart from that there was nothing but the barren wilderness of the Kalahari desert – stretching for mile after mile north and south and west.

'Let's look closer. Any section will do but we might as well use one that contains the coordinates. If you please, Mr Liddell—'

Schlietvan pointed at the desk. Liddell went over and returned with the telex copies of the document the pilot had

11

found at the camp.

In the ransom demand the terrorists had stipulated that the British government's reply was to be dropped by parachute in a canister at a point in the desert for which they'd given map co-ordinates. Instructions for the delivery of the weapons would be left for collection in the same canister the following day. Any attempt to approach the point on the ground by a rescue force would result in the immediate death of their captive.

Schlietvan looked at the telex sheet, consulted a chart by the frame and tapped the button again. A further series of images flashed across the screen, stabilizing finally in a pattern of green and brown and grey. Liddell leant forwards. It was a colour-imposed aerial photograph – the desert was too big and too uniform to make a ground survey worthwhile – showing a number of round grey depressions, the pans, some coils and patches of green, the scrub, and linking them all the flat brown spaces of sand.

Nothing else, not even a contour line. Just that abstract pattern of washed-out colours which represented a single section of the vastness of the Kalahari.

'In fact, the precise point is here,' Schlietvan's stubby finger on the Perspex once more. 'Inside the central game reserve as it happens. But it could be anywhere — '

The South African stepped back, his face momentarily shadowed against the morning light from the window.

'I know that desert well, Mr Liddell. As a young man my father took me there many times to hunt. There is a rare breed of person who falls in love with places like that. He was one such; I was not. It is hard, wild, dangerous – in my view full of stupid unnecessary dangers. One year I was proved right and we almost died — '

Schlietvan turned and Liddell followed him back to the desk as he went on talking.

'There were five of us on safari. My father, myself, three boys. Two days out my father decided to zero a new rifle he'd bought. He put up a target not far from the truck, fired maybe a dozen shots, then we went on. Half an hour later the truck came to a stop. We discovered one of my father's shots had ricocheted a full fifty yards off a rock and punctured the underside of our main gasolene tank. We had lost sixteen gallons. In our reserve cans we had just ten—'

He sat down and paused, waiting to see if Liddell understood. Liddell shook his head frowning.

'Water, Mr Liddell, water. That was what was important, not the gasolene. We had supplies for three days' driving to the next well. Only now we could only drive half the way, the rest would have to be on foot and take twice as long. So our water supplies would run out before we got there, *if* we got there—'

Schlietvan shrugged. 'We were lucky. One of the kaffir boys collapsed with heat exhaustion. He never worked again. My father spent a month in hospital recovering from dehydration. But we all made it, we all lived — '

Schlietvan pushed everything aside and leant forwards over the desk.

'In the Kalahari water is always desperately short, Mr Liddell. At this time of year it's scarcer than ever. We're approaching our African mid-winter and the last of the rains are drying up. It was like that during our trip. Had there been one more of us then, six and not five, the ending would have been very different.'

Liddell thought for a moment and said, 'Are you suggesting that, whatever group it is who've grabbed this woman, there aren't likely to be many men involved?'

Schlietvan nodded emphatically. 'Ten perhaps, certainly no more. Logistically, it would just not be possible to support them.'

Liddell frowned again. 'Whether she's being held by an army or a mere handful, the problem's the same.'

'I think not, Mr Liddell, but first let me put it like this. We both want this Welborough-Smith woman out of there alive. I, because I wish to learn what she knows about Mlanda – he may even have led the operation himself. You, because you can't either afford to pay the ransom or not to pay it, right?'

Liddell shrugged.

Of course that was the case. And furthermore, as they both

13

knew, the Botswana government couldn't be involved in any attempt to release her. Committed to black nationalism yet economically dependent upon the white regime to the south, it would be paralyzed.

'Ten blacks, young, probably inexperienced, maybe even out on their first mission — '

Schlietvan's voice was quiet now and speculative.

'That shouldn't be impossible. Not for a good man, a white, of course. A man who knew the desert, who could reach the drop-zone on foot, hide up there, follow them after they've collected the canister to wherever they've taken the woman, and then launch a surprise attack on their camp. Maybe a couple of reliable natives with him to provide back-up fire-power. But that's all he'd need — '

He stopped and Liddell looked at him intently. He suddenly understood what the South African was proposing and it made sense, total sense. More than that, he could see it was the only possibility.

'And you've got someone who could try that?' Liddell asked.

'From the Bureau?' Schlietvan listed his hand in mock horror. 'Mr Liddell, with our new policy of détente with black Africa the most I'm allowed now is a few low-profile observers up there. If something went wrong with this and we were found to be involved — '

He closed his eyes briefly and shook his head.

'Who've you got in mind then?'

'Well, he has to meet certain conditions,' Schlietvan rapped them out with his thumb on the desk. 'Know the desert backwards; have the training, nerve and experience to tackle an operation like this; above all, be in a position where he couldn't refuse to take it on – at least not if the offer came from you.'

Liddell stared at him, puzzled, but before he could say anything Schlietvan chuckled and continued.

'Part of my business, Mr Liddell, is keeping up to date on people in trouble,' he said. 'I'm thinking of a man in very serious trouble, a man you can do a great favour to in return for the woman. If he's successful, I get just a few hours with

14

her afterwards. Let me explain — '

Schlietvan switched on the intercom and spoke to his secretary again. Then he started.

3

'Give me a Castle.'

'Yes, sir.'

The African barman reached under the counter and pulled out a bottle, wet with condensation from the ice-box. He snapped off the metal cap and started to pour the beer into a glass tankard.

'Hell, no, leave it inside.'

Haston reached over, took the bottle and drank straight from the neck, draining it in a few seconds and beckoning for another. Then he glanced round. No one else yet at the long horseshoe of stools in the dusky light but they'd arrive soon enough. No hour was too early to start drinking in Gaborone, but ten in the morning was an accepted norm and there were only a few minutes to go.

The second bottle clunked down on the counter, spraying drops of water across the mahogany, and Haston picked it up. His wrist was shaking as he drank again, his mouth felt raw from the ash and sour wine of the night before, and his head throbbed savagely. He lowered the bottle half-empty, started to swear under his breath, then stopped as the door clattered open behind him.

Footsteps rang on the space of tiled floor between the door and the carpet and someone laughed. Haston sat resolutely facing the bar. Then a voice called out.

'Jerry!'

He turned round. It was Andy Vaughan, and Haston felt a wave of relief relax the tension in his shoulders as he saw him.

Andy, a pilot and an old friend, was all right. In fact, Andy had been the first to know and was still the only person Haston had spoken to about it. Andy had flown Haston out of the camp and Haston had told him everything, sitting slumped in the passenger seat with a cargo of trophies stinking behind them.

16

That was three days ago. Since then Haston had stayed shut-away alone in his apartment with some cartons of cigarettes, crates of drink and a bitter drunken fury.

'So you've emerged at last,' Vaughan came over and clapped him on the back. 'How are you doing, old son?'

Haston lifted the bottle. 'Manual for survival.'

He grinned and Vaughan said, 'That's the spirit. Look, I've got a couple of clients who want me to do some runs to Ghanzi.' He indicated two men who'd come in with him. 'Soon as I've settled the details I'll be back and we'll have a few together.'

'Okay, Andy, take care.'

Vaughan went off and a few minutes later the door clattered open again. A group of visiting Japanese businessmen. They didn't matter. But the ones who did wouldn't be far behind, the ones he'd lived and drank and talked and hunted and laughed with for seven years.

They weren't far behind. Bill Roberts was the first, another pilot who worked the Jo'burg-Capetown route and had often flown Haston down for weekends in the south. He crossed the floor and waved casually.

'Good to see you again, Jerry. I'll be with you later.'

Haston waved back. Normally, Roberts would have joined him right away. This time he sat down on the far side of the bar and occupied himself with a copy of the *Rand Daily Mail*. Unlike Vaughan, who'd meant what he said, Haston knew that Roberts wouldn't join him later.

He lit a cigarette and inhaled the smoke slowly, steadying himself with a deliberate act of will against the recurring waves of anger. It wasn't Roberts' fault and Haston didn't blame him. It was just that the community was too small, the amount of business too limited, the competition too fierce, the tensions and pressures to strong. Reputation was everything, the word-of-mouth recommendation that was passed around and secured the few jobs going – whether they were for a hunter or a pilot.

For Roberts to be seen drinking with Haston now was to run one hell of a risk, an unacceptable risk, the risk of being associated with what he'd done. Sense. Simple hard commonsense. A

17

good hunter was a magnet because of the other services his clients needed. A hunter who'd lost his licence was a leper. Only three days ago he'd been in the first category. Now to all intents and purposes he was in the second.

Haston smashed his palm upwards against the base of the counter and felt ripples of pain travel up his arm.

Why? What in the name of Christ had got into him? It would have been so simple to have left it alone, to have said sorry but that's the way it goes. Clients weren't guaranteed a trophy whatever they paid for their safari. They accepted that and no one was going to blame him that the hyenas – or more likely those little yellow bastards, the bushmen – had taken the leopard bait three nights in succession.

But he hadn't left it alone. He'd fired that one wild crazy shot and Anderson had discovered and exactly an hour later he was on the supply flight out. It wasn't Anderson's fault either. If Anderson hadn't dismissed him instantly and made a report to the Game Department, he'd have put the whole concession at risk. It was nobody's fault but his own and he cursed again, spitting the words out silently between his teeth, at the blind mindless stupidity of what he'd done.

'Hullo, stranger — '

Haston swung round. Gail Black from the pharmacy on the Mall. Pert and blonde and smiling – she was wearing rope-soled sandals and he hadn't heard her come in.

'What are you doing here? I thought you'd got another week out in the wilds.'

'You didn't hear?' He looked at her puzzled.

'Hear what?' She frowned. 'I just got back now from ten days in the Cape. What's been going on?'

'You go get yourself a Castle,' Haston said firmly, 'Talk to a few people and find out. Then, if you still feel like it, come back and I'll buy you one myself. But not before.'

She looked at him uncertainly and walked away.

Haston watched her go. Slim legs, firm buttocks under her denim skirt, thick yellow hair bouncing on her shoulders. He'd had his eye on her for a couple of months and she might come back even when she knew, but not for what he'd planned, what he'd done with all the others. That was something else which had gone now.

Christ, how many had there been? He couldn't remember and it didn't matter because the number was carved on the door of his apartment, a notch for each of them cut on the frame with his hunting knife after he'd turned them out. But seven years as a professional hunter, say, five full safaris a season – he'd never turned in a safari without scoring a new one – and then all the others. The ones he'd pulled in the summer months when the concession areas were closed, the ones on weekends in Jo'burg or the Cape, the others he'd collected when he lit home for the States each year.

Maybe damn close on eighty in all. Eighty little pussy-cats that he'd spoored and dropped and humped. Well, Miss Gail Black wasn't going to get laid that way and the rage came once more as he thought about it, coiling viciously inwards and blurring even the hangover.

They came quickly after Gail. Clark Bishop, small, paunchy, wise-cracking, an Australian who ran one of the local travel agencies. Piet Sturmer and Larry Verney together, both hunters with another concession company, Botswana Game, resting between safaris. Val Archer, the girl with the biggest tits in town who drank herself blind regularly every Friday night and laid a different man each week. Meadows from the Dodge garage, Walsey of the Land Use Department, Ric Sheehan, another American like himself, on loan from the UN for a cattle study programme.

Maybe twenty in all, virtually everyone he'd known well since he'd settled in Gaborone. And from each of them, in different ways, in different degrees, the sequence of reaction he'd expected. The surprised greeting, from some a fumbling expression of sympathy, from others an embarrassed avoidance of the whole subject, a booming over-hearty disregard of what they'd heard, from others still a lamely confident declaration that it was all a misunderstanding and everything would still turn out fine.

But invariably at the end the excuse and the awkward movement away – leaving Haston sitting there alone with a circle of empty stools round him.

He took it all, talking, laughing, shaking hands, watching them leave, and then drinking the beers that he was calling for, faster and faster. Throwing them down, his mouth still raw but his head muzzy now, to dull the acid sense of contempt, disgust and waste.

'You back already, Jerry — ?'

Haston's head jerked up and he swivelled on the stool.

Walt Meegeren. He'd have known anyway without looking from the smell of gin which reached him the next moment. In his late forties. Plump, brick-faced, jovial and plausible. A smart-assed wheeler and dealer who lived off the pickings of others and happened to hold a hunter's licence, although the concession companies only employed him as a last resort when no one else was available.

The rest of them round the bar, even if they were reluctant to sit with Haston now, would be genuinely sorry for what had happened. Not Meegeren. Meegeren would be delighted and not just because every hunter less increased his chances of a safari, but because Meegeren was a four-square, copper-bottomed, through-and-through bastard.

'Of course, I'd forgotten,' he shook his head solicitously. 'I was sorry to hear about that, Jerry, truly sorry.'

'To hear about what?'

Haston kept his voice level with another conscious act of will.

'Why, that business down near Tshane — '

'What business near Tshane?'

The control was going now. He tried to hold onto it, keep it tight and close and casual as he'd promised himself he would, as he'd managed to do with the others. But looking at the bland ingenuous face, hearing the empty gloating words, he could feel it remorselessly slipping away.

'Oh, come on, Jerry, don't take it so hard. What are you kidding about? Everyone knows — '

'Listen, you little bastard — '

Haston came off the stool fast, seeing Meegeren suddenly through a surging red haze, reaching out with one hand for his shirt collar, clenching the other to smash it into his mouth.

20

'What happened at Tshane's my bloody business, no one else's. One more word from you — '

'Cool it, fellow!'

Another voice, a figure between him and Meegeren, an arm against his chest pushing him back towards the bar. Andy Vaughan.

Haston held onto the shirt for a moment longer. Then he slowly loosened his fingers, let go and stepped back still shaking as the pent-up fury drained away.

'Why don't you go somewhere else, man, like a long way off,' Vaughan said.

Meegeren shrugged and walked away, and Haston climbed back on the stool.

'Thanks, Andy, and sorry.'

'The hell with it!' Vaughan signalled the barman to bring another beer. 'He's a little creep, but that's not going to help anyone. Get outside this instead.'

The bottle slid along the counter, Haston lifted it and took a long swallow.

'I'm almost through,' Vaughan went on. 'But it'll be another few minutes yet. We'll talk about it then. Meantime you stay here and don't try anything else. Promise?'

Haston nodded. 'Okay, promise.'

Another calming tap on his shoulder, then Vaughan was heading back across the floor to rejoin his clients.

Haston finished the bottle and gazed down at his shadowy reflection in the polished mahogany. Strangely, the flare of violence had cleared the muzziness; the ache in his temples had gone and even his wrists had stopped trembling. In a way it had left him feeling worse. Before there'd been the muddled rage to feed on, the self-pity to fight down, the façade of light-hearted defiance to keep up as he faced the others.

Now all of that was spent and instead there was just a dull weary nothingness.

'You Mr Haston, sir?'

The boy must have been watching from the door, waiting until the incident was over. He'd come silently up to the stool and was standing beside it, lanky, diffident, a barefoot black

21

teenager.

'What the hell do you want?'

'Gentleman ask me to give you this, sir.'

It was an envelope with his name typed on the front. Haston ripped it open, pulled out the single sheet of unheaded paper and read the few lines.

'Your name has been given me by a mutual friend. I am interested in arranging a safari at rather short notice, and would like to discuss this with you.

'Unfortunately, my car, a cream Ford, has broken down on the side road to the dam. Would you be kind enough to meet me there, where I am waiting for a repair truck.

'For reasons I will explain I would ask you not to mention this to anyone until we have spoken.

'I should add that I believe I can help you solve your recent difficulty.'

There was no signature, just an indecipherable pair of initials at the foot of the page. Haston read the letter twice, then he looked at the boy.

'Who gave you this?'

'Gentleman, sir.'

'What sort of gentleman?'

The boy shrugged. '*Morena*, sir.'

Morena. 'Chief'. The Setswana term for any white man of authority.

'And where did the *Morena* give it to you?'

'On the road here, sir,' the boy pointed towards the window. 'Right now.'

Haston thought for a moment. Then he fumbled in his pocket, found a fifty-cent coin, gave it to the boy and waved him away. Afterwards he read the page again.

It stank, everything about it. The unnamed mutual 'friend'. The car that had conveniently broken down on the side road to the dam, a hidden rocky track Haston knew well – the place you went to with a girl for a quick one because few other people used it even at weekends. The *morena* who had somehow managed to

22

give the boy the letter a few minutes earlier just outside, although his car was immobile several miles away.

Haston crumpled the sheet, balling it between his fingers until his knuckles were white.

The bastards, both of them, the cheap bastards. The one who'd come up with Haston's name and the one who'd written. Because he knew what it meant, what was involved. Someone, a visiting businessman probably with a couple of days on his hands, wanted to knock something over. Elephant or lion or buffalo, the expensive ones, that's what they usually went for. Only they hadn't time to get a game licence and they didn't want to pay the fee. They just wanted the trophy – and a hunter to find it for them.

A bent hunter. Haston glanced along the bar. None of them there would have done it except that little swine Meegeren perhaps. But even if it wasn't Meegeren, someone else. Someone knew he was in trouble and, when this figure had asked around, had told him Haston would do the job with no questions asked for a cash payment on the side.

He swore, tossed the crumpled letter into an ashtray, tilted his cigarette and jabbed the burning end into the wad of paper, watching it smoulder and glow.

Then he stopped. There was something else, something that made no sense at all.

'I should add that I believe I can help you solve your recent difficulty.'

Why that? Money, yes, that would have figured – even on regular safaris hunters were sometimes offered a 'special present' by some punk of a client hell-bent on returning with his trophy. But Haston's 'difficulty' wasn't just money – it was the licence, something no amount of cash was going to solve. And the man must have known that when he'd written the letter.

So why in the name of fortune waste time in holding out an inducement Haston could establish was worthless within minutes of meeting the man – long before there was any possibility of agreeing to take him out?

Haston waited until the paper dissolved into a pile of grey ash and the trail of smoke had drifted away. Then he pivoted on his stool again. The bar was packed now with the full lunchtime crowd, talking, laughing, jostling each other. Through the throng of figures he could see Vaughan still closeted with the couple who wanted to fly to Ghanzi – the negotiations were obviously taking longer than Vaughan had imagined.

He frowned and hesitated. Then he threw a five-rand note on the counter and walked quickly out through the hotel towards the sun-baked space of gravel where he'd parked his car.

Midday now. The sky a brilliant unbroken blue and the heat strong and clean and dry.

Haston turned left out of the entrance, drove past the airfield with its single clay landing strip shimmering dusty red in the sunlight, and headed south on the Lobatse road. The dam was only three miles outside Gaborone but as always it took him twenty minutes to get there; the metalled surface ended at the town limits and afterwards there was just a sandy cratered track. He bumped carefully along it until he reached the junction with the side road, cut the engine and got out.

The cream Ford was parked where the letter-writer had said, about fifty yards up the side road under a tree with the dam water glittering through the thorn scrub beyond. A man was leaning over the hood, tall, moustached, incongrously dressed in a thick tweed jacket and dark grey trousers. He seemed to have been gazing at the water, but when Haston appeared he glanced round and stood up.

Haston looked at him for a moment. Then he walked up to the car.

'Haston,' he said. 'Jerry Haston.'

The man held out his hand. 'I'm pleased to meet you, Mr Haston. My name's Liddell.'

Haston shook hands. The accent had been English, the clear precisely-modulated English that the High Commission people spoke, only he knew all of them and he'd never seen this one before.

'You wrote that note?'

24

Liddell nodded. 'Thank you for coming so promptly. I'm sorry it was at such short notice.'

'What can I do for you – or what might I be able to do for you?'

As he spoke there was the roar of a truck on the Lobatse road. The junction with the track was out of sight, hidden by a screen of bush, but Liddell frowned, followed the sound, head cocked to one side, until it faded away, then looked back at Haston.

'Would you mind if we talked inside the car? I don't want to appear unnecessarily secretive, but I do wish to keep this quite private.'

Haston hesitated. If the man really did want to fix up a quick game safari without a licence, then the request was reasonable enough. After what had happened at Tshane, Haston was poison and anyone seeing a stranger talking to him in a place like that wouldn't just start wondering – they'd start talking.

Yet he was bewildered. There was a type who wanted that sort of safari and he knew them and this one just didn't fit. Not with the tweed jacket, the quiet English voice, the military moustache, not in any way. Liddell didn't want game – he was after something else.

Haston shrugged. 'It's the same to me.'

The Ford had had a trailer conversion unit built onto the chassis, a metal-frame cabin behind the driving compartment with large unglazed windows like the ones made for game-viewing vehicles except these had plastic curtains tacked over them. Liddell lifted the tailgate and another man climbed out, younger and fair-haired but also wearing a jacket and dark trousers.

'This is my assistant, Mr Kennedy,' Liddell said. 'He'll keep an eye open from the front just to make quite sure we're not disturbed.'

The new one, Kennedy, smiled pleasantly, went round to the hood and propped himself against it in the place where Liddell had been leaning before.

'Please—'

Liddell gestured inside and Haston clambered up. A folding table ran down the centre with a padded bench on either side.

As Haston settled himself on one of the benches, Liddell inspected him quickly.

Medium height and lightly built but with a hard wiry body, sun-tanned and sinewy, under the faded bush shirt and shorts. Corn-coloured hair, pale-brown eyes flecked with green and a strong mouth in a lean fierce face, almost hungry in its thinness. A compulsive and inveterate womanizer, Schlietvan's file had described him, and Liddell could see instantly why the American would be so successful in that direction.

He wondered whether the rest of the assessment was as accurate: impulsive, reckless and short-tempered, but immensely resourceful, a first-class hunter and outstanding shot — in short a 'superbly-equipped natural killer dedicated to his profession', the summary had concluded. If that was right, then, as Schlietvan himself had said, Haston might be the ideal man for the job.

'Mr Haston,' Liddell sat down opposite him, 'I don't want to waste your time, so I'll get straight on with what I'd like to discuss. I work for a department of the British Foreign Office. I understand you're in a certain amount of trouble. As I said in my letter, in return for your cooperation over something else, I believe I can solve that trouble for you.'

'Now just a moment,' Haston interrupted. 'What the hell is this? First of all are we talking about something private or official?'

Liddell thought for a moment. 'In one sense I suppose you could call it official. In another, and much more importantly, it's private. In fact, it's so private that if I discovered you'd even mentioned this conversation to anyone else, I would immediately use our very considerable influence in this country to — well, I don't imagine I need spell it out.'

He didn't. Haston gazed at him across the table in the chequered dust-moted light and once again the anger came welling up.

It was his day for bastards and this was another — not the one he'd been expecting, the crook trophy client, but a bastard all the same. Maybe even a bigger one. Sleek and polite and unctuous who thought he could blackmail Haston into taking on whatever cheap little scheme it was by threatening to have him thrown out of Botswana if he didn't.

Well, Mr Liddell had got it wrong – he'd got it badly wrong.

'Listen, I can save you some breath, mister,' Haston stabbed out a finger. 'I don't give a damn for you or your bloody influence. You've made a mistake. The problems I've got are going to get me declared a prohibited immigrant anyway. There's nothing more you can toss on top of that. So you can take your tricksy little safari, whatever the hell it is, and ram it up someone else's orifice. Meantime, I'm going right back to the hotel and I'm going to tell anyone who's interested there's a couple of UK Foreign Office figures hanging around the backside of the dam handing out bent proposals. Maybe you can "discuss" that with the Gaborone police.'

Haston stopped, slid down the bench and stood up beside the open tailgate.

Liddell watched him. Then, as Haston was about to jump down, he said quietly, 'You'd be rather silly if you did, Mr Haston. You see, I think you're forgetting British influence out here can work both ways.'

Haston checked, hands gripping the roof bar, knees already bent for the leap to the sandy whiteness of the track.

Outside a roller swooped down, plucked an insect from the air and vanished in a swallow-tailed dazzle of turquoise wing feathers. A lizard skittered through the dust, the shadow of a passing eagle rippled over the thorn, somewhere a lauri-bird called – raucous and insistent.

Haston waited immobile, a crouching silhouette against the square of sunlight. Then he lowered his arms, straightened up and turned slowly back towards Liddell.

'What is it you want?' he said.

The surge of anger, the exhaustion after the night before, the lingering strain of facing the people at the bar, everything had momentarily made him forget the curious statement in the letter and Liddell's echo of it at the table. Now he remembered – and he understood.

'Let's be clear what you want first,' Liddell waved him back to the bench. 'You're a licensed professional hunter, one of

27

about forty in this country, I believe. I'm not familiar with Game Department regulations, but I gather three days ago you shot a buck as leopard bait for one of your hunting clients. The buck was in excess of your quota, apparently a serious offence. The managing director of your safari company discovered, he fired you and made a report to the Department. In short order, they'll take away your licence; as you say you'll be told to leave the country; and furthermore you'll never be allowed to hunt professionally again anywhere else — '

He paused. 'Unless of course someone intercedes on your behalf.'

Haston said nothing. Someone. Someone powerful enough to overrule the report and silence the Game Department. Someone who in Botswana could only be the British — the country's administrator for almost a hundred years before Independence and still by far its largest source of foreign aid.

'Mr Haston,' Liddell leant forward, 'I'm prepared to make that intercession. I can guarantee you'll keep your licence. I can also guarantee you'll get your job back with Anderson and Mahoney as if nothing at all had happened. In fact, I think I can guarantee just about everything you want at this moment.'

'Because you've taken a sudden fancy to my pretty face for instance?'

Liddell ignored him. Instead he pulled out a photograph from his wallet pocket and unfolded a map that had been lying on the table.

'She's called Alison Welborough-Smith,' he handed Haston the photograph. 'And she's somewhere here — '

Liddell touched a spot on the map, and started.

There wasn't much to tell. What there was he told quickly and simply: the capture, the discovery of the ransom demand, the site for the canister to be dropped, the suggestion that one man, Haston, with a couple of Africans to support him could trace the terrorists to their camp in the bush, launch a surprise attack and rescue the woman.

All he left out was Schlietvan's contribution and the woman's connection with Mlanda. The first because, as the South African had said, if Haston had any idea the Bureau of State

28

Security was involved, he wouldn't even hear the proposal out: in independent black Botswana, if there was one thing worse than breaking game laws, it was to be connected with BOSS. Mlanda for the same reason. Given Mlanda's reputation Haston might have guessed BOSS was bound to be involved anyway.

There was a third factor he omitted too, of course: the necessary and logical consequence of the whole operation. But that was something very private, something for him and Schlietvan alone.

'What did you say her name was?'

Liddell had finished. Haston had listened to the story in dazed bewildered silence. Now, instinctively, still not really understanding or taking it in, he reached for the photograph again.

'Alison Welborough-Smith.'

'Jesus, what a mouthful!' Haston wrinkled his face. 'And those coordinates for the drop-zone?'

'Here.'

Liddell had written them on a piece of paper. He pushed it across the table, Haston took it, swivelled the map round and found the place – a little pan north of the Moretse depression in one of the Kalahari's great areas of emptiness.

Haston studied them both. The woman's face with the curling black hair rolling off the high-necked blouse, the infinitesimal speck in the desert where the canister was due to be dropped. Studied them, tried to find some link between the two, himself and the Englishman's bizarre proposal, made in that calm imperturbable voice, and gave up – shaking his head helplessly.

'Listen,' he glanced up. 'Just so I've got it right, just so I'm not going crazy or something. You really expect me to take an armed safari up there, find this bunch of black hoods when you unload that parachute, and somehow bring this lady back – like neatly packaged in Macey's Christmas wrapping, maybe?'

'It's an offer, Mr Haston.'

'And how the hell did you figure I was even going to set the safari up? Trucks, men, guns. What was I supposed to do –

29

wave a wand and they'd appear by magic?'

'I think I said an offer, not a picnic.' Liddell cool, quiet, the moustache barely moving as he spoke. 'You're not naïve, Mr Haston. Although I'd deny it ever took place, you must know I'm taking a considerable risk in even having this conversation. But that's the absolute limit of the risk I'm prepared to take. If you accept, everything else, the supplies you need, the way you handle it, will be entirely up to you. I understand you're not without ingenuity, so I don't imagine the details will be too difficult. But they'll be your concern – not mine.'

'Jesus Christ!' Haston shook his head again. 'You're so far off base, I don't even know where to begin. I'm not some goddam soldier, I'm a hunter —'

'Are you, Mr Haston?' Liddell lifted his wrist and looked at the date window on his watch. 'Yes, I suppose technically you're right – as of this moment. It's Tuesday today. I rather wonder what will be the case at the end of the week.'

Haston sat quite still. The air inside the Ford, trapped by the metal roof and sides, was thick and close. Out of the corner of his eye he could see Liddell's assistant leaning over the hood: a rivulet of sweat gleamed on the back of his neck and there were dark patches at the shoulder-seams of his jacket.

It was insane. Totally, utterly insane. This was a job for the military, for one of those specialist anti-terrorist units like they'd used in Rhodesia, not for a solitary hunter. Then there was the equipment needed – above all the weapons. High velocity hunting rifles wouldn't be any use; you wanted Army-issue repeaters, Schmeissers or the Czech Brnos, guns you couldn't just walk into a gunsmith's and buy off the shelves – Christ, there weren't even any gunsmiths in Botswana!

And the plan itself, that was the craziest part of all. To hide up near the drop-zone, track the terrorists back to their camp, mount an ambush and pull the woman out. They'd kill her before he got within a mile of the place – if he even managed to tag onto them after the canister was dropped. And then they'd simply go gunning for him.

No, the whole scheme was impossible, lunacy, suicidal madness. He opened his mouth to tell Liddell – and he stopped.

30

It was lunacy – but it wasn't impossible. Liddell had said there'd be ten of them at most. He was right. There wouldn't be enough water or provisions for more. Then they'd be urban kids from the ghettoes, they always were. Confused, jumpy, lost. Even the few scouts they'd be able to deploy round the drop-zone wouldn't really know what they were looking for, or what to do if the instructions in the ransom note weren't followed and a ground force was sent after them.

A ground force! Himself, a couple of men, a truck, a few guns. It sounded laughable but Liddell was right; it was the only chance, the only way. And Haston knew he could put it all together too. By turns it would be embarrassing, humiliating, he'd probably even have to crawl, but he could get everything he needed right here in Gaborone – even the repeaters.

Put the safari together and set out and maybe, just maybe, pull it off. With his licence back if he did – he believed the Englishman there – and if he failed at worst a bullet in the gut, at best nothing more than he was facing now – deportation and never being able to hunt again.

In fact, he'd even got that the wrong way round. The bullet in the gut wasn't the worst. You took that risk week after week, every time a jittery client nudged the sight off-centre and you ended up following some wounded animal into the bush. A dirty old buffalo bull with a broken shoulder, a lion with lead in his ribs, an elephant who'd taken three straight magnums through his neck and would still hold himself upright for hours against a tree – waiting for you.

Horn and claw and murderous trampling weight. They were just as lethal as bullets. But you accepted them, you took them on and survived. Survived because you had a weapon which matched theirs, and gave you, if you were cunning and skilful and brave enough, superiority over them. A gun – and the licence that went with it. Without that licence, as this bastard Liddell knew, you had nothing.

Blackmail. It came right back to that. Nothing more, nothing less.

If you don't accept, Mr Haston, you'll almost certainly be thrown out of this country in any event. But if there's the slightest doubt, be quite sure I'll

31

personally see it happens. On the other hand, if you do agree, you can stay here and continue as before.

Haston gripped the table and glanced at the hinges joining it to the front seat support – readying himself to wrench the wooden panel from the metal frame and hurl it in Liddell's face.

'I doubt whether that's really worthwhile, Mr Haston,' Liddell half-smiling, stroking his moustache. 'Instead, why don't we look at those coordinates again and work out a schedule for the canister-drop?'

Through the open tailgate the eagle's shadow was still planing over the thorn. Haston held the table for a moment longer, fingernails gouging the underside of the wood.

Then slowly he let go, leant back and listened.

4

The door opened, the sunlight outside blazed for a moment, then it closed again and the shack was in semi-darkness once more.

'Just come, George.'

The boy who'd entered gave Mlanda a piece of paper. Mlanda read it quickly. It was the weekly report from the camp – a few simple code-words radioed down by relay to the receiver hidden outside the township, and brought in from there by courier.

'That's fine,' he said. 'You tell them there's nothing to go up.'

The boy went out and Mlanda walked across the earth floor to the back of the shack.

It was savagely, mercilessly hot. The heat came up with the dust from the ground, through the cracks in the walls, worst of all almost tangibly like a grill from the low corrugated-iron roof – so hot that if he reached up and touched it his hand blistered. He wiped the sweat from his face and listened.

Outside there was the usual daily cacophony – ancient grinding trucks, blaring horns, shouting children, snarling dogs. The sound mingled with the heat and throbbed in the sticky air. At night they'd change – the screams of a woman as her man beat her senseless, drunken voices bellowing in argument, the vicious grunts and shrieks of a knife-fight followed by the drum of running feet and occasionally the howl of a police siren. But never once, throughout the twenty-four hours of each day and night, was the township quiet.

His home but, Christ, how he hated it. For what it was, for what it did to people, for everything it represented. All the country's filth and squalor, crime and violence, shovelled away like dirt under a carpet in the endless rows of broken-down huts that stretched for miles all round. Festering, feeding on itself, breeding maggot-like in misery and apathy. Only twenty miles away in Jo'burg there were fine tall buildings, gaiety, laughter and hope. Here nothing but stench, noise, brutality and despair.

Mlanda shivered uncontrollably. Sometimes the feeling of hate was so powerful it was like an illness – paralysing him so he couldn't think or see or move. It happened now. He forced himself to relax until the tremors passed. Then he glanced across the floor.

'How long are you going to be, man?' he asked curtly.

'Patience, my friend, patience — '

Josh Valdez lifted his head from the map and flapped his withered hand soothingly.

'To find five places like you want, now that takes time – even for me. I'll tell you when I'm ready.'

'For Christ's sake get on with it,' Mlanda snapped.

He watched Valdez with distaste, angry once again that he'd had to use him but knowing as before he had no choice.

Valdez – old, crabbed, rheumy-eyed, alcoholic – was technically a 'coloured', a half-breed who inhabited the shadowy no-man's-land between white and black. To Mlanda, more specifically, he was trash, human wreckage, a piece of flotsam washed up by accident to die in the township. Yet Valdez was educated and for years he'd been a collection agent for a British trading company with a chain of stores strung out across Botswana. Mlanda remembered that when he learned the woman had gone there to study her leopards. He formulated the outline of the plan. Then he slipped back into the township, found Valdez and bought him with money and cheap gin to tell him how it could be carried out.

Now the old man was choosing sites along the border where the arms could be dropped.

'I tell you, it's one big country, that — '

Valdez was sitting on a crate behind a small rickety table. He belched, fumbled below the table and drank unsteadily from the neck of a bottle, liquid running down his scrawny mottled neck.

'One big bastard of a country. You think you know how to handle it, you think you got it measured, you got water, guns,

34

everything, so you're on top. Then, suddenly, man, it comes right up behind you and kicks you in the arse. I remember once we camped on a puff adder nest. We didn't know and that night—'

'Just do the work, man,' Mlanda cut him off.

'Why? That desert bugs you, does it?'

'For Christ's sake!'

Valdez chuckled, a hoarse wheezing rattle, and Mlanda turned and paced angrily round the floor, bare feet scuffing softly in the dust.

Valdez was right – and the old man knew it. Mlanda had been shaken by his one brief experience of the Kalahari. The township, yes, he hated that but for reasons he knew and understood. The desert had been different – different from anything he'd ever known or imagined. Its vastness, its ferocity, its loneliness. The menace of a fleeting shadow behind thorn, the silent presence of the circling eagles, the terrible dry heat – no stronger than in the shack now but somehow pitiless and deadly.

He'd only spent two weeks there, but it was enough. In spite of what he'd told the woman and the others he wasn't going back. There was no need. They had good radio contact, B'Volu – his second in command – could collect the canister, he was better employed monitoring the drop-sites for the arms. That was how he'd rationalized it and it was all true. Except he knew it wasn't the real reason.

The real reason was that for the first time in his life Mlanda had been afraid.

He cursed under his breath, tugged at his beard and prowled restlessly to the door. Through the crack in the lopsided frame he could see a ten-ton cement-carrying Ford lumbering by, wheels raising billows of choking grey sand and exhaust trailing smoke and diesel fumes. A child raced up to the front axle, bent down, scooped a stone from the rutted track and hurled it into the driving cabin. There was a cry of pain, the truck slewed sideways and the child ran off – rake-thin, raggedy, blank-faced, mindlessly uncaring.

'I get you, you young bastard, I get you for ever — !'

The driver's door opened and the driver stumbled out, hand to his forehead where blood was streaming down between his fingers.

'You hear me? I break all your knees and rip all your balls off—!'

The driver disappeared up the track and Mlanda turned away. He'd seen it all, heard it all, a thousand times before. Nothing was going to change that – except what he was doing.

'They tell me you got a prize — '

Valdez had picked up the bottle again, speaking through the gin as he slurped it into his mouth.

'One big bastard of a prize. Big and fat and beautiful. That right?'

'Who told you that?'

'I hear,' Valdez lowered the bottle and shrugged. 'I also hear she's a prize to be enjoyed every way.'

There was a leer like a snail's track of slime in his voice.

'You listen to me, man — '

Mlanda crossed the floor to the desk, reached over, caught Valdez by the collar of his filthy shirt, lifted him up and shook him furiously.

'You forget anything you ever heard, right? Because I tell you this. I ever catch you mention her again and I break your filfthy neck!'

He hurled Valdez away and the old man tumbled off the crate onto the ground. Then Mlanda walked to the back wall again.

The boy must have talked, boasting to the old man about what he believed Mlanda had done. That was bad enough – that Valdez knew about her. He'd have to speak to the boy but Valdez wouldn't say anything else – he'd be too scared. No, that wasn't what had caused his flare of temper. It was Valdez' tone and the dirty lascivious chuckle.

Alison Welborough-Smith. Whenever he thought about her it was always the same, a tangle of memories, impressions and feelings, all of them warring and colliding against each other. She was white. She was rude, arrogant and abrupt. She trampled over everything and anyone that stood in her way as ruthlessly as any *verkrampte* Boer farmer taking a whip to his plough-boy.

She was also the most extraordinary woman, white or black, that he had ever met. Within minutes, that first day at her camp in Tanzania, she'd casually instructed him to fetch her something. He'd bristled instantly, blood rising in anger at the insult. Then he'd suddenly realized it had nothing to do with the colour of his skin. She simply hadn't noticed. To Miss Welborough-Smith there were just two categories of life: animals and people. She made precise distinctions about the former, none whatsoever about the latter.

He'd stayed there for two weeks, mesmerized by her. She'd talked to him, lectured him, for hours, telling him stories about Africa and its history and its wildlife that he'd never heard, never considered before. And he'd listened hungrily as whole dark areas of the continent's past, his past, came into focus and light. (He'd never screwed her. Christ, you didn't screw women like Miss Welborough-Smith. Those stories were just for the men. They loved hearing them – it gave him and them status to have had a white woman.)

Then when he'd gone to her new camp in the Kalahari – and it was now that the confusion, the ambivalence started again – he found himself, embarrassed, more of a suppliant than a captor. She'd greeted him, he'd explained fumblingly what he wanted to do and she'd accepted immediately – providing of course it didn't interfere with her studies. And now she was out there, five hundred miles in the wilderness to the north, carrying on as if nothing had happened.

'Move, man — '

The door opening again and the boy's head against the glaring sun.

'Patrol up the road heading this way.'

The door slammed shut, Valdez hurriedly tucked the map down his tattered gaping shorts, and Mlanda slipped in behind the screen that covered the rear exit to the shack.

Police patrols were common. Most likely this one would just pass by. If there'd been a tip-off – the possibility he lived with day and night – then he'd have no chance, the shack would be surrounded. But if they stopped to make a random check, then at least he could make a break for it – running through the dense squalid huddle of the township.

He pressed himself flat in the darkness against the wall, listening to the wheels and thinking of the woman. Whatever else, as Valdez had said, she was a prize. The biggest prize of all. A prize worth venturing everything for.

The wheels trundled closer. Through a chink in the crumbling bricks he could see Valdez shivering and sweating. Mlanda waited.

5

The baboon was a two-year-old male like half-a-dozen others in the pack – except this one was bigger and stronger, more aggressive and adventurous than its peers.

He had been watching the female for a week. Watching and smelling her – because the baboon's interest had been aroused first by the scent she gave off – rich, acrid and musky, deeply and disturbingly exciting. For a while, the male wasn't even sure exactly where the smell came from, only that it enveloped her body in a thick invisible haze. Then one morning, suddenly linking the visual signals of the dark hair bobbing on her head with the equally dark hair round her groin as she cleaned herself, the male traced the specific source – two small glands on either side of the female's vagina.

After that, intensely curious, pulled forward by a desire he didn't understand, the young male made several attempts to approach her – to touch and lick and explore the area from which the scent flowed out. Each time he was attacked and sent whining away in terror, once with a mauled and bloodied ear, by the pack's dominant male, a massive and grizzled fifteen-year-old animal. Yet as soon as the terror faded the curiosity and desire would return, and the young baboon would start watching the female again – waiting for another chance to investigate the smell.

That afternoon the old male was dozing, haunches spread wide, scarred head sunk on its breast, fur glistening grey-white in the lowering sunlight. Round it the rest of the pack were foraging for grubs and roots in the dry grass, while two sentinel baboons – perched on outcrops of rock – kept watch against predators.

The young male studied the female carefully. She was some distance from the others, squatting in a little dust-bowl and searching her skin for ticks. The smell spilled out over the grass towards him again – vivid and magnetic and baffling. The male scratched his stomach, shivered and gave a quiet tentative bark. The female looked across at him, passive, enticing, wrapped in warmth and the strong bewildering odour. Then the male made up his mind. He rocked forwards, circled away trotting towards the west and began to approach her from the rear.

The leopard moved at the same instant.

For two hours until then, unnoticed by any of the pack, it had been nothing more than a bar of blackness in the tangled lengthening shadows of a heap of stones. Now, in a single fluid movement, it lifted itself from the ground and raced forwards with an explosive burst of speed. The baboon never heard the leopard but the sound tremors from its paws rippled across the earth and registered on the young male's pads. He whirled round, his neck bristles snapped up, he made a frenzied scrabbling charge back towards the pack, then he stopped – spitting and chattering.

The angle of the leopard's run had bisected the line between the young male and his companions.

The leopard slowed and dropped down onto its belly. Behind it the rest of the baboons were barking and screaming in a tumult of fear and impotent rage. Together as a pack, ringed defensively, slashing with their great yellow incisors, hurling rocks and logs, they might have driven the leopard off. But once one of their members was separated from the others, as the young male had been, the animal was doomed.

The leopard came forwards very slowly, prowling, undulating over the ground, its black mask expressionless but its yellow eyes narrowed and unblinking. In front the baboon reared up, hind legs churning the dust, mouth distended in aggression, helpless but screaming defiance. Three feet away the leopard stopped. It watched the baboon for a moment. Then it reached out one paw and struck casually, almost lazily at the baboon's head like a farm cat swatting at a fly.

The baboon's fangs cut down at the black paw but the paw was no longer there. Instead the leopard was springing, a great surging bound that raised it clear of the earth and brought it smashing down on the baboon's back. Its jaws closed over the

40

young male's skull, crushed tight and the animal was dead.

The leopard snarled then, the first sound it had made since the hunt started, and glanced over its shoulder. The rest of the pack were already in retreat, their screams and barks growing fainter as they vanished into the bush. Its head moved in an arc checking the rest of the surrounding terrain: there was no sign of a competitor, no feral spore on the darkening air, no tremor of sound coursing through the earth.

Finally, it licked the blood from the crumpled skull and settled down to eat.

Half a mile down-wind to the south the woman listened intently. She'd heard the sudden chorus of terrified barks, the hysterical chattering of the isolated male, the sudden silence, then the fading screams of the pack – and she knew what had happened. Now it was a question of waiting.

She gave it twenty minutes. Then in the dusky light of early evening she walked forwards through the scrub.

The leopard had gone but the remains of the kill were just where she'd fixed it by ear. Too small to be worth removing and storing in a tree, the leopard had eaten its fill and left the stripped carcass on the ground. As she came up, a jackal was nuzzling at the scattered entrails. It growled hesitantly at her once, then turned and ran silently away. The woman knelt down, studied the mangled creature for a while and felt in her shirt pocket for her note-book.

A two or three-year-old male – the bone size and fur colour gave its age, the torn genitals its sex. Weighing between thirty and forty pounds, of which nearly one third had been taken as food. Killed at exactly ten past five – she'd noted the time of the smothered scream on her watch. Killed probably because it had strayed from the pack. Terrain: open plain with scattered bush and rocky outcrops. Weather: fine and clear with light southerly wind.

She wrote quickly but carefully, systematically recording every detail. On their own they'd provide nothing except another picture of another kill by yet another feline predator. But together with the other records something would emerge, something *had* to emerge. A profile, a pattern, an answer to the

41

apparently inexplicable behaviour of an animal which wasn't just another feline predator – but, in all probability, the rarest creature on earth.

The light drained, stars began to fill the sky, the eyes of other waiting jackals glowed nervously in the bush. Engrossed, frowning in concentration, mindless of everything – the darkness, the constellations, the circling eyes – the woman wrote on.

All she saw were her own scribbled notes, the bloodied carcass, the deep pug-marks round it – and somewhere in her mind's eye the form of the dark taloned animal who'd killed, eaten and vanished.

6

For a couple of minutes Haston thought the boy at the house must have been wrong.

There was a newly-delivered pile of tyres by the garage door, a stripped-down Ford on the maintenance ramp at the centre of the dusky shed and a litter of tools on the work benches round the walls. But that was all – there was no sign of the mechanics or anyone else. He stepped over the tyres and looked into the adjoining shed where the spare parts were stored. A jumble of body panels, cam-shafts and gear-boxes, oily and hot under the low corrugated roof, but still no one.

He turned back. Then as he was about to walk outside again, he remembered the office – a glass-partitioned cubicle at the rear right-hand corner. Normally, he'd have seen straight into it as he entered the garage. Today the blind had been pulled down inside and it had almost disappeared in the dim light.

He walked forwards, rubber-soled boots silent on the dirty concrete floor, and looked through the half-open door. She was sitting behind the desk entering up a ledger, so absorbed with the columns of figures she didn't notice him standing there only a few feet away.

Haston waited, watching the pen travel neatly across the blue-ruled page as the tiny accounts built up.

Three o'clock. Less than an hour since he'd left Liddell by the dam and walked back up the track to his car. The last of the anger had long since ebbed. Afterwards had come resentment, sullen cold resentment at the blackmail he had no choice but to accept. And then, as the Englishman talked, as they agreed a plan and a date for the canister to be dropped, even the resentment went.

Now there was just urgency.

The terrorists had set a deadline of fifteen days from the pilot's arrival. Three of those had already past. He'd need at least another three, driving hard north-west across the desert, to reach the general Moretse area; two more to approach the drop-zone on foot; and maybe two more still to track the men after the canister landed, find their camp and launch the attack.

It left him a bare margin of four days for contingencies, to repair a broken axle if the truck hit an ant-eater burrow, to wait out in the bush if a sudden winter storm forced the flight to be postponed, to spend hours casting left and right if he lost the men's spoor on an outcrop of limestone – as happened so often with game. They were the usual accepted hazards of the Kalahari. On safari out there four days either way didn't matter.

Not this time. Liddell had shown him the ransom note but he'd have believed it anyway. He knew those bastards, every white man in Africa did. When the fifteen days were up they'd murder the woman – raping her first, all of them, if they hadn't done that already. A gang of simple barbaric butchering swine with nothing to lose from killing her and everything to gain – a bloody final warning about what would happen to future hostages if their demands weren't met.

Four days as a margin, and even to get them he'd have to leave that night. So everything had to be organized over the next few hours. He'd known in the Ford how he could do it, that sickening revulsion as the realization came to him, and he'd chosen Mary first because of the three he knew she'd be the least difficult. Compared to the other two, she should be easy.

'What do you want — ?'

She'd glanced up from the ledger, noticed his silhouette shadowed in the doorway and, startled, half-rose. Then she saw who it was.

'Jerry! What are you doing here?'

No trace of hostility in the voice, just surprise and a certain awkwardness. He tried to remember how long it was since he'd seen her. Eight months maybe, no nine. Anderson had offered him a client who'd arrived suddenly late at the end of last season. He'd had to make up his mind there and then. He'd said yes, left her a note – she'd been out at the garage – and he'd gone.

Three weeks later when he came back from the safari, he told

44

her. In fact, he hadn't told her, he couldn't bring himself to do it face to face. Instead he'd written another note and slipped it under her door when she was asleep.

'I just sort of wondered how everything was going.'

It sounded lame and improbable, but she didn't seem to notice. She pushed the ledger aside and came round the desk. She was wearing stained mechanic's overalls and there was a smudge of grease on her cheek.

'If the bloody government settled their bills, we wouldn't be in too bad shape. But they'll pay up sooner or later. Meantime,' she smiled. 'Well, we get by.'

'That's good to hear —'

He stopped.

She was English. In her mid-twenties with an English rose prettiness: bright-eyed, clear-skinned, shy and vulnerable and blushing. Or that was how he'd seen her the first time. Three years ago at a party Pete Travers gave to celebrate her arrival in Gaborone from England as his bride. Two years later Travers bent down to reach under a truck, stiffened and toppled sideways – dead instantly at thirty from a massive coronary.

Haston had fancied her from the moment he was introduced – or that was what he'd thought. There was something in the demureness, the graceful movements, the slender fragile figure, something delicate and private that he'd wanted to break open and touch and discover. He'd waited a couple of months after Travers' death. Then one evening he went round to her house. Mary was there alone. Chalk-faced, shivering, holding back tears as she opened the door.

He'd brought a bottle of gin and he'd made her drink it, sympathetic, consoling, encouraging, slug after slug until she couldn't stand. Then, ignoring her slurred protests, he'd undressed her and screwed her on the floor while Travers' dog, an old black Labrador, snuffled puzzled round them. Afterwards, she'd clung to him, sobbing, arms clenched round his neck, tears pouring out and wetting his chest.

It had been a mistake, a catastrophic mistake – not for her but for him – and he hadn't understood why. Maybe the memory of Travers. Maybe the depth of her vulnerability, far

45

deeper than he'd guessed, and the way he'd exploited it with the gin. Maybe just the bewildered whining snuffles of the old dog.

All he knew was he'd felt ashamed the next morning, and the Anderson job had been a God-given let-out. He'd run, parlayed off the goodbye and taken care to avoid meeting her since. Now the shame was still there but the rest was different. He hadn't ever dreamed he'd need her, he hadn't dreamed he'd ever need anyone come to that, but now he did – and badly. All three of them but in a way Mary most because without wheels he couldn't even begin to plan.

'Listen, Mary, I screwed up.'

'Which particular direction are you referring to?'

She smiled and Haston felt a surge of relief. At least she wasn't bitter, she could even make a joke of it, and that was one hell of a start.

'You heard the story?'

She nodded, leaning against the door-frame. 'I can't remember who it was, but someone told me yesterday. I'm sorry, Jerry.'

'Hell, it doesn't matter. I'm a survivor. I'm such a goddam expert in screwing up I have to be — '

He grinned. Normally, it came naturally, this time he had to force it. But the effect would be the same, it always was – boyish, spontaneous, charming, a weapon he could turn on and off like a tap.

'No, I meant that night with you. Know what happened?'

She looked at him puzzled. 'What do you mean?'

'Know why I chickened out?'

She shook her head still puzzled. 'I know what you wrote in that note.'

'That was crap. No, I mean the real reason. I'll tell you. I'm allergic to dogs.'

Mary gaped at him. 'What on earth are you talking about?'

'It's true, promise. Any time I get into that sort of activity with domestic animals around, I come out in a rash. Green spots under the armpits, yellow ones on the nose and purple zig-zag stripes across the chest. Happened next day. First thing

I knew they were trying to haul me up the flag-pole over the UN mission. I was so scared I went into hiding. It's only just worn off – that's why I haven't shown again until now.'

He stopped and grinned again. Mary waited a few moments frowning. Then she burst into laughter.

'You're an idiot, Jerry, a complete bloody idiot!'

Haston laughed too.

It had been a gamble, a calculated gamble. Either the reference to the dog, Pete's dog, and the fantasy he'd woven round it would have touched some still-raw nerve, brought back the anguish of those months and the resentment she might have felt at what he'd done. Or the absurdity of the story would have defused the memory, made the incident funny and not painful, and she'd have realized that and laughed.

She had laughed and the gamble had paid off and now he leant forwards and touched her lightly on the cheek.

'I'm sorry, Mary. I guess I got myself in a tangle and just walked out on it. But it was good and I didn't forget and it's been with me ever since.'

His voice was serious, quieter, and he made himself go on smiling. It hadn't been good, it had been a nightmare, and nothing would change that. Except he had to pretend otherwise – and more, that there was better to come.

'Don't pretend, Jerry, there's no need to.'

She shook her head, but she'd flushed slightly and there was something almost wistful in the words.

'I'm not,' he said. 'Either about the good or the bad of it – the last part being me. But things change, truly, and I reckon they have. Now, listen again because this is a bribe and whatever else bribes have to be considered seriously — '

He lifted his hand and ticked off the points with his fingers, relaxed, light-hearted, still smiling, making her laugh again as he spoke.

'Time we've got. Well, the hell with it I've got time and you can make space. So for openers I figured Sunday up on the dam. We'll leave early and snatch Sid Marais' boat. I'll bring a crate of Castles, ice and a basket of goodies. You, just yourself, swimsuit and chaperone – that's if you're still wary about my

47

designs. If you're not, sensible lady, don't even bother with the swim-suit — '

Mary tried to interrupt him but he waved her into silence.

'Monday we do Gabs and sin city gets the grand tour. Tuesday it's down to the Cape. To be honest, there's a small qualification here. If I haven't convinced you by then, if that chaperone's still on the team, then you fix her fare. The rest – the bridal suite, the orchids, the oysters – they're all on me. But that hatchet-faced old cow, whoever she is, she's part of your personal baggage. And once we've lost her in a mine-shaft disaster – believe me, lady, we will – it's Europe, Acapulco, Montego Bay, you name it and we'll be there. Listen, we're going to have the whole goddam world for breakfast — '

'Jerry, for Christ's sake!'

She'd been laughing almost uncontrollably. Now, finally, she managed to make him stop.

'What's the matter? Don't you buy it?'

'Oh, yes, I'll buy it, Jerry, I'll buy it all,' the laughter had brought tears and she wiped her eyes. 'Only, before you collect the tickets – can you tell me what you want?'

Haston shrugged and grinned once more.

Another fantasy. He knew it and she knew it and it didn't matter, it was utterly unimportant. There were things called loneliness and grief and fear and trust, and fantasies made them all bearable, even trust however many times it was broken. Because at the end there was always the slender outside possibility that for once the trust would be kept and the fantasy made real – maybe not in full but enough, just enough, to warrant the risk of trusting.

The acid test of whether anyone would take that risk was laughter and Mary had laughed again.

'Look, I need — ' Haston hesitated, 'Well, a favour really. I want to borrow a truck.'

'A truck? What's happened to the Dodge?'

'I had to leave it down at Tshane until the safari's over.'

She nodded understanding. While the safari companies paid a salary and all expenses, every hunter had to provide his own vehicle and trackers. Haston's Dodge and his boys were still at the camp. Frank Yerby, his replacement, would drive them back when the safari ended.

'Is it for running around here?'

Haston shook his head. 'I've got to take it out.'

'Out' meant the desert and that in turn meant four-wheel drive. Another Dodge, a Landrover, a Chevvy, a Toyota Land-cruiser. The only vehicles that could stand up to the merciless bone-bruising terrain of the Kalahari.

Mary frowned. 'Apart from the one on the ramp I've only got two now and they're both out on contract to Land Use. How long would you want it for anyway?'

'A couple of weeks maybe.'

'Two weeks! But you'll have the Dodge back well before then, won't you?'

Haston winked but said nothing.

He couldn't explain and there was no point in inventing a story. As with everything else, Gaborone was too small and she'd learn within days that whatever he told her wasn't true.

He waited. There was another possible vehicle and they both knew it. Travers' own Toyota which she'd kept when she took over the garage and used for the drive in from her house on the outskirts of the town. Without that she'd have no transport her-self unless she rented another car. She couldn't take Haston's — that would instantly lead to questions — and he couldn't rent one for her. Anderson had cancelled his salary cheque when he fired him.

'And I suppose I'm not to tell anyone, right?' she said. 'If I'm asked what's happened, I've got to say it's having a major over-haul, something like that?'

'You've got it.'

Mary had guessed as Haston knew she would, guessed he wanted the Toyota and wanted it for something illegal, some-thing that could even conceivably get her into trouble. A bent hunting trip for some quick cash maybe, as he'd imagined Liddell's note was proposing. Or a smuggling run across one of the borders. But something bad.

'Jerry, you're impossible, quite impossible — '

She shook her head and smiled, a private speculative smile.

'You arrive at my house nine months ago, you behave quite disgracefully, you make me drunk, you take advantage of me, then without explanation you disappear. And now you've got the nerve to turn up again with a totally outrageous request and a whole lot of nonsense to see you get it.'

'Truly, I meant what I said about the oysters.'

'You didn't mean any such thing!'

'Sure I did. I only just remembered how good that advantage you mentioned felt. I figured it was worth trying again.'

Haston forced another grin and she laughed and then he waited, gazing at her face.

She'd changed over the nine months since he'd walked out. The fragility was still there but there was strength now too. In the set of her mouth, in the way she held herself, in the quiet humorous way – neither self-pitying nor accusing – she'd described what had happened between them. She'd come to terms with Pete's death and thrown herself into making a success of the garage and the experience had given her something that hadn't been there before.

Somehow it unsettled him more than if she'd been bitter and hostile.

'All right —'

She moved away from the door-frame and rubbed her cheek, spreading the smudge of grease across her nose.

'It's outside by the storehouse. The keys are in the ignition. Leave it back there when you've finished.'

'Thanks, Mary, that's – well, just thanks.'

Haston paused. He could smell the oil on the floor and hear the chatter of the returning mechanics in the street.

'There's one other thing,' he went on. 'I don't need it until to-night and I don't want to be seen driving it. On your way home this evening, can you leave it in that clump of trees back of Van Rhensdorf's place? He's down in the Cape right now and no one goes there. I'll collect it later.'

'It'll be there.'

Mary turned towards the cubicle. Haston reached out and ruffled her hair.

'I've got half an hour before my next date,' he said, 'I'm going to use it to book that bridal suite and those oysters.'

'I believe you, Jerry. I'll be waiting.'

A final smile and she'd gone, making the blind ripple against the glass as she closed the door.

Haston got into his car. Mary didn't believe him but against all odds, all belief, she would be waiting. She should have been the easiest of the three. Yet as he spun the wheel, tyres slithering in the turn on the sun-melted macadam, he found his arms were shaking almost uncontrollably.

He pulled into the side and waited until the tremors passed. Then he set out for the other side of the town.

Sweetness first. The thick fragrant warm scent. He didn't know where it came from, what mingle of spices caused it, he'd never asked. But it had been the first thing he'd noticed when she invited him to the house, and each time he returned he'd felt it wrap itself round him like mist, lingering for hours after he left in his clothes and hair and nostrils.

It came out towards him now, seeping through cracks in the door and swirling in the air. He knocked and waited. Dogs were howling in the shacks across the road and a black cycled past, handle-bars jerking wildly as he bumped over the ruts.

There was a faint shuffle inside and the door opened.

'Please come in.'

No hesitation, no surprise, nothing. Just the hands raised and held together, the small bow of greeting, the soft clear voice.

Haston climbed the wooden steps and went in. The room hadn't changed in the two years since he'd been there last. The damask-covered table at the centre, the polished brass plates on the walls, the hard little couch, the religious paintings on either side of the doorway at the back – the many-armed goddesses in bright primitive Indian colours. Everything neat and tidy and spotlessly clean, unlike the squalor of the African houses all round.

He turned. Vasha had closed the door and was watching him, not curiously but with a polite passive stillness. She lifted

51

her arm, brown and slim and graceful under the blue sari, and pointed at a chair.

'Sit down, please.'

Haston went to the table and sat while she settled herself opposite him.

Vasha. Like the room she hadn't changed either – if anything she was even more beautiful now than then. Two years ago. He'd come out to the township – one of the poorer areas on the fringe of the capital – to buy some bush shirts from another Indian merchant who had a shop there. She'd been in the shop when he walked in – and Haston instantly thought he'd never seen anyone as lovely in his life.

She was eighteen. Small and slender with great lustrous black eyes, long hair so dark and fine it glowed like shadowed water, and a mouth that, when she accidentally jogged his arm and shyly apologized, broke into a dazzling enchanting smile. Yet more than that there was the way she moved, the movements of a dancer, supple, sinuous, incapable of a single awkward gesture and charged always with a gentle soaring gaiety.

For five minutes Haston had simply gazed at her mesmerized. Then when she left the shop, he'd run out and caught up with her in the street. He offered to carry her package, began to talk and it had started from there.

'How are you, Vasha?'

'I'm very well thank you, Jerry.'

'That's good to hear — ' the words as strained and meaningless as when he'd greeted Mary.

'Look, I'm sorry about the money. It hasn't been easy for a while, with all the troubles the clients are cutting back each season. And just recently it's become really bad.'

That wasn't true – apart from the last part. The past two seasons had been excellent, the clients didn't seem to give a damn about the unrest in South Africa to the south, and he'd made a hell of a lot. Somehow it just all went; he wasn't sure where or why although none of it had gone to Vasha.

'That doesn't matter. We manage.'

'Fine. Well, if things improve I'll really see what I can do — '

He stopped. It was becoming more difficult every moment,

but he had to go on and sooner or later, before he asked, he'd have to face it. He did so then.

'And how's little Ramsingh?'

She didn't reply. Instead she got up, went out through the rear door and came back a few minutes later with something in her arms wrapped in a woollen shawl. She held the bundle out to him, Haston took it and looked down.

The face of a sleeping child, an eighteen-month-old boy. Brown curling hair, long eyelashes, skin much fairer than hers, a little chubby hand gripping the wool, the smell of baby oil and the steady murmur of breathing like a small resting animal. Ramsingh Gopal – he'd been given her name – but Haston's son.

Haston held the boy for a moment. Then he handed him back to her.

'He's a great-looking kid, Vasha.'

'Thank you.'

She went out again and Haston swung back towards the table.

It had sounded crude and hollow, but it was all he could think of to say. And with it everything came flooding back, everything he'd held himself against remembering.

The day she'd told him she was pregnant, her face beaming with the news, and the simple happy question – when would they get married? Her disbelieving shock, the colour going from her cheeks, her eyes glazing over and her throat trembling, as he tried to explain to her he couldn't get married, he didn't want to, that for him it had been fine but different – a friendship, an affair between hunting trips. And then the terrible silence as she backed out of his apartment and left.

Afterwards, equally appalling, the occasion a few evenings later when her aunt came to see him. There were no threats, no blackmail, no accusations. Instead a quiet courteous explanation as if he as a foreigner hadn't understood. He didn't have to live with Vasha, he didn't even have to see her again. All he had to do was go through the ceremony of marriage. That would protect her in the eyes of their community. If not, she'd be a broken woman, a whore, with shame on her and the child

53

and the family for ever.

Haston had blustered, shouted, offered money, made other promises he hadn't kept, but flatly refused even to consider it. He wasn't going to shackle himself to some little Indian girl who however pretty, however great in bed – and she'd been stunning there after he taught her – was basically just another lay. She'd gone into it with her eyes open, if she'd got herself knocked up that was her responsibility, not his.

The aunt had bowed and left, fatalistically accepting it with the same grace as she'd spoken. Finally, months later still, he'd come back from safari to find a letter under his door. Misspelt but elegantly written and still without any hint of reproof, it told him that Vasha had had a boy and both were well.

He'd sent off a small cheque then, vaguely reminded himself to do so again after the next trip and promptly forgotten about it. Until now when, like Mary and Jo, he needed her. Haston closed his eyes and shuddered.

Then she came back into the room and sat down, waiting patiently for him to speak. Haston crossed his arms awkwardly on the table.

'Vasha, I've got myself into a whole load of trouble.'

'I know that, Jerry. May I say I am very sorry?'

Three days, that was all, and the story had even reached this little house on the edge of Gaborone. Well, at least he didn't have to go through it again.

'There's a possibility I can unscramble it,' he went on. 'But I'll need something from your uncle — '

Her uncle. Old Gopal. Dealer, agent, merchant, fixer. The man who with his wife had brought Vasha up after her parents died and who, for the dishonour Haston had brought on her and his name, had better reason to hate him than anyone in the world.

'Is he here now?'

She nodded. 'He's up in the store-room.'

Gopal's house had two levels. The lower, where they were sitting, contained the living quarters. The upper was a single large attic where Gopal kept stocks of the merchandise he sold in his shop up the street. His wife, Vasha's aunt, was probably over at the shop now counting the day's takings.

'Vasha, what I want is going to be difficult, maybe dangerous, even for him to get. And I know I've got no reason for asking you to help, you less than anyone. But if it all works out, if I can hang onto that licence, then I promise I'll try to do something, Christ knows what, but something to make things better in the future. So I'll ask anyway – would you speak to him for me?'

She smiled. The first time since he'd come in and not the smile he remembered, the great joyous expression of happiness and laughter. But gently, fleetingly.

'You don't need to promise anything, Jerry,' she said. 'Of course I'll do it.'

Before he could say anything else she was gone, bare feet rustling on the stairs, sari brushing against the banister rail as she climbed up to the attic.

Haston waited, tracing the pattern in the damask with his finger.

Gopal might hate him but the merchant adored Vasha, his only niece. At her request he would do anything, even if it meant accommodating Haston. And without question or comment she'd gone to make the request. After everything that had happened, the shattering of her faith, the disgrace, the two-year silence, even the broken promises about money, she'd simply smiled and got to her feet.

Haston shuddered again. Then she was back, as silently as she'd left.

'Go upstairs, Jerry.'

He stood up. 'I'll never forget again, Vasha — '

'You can forget,' the fugitive smile again. 'You gave me another boy. He's enough now.'

She made the small bow, turned and went into the back room where the child was sleeping. Haston hesitated for a moment. Then he climbed the rickety flight of stairs.

'Mr Haston?'

Gopal's voice. The attic was in darkness and the Indian was somewhere in front of him. The fragrant scent was even stronger here and mixed with others, herbs and spices and tallow and pitch and grease.

'Here please, sir.'

A torch flickering, beckoning him forwards. He went in. Dimly he could see shadows cast by bales and sacks and great mouldering mounds of clothes. The torch traced an arc, hinges squeaked and the door closed behind him.

'Jesus Christ, Gopal, don't you ever air this place?'

Whatever the past, whatever the private bitterness, Haston knew he had to start and continue like that – the standard unchanging tone of *Morena* to servant, master to tradesman, European to Indian. Gopal would expect it too.

Blinds scratched down, another door closed, then a switch clicked and a naked bulb glowed.

'Good heavens, Mr Haston, if my neighbours saw my stock I'd have nothing left by morning.'

Gopal giggled and Haston saw him. Ancient, bent, gold-capped teeth white in a puckered walnut-coloured face. Moving round the walls like a secretive avaricious mole as he latched down the blinds – shutting out the sunlight and the eyes.

He tugged down the final piece of frayed linen and pushed forward a cane chair.

'You like to sit here, sir, please — '

Haston sat down while the old man hunched himself on a roped bale.

'Yes, please?'

The question simple, direct, unprefaced by any ritual exchanges about the weather or the country or the hour.

Where did they come from, these people, Haston wondered. Not geographically – but in mind and spirit. The links and cogs and go-betweens who'd colonized the world far more efficiently, more lastingly than any imperialist power. Who would listen and arrange anything and take their money and keep their silence. Spreading out, marrying the local population, attending their churches, bearing their children and yet remaining untouched, inviolate – except to trade, to barter, to the ring of coins that for them was what power or fame or lust were to others.

56

He had never understood them, but he knew they were the oil that lubricated the machinery of commerce and intrigue throughout the entire continent – and that only one of them, a man like Gopal, could produce what he wanted now.

'I have a friend, Gopal. A powerful well-connected friend. So powerful that he can even get me out of the difficulty I'm in – and I don't need tell you about that.'

Gopal dipped his hand into a sack, cupped some grains of maize between his bony talon-like fingers and scattered them slowly on the floor. Dust snapped upwards in little puffs where they fell.

'What does your friend want, Mr Haston?'

Yes, Haston thought, he would frame it like that. Not as something direct between the two of them but a transaction on behalf of an unnamed 'friend' – with Haston merely the intermediary. Even the pretence of distance, of a third party, was enough. It was part of the pattern of thought which allowed Gopal and his people to survive where others didn't.

'He wants some guns, Gopal. A pair of automatic repeaters. Schmeissers or Brnos or even the old Sterling. And an automatic rifle, too, either the FN or that new Israeli model whatever the hell it's called.'

The Indian lifted his head and laughed, a thin tinkling noise.

'You are joking with me, Mr Haston.'

'I'm not joking, Gopal. My friend wants those guns and he wants them now – tonight.'

'And even if you are not joking, sir, where do you think I would get such things?'

Haston shrugged. 'I wouldn't even want to guess. But if I had to, I'd say right here in Gabs. Because of what's been happening.'

He had banked everything on that. Fear. The fear that had always been there but had doubled, trebled now after the civil war in Angola and the events in Rhodesia. Fear in the white community, among the coloureds, among the blacks. The fear and its fallout – the caches of guns that were being built up against the day when the country might either become a battlefield itself, or be forced into combat with South Africa.

57

If anyone knew where those stocks of weapons were being hidden, it would be Gopal. To him they'd simply be another commodity, another line of merchandise for barter, exchange and profit when the moment came.

The little Indian sat cross-legged, silent, studying Haston's face. Haston stared back, trying to guess what was going through his mind. The legacy of bitterness about Vasha? The incident at Tshane and the vengeful pleasure he'd get when Haston's licence was revoked? The identity of the 'friend' he'd so swiftly converted into the principal in the discussion? The purpose for which Haston needed the guns so urgently?

Gopal's hand made lazy circles in the maize, his face was expressionless, his eyes rheumy, dreaming and blank. It was impossible to fathom even one of the thoughts that might have been circling there and Haston gave up. He reached for a cigarette and lit it, coughing as the smoke mixed in his throat with the attic dust and the smells from the bales.

'You came here tonight, sir, to buy some safari boots — '

Gopal suddenly levered himself off the bale, scuttled to a table in the corner and came back with a tattered invoice book.

'Six pairs because the price is most excellent and the stocks won't last,' the high-pitched giggle again as he scrawled on the page. 'Sign here, please, Mr Haston — '

Haston took the book and signed.

'Thank you,' Gopal reached for it again. 'And because you are in a hurry for them, I shall have them packaged and delivered – where, sir?'

Haston looked down at him dazed. He didn't know how the decision had been made or why. All he knew was that Gopal was giving him what he'd asked for.

'Behind Mr Van Rhensdorf's house,' he said. 'There'll be a Toyota there in the trees any time from six on. The – boots – can be left in the rear tool-locker.'

Gopal nodded. 'Very good, Mr Haston. They will be there before midnight.'

'Thank you, Gopal — '

He hesitated still bewildered. While he might never know why Gopal had agreed, there was something missing. The single inevitable unchanging factor in any transaction with Gopal's race. Money or barter – and he'd been asked for neither.

'Look, this friend of mine can't pay you at the moment. But as soon as he's finished — '

'Please, Mr Haston,' Gopal lifted a skinny hand. 'Sometimes we buy things and we pay for them in other ways. You tell your friend, sir, I don't want any money or exchange for the boots. Maybe he thinks about that and maybe he finds another way of paying. Maybe he just pays to himself — '

Gopal's withered teeth flashed in a benign gold-and-white smile, he bowed and opened the door.

'Good day, Mr Haston, sir.'

The blinds had been drawn in the lower room too and it was dusky on the stairs. Walking carefully down Haston felt his cheeks burning fiercely.

The fence, thick double-strand wire on stakes, started fifteen miles east of the town. No one knew quite where it ended. Not even, by repute, Gardner Marshall himself, one of Botswana's few legends – the old man was supposed to be among the biggest landowners in the world.

There were certainly almost a million acres here, half as much again up round Ghanzi and other holdings scattered across the country. Harsh raw Kalahari land that even at its richest and in the years when the rains didn't fail, could only support one head of cattle on every fifteen acres. It still left Marshall a very wealthy man indeed.

Haston followed the fence for a further ten miles after he first reached it. Then he saw the gate on his right, stopped for the African herder to open it and drove through. The farm was another mile down a sandy track, level and graded unlike the national ones – the Marshall millions saw to that. Sixty yards before the compact white-washed building he turned off into an acacia grove, parked the car and got out.

The stables were in front of him, dazzling white like the farm through the leaves. He waited in the shadow. He didn't want

59

the old man who anyway would be working at his office in the big house way over to the west. He was looking for someone else – someone who, if he was right, would just have finished the afternoon tour of the troughs and be heading back to the farm for tea.

He was right. After a few minutes he heard a voice calling, loud and imperious, the answering shout of a groom, the creak of saddle leather, then a figure was coming towards him through the trees.

'Christ, you — !'

She'd almost walked straight into him. She checked, blinked in the dappled shade after the brilliance of the sunlight, then the words came – acid and contemptuous.

'What the hell do you want?'

'I'd like to have a talk, Jo.'

'With me? What the hell have you got to talk to me about?'

'Maybe we could go in and I could explain there — '

'Explain?' She laughed, a quick bitter sound in the stillness of the acacias. 'What have you got to explain, Jerry Haston? Like the trouble you're in really isn't your fault at all? Or who you're screwing now and why? It's that bit who works Natural Resources, isn't it, the one with acne and the drooping boobs? So what's the problem? She lost her diaphragm and wants to borrow mine — ?'

She stopped, rigid, white-faced, the riding-crop switching furiously against the leg of her jeans.

Haston didn't answer. She knew about Julie, a secretary in the Natural Resources building who'd been the last one before the safari. That could only be good: she still minded enough to find out who he was sleeping with, minded enough to be enraged.

'You've got nothing to explain to me, Jerry, but I'd be happy to explain something to you. You want to know how I feel about what happened at Tshane? I'm glad, that's what I am, I'm truly bloody glad!'

'I figured you might be,' Haston forced a grin. 'I just came by to give you the full bad news so you wouldn't miss out on any of the gory details.'

60

'You cheap no-hoping little creep — !'

He didn't know what she was going to do but he stepped forward and caught her, holding her tight against him, working his hands down her back and inside her jeans and then gripping her buttocks. Strong and smooth with nothing under the cloth except the warm skin.

For a moment she was stiff and unyielding. Then she relaxed and curved towards him. He began to move his hands upwards, over her hips, her ribs, the taut knuckled bow of her spine. Pressing with his finger-tips, scratching lightly with his nails, stroking and probing and rubbing in the way he knew she loved.

He reached her shoulders and began to turn her, stretching round for her breasts. As he did so she ducked suddenly, rocked back, lifted the crop and slashed it down across his face.

'You bastard!'

The tip of the crop had touched his eyelid and Haston swayed away, hands to his face, blinded, feeling the thin welt of pain and the blood trickling between his fingers. He rubbed hard until the pain went and he could see again. Then he looked up.

She was still standing there, pale, breathing heavily, glaring at him, but even before she spoke again he knew that briefly the anger had spent itself.

'The hell with it!' She turned towards the house. 'Let's go inside.'

He walked behind her through the trees and across the courtyard to the heavy studded door.

'You want a drink?'

Haston nodded and she pointed at a cabinet.

They were in the drawing-room, cool and dim and comfortable with lilac-coloured curtains and deep soft cushions on the chairs. Haston went over to the cabinet and got out a couple of glasses. He didn't need to ask her if she wanted a drink too. She would and it would be the same as always, as before. He filled the glasses with ice, poured in the vodka and squeezed a spray of lemon over the surface.

'Why, Jerry, why?'

She'd taken the glass without thanks and drained half of it. Her voice had changed now, the bitter edge had gone with the anger and she sounded almost weary.

Haston shook his head slowly, and lit a cigarette, but didn't answer.

Why? Not why had he come back now – but why had he done what he did before? He couldn't answer because he didn't really know, any more than he knew with the others. Except Jo Marshall wasn't one of the others; she was different, she was special. He looked at her leaning back on the cushions where he'd seen her so often before. Lithe and young and beautiful. The long golden hair, the strong independent face, the fine breasts lifting under the white shirt, the straight brown legs showing as the jeans rode up her calves. Not some dewy-eyed fumbling virgin but as she'd been from the start, passionate, experienced, funny, the best there was, part of that country, loving it like he did and sharing it all with him.

And everything was still right there in front of him. Not just herself but the great farm that her father, old man Marshall, had given her, the money that went with it, the horses, the hunting, the lying by the river in the sun, the ease of never having to work again. Even now one movement forwards, one offer, one apology and promise – and she'd forgive him and it would all come back.

Except the promise wouldn't be kept, it would happen again and then it would be even worse than before. He couldn't explain why but he knew it, and all he could do was shake his head in silence.

'Christ, don't bother!' She lit a cigarette for herself, 'Just tell me what it is, Jerry.'

'I've got a problem, Jo.'

'I heard that. So what else is new?'

'This one's different, a way of solving the other one. Someone's offered me a chance — '

'To straighten out the Game Department?' She looked at him incredulously. 'You've got to be kidding. No one's going to bend them – not until they make some hot little mama chief ranger and you get round to poking her.'

'It's true — ' Haston hesitated. 'Well, put it like this, if I don't pick up the chance the licence goes and I get thrown out anyway – just like that.'

He snapped his fingers. She finished her drink, gave him the glass to refill and went on watching him curiously.

'You're really in it bad, aren't you, Jerry?'

Humour, puzzlement, almost wistfulness in her voice now. A sense of disbelief that he, Jerry Haston, had finally reached that point.

'Right.'

He gave her back the glass, chill between his fingers.

'Jesus, that must be strange, for you I mean. The Jerry Haston who was everybody's best friend and suddenly no one wants to know any more. Aside from a few scrubbers maybe — '

She shook her head, smoke lifting in the air, and crossed her legs.

'What do you want?'

Haston stubbed out his cigarette.

'Ben and Charlie with your word to them for me – and nothing to anyone else ever.'

He spoke slowly and deliberately, putting all the emphasis and urgency he could summon into the simple flat words.

Ben and Charlie. Ben her farm manager, Charlie her livestock foreman and senior tracker. Two of the best blacks he'd ever known, far better for what he'd taken on than his own boys – even if they'd been available. Both in their early forties, both former policemen who'd been trained by the British before Independence, both now bound irrevocably by loyalty and custom to Jo – a loyalty that with her given word could be transferred to him.

He stood in front of her waiting for her answer. She put down her glass and stared at him.

'You sure you don't want the ranch too, Jerry?'

Beyond the windows there was the distant rasping murmur of cicadas. Inside the room there was nothing – except silence and sunlight patterning the floor and the frozen bewildered oval of Jo's face.

'And if I asked why, you wouldn't say—'

She stood up, lit another cigarette and started to pace restlessly between the chairs.

'I could say you amaze me, Jerry Haston, only even that wouldn't be true. You don't amaze me. You stopped amazing me that day and in what I learned afterwards and then in everything I ever heard since. But Ben and Charlie – Jesus!'

She smiled and although she was still speaking out loud, it was more as if she was talking to herself.

'You know what you could do? Christ, sure as hell you must have done, for me or anyone else I guess. But I'll say what it was just for me. You could make me laugh and cry and see things and do things and have fun and come, come like there was no tomorrow, and then want more. And I believed you, I believed you all the way, right down the line, like there couldn't be anything else or anyone else ever again. Not just for me but for both of us — '

She paused then but he knew what she was remembering.

He'd given her a key to his apartment when they'd started going together and he'd forgotten about it. One night, maybe six months later, he'd come back from safari, called the farm and been told she was away with her old man down in Jo'burg. He'd left the key off the lock and he was in bed with someone else when Jo had walked in. She'd flown back on the early flight, learned he'd returned and had come over to have breakfast with him.

Haston, half-asleep when the door clicked open, had thought it was the dhobi girl and had drowsily called for her to collect his shirts. There was no reply and he'd raised himself up to see Jo standing there – looking at him, at the bed, at the other figure curled beside him. She'd said nothing then and he hadn't had time to speak either. She just turned and walked out.

Later that morning he'd gone to the farm. She'd met him at the door, very calm, very composed, although the moment he saw her face he should have known it was impossible. There was no way any woman was going to understand – least of all Jo with her pride and fierceness and the total commitment she'd given. She listened to him for a time, standing four-square in the doorway. Then she'd spat in his face and kicked at his groin.

64

Until half an hour ago he hadn't seen her since.

'And now you want Ben and Charlie with my word for them,' she went on. 'You know, Jerry, if I asked you to tell me the truth just for once and you said you wanted them for – what did you use to call it? "Hunting pussy", right? Even if you said that at least it would be something real between us. Like I'd know where I was, helping get another notch on the door.'

'I'm not hunting pussy. I don't want any more notches on the door. I just want to keep my licence.'

Haston seldom flushed but for the second time that day he knew his face was hot and red.

Hunting pussy and the notches he carved each time he scored. He'd told her about it one afternoon after they'd made love in her bedroom overhead. Laughing, as a joke, thinking it would somehow make him more glamorous to her. Making her believe it was all over now and the last one had been cut in the wood. Although even as he spoke knowing he was lying.

'Is there anything else you want?'

'Not from you, no —'

He should have phrased it differently and he broke off, but it was too late.

'Not from me?' she said. 'So who else is going to get lucky? What are you doing, Jerry, making the rounds of everyone you've screwed and lied to and dropped, like you're collecting for a jumble sale? Christ, you must be having fun.'

Haston's cheeks burned even hotter. 'I need Ben and Charlie badly. That's all.'

'Oh, the hell with you, Jerry —'

Jo was by the fireplace. She gazed at him and suddenly, briefly, there were tears in her eyes.

Haston knew the reason and glanced away, unable to look at her. With Mary it had been loneliness, the memory of the comfort he'd given, however quick and spurious, and the distant fragile hope there might be more. With Vasha, passive undemanding Vasha, it was dominance: he'd charmed, enthralled and overwhelmed her – and somehow the legacy of the child had been enough. But with Jo there was something else. Jo had loved him and stronger even now than the anger, the sense of betrayal, the wounded pride, she loved him still.

Haston lit another cigarette and started to speak, but she whirled round, jabbed at the bell-push on the wall and instantly her housekeeper appeared – fat and wrinkled and humpbacked.

'Majuliette, I want Ben and Charlie right now. You send one of the kitchen boys to get them quick. Understand, Majuliette?'

'Yes, Majo.'

The housekeeper shuffled out, the door closed and there was silence again apart from the cicadas and the afternoon bees humming in the banks of lavender outside.

'Listen, Jo, I'm telling you the truth — '

'For Christ's sake, Jerry,' she cut him off and moved to a window. 'Don't bother. I don't care a damn whether it's the truth or not. You can have Ben and Charlie and my word for them. Jesus, I don't know why but you can. Only there's one condition — '

She propped herself on the sill and her finger stabbed out towards him.

'Whatever you pick up along the way, however you do it, wherever you screw her, you tell her this – it's courtesy of me. And when you make that notch I want my initials cut alongside it. J.F.M. Jo-fucking-Marshall. She paid for this one, right?'

The door opened again then and Majuliette came in to say Ben and Charlie were on their way up from the stockyards.

Haston stood waiting in the middle of the room while Jo spoke to her. Then he glanced down at his hands. Unconsciously, he'd been plucking at something round his wrist – a plaited fibre bracelet. Jo had made it for him one afternoon by the river, laughing with delight at the skills she'd learned as a child from the African trackers while she separated the tough strands from the fleshy cactus leaves, wove them together, knotted the two ends and finally slipped the band over his outspread fingers.

He'd forgotten about it for months, forgotten too what she'd said when she gave it to him, but he remembered now – the occasion and the silly joking words and the sunlight hot on the rocks by the ford and a malachite kingfisher skimming the water. He looked up and Jo was still watching him and he coloured again.

Then he walked over to the cabinet and filled his glass from the vodka bottle. Haston didn't want the drink. He just wanted to rinse the sour dry taste out of his mouth.

7

Once the woman thought she'd lost the animal.

She'd woken suddenly one night, felt agonizing cramps in her stomach, crawled out of the tent and then for half an hour she'd been violently sick. Later, lying dizzy and still convulsed by pains on her camp bed, she realized she must have caught some streptococcal infection – probably from the meat of a buck one of the boys had shot and hadn't cooked properly.

The infection racked her body for three days, leaving her spent and helpless in the tent. On the fourth night it passed and next morning she forced herself to get up, weak, emaciated, stumbling as she moved but able to walk again. Instantly, she went straight over to where she'd seen the leopard last.

Throughout the illness she'd thought of almost nothing but the animal. Even when the pains were at their worst, when she'd been sweating, choking and retching up bile, it had been with her – a black feline silhouette prowling relentlessly through her giddy and aching brain. Never once, lying awake in the midday heat or dozing fitfully at night, had she been able to forget it. Now, unsteady and shivering in the bright morning air, she reached the tree where the animal had made its last lair and stopped.

The sand below was patterned with the huge familiar pug-marks but the leopard had gone.

She knew that immediately, instinctively, with such complete conviction that she walked forward to the trunk and looked up – a certain invitation to an attack if the animal had been sleeping above. There was nothing in the dusky tangle of branches except hanging shreds of raw wood where the leopard had sharpened its talons.

Then she turned and examined the spoor. She knew as little about tracking as the rest of the boys in the camp, but she could see that the pug-marks were stale and cold: instead of being crisp and firm the prints were blurred and the rims crumbling. Sometime after she fell sick, perhaps the night it happened, the leopard had climbed down the tree and moved on to find yet another hunting territory. All it had left were these fading marks.

She spent the next three days searching the bush to the north of the camp. Sometimes two of the boys went with her but they were no more experienced than she was, and more often she set out alone – rising at dawn, driving herself for hour after hour through the scrub, still weak and enervated from the infection, as she scoured the ground for tracks, then returning trembling with exhaustion to the tent as darkness fell.

It was a hopeless impossible task. The trail was days old, she'd never followed animals except by sight, the sand was criss-crossed with other spoor-lines – antelope, buck, warthog, zebra, wildebeeste, mongoose and civets, a dizzying confusion of prints – the thorn lacerated her clothes and skin, the desert stretched limitlessly ahead.

Yet she never considered giving up. Not even when she fell, reeling with tiredness, into some anteater burrow or collapsed, almost fainting from the heat, into the shadow of an acacia copse for a brief rest before she went on again. The leopard was somewhere out there in front of her. She'd watched it, kept pace with it, lived with it for three months. Now with the same inflexible purpose she'd search until she found it once more – and then continue as before.

On the fourth evening after she'd recovered from the infection she climbed a low ridge and came out above a stretch of grassy plain. Below her, herds of springbok and sable were grazing undisturbed in the waning light. She watched them for a few moments. Then, as she turned to head back for the camp, she checked. The herds had suddenly started to scatter. Beginning at the left, at the farthest point she could see, they were breaking in successive waves and galloping towards the horizon.

She waited, puzzled. A pair of cheetahs or a pride of hunting lions were the obvious explanation – except they'd only disturb the game in the immediate area where they were trying to kill.

69

Here the whole plain was moving. The parting waves built up, lapping closer like an incoming tide, the earth throbbed to the drum of hooves, dust spiralled into the air, animals were racing terrified on every side – and then she froze.

Behind the waves something was moving towards her across the plain through the tall tawny grass. Indistinct and shadowy at first, a fugitive shape glimpsed between the dry stems. Then, as it drew nearer, taking form and substance between the clouds of dust. Something immense and black and menacing – padding over the baked winter earth as remorselessly as it had prowled through her mind.

The woman registered its direction and course. Then, as the leopard passed beneath her, her legs folded and she crumpled to the ground and wept.

8

'Are you ready, Ben?'

'Yes, sir.'

The African's teeth white in the darkness of the copse. No moon, the leaves rustling softly overhead, the air raw and chill with the night's frost.

'You, Charlie?'

'Ready, sir.'

The voice more distant this time and muffled by the Toyota's canvas sides. Haston and Ben were standing outside by the hood, the other African had already climbed into the back.

Haston glanced at his watch. Just after three. Three hours before dawn – and three hours before they'd have to be the far side of Letlhakeng. They could do it but they'd have to move.

'Right, let's go.'

Haston got into the passenger seat and Ben settled himself behind the wheel. The engine roared, the headlamps blazed, the tree trunks leapt up, a wall of black lances against the sky, and they rolled down to the road.

Haston had given Ben the first shift partly because he was exhausted and wanted a few hours' sleep, but mainly because the run to Letlhakeng was the only part of the journey they'd be able to make on a track. After Letlhakeng – and daylight – they'd have to switch to the bush. He was even taking a chance now that some night traveller might recognize Mary's truck and wonder what the hell it was doing out at that hour. The risk was acceptable in the darkness, not by day. That meant the bush and there he trusted himself more than the black to avoid the rocks, craters and burrows which could shatter an axle and wreck the fragile structure of the timing.

He stretched out his legs, slumped back against the padded foam rubber and dozed fitfully.

'Letlhakeng, sir.'

Ben's hand on his shoulder shaking him awake. Haston sat up stiffly, yawned and looked out.

Ben must have driven fast because the coming day was still only a cold blade of paleness on the horizon. Ahead in the greying darkness were circles of mud huts, the gas station and the low white block of the single trading store with a lamp burning above the doorway.

'Straight through, Ben,' Haston said. 'I'll take over a couple of miles the other side. Did we pass much on the way down?'

Ben shook his head. 'Two trucks coming from Ghanzi, sir. Nothing going our road.'

That was good. He'd expected night trucks from the cattle ranches round Ghanzi – heading in the opposite direction towards Gaborone. They weren't a problem because to their drivers the Toyota would simply have been a brief dazzle of passing light.

'Right here, Ben.'

Ten minutes later they pulled off the track, Haston got out and stood for a moment shaking the stiffness out of his arms. The light was changing fast now. The gun-metal grey had already gone and the sky was patterned with rose, flamingo-wing rose that came before the sun. Next would be the first golds, the clear fresh golds of a Kalahari dawn. And, finally, in fifteen minutes, the sun itself. Ferocious, implacable, cleansing. Scouring the frost from the ground and within a few hours raising the temperature from below freezing to an arid ninety degrees in the shade.

Christ, how he loved this country! The wildness and immensity of it all. The barren sand dunes in the south. The great desert of rock and sand and thorn and plain sweeping across the centre – they were on the edge of that now. The vast delta to the north, ten thousand square miles of lagoon and reed and game. A man's country all of it, a country to hunt, a country that challenged you and fought you inch by inch for the prey it harboured – and if you won yielded with brief good grace only to fight you more harshly, more violently, the next and every time you took it on.

Haston shivered in the chillness. For the quarry he'd been

given on this safari, he'd fight back harder than he'd ever fought before. This time there was no returning without the trophy.

He got in behind the wheel and set off again, the thorn parting like breaking waves as the Toyota rocked and crunched through.

'We'll take a break — '

Midday. The cold of the night long since gone, the sun high overhead, the heat shimmering hazily above the earth.

Haston stopped in the shade of some mhata trees, leaves dusty grey against the violet sky, and glanced at the mileometer. In the six hours since Letlhakeng they'd covered seventy miles – exactly what he'd guessed. He got out, still stiff and tired but as always when he went into the desert feeling his mind clearing, senses sharpening, energy starting to pour back.

Ben and Charlie were squatting on their haunches in the tree shadow, talking to each other in Setswana, the voices deep and unhurried. Ben, massively built with immense shoulders and long arms corded with muscle, a reserved methodical man who spoke seldom and smiled rarely. Charlie, taller, thinner, almost gaunt in the green safari overalls they were both wearing. Charlie liked telling long rambling stories, punctuated by bursts of laughter, in which he figured as a buffoon. In reality Charlie was no buffoon. Apart from the little yellow men, the bushmen, he was the best tracker Haston had ever seen working.

Neither of them knew yet where they were going or why. Jo had simply told them to accompany the *Morena* Haston, they'd nodded expressionlessly, collected their blankets and joined him in the copse at midnight. In a moment he'd explain. Meantime, as the heat scorched out the tiredness, he systematically checked everything in his mind.

Liddell first, the urbane moustachioed Englishman who'd sketched out the plan. At ten on the sixth morning after Haston left, a plane would fly in over the drop-zone and unload the canister. By then the three of them should be lying up close to the site. The reply parachuted down would say the ransom would be paid but another week was needed to assemble the weapons demanded.

Liddell guessed the terrorists would take the canister back to wherever they were holding the woman. Haston would spoor them with Ben and Charlie, reconnoitre their camp and mount his attack. Afterwards, if he was successful, he'd trek back with the woman to the Toyota and then head straight for Gaborone.

That at least was the idea. If it was to have any chance of working, the critical factors would be total surprise and instant overwhelming firepower – and little Gopal had kept his word about the guns. They'd been there in the Toyota's tool locker when he'd collected it from the copse. Two new Schmeisser submachine guns and a Belgian Urtzi automatic rifle. The three weapons packaged in cardboard cartons and labelled, as Gopal had entered them in his invoice book, 'safari boots'. And beside them something else, something essential that after the turmoil of the day Haston had forgotten to ask for too – a fourth carton of ammunition.

On the extra carton Gopal had written 'spare laces for boots as supplied – no charge'.

Haston had only glanced at the guns last night. Now he reached over the tailgate to pull one out. He had the flat cardboard box in his hands when he hesitated. As soon as the Africans saw what he was doing they'd start wondering. It was time to tell them.

'Ben, Charlie — '

He left the carton in the truck and squatted down opposite them, balancing himself on his heels.

'Miss Jo gave her word for me for anything, right?'

They both nodded, black faces shining with sweat, hands trailing idly between their spread knees in the sand.

'Well, we're going hunting but this time it's a different sort of safari — '

He told them the story slowly and factually, talking in English – the country's common language – which they spoke more fluently than Haston did their native Setswana.

When he finished there was silence. Both of them had watched him while he was speaking, now they were looking at the ground. Haston had no idea what they were thinking. He'd never been close to any African, not even his own boys. In

74

theory they were equal, black or white. There was no segregation in Botswana: it was a republic where everyone was treated the same under the law. In practice it was different. There might be cooperation, trust, even affection. But between the European and the African there would always be distance.

'These men, sir,' Ben finally, slow and thoughtful, still looking at the earth. 'They from outside?'

Outside. Not of the country but the tribe, because the tribe was all that mattered. Both Ben and Charlie came from the Batawana in the south. Only the prospect of firing on their own people might have collided with their loyalty to Jo.

Haston had anticipated the question and he answered it in the only way he knew they'd accept – openly and truthfully.

'Ben, I don't know for sure who the hell they are,' he said. 'But have your people, Charlie's people, the Batawana, have they ever been into things like that?'

They both glanced up now and Ben shook his head. Like the seven other Swana tribes in the country the Batawana were a peaceful people, who'd avoided being drawn into the guerrilla wars that flared all round them.

'Right,' Haston went on. 'So while I can't promise you, I'd say it's ninety-nine-per-cent certain they're not just from outside, they're from over the border – like down from the north maybe. We'll find that out when we spoor and see them. But one thing I will promise you. If I'm wrong, if they are Batawana, then I'll strike out Missy-Jo's word and you can come back and I'll go on alone. Okay?'

'No, sir — '

It was Charlie this time, speaking for both himself and Ben although neither of them had looked at each other since Haston started.

'You told us the truth about these fellows. If they am Batawana, they doing bad things for our people. We go with you anyway, *Morena.*'

'Thanks Charlie, Ben — '

Haston shook them both by the hand and they beamed. Then he stood up.

'Well, we'd better start by checking what we've got in the

way of guns.'

He went back to the truck and told them to spread out a big ground sheet – a spare he kept in his apartment – on the sand. Then he pulled out the cartons.

The two Schmeissers, stubby and black, were coated with a thick layer of protective grease. He gave the Africans one each and told them to clean the weapons with gasolene-soaked rags. The Urtzi didn't need cleaning; apart from a film of oil round the breech it was in immediate working order. It was about two years old, Haston guessed, and had probably been picked up and sold as plunder in the aftermath of the Angolan civil war.

He flicked the regulation catch to single shot, lifted it to his shoulder and sighted on a boulder fifty yards away through the scrub. The balance was good and the heavy metal stock felt cold and steady against his cheek, but he was swearing as he lowered the barrel. When the time came he'd be snap-shooting, maybe in poor light. At fifty yards, even twenty-five more, the target wouldn't be a problem. But for anything beyond that he'd need a telescopic sight to be certain – and the Urtzi hadn't got one.

His own Redfield scopes would have been ideal – only they were still clamped to his hunting rifles in the camp at Tshane. He'd just have to do without and hope to hell he could get within open-sight distance of the terrorist base before he started firing.

Haston put the Urtzi down and waited until Ben and Charlie had finished cleaning the Schmeissers. Then he tested the breech mechanisms with an empty magazine. They were still slightly sticky, partly clogged with remnants of grease which would have to be dissolved, but both actions snapped firmly and smoothly as he worked the triggers.

'That'll do for the moment,' he said. 'We'll tidy them up and give them a run-through when we're further out in the bush. Meantime, pack them away where they were before.'

As the Africans stowed the guns back in the tool locker, Haston checked the rest of their supplies.

Two ten gallon jerry-cans of water which he'd filled from the tank in Van Rhensdorf's yard. A crate of assorted canned food containing everything that had been on the kitchen shelves in his apartment. His reserve 12-gauge shotgun, a box of cartridges, an old sleeping-bag and a big canvas utility sack full of tools, cable, rope, screws and sundry spare parts – standard equipment for any vehicle used in the desert.

That was all. A meagre enough collection but as much as he'd been able to assemble in the time. The food he could supplement by shooting guinea fowl or sand grouse. Water too wouldn't be a problem, at least for the first stage of the trip; there were occasional bore-holes near their route and he could send Ben off to refill the cans. It would be very different of course after they left the Toyota and continued on foot. Then they'd be deep in the central Kalahari, back-packing as much as they could carry and eking it out for five or six days.

Haston stepped back. The guns were packed away and Ben and Charlie were waiting. He glanced up through the leaves. The sun was at its peak and the heat intense outside the little cone of tree shadow. Normally, he'd have taken an hour's break now for food and rest. Today there wasn't time.

'Open a couple of cans from the stores, Charlie,' he said. 'We'll eat on the way.'

He got into the cabin again, gunned the motor and the truck moved forwards through the thorn.

They'd covered a further hundred miles when Haston decided to make camp at dusk.

The going had been easier than the morning with some stretches of track between the Weneng cattle stations. Although there was little chance of meeting anyone except an African herder, he'd skirted the stations themselves but used the tracks that linked them whenever he could. They'd left the last one in the late afternoon and the final hour had been rock, sand and scrub again. From now on it would be like that until they reached the drop-zone.

Haston sat on the lowered tailgate while Ben set up camp and Charlie built a fire. Every muscle in his body was quivering with the vibrations transmitted through the chassis during the eighteen-hour drive, and he felt limp with exhaustion. Yet the elation was still there, the sense of alertness and excitement which had started stirring at dawn when they turned off the Ghanzi road.

A spurt of flame lifted from the kindling. Charlie swayed back on his heels, reached for a pile of bone-white mhata branches and stacked them carefully over the blaze. Above him the sun was setting, an orange coin framed by trails of evening cloud against the darkening sky. A distant jackal gave a first hesitant call. Nearer, a lion growled a reply – not a territorial roar yet but an irritable warning it was there and preparing to hunt. Somewhere between them a hyena bayed its presence and for a few moments the calls mingled. Then they rumbled away into silence.

The desert. Familiar, reassuring, safe – far safer even with its threatening night sounds, its curving daggers of thorn against the last light, its cold brilliant stars, than anywhere else he'd ever known. He'd chosen and made it his own, his landscape and country and home. For those few sickening disbelieving days he thought he'd lost it. Not now. He was back where he belonged and he'd walk through hell to stay there. Find the goddam English woman with the fancy name. Pull the silly bitch out. Cart her back to the suave bastard Liddell and then go on as before – except he'd learned his lesson and he'd never put it all at risk again.

'Stew, *Morena*—'

He took the billy-can from Charlie and spooned the hot soupy mixture hungrily into his mouth. Charlie asked him if he wanted coffee but all Haston wanted now was sleep.

He finished the can, climbed off the tailgate, walked over to his sleeping-bag and got inside. For an instant he could hear the low voices of the Africans by the fire and a little owl screeching overhead. Then he was asleep.

For the first time since he'd been flown out of Tshane he slept easily and deeply through the night.

'Here, *Morena*—?'

Ben, the next afternoon. They were two hundred and fifty

miles from the Ghanzi road turn-off, far beyond the last settlement, and Haston had decided to test the guns.

He'd given Ben three oil-rags and sent him over to a group of trees fifty yards from where he'd stopped. Charlie had got out the Schmeissers and the Urtzi and laid them with the ammunition carton on the hood.

'Right,' Haston called back. 'Nail them waist-high a couple of yards apart.'

Ben tacked the rags to the tree trunks and came back. There was a light breeze and the rags fluttered dirty white against the darkness of the wood. Haston picked up a box of shells, fed a dozen into a magazine, slapped it into the breech of one of the Schmeissers, fully cleaned of grease now, and held the gun forward above his hip. He aimed at the left-hand rag and squeezed the trigger.

There was a short hammering burst of sound, a throb against his ribs and the smell of cordite. He lowered the Schmeisser, filled another magazine and fired the second gun – aiming at the centre rag now. Then he walked forwards and examined the two targets.

Both the rags had been shredded by compact clusters of bullets and splinters of wood littered the sand below the trunks. There was nothing wrong with either of the repeaters, they were each perfectly balanced and the empty shell-cases had flicked smoothly clear of the breeches as they pumped through. Haston rearranged the rags, folding them over so the surfaces were untorn, and returned to the truck.

'You first, Charlie.' Haston gave him a Schmeisser and a magazine. 'You know how to load it?'

Charlie nodded. 'Yes, sir. I think this same as the Sterling we used with the police.'

Haston watched him fill the metal clip with shells, pressing them down one by one against the discharge spring. Charlie was right. The loading mechanism hadn't changed in years – even the Urtzi operated on the same principle.

'Fine,' he said when Charlie was ready. 'Three bursts going from left to right with a few seconds between them. The barrel always pulls right when you hit the trigger so remember to keep your left hand firm to stop it drifting off.'

Charlie, tall, angular, face intent as he gazed at the targets, put one leg forward, crouched slightly and fired off the three bursts.

Haston walked over and looked at the rags again. There weren't the same small groups of holes as he'd registered, but each piece of cloth had been ripped at least twice. If Charlie had been swinging the gun, he'd have scythed down everything in the arc it covered.

'Hell, Charlie, that's professional stuff,' Haston clapped him on the shoulder. 'Keep shooting like that and we'll have you drafted to the president's bodyguard.'

Charlie grinned happily and Haston gave the other gun to Ben.

'You're turn now, fellow,' he said. 'And you're up against some heavy competition.'

Ben was even better. When Haston checked the rags for the third time they'd almost disappeared – only a few ribbons of cloth were still dangling from the gouged and pitted trunks. He didn't yet know exactly what he'd need the Africans to do; he wouldn't be able to work that out until they found the terrorist camp. But the guess he made when he went to Jo had been right – he'd probably got the two best men in the country for the job.

'Hell, this isn't a safari,' Haston laughed. 'It's a goddam army. Right. Now let's make sure there's nothing we don't know about the way these things work.'

Chuckling, Ben and Charlie squatted down to strip the Schmeissers, check the working parts and assemble them again.

Half an hour later, after Haston had test-fired the Urtzi, they were off again.

The rest of that day was like the day before – and the one that followed. So too the nights between them. An unchanging pattern of waking at dawn under the fading stars with frost thick on the earth and furring the Toyota's windshield. Black coffee by the smouldering fire. Packing up camp and then driving hour after hour north-west through the desert as the sun rose and the heat returned.

Sometimes they'd break through a barrier of thorn to find a

pan in front of them, a shallow open bowl of baked mud with a layer of mineral crystals sparkling white on the surface. Then Haston would stamp on the accelerator and for a mile or two they'd race across it, frightened buck breaking on either side like a bow-wave ahead and great plumes of silvery dust billowing behind. Afterwards, there'd be scrub again, thorn slashing through the open windows, stones smashing against the axles, sweat pouring down and pooling on the seat, arms aching and straining to hold the wheels straight.

Haston had done it before. There were always those few hours between leaving camp with a client until you reached the point where you'd start to spoor on foot. But never like this, never for three full days in succession with barely even time to stop and eat, never with the same unremitting urgency.

Occasionally, he'd hand over to Ben for a while – reluctantly but knowing his concentration was slipping from the effort and the African would be safer until he'd rested. Then, slumped back drowsily against the bouncing headrest, he'd wonder vaguely about the woman. Alison Welborough-Smith. The vague face in the photograph above the high starchy blouse.

It wasn't difficult to figure what she'd be like. Earnest, prissy, humourless, reckoning she knew more about the desert after a few months than people who'd worked and hunted it all their lives. He knew the sort. He'd met them in Gabs, sassy little figures in their crisp new safari suits who'd lecture anyone they could corner about 'conservation' and 'ecology' and all that crap – crap because when it came down to the Kalahari they didn't know their arse from their elbow.

All that made Miss Welborough-Smith any different was being a woman. An uptight spinster college lady who'd treated the desert like an English country garden, and until she got her come-uppance had no doubt been laying down the law about it in a high-pitched schoolmarm's voice. Well, she'd sure as hell discovered it wasn't a country garden. She'd been jumped, dragged off into the bush and was sitting somewhere out there now scared witless.

If he did get her out, there was one thing Haston knew for certain. She'd never come back to the Kalahari again. From now on she'd study her beloved pussy-cats in the safety of some dusty library.

The truck slewed and juddered violently over a dry rain channel, hurling Haston – half-asleep in the passenger seat – against the metal dashboard. He swore, rubbed his forehead where it had struck the rim, settled back and closed his eyes again.

'This will do fine — '

Dusk on the evening of the third day. Almost four hundred miles from Letlhakeng now and as far as Haston had agreed with Liddell they could safely use the Toyota. From here on they'd be travelling on foot.

He walked round the copse beside which he'd stopped the truck. The trees were bunched close together but there was a clearing in the centre. He measured the space between two trunks in the outer ring, found it was just wide enough to let the truck through and backed carefully inside.

'Ben, get your panga. I want it covered with branches from roof to wheels so there's no trace, right?'

Ben nodded, collected his panga and started hacking at the scrub outside the copse.

The chance of anyone else passing through that particular part of the desert was remote – the only possibilities were a group of bushmen or a gang of black poachers after game. If some of the little yellow men were in the area, any attempt to hide the truck would be useless; they'd pick up the faintest tyre impression miles away and follow the spoor until they found it. But at least the scrub would conceal the Toyota from a poaching gang who'd strip it to a bare chassis.

Haston turned to Charlie who was unloading the guns and the other supplies.

'Make up three packs, Charlie,' he said. 'Food, ammunition, rope, knives and so on in two of them, one of the jerry-cans in the other. Take the second jerry-can and everything else and bury it deep somewhere close.'

That was a toss-up. Leaving everything they weren't taking

inside the truck meant the risk of losing it to bushmen or poachers. Burying it on the other hand gave the hyenas a chance. With their immensely powerful shoulders and jaws they'd dig down several feet if they scented something below and grind up whatever they found. On balance, Haston preferred to risk the hyenas.

'What do I use for packs, sir?'

Haston thought for a moment, snapping his fingers irritably. Normally, he'd have brought several big canvas back-packs with him, but that was something else he'd forgotten in the urgency of leaving.

Then he said, 'Cut up the ground-sheet. Fold three lengths double and stitch them up the sides with wire. Then put some shoulder-straps on. They won't be comfortable, but they'll do.'

Charlie dragged out the ground-sheet and set to work.

It was two hours before they were ready. The truck had vanished beneath a mound of branches, Charlie had made and filled the packs, the other supplies had been buried beneath a cairn of stones, and Ben had brushed out as much of their spoor as he could within fifty yards of the copse. By then it was eight o'clock and dark with the cold settling and a half-moon rising over the horizon.

'We'll work it like this — '

Haston was sitting opposite them by a small fire, the last they'd be able to make before they got back to the Toyota.

'I figure we're about forty miles from the drop-zone. You agree with that, Ben?'

Ben nodded. As Jo's farm manager, dealing with herds of cattle over vast tracts of land, he was used to working from maps and he'd helped Haston navigate from Letlhakeng. The drop-zone itself shouldn't be difficult to find. In order not to risk losing the canister in the bush the terrorists had been forced to specify a pan and the little one they'd chosen was the only one inside the co-ordinates.

'So forty miles and two nights to cover them in, because from now on we move by night and sleep up by day. Whatever guards these guys have got out, they won't be more than a few miles from the pan. That means tonight should be fast and easy

83

and we want to make the most of it. You'll lead Charlie, Ben in the middle, me at back. Tomorrow night's going to be different. We'll be close to the drop and Christ knows what they'll have strung out round it. Okay — '

He glanced at his watch. Eleven hours to daylight. One for a rest now would leave them ten for the twenty-five miles before dawn. It would be a hard non-stop trek in the darkness but with Charlie following the game-paths they could make it.

'You've got sixty minutes. Then we're off.'

Haston leant back against his pack. He could feel the warmth from the fire on his face but overhead the Kalahari winter wind, sweeping down from the mountains to the south, cut raw and cold through the trees.

9

The woman had sensed it was about to happen again three days earlier.

By then the leopard had spent two weeks in the same place, the longest period since it had started to move north, and she was beginning to believe she might have been wrong, that it wasn't a journey after all, simply a restless search for a new and better hunting territory which the animal had finally found.

The leopard's base was a large baobab tree, gnarled and writhen and shadowy. She'd gone there every day at dawn and dusk, stationing herself in some rocks thirty yards away from where she could watch the tree unseen through her binoculars. On most evenings she missed the animal's departure to hunt. The leopard would wait until darkness and she'd never know the moment it dropped to the ground, silent and black against the night-black thorn, and pace away across the plain – although some nights she'd see it later drinking from the pool in the pan.

The mornings were different. The leopard would return regularly within fifteen minutes of the early light breaking, circle the trunk, stand for a moment sniffing the air, urinate, and then leap in one surging bound upwards to disappear among the branches where it would sleep out the long hot hours of the day.

The morning she sensed the animal might be preparing to move once more began with something unusual – she saw the leopard kill.

She'd watched it take prey twice before, but both times at night and both at a distance. All she'd seen then was the blurred shape of a racing form under a full moon, an antelope's body wheeling, pale and broken, up from the grass, and afterwards spirals of slow-drifting sand. Nothing more. But she knew she was lucky even to have witnessed that. Leopards seldom killed on open plain, preferring to hunt in the thick cover of tree and thorn scrub.

To have seen one, let alone, two kills in the open was rare enough. That morning the kill was made in full daylight and only thirty yards from where she was watching.

The leopard returned much later than usual. The sun was already clear of the horizon, the dew was beginning to lift and she was about to leave – thinking the animal must have climbed back into the tree while it was still dark. Then suddenly it appeared. At the same instant a male warthog came into sight, trotting slowly, heavily, through the grass oblivious of the leopard's presence.

The leopard froze, the blackness of its coat blending with the dark trunk so that it might have been a sinuous carved root arching out of the earth. The warthog lumbered on, stopped, snuffled at the ground, lifted its head, tusks smeared yellow and mud-brown, and grunted. Then the leopard sprang.

The woman heard the squeals for half a minute. Desperate, helpless screaming calls as the warthog was hurled from side to side like a rag-doll while the leopard fought to find the jugular vein. It caught the vein, there was the sound of tearing flesh, the reflex twitch of muscles churning the sand, then silence – broken only by soft purring growls.

The leopard raised itself slowly, sniffed round the warthog's body and took a few cursory bites from its stomach. Afterwards, without moving the prey or even marking the kill, it leapt up into the tree and vanished.

The woman remained in the rocks until midday when one of the men came to find her. By then a pair of hyenas had gorged themselves on the carcass, several little meercats had darted in to seize scraps of meat and a flock of scavenging maribou cranes had gathered to feed. And throughout the morning, as its prey, was systematically plundered, the leopard nine feet above hadn't issued one single challenge or warning.

She walked away bewildered. The only reason the big feline predators killed was for food or in the face of aggression from a competitor. The warthog hadn't been a competitor; he was a herbivore whom one growl would have driven terrified away.

Yet he hadn't been killed for food either. After those few casual mouthfuls the leopard had abandoned the body virtually untouched to all the other lower carnivores and scavengers of the desert. No other big cat she'd ever watched had behaved like that.

She returned that evening and then at dawn and dusk again for the next two days, but there was no sign of the leopard. No spoor in the sand, no trace round the warthog's skeleton, picked clean now and swarming with flies drawn by the last scattered fragments of skin, nothing. Then in the half-light of the third morning she saw the animal once more.

It jumped from a branch to the sand, stood briefly tense and erect in the low mist, then confidently and quickly padded away towards the north. The woman lay still in the rocks. There was nothing she could do, no way she could follow the spoor even if she knew how to read the tracks. All that was left to her was to wait. To wait and guess and hope.

At eleven, with the sun arcing high, the guess was proved right and the hope realized. The leopard appeared again, panting, moving more slowly, the long pink tongue hanging limply down over the dark muzzle. Whatever its instincts, whatever its desire, whatever was the cause of the strange magnetic pull towards the north, the soaring day temperature of the Kalahari had been too fierce and strong.

The animal circled the baobab trunk twice. Then it climbed wearily into the coolness of the upper branches.

The woman stood up. She'd half-known the morning of the warthog kill. Now she was certain. The leopard was confused and disorientated. That was why it had attacked the warthog. Not for food or as an aggressor but because at that moment the warthog had stumbled, a hapless unwitting distraction, across the path the leopard was plotting in the delicate mechanism of its brain.

Today the animal would rest. But tonight, tomorrow night, the night after, when the impetus had built up again, it would set out once more – this time under the chill screen of darkness when its body wouldn't be exposed to the shock of the day's heat. And when the leopard moved she had to be behind it.

She stepped over the rocks and ran towards the camp above the pan.

10

Haston squatted at the centre of the bush.

Ben was beside him. He couldn't see the African but if he leaned sideways he could feel his shoulder pressing against his own. A few yards in front of them the ground shelved down steeply before levelling out onto the flatness of the pan. Beyond, half a mile away on the far side, there was another bank rimmed with scrub. But between the two nothing except an empty sheet of dull silver under the lowering moon.

He turned his head and listened, straining to catch any sound in the darkness. The whirring of moths, a far-off jackal chorus, grass rustling. That was all. Then he heard Charlie, the dry branches crackling softly as they parted to allow him into the hollowed-out bush.

'What did you find?'

Charlie had crawled up to him on the other side and Haston whispered in his ear.

'Nothing, sir,' Charlie whispering back. 'I went maybe a hundred yards either way. Plenty of spoor, men's spoor, but it's all old, like from yesterday or before. No one's been round here tonight.'

'Okay. We'll take it easy until daylight — '

Haston lifted his watch. The luminous dial showed six o'clock. An hour to go before dawn.

'Twenty-minute shifts. I'll take the first one, then you Ben, then Charlie.'

More quiet rustles as the two Africans stretched themselves out on their stomachs. Then silence again. Haston remained squatting on his haunches, gazing out across the deserted pan.

They'd reached it at four, only just over thirty hours since they'd left the truck. The first night had been relatively easy. The scrub was sparse and criss-crossed with game tracks, and they'd covered Haston's target of twenty-five miles without incident. They spent the next day sleeping in the shade of another copse, taking four-hour spells on watch. There was no sign of anyone else and at dusk they went on again.

The second night was more difficult. They were only fifteen miles from the pan and soon after they left the copse a lightening storm flared briefly. The storm passed without rain but for several hours low cloud trailed in its wake obscuring the moon. In one way the thicker darkness was a help – making it more difficult for any terrorist guards to spot them. But it also slowed their own progress badly and by midnight, five hours after they'd started, they'd travelled barely seven miles.

Then the cloud lifted and Haston decided instantly to press on hard whatever the risk. If they weren't in position above the pan well before dawn so they could watch the canister drop at ten, the entire journey would have been pointless. He called a ten-minute break, they rotated the packs – the one containing the jerry-can of water was much heavier than the others – and set off once more.

The last hour was the worst. At two, according to Haston's reckoning, they were less than a mile away. He sent Charlie forward to find the pan, reconnoitre the immediate area round it and choose a base. Charlie returned at three. The pan was directly in front of them and he'd cut out a space in a bush on its rim as an observation post. But there were tracks on every side and for the last four hundred yards the height of the scrub dropped to a few feet, so they'd have to crawl to hide their silhouettes against the sky.

When they finally reached the bush Haston's shirt was drenched with sweat in spite of the frost, his kneees raw and bruised, and his arms shaking. He ordered another short rest. Then he sent Charlie out again. Now Charlie had just come back with the news that as far as he could tell there were still no guards within a hundred yards on either side of them.

Haston was puzzled. From the tracks Charlie had found a number of people had been there within the past forty-eight hours. Yet the night before the drop it appeared the place was deserted. He pulled his binoculars from the pack and searched the perimeter of the pan, looking for the glow of a cigarette, the flutter of a shirt, a figure pacing for warmth in the bitter cold that already had him shivering. There was nothing. He draped the sleeping-bag across his shoulders and settled down to wait.

The sky lightened soon after seven. By then Ben and Charlie had done their shifts and all three of them were squatting now – gazing out across the pan as its surface changed from silver to crimson and later, as the sun rose, to a harsh gritty white. Eight o'clock passed, then nine, the heat began to filter down into the shadow of the bush, the pan glistened and shimmered – and still there was nothing.

'*Morena* — '

Charlie's hand on Haston's arm. It was five minutes before ten. Charlie had inevitably picked it up first. Haston listened and heard it too – a faint hum somewhere to the south. The drop plane.

Briefly, it seemed to be circling. Then, exactly on the hour, the noise grew stronger and an instant later it came into sight. A pale-blue Cessna flying low and fast from the east with the sun dazzling behind. Haston screwed up his eyes at the glare. Dimly he thought he could make out on the fuselage the black double-arrow emblem of Kalahari Air – the charter company Andy Vaughan flew for.

The Cessna crossed the pan in a drumming roar of sound, banked steeply above them, circled back east and vanished over the horizon. Haston had been following the plane. Now he glanced down at the pan. He hadn't seen the canister being thrown out but it was just striking the earth, a metal cylinder with a small yellow parachute floating above. The cylinder bounced along the surface raising little puffs of dust behind it. Then it came to a rest and the yellow silk rippled slowly to the ground.

'Look, sir — '

Ben this time, his arm pointing through a gap in the leaves.

'Over there on the left.'

Haston lifted the binoculars and swung them round.

A young black in a singlet and ragged shorts was loping down through the scrub on the edge of the pan. He ran out onto the surface, stopped, turned and shouted something. A moment later two others appeared and joined him. All three were dressed the same and none of them was carrying a gun. Haston tracked them for a moment as they approached the canister. Then he gave the glasses to Charlie.

'See what you can make out.'

Charlie studied the group. With a few exceptions like the Zulu, all Africans to Haston were identical – Bantu. He couldn't tell the difference between the various tribes any more than he could pick out an individual buck in a two-hundred herd of impala. For Ben and Charlie it was different. Even at four hundred yards they'd be able to say whether the men were Swana or not.

Charlie handed the glasses over to Ben, Ben examined the group too, then there was a short conversation in Setswana between them.

'They from outside, sir – right outside.'

Charlie's statement was emphatic and Ben nodded in agreement. Haston closed his eyes in relief; whatever else happened at least there'd be no problems about using the Schmeissers on the terrorist camp.

He took the glasses back and looked at the pan again. The three blacks had reached the canister and an argument seemed to be going on. Eventually, one of them, pushed forwards by the other two, prodded it cautiously with his foot. The canister rolled away, the Africans scampered back, then there was a burst of laughter. Obviously, they'd been frightened it was booby-trapped. The first black came forwards again, gripped the canister confidently now, shouldered it and set off back for the scrub. The other two gathered up the parachute, followed him and the three disappeared over the slope.

Haston put the binoculars down, rocked back on his heels and wiped the sweat from his face.

He was even more bewildered. No guards round the pan and now this – three unarmed young Africans laughing and chattering as they collected the canister as if they'd been kicking a football around on a Sunday afternoon in a Jo'burg township. For a terrorist gang they were either hopelessly inept, which didn't

92

square with the vicious rhetoric in the ransom note, or so sure of themselves they didn't have to take the most elementary safeguards.

He glanced at Ben. 'What do you figure from that?'

Ben frowned and rubbed his jaw. 'I don't understand, *Morena.*'

'Charlie?'

Charlie shrugged but said nothing. They were both as puzzled as he was.

'Well, there's nothing we can do until tonight,' Haston stretched out. 'As soon as it's dark you check out the spoor line, Charlie, come back and collect us and we'll see if we can find their camp.'

They slept in shifts like the day before until the late afternoon. Then at four Haston woke to find Ben shaking his shoulder. It was Ben's turn to watch but Charlie was awake too, leaning forwards intently at the front of the bush.

'What is it?'

Haston sat up, rubbed his eyes and peered out. The pan, wreathed with heat haze, was deserted and he couldn't see anyone round its rim.

'Smoke, sir,' Ben said. 'Camp fire smoke.'

Haston sniffed the hot dry air. There was nothing except the powdery scent of the dry grass and the stronger smell of resin from a broken moretla branch.

'Are you sure?'

'Sure, sir,' Charlie leant back, parted the branches and pointed. 'Coming from over there. That dead tree by where those fellows went. To the left and back, maybe two hundred yards. Two fires. You can see the smoke over the scrub.'

Haston looked out again. He found the dead tree which the Africans had climbed past with the canister, but he still couldn't see or smell any trace of a fire. That didn't surprise him – Ben's and Charlie's senses were infinitely sharper than his own.

'Maybe it's just a bush blaze starting?'

Charlie shook his head. 'No, *Morena.* That's two thin lines of smoke. Bush fire there'd be clouds all over. That's where they

93

got their camp.'

'Jesus Christ —'

Haston sat back. The lack of guards, the casual behaviour of the three blacks, now their camp sited right on the edge of the drop-zone – when he'd been expecting to have to spoor them thirty or forty miles deeper into the bush. None of it made any sense at all.

'Okay, Charlie, it's over to you. Three hours and you find out what the hell this bunch of freaks are up to.'

The three hours passed, the sun slanted down, then as soon as there was darkness over the pan Charlie left – sliding noiselessly out of the tunnel into the bush and vanishing round the rim.

It was seven when he set out and eleven when he returned, crawling into the hollow as silently as he'd left.

'Small camp, sir. Those two fires, they got them low but there's enough light all over. One tent, eight or nine boys all talking or eating, a handcart with some rifles inside —'

Sweat dripped off him as he crouched between Haston and Ben with the moon lighting his face.

'And the lady. I damn near bump into her before I get there.'

'What the hell do you mean?' Haston said. 'Isn't she under guard?'

'No, sir. I go round the pan, pick up those fellows' spoor from this morning, follow it past the tree. Then, bang, she's walking right in front of me. I don't know from where, she's just walking and she doesn't have no one with her. I stick in behind and she goes into the camp and starts eating with the boys.'

'What happened then?'

Charlie shrugged. 'Nothing, *Morena*. I watch them a time, go round the camp in case they got guards out, none that I can see, then I come back. That lady she's still by the fire when I go.'

'Draw it out for me.'

Haston shuffled back and smoothed a space on the sand between them. The moon was high now and with Ben holding the branches aside the ground shone pale and flat.

Charlie took a twig and sketched out the terrorist camp site. An open oval surrounded by scattered clumps of bush. The handcart at one end. The two fires, fifteen yards apart, with the terrorists grouped round them at the centre. The tent set back at the other end.

Haston studied it carefully. The tent was obviously for the woman. But what the hell was she doing roaming around at night on her own and why even at the camp hadn't they got any guards posted? All he could guess was that it was confidence, total overweening confidence. The woman's will broken after a month in captivity and knowing she hadn't a chance in the desert if she tried to run. The gang so utterly sure no one would follow them out there that they'd even dispensed with lookouts at their base.

Whatever the explanation there was only one way to find out.

'Right, let's get ready to move,' Haston said. 'We'll go straight over there. If the situation's still like you say, Charlie, we'll hit them at dawn. Give me the grease, Ben.'

Haston had blackened his shirt and shorts with oil before they left the truck. He'd also put a tin of axle grease in the pack which he mixed with sand now, and spread on his legs, arms and face. Then he checked the three guns. There were full magazines in both Schmeissers and Ben and Charlie each had a couple of spares. He'd put a clip of twelve bullets in the Urtzi and another thirty in his pocket, tied in a piece of cloth to keep them from rattling.

There was plenty more ammunition in the carton but that should be enough. A prolonged fire-fight was out of the question. It was either surprise, shock and a few fast devastating bursts – or nothing.

'Okay?'

Ben and Charlie nodded and they all crawled out of the bush.

The scrub on the left-hand rim of the pan was thicker and taller, and after the first hundred yards they could move upright. Forty minutes later, Charlie, who was leading, lifted his hand, beckoned them to the ground and disappeared.

He was away fifteen minutes. When he came back he whispered in Haston's ear, 'Same as before, *Morena*. The lady, she's gone and the tent flaps closed. There's one fellow walking round in the middle. The others sleeping by the fire.'

Haston nodded and nudged him on again. They covered another short stretch of scrub. Then Charlie crouched, edged carefully through a thorn thicket and stopped. Haston, bent forwards, went up to his shoulder.

The camp was in a shallow dip in front of them – exactly as Charlie had sketched it. The silhouette of the handcart to the right, the two smouldering circles of flame surrounded by sleeping bodies in the centre, the outline of the tent some distance away to the left, and a solitary figure pacing slowly from one end to the other.

Haston gazed down, head moving slowly from side to side as he tried to print every detail, every rock and tree and bush, on his mind. Then he drew back.

'I'll take the guy on watch — '

They were on the rear side of the thicket, heads close together as Haston whispered the instructions.

'You two work your way along to the right, get as close as you can to the fires, then sit tight until you hear my shot. When that happens all hell's going to break loose. Ben, you deal with anyone who breaks for the cart. Charlie, you hold back in case there's something we don't know about or anyone heads the other way. I'll go straight for the tent and grab the woman. Then Ben and I'll take her back to where we left the packs. You stay behind, Charlie, for five minutes to give us cover if anyone tries to follow. Afterwards, join us at the packs. Clear?'

They nodded and Haston glanced at his watch. It was almost two.

'I'll fire as soon as I reckon there's enough light, say just before seven. That's five hours. Don't start moving close until the moon's down but make damn sure you're in position by six. Okay, let's go over it again.'

He made them repeat the instructions in turn. Then he sent them off.

Four hours later Haston was lying by a termite mound less than thirty yards from the tent. The air was chillingly cold, the ground thick with frost and in the darkness after the moon had set he could only just see the single guard in front of him. He wasn't the same man who'd been walking round the camp at two. That one had been relieved when Haston was in the middle of an open stretch of sand between the thicket and the mound. He'd lain pressed against the earth while the voices drifted yawning and sleepy towards him. Then, after the change had been made, he'd crawled on.

Now he was watching the replacement. Every few minutes the man would stop and warm himself by the fire. Then he'd stroll to the tent, head and shoulders flickering against the stars in the gaps between the bushes on the far side of the camp, circle it, return to huddle over the fire again, and start once more.

Haston slid the Urtzi forwards and began to rub his hands, aching from the icy metal, to keep the blood circulating. Apart from the cold, he felt nothing he hadn't felt on safari a hundred times before. A small knot of adrenalin tension in his stomach, the total alertness that always came at the end of a long stalk, complete certainty in himself and his gun, readiness for anything that might happen after he fired.

It made no difference that this time the target was a man and not an animal. He was hunting again, on his own, out in the desert he knew, surrounded by its smells and sounds and textures – the scent of the night air, an owl calling, sand grating harsh and rough against his skin. When he squeezed the trigger it wouldn't be a man's head framed in the sight – it would be just another trophy. Only this time the most valuable trophy of all. His licence.

He crossed his arms, tucked his hands under them for warmth and waited. Then he suddenly stiffened.

It was still half an hour before dawn with no sign yet of the coming day, but a light had gone on inside the tent. Haston picked up the Urtzi and crouched by the mound. The light moved backwards and forwards, a pool of orange behind the canvas. Then it snapped off, there was the noise of a zip being pulled down and a figure came out.

'Nelson —'

A woman's voice calling softly. She stepped forward and Haston saw she was dressed. The guard, who'd been squatting by the fire, jumped up and ran towards her.

'I'm going over there now. If it moves when the sun comes up, I'll come straight back — '

When the guards had changed shift at two, they'd talked in a dialect Haston hadn't understood. Now the woman was speaking in English and he could hear every word.

'Otherwise, I'll wait until eight and be back then. You tell B'Volu when you wake him, all right?'

The man nodded, the woman ducked back into the tent and the torch went on again.

Haston, bent low in the darkness beside the mound, had no idea what was going on. The woman, the hostage, had spoken to the guard like a servant.

The torch wavered again behind the canvas – presumably she was collecting something she'd left inside the tent. Haston hesitated a moment longer. All he knew for sure was that in a few seconds she'd reappear and walk away – and the entire operation would dissolve in chaos.

Then he decided. He stood up, flicked off the safety catch and ran forward.

The man, standing by the tent flaps, didn't hear him until he was ten yards away. Then he swung round, peered into the darkness and opened his mouth to shout. At the same instant Haston lifted the rifle and fired. The sound of the shot in the pre-dawn silence was deafening and the guard was hurled back as if he'd been kicked in the chest. Haston pumped another bullet into the chamber, swerved left towards the tent and snatched at the flap.

'Get out, quick — !'

The woman was kneeling on a ground-sheet with a pair of binoculars in her lap. She must have been cleaning the lenses when he fired – she had a tissue in one hand and a small brush in the other. Now she looked up at him, pale-faced, confused, black hair falling across her shoulders as she shook her head in bewilderment.

'For Christ's sake, come on — '

Haston grabbed at her wrist, heaved her to her feet and pulled her stumbling outside. Behind him he heard shouts and the throbbing roar of an automatic, and vaguely registered that

Ben must have opened on the group round the fires.

He raced to the termite mound, dragging the woman after him, pushed her down and knelt beside her. The camp was a wild confusion of terrified screams, running figures, hammering bursts of gunfire and flashes of light from the detonating shells. As he watched one of the terrorists seized a blazing branch from the flames and hurled himself blindly, aimlessly towards the mound, eyes rolling and mouth distended in panic.

Haston waited until the man was almost on top of them. Then he swung up the Urtzi and fired from the hip. The heavy magnum bullet caught the African in the throat, tossed him backwards like the guard and sprayed the ground with blood. The branch rolled away, came to rest against a dry thorn bush and instantly blazed up again.

'What's this? What's happening — ?'

The woman's voice, bemused and trembling.

'It's all right,' Haston said. 'You're safe. Don't say anything, just do exactly what I tell you.'

He glanced to the right, where he could see the breech flashes of the Schmeisser, and swore. There was no chance of linking up with Ben in the darkness and he wouldn't be able to find the track they'd taken round the rim of the pan. All he could do was head for the pan itself, trust that Ben would guess what he'd done and double back to meet Haston there. It would mean exposing themselves on the open surface, but there was no other way he was going to find the hollowed-out bush and the packs again.

'Hold my hand, keep as low as you can and run like hell.'

Haston pulled the woman up and set off through the bush, leaping, sliding, tripping as he tugged her behind him through the thorn and over the hidden rocks.

Ten minutes later, panting and sweating, he stopped. The pan was below them and the first faint glow of daylight was seeping across the eastern sky. Haston rubbed his face, feeling the clotted grease between his fingers, shifted the Urtzi to his other hand, gripped the woman's arm, and plunged down the bank.

'Ben! Ben!'

He shouted upwards at the still-dark barrier of sand and bush above them.

They were twenty yards out in the open now, isolated and vulnerable as the fast-growing light washed scarlet and rose over the pan. If one of the terrorists had escaped from the camp with a rifle and hidden up in the scrub, they'd be helpless targets.

There was no answer and Haston shouted again, hoarse and urgent. Still no call in return and he tried once more, voice echoing in the silence now that the firing in the camp had stopped. Then, just as he was about to give up, he heard a distant shout to his right.

'*Morena!*'

A great wave of relief swept over him. Ben had guessed what he'd do and was somewhere up there in the bush on the rim.

'Down at the edge, Ben, fast as you can,' he called back.

Haston caught the woman's arm again and sprinted back to the shelter of the bank. Moments afterwards the branches crackled and Ben appeared, Schmeisser held head-high as he forced his way down through the scrub towards them.

'Thank God!' Haston greeted him. 'Are you all right?'

Ben nodded imperturbably. 'Fine, sir. I dropped maybe three or four of them. The rest, they gone running all over the place. Then I come looking for you.'

'And Charlie?'

'He's okay too, sir. He's waiting like you said. Then he'll go to the packs.'

'Well, let's get the hell over there. You reckon you can find them?'

Ben nodded again and they moved off, half-running, the woman stumbling behind Haston, round the base of the pan.

The hollowed-out bush was only two hundred yards from the point Haston had climbed down the bank. Ben cast ahead, then back and finally found it. They struggled upwards and stopped on the reverse side. Haston listened for a moment. The dawn was spreading across the whole plain now but he could hear nothing except the small morning sounds of the desert waking.

'Who are you?'

Haston swung round. It was the woman. She hadn't spoken since the confused questions in the darkness by the mound with the Schmeisser drumming and the terrorists screaming, and in the turmoil that followed Haston had barely glanced at her.

Now he looked at her properly for the first time. Tall, perhaps even slightly taller than he was, in safari boots, faded jeans, check shirt and with a thick sweater knotted round her neck. The long curling black hair and the strong-jawed face were as he remembered them from Liddell's photograph. But the mouth and eyes were different. The mouth not smiling, but hard and determined. The eyes no longer vague but dark, intense, unblinking.

Haston touched his jaw awkwardly, suddenly conscious of the grease and sweat and thorn-ripped shirt. He'd imagined her as a slightly scatty academic. Whatever else she wasn't that. She was still pale and her chest was heaving from the strain of the run. But in a few bare minutes after the traumatic experience of the raid and her rescue, she'd composed herself utterly and she was watching him without a tremor.

Miss Welborough-Smith was obviously a very formidable lady indeed.

'Haston, ma'am,' he said. 'Jerry Haston. And I believe you're — '

'My name is Alison Welborough-Smith,' she cut him off abruptly. 'I imagine you're aware of that. What I'd like to know is precisely what you think you're doing?'

The question came in an icy upper-class English voice, the hostility and barely-controlled anger behind it unmistakable.

Haston gaped at her, opened his mouth to answer, closed it again and shook his head. He'd travelled five hundred miles across the Kalahari, pulled her out of the hands of a gang of black thugs who were threatening to kill her, and her response was to treat him like an impertinent and unwelcome intruder.

'Listen, miss, maybe after all that you'd best sit down and rest a moment — '

He fumbled for the words.

'I'm sorry it happened so suddenly. I'm sorry too for the way I look,' Haston forced a smile. 'But the important thing is that we got you out. We're not clear yet, but in a couple of days with a bit of luck — '

She interrupted him again. 'Just answer my question, please.'

Haston shrugged helplessly. 'I was sent to see if I could get you free.'

'Who sent you?'

'Your people, the British Foreign Office, I guess.'

'And they told you to do that — ?'

She stepped towards him, stabbing out a finger, and Haston recoiled.

'They told you to kill and murder like some drunken bunch of hooligans, did they?'

The voice bitter, accusing, shaking with fury now as the control started to break down.

Haston shook his head again incredulously. 'They said you'd been kidnapped by some terrorists and they asked me to do everything I could to get you away.'

'Oh, they did, did they? Well, let me tell you what I think of you and what you did — '

She shivered and lifted her hand.

'I think you're a filthy sadistic little bastard!'

Then, before he could move, she slapped him twice with all her strength across the face.

11

He'd rocked back and almost fallen. Then as he straightened up again a wave of anger replaced his amazement at the ferocity and unexpectedness of her attack. She'd tried to go on talking but he cut her off violently.

'Anything you've got to explain, you can explain later. Meantime we're getting out of here — '

Haston swivelled round, crossed to a gap in the bush and looked down over the pan, searching for Charlie. He saw him immediately, loping steadily round the perimeter with his Schmeisser cradled against his chest. As he watched Charlie cut off to the right and climbed the bank.

'How did you make out, Charlie?'

'No trouble, sir — '

Charlie had stopped in front of him, face glistening with sweat but his breathing level and slow.

'They gone running every which way when Ben fired. Afterwards I didn't see no one. I stayed five minutes, then I made a circle round where you were. Still no one and no spoor heading this way. I reckon they all gone east.'

'Let's hope to Christ they're still running,' Haston said. 'But we're not going to chance that. Even with the ones we took out there must still be four or five left. They could stop, regroup and come after us — '

He glanced upwards. Full dawn now with the last stars gone, the pale sky deepening into violet and the sun clear of the horizon. Two more hours of coolness before the day's heat.

'We'll pack and trek until nine. That should put us eight miles away. Then we'll figure out how to stage it next. Ben, you take point this time with Charlie covering the rear — '

The two Africans nodded and Haston swung back towards the woman.

'You'll travel with me in the centre, Miss Welborough-

103

Smith. It's like before. If anything happens, you do exactly what I say.'

She glared at him, furious, hands clenched and quivering, knuckles showing white against her jeans.

'I've not the slightest intention of going anywhere at all with you—'

The same cold contemptuous voice with the words deliberately spaced out in rage.

'I am staying right here.'

Haston ignored her. He slung the Urtzi across his shoulder, hefted the pack and gestured Ben to move off. Then he looked round again.

'I doubt it, miss, I really doubt it. You either walk sensibly aside of me or you get trussed like a chicken and toted. What's your pick?'

He'd forgotten about everything now: amazement, anger, the unanswered questions about the guards and the camp and the woman's behaviour. For the moment all that mattered was to get away from the pan into thick cover before there was any chance of the terrorists striking back.

She went on gazing at him, trying to make up her mind whether to resist. Something in his face or his words must have convinced her it would be pointless. She hesitated, turned suddenly and set off after Ben who was already trudging away through the bush.

They travelled along the route Charlie had chosen two nights before on their approach to the pan. Then it had been slow and exhausting, with pauses every few minutes to listen for sounds in the darkness and the last four hundred yards a painful crawl on hands and knees. Now upright in the crisp morning air it was much easier and soon after nine Haston guessed they were a good eight miles from the hollowed-out bush.

He found an outcrop of rocks overhung by a tall umbrella acacia tree and summoned Charlie forward. Charlie examined the bare trunk, nodded and swarmed up into the dome of spreading branches at the top. From there, twenty feet above the ground, he could watch the scrub for half a mile on every side.

Then Haston checked the jerry-can of water. There were about five gallons left, say eight or nine pints for each of them to last the two days and nights until they reached the truck. It would be tight but, providing they only moved by darkness, it should be enough.

He told Ben to build a small bark fire and make coffee. Then he went over to the woman who'd sat down on a rock at the edge of the tree-shadow.

'How are you doing, ma'am?'

She hadn't spoken once since they'd left the pan, striding swiftly ahead of him without even glancing back. At least the journey had disposed of one worry – that she might have difficulty in making it to the truck. From the way she'd moved the remaining forty miles would be no problem at all.

'I wish to talk to you, Mr Haston.'

'I figure maybe we'd both better have a talk — '

Haston squatted down opposite her. With the rest of the march in front of them he decided to ignore her attack and start by being conciliatory.

'Look, I'm sorry for what I said back there at the pan. Trouble was, with those thugs less than a mile off, we just had to move – they could have lit out after us any moment. I guess you were all shaken up, I was in a hassle to shift and, well, I'm just sorry it happened that way.'

She looked at him indifferently.

'I was not remotely what you call shaken up,' she said. 'I do not consider those people thugs. And furthermore I'm not interested in your apologies.'

The chilling voice again, the clenched jaw, the pale furious face. Haston shook his head helplessly as the bewilderment flooded back.

'Then can we just get a few things straight,' he said. 'Am I crazy or were you kidnapped?'

'In a sense I was kidnapped, yes.'

'Hell, I don't know about senses. Far as I'm concerned if people get kidnapped, they get kidnapped. Anyway, that's what they told me about you and they asked me to get you out. Which is just what I did, right?'

She stood up, walked over to the tree, circled the trunk and came back, but didn't answer.

'Listen, Miss Welborough-Smith,' Haston went on. 'Maybe I've got it all wrong, maybe there's things I don't know. But whatever, none of this adds up. Why don't you tell me what happened?'

Ben appeared with two mugs of coffee. She took one and sipped. Then she lifted her head.

'What do you do, Mr Haston?'

'Right now, all I'm doing is trying to get you safely back to Gabs.'

'I don't mean now, I mean normally.'

Haston felt for the pack of cigarettes in his shirt-pocket, pulled one out and lit it, the first in three days. He inhaled and hunched himself forwards as he let the smoke out.

'I'm a hunter,' he said. 'A professional hunter.'

'Oh, my God —'

She laughed quickly, mirthlessly, and hurled the coffee onto the sand.

'What an obscene irony! But of course how appropriate, the obvious choice to send for something like this! And how much did they pay you for that particular piece of butchery?'

Haston didn't reply. He couldn't see her face – he was gazing at the ground – but her shadow jumped across the chequered earth as she paced, tense and restless, between the rocks.

'All right,' the shadow was still. 'I'll endeavour to explain. I very much doubt you'll understand but I'd ask you to afford me the elementary courtesy of listening —'

She sat down on the rock again. Haston glanced up and waited.

'I came out here four months ago, Mr Haston, to study certain mammals. In particular one species of the larger carnivora, *Panthera pardus*. The animal you will no doubt know as the African leopard —'

Four months ago, she'd set up camp in the bush just as Liddell had described, not by the pan but a hundred miles farther south. Initially, there were four of them in the party. The woman, a young research assistant, a cook and a tracker. The research assistant had contracted tick fever soon after they arrived, and the charter pilot had flown him out on the first of his supply flights.

When the terrorists appeared she'd been alone in the camp with the cook and the tracker.

'They came one evening about six weeks ago,' she said. 'Eleven of them just before dusk. Nothing happened, there was no silly drama or trouble or shooting. They just walked into the camp and said what they were going to do.'

Haston frowned. 'Who did the talking?'

She hesitated for a moment. Then she said, 'The man in charge of them was an African who spoke excellent English. He stayed a week and organized everything, then he left. He was due back ten days' ago, but for some reason he didn't return.'

Haston nodded.

He understood the gang's extraordinary behaviour now – the casualness, the lack of guards round the pan, the terror and confusion when he'd attacked. Without direction after their leader had gone the rest of them had simply reverted to type – indolent, stupid, undisciplined young urban blacks. It was a miracle they'd managed to organize even one night look-out and that was probably from fear of lion.

'And just what did this fellow say was going to happen?' Haston asked.

'He told me I was going to be held until he got a reply to the letter he left for the pilot to collect. Then I could go.'

'Meantime what were you supposed to do?'

She hesitated again, unknotted the sweater tied round her neck – the morning's heat was rising now – and folded it in her lap. Then she suddenly leant forwards.

'Do you know what I mean by a black leopard, Mr Haston?'

She was gazing straight at his eyes. The anger had gone and her voice had an urgent probing intensity.

'Sure.'

'But you've never seen one?'

Haston shook his head.

Of course he hadn't seen one. Black leopards were creatures of dream, legend, mythology. In the past thirty years, two were

107

supposed to have been killed by bushmen and their skins bartered for fortunes in tobacco at desert trading stores. As far as he knew, those were the only reports of the animal in living memory. He'd never met anyone who'd even claimed to have seen the pelts, let alone a specimen in the wild, and the stories about them were hazy, ancient, clouded by cynicism and contradiction. No one knew for sure whether the creature still existed – or precisely what it was if it did.

'I have seen a black leopard,' she went on. 'In fact, I've seen it daily for the past three months. The last occasion was yesterday evening. Unless it's moved since then it will still be within ten miles of where we are now. I know that because I've followed the animal from the moment I first saw it — '

Haston listened in growing amazement as she told the story.

Six weeks before the terrorists arrived her tracker returned to the camp one afternoon with the news that he'd found fresh leopard spoor in the desert to the west. She immediately went out with him again, picked up the line of the spoor and followed it. The pug-marks, the biggest both she and the tracker had ever seen, eventually led to a large acacia tree. They waited there throughout the evening and shortly after midnight the animal jumped down.

'There was a full moon and we saw it clearly for several minutes before it moved off to hunt,' she said. 'It was as big as the tracks had indicated, a female of almost two hundred pounds – or that was my guess. If I'm right, that would make it among the largest specimens ever recorded. And it was totally uniformly black — '

She stayed by the tree all night, saw the leopard return at dawn, then the following day she set up a proper observation post with a hide and a mounted telescope.

She watched the animal for three weeks. Then one morning it didn't come back to the tree. She and the tracker spent two days casting in circles through the surrounding bush before they found its spoor again, and discovered the leopard had moved its base to another tree a few miles north. The observation post was moved, she continued her twice-daily watches, then the pattern was repeated – the leopard vanished and after another

108

search they located it again at yet another base further north still.

A week later the terrorist gang walked into her camp. Here Haston started shaking his head again in disbelief. According to the woman, she'd explained to their leader what she was doing, and asked to be allowed to carry on her observations while they were waiting for the reply to the ransom note.

'And he agreed to that?' Haston said. 'He let you go on just as if nothing had happened?'

'He did more,' she said. 'By then it was clear to me the animal's movements weren't random. They had a coherent pattern – for some reason it was systematically travelling north. To follow it required moving camp whenever it moved. I explained this and he volunteered to change camp sites as necessary. That was why I was at the pan last night, we arrived there two weeks ago simply because it was on the leopard's route. Had that canister been dropped a few days from now, I'd probably have been further north still.'

She stopped and Haston gazed at her in silence.

Somehow this gaunt implacable-looking woman, dark eyes still unblinking but face streaked with dust and sweat now, had persuaded a murderous bunch of black terrorists not merely to let her continue her studies of the leopard uninterrupted, but actually to alter their arrangements to accommodate her. And this while she was ostensibly their captive under threat of death.

It was almost unbelievable. Yet it had happened, it explained the last unanswered questions – such as her fury after he'd pulled her from the tent – and in a way there was a certain crazy logic to it. For the terrorists, after she'd convinced them she had no other interest apart from the leopard, a cooperative hostage who didn't even need guards must have been a much more attractive proposition than a terrified prisoner who might well have tried to kill herself rather than endure captivity in the desert.

Bizarre, crazy, but plausible. More than that it was a fact – and Haston hadn't any doubt she was speaking the truth. Single-minded and obdurate, obsessed by the animal, she'd simply ignored the threat, manipulated the situation to her own advantage, and converted her captors into servile allies.

And now, awed, baffled and exhausted, he was landed with her.

'Mr Haston—'

She got up from the rock again and stood with her back to him looking out over the bush.

'As a hunter I don't need tell you how rare that leopard is. Certainly one of the rarest animals on earth, possibly the rarest. Zoologists have spent years searching for it without success. My own observations over these three months have been unique, but they've still barely scratched the surface. Most important of all they haven't yet established exactly what it is I've been studying—'

She swung round, fingers plucking at the folded sweater.

'Do you understand the term melanism?'

Haston nodded.

Melanism. An abnormal darkness of colour in certain animals, birds and insects just as albinism – for the same unknown reasons – caused abnormal whiteness in others.

'There are only two possible explanations for that leopard's colouring, Mr Haston. Either it's an example of melanism, a freak. Or—'

She hesitated.

Haston lit a new cigarette from the butt of his last one and ground out the smouldering end in the sand. She didn't need to go on because he could guess what was coming.

'Or it's a separate species,' he said.

'Good Heavens, I wouldn't necessarily go as far as that—'

She was instantly the scientist, cautious, sceptical, wary.

'It may be just a sub-species, even a variant of the normal form. But, yes, an entirely separate species can't be ruled out of the question.'

'And how did you propose deciding what it was?'

'I told you the animal is moving north,' she said. 'None of the big feline carnivores change territory without cause. Here the usual reasons – competition for prey, shortage of game or water, human and cattle encroachment – simply don't apply.

110

So there must be something else. I'm guessing but I think I may have the answer. I believe that leopard may be searching for a mate.'

'A black one?'

She nodded. 'If it's just melanistic, of course, it'll breed with any ordinary-coloured male – they'd both belong to the same race. But if it is truly different, if the black leopard is distinct, then it will only mate with one of its own kind. In that case this one will ignore the ordinary males and go on until it finds another black.'

And if Welborough-Smith had witnessed that she'd have made scientific history. The shadowy prowling creature of legend would have become fact, made flesh and blood, studied and photographed and written about, no doubt even classified under her own name – the ultimate dream of any naturalist.

Haston understood everything now – except what happened next.

'You were sent to free me, Mr Haston,' she said. 'Isn't that correct?'

She was still standing above him, the sweater in her hands, the dust on her face clotting into dry flakes with the heat. Haston glanced up.

'Sure,' he said. 'I just did what I was asked to. I'm glad we've got it straightened out at last.'

'Well, I wish to apologize for my own reaction afterwards. You obviously couldn't have been expected to know the circumstances of my capture and I was perhaps a little over-wrought. I realize that now and I regret both what I said and did.'

'Hell,' Haston shrugged embarrassed. 'Don't bother about that. Anyone might have done the same.'

'However — '

She went on as if she hadn't been listening to him.

'Now that you have freed me, your job is clearly finished. If you can spare me a little water for the journey back to the pan, I would appreciate it. If not I'll manage without. Once I'm back there's no problem – there's still ample in a pool left by the winter rains.'

For a moment Haston thought he must have mis-heard her.

Then he said slowly, 'Are you trying to tell me you want to go back there?'

'Naturally,' she nodded incisively. 'As I've just taken pains to explain to you, I've been given a chance such as no one else has ever been given before. A chance to identify and perhaps guarantee the survival of a new species of leopard. That is an immense responsibility, for me personally, to the scientific community, to the entire fauna of this continent. Under no circumstances whatsoever can I pass it up.'

'Miss Welborough-Smith,' Haston got to his feet, 'there are still half-a-dozen terrorists out there, maybe more —'

'I doubt it,' she cut him off. 'I imagine after what you did they're already on their way back to wherever they came from. But even if they are still there I can handle them. I've done it once, I can do it again.'

'And how do you figure on surviving alone in the desert?'

'There's a large quantity of supplies at the camp,' she said. 'They certainly won't have taken all of them. Also it will only be for a matter of a week or so. By then you and your men should be back in Gaborone. As soon as you inform the High Commission they will organize a flight out and I can make arrangements for re-equipping my expedition.'

Haston was silent.

She was mad, he realized that at last. Mad with the blind confidence and terrifying half-logic of the totally insane. A single animal – an extraordinary rarity but in essence no different from the big cats he set up for his clients to shoot each safari – had become such an obsession that her reason had snapped.

It was just conceivable the rest of the gang were already heading back for the border. Far more likely they were preparing a pursuit: by now they'd know from the tracks they only had three men to deal with and the woman was too valuable a prize to surrender without a fight. If she fell into their hands again, there'd be no question of co-operation – all else apart there would be vengeance for the ones who must have died in her rescue.

But even if, against all probability, the gang had gone there was still the desert. Before she'd had a fixed camp and two experienced Africans to look after her. Now she was proposing to set off with a few provisions and maybe a flask of rainwater, alone, unarmed, to spoor the leopard across the width of the Kalahari. Twelve hours, he'd give her, maybe twenty-four if she was lucky and survived the first night. Afterwards, there would be just jackal and swollen-bellied maribou and another small litter of white bones on the sand.

Except he couldn't even give her the chance of twelve hours because Liddell would never believe him.

'Ma'am, you and I together, we're going back to Gaborone,' he said gently. 'Soon as we're there you can fix up whatever you want.'

'By which time it will be too late. The animal will have moved on. I won't find it again, you know that as well as I do — '

Her cheek was twitching but her voice was still quiet and urgent.

'How much are you being paid, Mr Haston?'

Haston flushed. 'I don't think that's really relevant — '

'It's very relevant,' she said. 'I'd assumed you were simply being paid a fee to free me. From your attitude I now deduce you won't collect the money unless you deliver me safe in Gaborone. In that case tell me how much and I'll guarantee to match it – to top it. You can take my word that I have considerable resources available.'

It wasn't an offer – it was a final desperate appeal made, Haston guessed, in the only way she knew how, in those clipped pedantic phrases. He shook his head.

'I'm sorry, miss, but I'm responsible for your safety.'

'All right — '

She lowered her shoulders and started to turn away. Haston, thinking it was over, lifted his head to call Charlie down from the tree.

As he moved she whirled back and flung the sweater across his face. Blinded, taken totally by surprise, Haston staggered back. Then, before he could remove the sweater from over his eyes, he felt an agonizing sickening pain in his groin. He crumpled and fell sideways, choking, retching, hands pressed against his testicles, dimly aware she must have kicked him there with the metal-covered tip of her safari boot.

At the same time he heard the rustle of grass and the drum of running feet.

'Ben — !'

He struggled to his knees and shouted hoarsely, saliva trickling down his chin and aching spasms gripping his stomach.

'Stop her, for Christ's sake!'

She was thirty yards away twisting and racing between the thorn bushes with her hair streaming out in a dark fan behind. Ben dropped the coffee pot, plunged past him and set off after her. A moment later Haston heard Charlie drop to the ground and saw his tall boney figure racing away too.

Haston, limping and shaking, caught up with them five minutes afterwards. By then they were a hundred yards from the tree in a clearing in the bush. The woman was lying writhing on the ground, face pressed to the earth, with Charlie kneeling across her legs and Ben holding her arms twisted up against her back. There was blood dripping from one of Ben's wrists and Charlie rocked backwards and forwards each time she heaved.

Haston ripped off his belt, knelt down beside them and lashed her hands together.

'All right, let her go now — '

The three of them stood up, Ben sucking at his wrist, and after a moment the woman clambered awkwardly to her feet.

'She take a bite at you, Ben?' Haston said.

'Yes, sir. But I got bitten by cats before and I always lived.'

Ben grinned and Haston turned to look at her. She was standing upright, hunched slightly forwards because of her arms tied behind her, panting, face chalk-white under the new smears of dust and sweat, eyes glazed and black and murderous with hate. Overwhelming hate, so fierce and concentrated that it came across like a physical charge.

Haston had never experienced anything like it and he stepped back involuntarily, forgetting briefly even his own pain and anger. Then he recovered himself.

'It's all over now, lady,' he said. 'No more talk, no more nothing. We're just going back to Gaborone.'

114

'You'll have to carry me every inch of the way.'

Her voice even more chilling, more bitter, more furious than before.

Haston shrugged. 'It's your choice, just like it was by the pan. You can either walk in reasonable comfort. Or you get trussed, bound, wrapped and gagged. Either way we'll get you there. And let me tell you something — '

His groin was throbbing and his own rage at what she'd done, at the mad violent bitch, came surging back.

'I hope you pitch for being carried. Because although that's going to be tough on us, it'll be nothing like as tough as it'll be on you. You'll feel every single step. And personally that's going to give me a whole load of pleasure.'

'You little swine — !'

'Ben, Charlie, come over here.'

Haston ignored her, took the two Africans to the far side of the clearing and explained. It was a combination of the leopard, the desert and her capture, he said. Together they'd made her temporarily insane, so much so that she wanted to commit suicide by staying out there alone in the bush. His responsibility was to return her safely to Gaborone – even if the three of them had to carry her to the truck.

Ben and Charlie nodded understandingly – they both knew what could happen to people exposed to the Kalahari. Then Haston sent Charlie over to the tree to collect one of the packs and returned to the woman.

'Which is it going to be?' He asked.

There was no answer, just the same terrible glare.

'Okay, I assume that means my way,' he said. 'Well, try it for a few hours and see how you fancy it.'

Charlie came back with the pack. Haston told him to empty its contents and tear the canvas into strips. Then they set about binding her.

Even with the three of them and her hands already tied it took several minutes. She fought every inch of the way, kicking, struggling, heaving, lashing until all four of them were drenched with sweat. But finally she was lying panting and helpless on the ground again, this time paralysed by the canvas strips which were bound round her from her ankles to her shoulders.

Haston looked down at her.

'Are you really going to force me to gag you, too?'

She was like a trapped animal lying there and for an instant he felt almost a sense of pity for the madness, the fanaticism. But her eyes were still remorseless, unyielding, vengeful and he knew the answer without her replying. If there was the slightest chance, even if it meant giving them away to the terrorists, she'd shout.

He got out his handkerchief and knelt down beside her. Then she opened her mouth, licked away the dust and lifted her head.

'You have probably just made yourself responsible for the extinction of one of the most beautiful animals on earth,' she said. 'You'll live with that all your life. And however long it takes, whatever I have to do, I'm going to see you pay for it.'

Haston dropped the handkerchief quickly over her mouth, knotted the ends behind her head and beckoned to Ben. Ben stepped forward and heaved her lightly onto his massive shoulder. Then they turned and set off back for the tree.

It was Haston's fault and he cursed savagely at his fumbling stupidity as he looked down at the wreckage. Or rather it was the fault of his exhaustion and the woman who'd caused it.

He glanced across at her, sitting silhouetted against the stars, and swore again. Ben and Charlie were watching him anxiously.

Two hours before dawn on the night after they'd left the tree. The day before they'd carried her in turn until the midday heat became unbearable. It was slower, of course, far slower, than if she'd been walking, but by the time they stopped Haston reckoned they'd put a further six miles between themselves and the terrorist base at the pan.

They rested until darkness. Then they'd gone on, taking turns to move her, a limp deadweight bundle, on their shoulders. For her, trussed, jolting, hands and feet numb from the constricted blood, it must have been torment and three times

116

Haston offered to let her walk. Each time his only response was silence and the staring hate in her eyes. Ben's shifts were much longer than Haston's and Charlie's, but even Ben's immense strength wasn't limitless and Haston had just finished a spell when it happened.

He called a rest and told Charlie to get out the jerry-can of water. Charlie put the jerry-can on the ground and poured some water into a mug. Haston drained it, stepped forwards to refill the mug and stumbled. Like the others, sweating from the walk and the effort of carrying the woman, he hadn't noticed the bitter cold.

The jerry-can wasn't one of the old-fashioned metal containers − it was made of light-weight injection-moulded polyurethene. Tough and pliable by day, it became rigid and brittle when the temperature fell to freezing-point at night. As Haston stumbled he knocked it against a rock. Instantly, there was a sharp splintering sound and seconds later all but a cupful of the water, held in the shattered base, had drained away into the sand.

He kicked the broken plastic fragments viciously. Then he looked at Charlie.

'How far to go?'

'To the truck, *Morena*? Maybe fifteen miles,' Charlie said.

Fifteen miles. Not just to the truck but also to the full jerry-can buried with the rest of their supplies under the cairn of stones beside it.

If the three of them had been on their own, he would have pushed straight on and chanced it. The last few hours, moving, sweating, dehydrating in the full desert heat, would have been hell, but they'd have survived that. The woman made it very different. With her as baggage, to go on now waterless would be suicidal. All one of them had to do was fold an ankle under her weight and he'd be lucky to get two of the party back alive.

'How are you feeling, Charlie?' He asked.

Charlie shrugged. 'I can make it, sir. You count on maybe midnight. I'll be back then.'

'Good for you, Charlie — '

Haston tapped him on the arm. Charlie had understood

117

instantly without any explanation. As a tracker he was the fastest, fittest, best-equipped of the three of them to do it. Use the cool dawn hours to reach the truck, lie up there through the heat, then make the journey back after dark with the spare can.

'Okay, take the pack and get going.'

Charlie shouldered the empty pack and loped away into the darkness. Then Haston walked over to the woman.

'Largely because of you, miss,' he said, 'we've just lost all our water. That means we're going to have to wait up here a whole day without any. If you've never gone dry for a day in the desert before, you'll find it's quite an experience. Also, Charlie, who like it or not helped save your life, is doing an extra thirty miles on foot to see we get out. I just hope you're happy.'

She sat motionless, rigid, saying nothing, just gazing at him with the same ferocious implacable eyes.

He leant down, unknotted the gag, then removed the strips of canvas binding her legs and arms.

Even anger was pointless now. She'd be too exhausted to make another break. All she was doing was getting a perverse masochistic pleasure of the pain she'd inflicted on herself, punishing herself as well as him for what had happened.

'I suggest you grab some sleep,' Haston straightened up. 'And if you've got any idea of running again – forget it. Either Ben or I will be awake all the time.'

He went back to Ben, told him to take the first watch and huddled down in a scoop of sand, arms wrapped round his chest against the cold. When he shut his eyes she was still sitting erect against the night sky.

Dawn came, then the sun, then the long scorching hours of heat. There were no trees for shelter, only patches of dusty patterned shadow under the thorn bushes which moved as the sun climbed. Ben, on an early foray, managed to find a few *tsava* melons – small juicy green fruit which Haston carefully rationed and distributed for them to suck at intervals throughout the day.

The rest of the time they lay still and silent in the scraps of shade, watching the bateleur eagles wheeling slow and high overhead. If it hadn't been for the melons, Haston doubted

whether any of them would have lasted through to the evening without fainting. When the light began to fade his head was dizzy and aching, his lips cracked, his mouth raw and parched, and his skin stiff with dry sweat.

The woman was extraordinary. She didn't speak once. She just lay, gaunt, dirty, white-faced, her hair tangled and clotted with sand, gazing upwards. Only it wasn't the eagles she was seeing, Haston knew, it was the image of the leopard – and her eyes never closed as she tracked it in her mind across the sky.

Then suddenly it was dark and just as quickly, it seemed, after the interminable hours of sun, midnight. Charlie returned thirty minutes later. He unslung the pack, lifted out the jerry-can and filled the mug with water – the sound of the splashes ringing cool and soft.

The woman drank first, then Haston waved the mug towards Ben. But instantly, inexplicably he wasn't thinking of himself, of his own raging thirst, of the water there to slake it – more than enough now, whatever happened, to get them all back to the truck.

He was watching Charlie. Charlie hadn't uttered a word since his return, he hadn't even looked at Haston. For some reason Haston couldn't even guess at something had happened while he was away – something very bad.

Haston drank at last, filling and draining the mug three times. Then he put it down. The two Africans had moved away and were talking to each other in Setswana. He walked over to them and squatted down.

'What is it, Charlie?' he said quietly.

Charlie's face was lowered and it was several moments before he answered.

Then he said, 'You tell us all the truth, *Morena*?'

'Sure I did, Charlie.'

'And there's no one else in this?'

'Apart from the British guy who sent me, no, of course not. Why?'

Charlie hesitated again. Then he looked up. Normally his face was calm and smiling. Now it was troubled, his forehead creased with doubt, his eyes restless and disturbed.

'That truck's closer than we thought,' he said at last. 'I get about half a mile from it and the sun, she's still not much up. Then I see a nice little steenbok away left in the bush. It's early, I still got the gun and I think we can use the meat. So I cut off after him. That buck keeps moving and I circle right round the trees where the truck's hidden and then suddenly I'm crossing new tyre spoor.'

Haston frowned. 'Have we got poachers out there?'

'That's what I think first, sir. So I follow the spoor, going careful. It takes me back towards the trees. Then I stop. There's another truck near the trees, a big new Chevvy, and five men. Four of the men, they got guns and they're white, sir. I don't know them. But the fifth, he's black and he's from Gaborone—'

Charlie dropped his head again.

'He's called Sitavu, *Morena*. He's a rich man with his own truck and a big farm. They say bad stories about him. They say he gets all this money because he works for the South Africans – for their police.'

He stopped and Haston closed his eyes and shuddered. Then he asked, 'What did you do, Charlie?'

'I watch them a time and it's like they're waiting – if I hadn't seen that buck I'd have walked right on them. Then I back off, find some thick bush and sleep. When it's dark I go round the other side of the trees where I buried the stores. Those men, they're all by a fire near their truck. I got the trees between and I left that jerry-can on top under the stones, so I don't have to dig. I take the stones off and get it. Then I come right back.'

Silence again. Ben had also kept his face carefully turned away while Charlie was talking. Now they both looked at Haston in the starlight.

'I don't know who those men are,' Haston said. 'But whoever they are, I was told nothing about them. If they're South African police, Charlie, like you think, and if I'd known they were going to be involved, I'd never have brought you into this. I'd never have come in myself. That's my word.'

He gazed straight back at them and they both nodded, silently accepting it.

'Okay. Well, just wait a moment while I figure out what the hell we're going to do — '

Haston stood up and walked away. He didn't know where he was going, he didn't care. He just desperately wanted time and silence in which to think.

He'd been conned, that was all he knew for certain. Conned, cheated, ripped off and lied to – all by that bastard Liddell. Liddell hadn't said he was working with the South African police, with BOSS. If he had done, as Liddell knew, Haston would have jumped out of the Ford, gone straight back to Gaborone and reported the Englishman to the authorities. To be connected with BOSS was as dangerous for him as for Ben and Charlie, who'd believed Haston had led them into it.

'Mr Haston — '

He turned. She'd walked over, feet silent on the sand, and was standing close to him in the darkness.

'I overheard your conversation. When you referred to those men as South African police, you meant they were agents of the Bureau of State Security, didn't you?'

It was the first time she'd spoken in thirty hours. The wildness and fury had gone from her voice and she was as calm again as when she'd been discussing the leopard.

Haston nodded. 'I guess so. Although I've not an idea in hell why they're there.'

'I think I can tell you,' she said. 'You looked astonished when I explained that the leader of my captors had allowed me to continue studying the animal. However, you never asked me his name, nor would I have told you then if you had. I will now. You've probably heard of him. He was once a friend of mine. He's called George Mlanda.'

Haston gaped at her.

Each time he thought she'd exhausted her capacity to astound him she did it again. Mlanda. The best-known and most-hunted terrorist leader in southern Africa. And a friend of Miss Welborough-Smith. Whatever her relationship with him, if BOSS had learned he was leading the ransom gang, they'd have risked almost anything to get information about him before the trail ran cold.

121

'Even for a prize like George Mlanda,' she went on, 'sending BOSS agents into Botswana is appallingly dangerous. If they were discovered to have been here, it would be political dynamite. Had you considered that?'

'Sure. But they obviously figure it's worth the risk.'

'The risk? I wonder how much of a risk. BOSS must be working with the people who sent you, that's how they knew where to find your truck. But apart from me, whom they no doubt assumed would be so thankful to be free that I'd keep silent about anything, the only other person who'd know of their involvement would be you — '

She paused. 'BOSS isn't particularly noted for its scrupulousness, Mr Haston.'

Haston said nothing. He stood there cold, numb, trying to take it in.

An agreement between Liddell and some figure in that tall grim building on Eloff Street. *We find you someone prepared to try to free the woman.* (BOSS had probably been the anonymous 'friend' who gave Liddell Haston's name.) *If he's successful, we have her for a few days to learn what she knows about Mlanda. And the man, well, we take care of him. Quickly, efficiently, discreetly, so there's no embarrassment for anyone. A bullet through the mouth – either just another lost victim of the Kalahari or at worst, if the body's found, a disgraced hunter who killed himself.*

So simple and so obvious – more obvious than she even realized because she didn't know about the licence. Haston breathed out slowly: there was sweat on his palms in spite of the chilling air and his legs felt weak.

'I think you've been set up, Mr Haston. In fact, I'm quite sure of it — '

The same crisp upper-class accent but growing confidence and strength now in her voice as she continued.

'Yet even if I'm wrong you will still have me to contend with. If those men do let you through alive, I will make quite sure it's publicly known you were connected with them, in league with them. However much you deny it you're not going to be believed. You'll be kicked out of this country so fast you'll scarcely know it's happened.'

122

She stopped and Haston waited. She hadn't told him all of this gratuitously, he knew that.

'Those BOSS agents are a matter of indifference to me,' she said. 'They'll learn nothing about Mlanda but I'll certainly be delayed – irretrievably as far as finding that animal again is concerned. However, you have a truck, provisions, an experienced tracker. I will give you a chance, Mr Haston — '

She was looking at him steadily, totally sure of herself now.

'Get hold of that truck, take-me back to where I last saw the leopard and help me find it again. Then you can leave one of your boys with me and go back to Gaborone. You'll be satisfied I'm safe and you'll have done your job. I in return will give you my promise never to mention your connection with BOSS.'

Haston gazed back at her. 'And how do you reckon I'm going to get the truck out from under the noses of those guys? Four of them, Charlie said, all armed and not bone-headed young blacks but serious, trained soldiers.'

'I'm not sure.' she said, 'That's for you to work out. However, owing to the fortunate accident of breaking that jerry-can, the situation's been completely reversed. We know they're there, so the element of surprise is on our side. I imagine if you came on them unawares you could disarm them, disable their vehicle and we could be away without a shot being fired — '

She paused again. 'I think you can handle it, Mr Haston. In fact you've got to handle it. For you it's not just a chance – it's the only chance.'

A gust of night wind raised eddies of sand round her feet and an owl called softly above.

Haston hesitated. Then he turned abruptly and walked back to where Ben and Charlie were squatting.

'How many hours to the truck? Charlie?' he asked.

'Moving fast about four, *Morena*.'

'If you get in a couple of hours' sleep now, can you do it again?'

Charlie nodded. 'Yes, sir.'

'Okay,' Haston said. 'You better get your head down right away. Because afterwards we're all moving. We've got a job to do first. Then we're going hunting leopard.'

Haston raised himself cautiously and looked across the open space of sand at the Chevvy.

It was twenty yards away with the copse where his own truck was hidden the same distance further back in a direct line behind. When he'd first seen it, guided through the bush by Charlie an hour earlier in the darkness, only one of the men had been awake, a guard standing by the hood. Now in the growing dawn light the other four were up, three whites and the black from Gaborone Charlie had recognized.

As he watched, one of them piled some branches over a low fire, fanned it to flame and put a billy-can on top.

'Five minutes, Pete, all right?'

The voice, flat, nasal, unmistakably South African, carried clear to him across the sand in the still morning air.

'Jeez, you take your time. Come on, man, I'm bloody freezing.'

The guard by the hood wandered over to the fire and stood gazing morosely down at the flames.

Haston lowered himself to the ground. Ben was lying on his left, Charlie on his right, both with their loaded Schmeissers in front of them. They'd left the woman in a clump of thorn on the far side of the copse: she'd wanted to come with them but in the end reluctantly agreed with Haston that if anything went wrong she'd only be an added liability. Haston lifted his hand, spread out his five fingers and glanced at the two Africans in turn. Both of them nodded. Then he checked the safety-catch on the Urtzi and waited.

'Get your mugs everyone – coffee up!'

The same nasal voice calling across the sand. Haston waited another two minutes, then he raised himself again. The guard had propped his rifle against the Chevvy's door and all five men were crouched round the fire drinking. He could see the steam rising from the mugs and even smell the coffee grounds.

'Ready,' he whispered.

Ben and Charlie crouched beside him, the barrels of their

autòmatics thrust forwards into the low screen of scrub.

'Now!'

They stood upright together. For a moment no-one noticed them. Then one of the men glanced casually round, froze and began to open his mouth.

'Don't move!' Haston shouted. 'Everyone just stay right where you are.'

He crossed the sand quickly, Ben and Charlie level on either side of him. As he reached the fire, another man, stocky and ginger-haired, tried to get to his feet. Haston checked and swung the Urtzi towards him.

'One inch more,' he said, 'and you get a magnum in your gut. Understand?'

The man dropped back onto his haunches and Haston went on again until he was only a few feet from the flames. All five were gazing up at him. He looked at each of them in succession. The black, Sitavu, had nothing but the four whites all had hand-guns buckled in holsters to their waist-belts. Then there was the guard's rifle leaning against the door and a pile of repeaters stacked inside the truck.

'Unbuckle your belts and throw them over there,' Haston gestured to his left. 'We got three heavy automatics. Anyone tries anything and you all go. Okay, one by one starting with you.'

The ginger-haired man again. He was about forty, older than the other whites and, Haston guessed, the group's leader.

'What do you want, man?' he asked.

'Christ!' Haston said, 'You know bloody well what I want.'

'You got the woman — ?'

There was no pretence, no effort to dissimulate. He just came straight out with it. Haston didn't answer and the man went on.

'Sure, I reckon you got her, man, otherwise you wouldn't be doing this. We only want to talk to her, man, a day, maybe just a few hours. Then you can all go on — '

'Don't give me any of that crap,' Haston cut him off. 'Get your belt on the sand and shut up.'

The man, face pocked with acne scars, tossed the belt over to where Haston had pointed and Haston gestured at the next.

125

Then he went round until all four belts lay in a pile out of reach.

'Get them, Ben,' he said, 'and the others. The way we fixed it up — '

Ben slung his Schmeisser, picked up the belts, then collected the rifle and the repeaters and set off into the bush. A minute later there was a series of single muffled shots at intervals. Ben was doing what Haston had instructed him on the trek to the copse: jamming the gun-barrels in the ground and then firing a shot to blow out the muzzle.

Ben came back, looked inside the cabin and checked through the gear in the back of the truck.

'I don't see nothing else, sir,' he said.

'Okay, let's get right on with the next part.'

Ben walked off in the direction of the copse and Haston moved slightly to one side, so that both he and Charlie had the group covered with an equal arc of fire. One of the men shifted slightly, his legs cramped under him, and Haston instantly jabbed the Urtzi forwards.

'Not even that, fellow,' he said. 'Just once again and it'll be the last thing you ever do.'

The rest of them sat very still. Then their leader glanced up.

'You planning on taking us back with you to Gaborone, man?' he asked.

'My plans are my own bloody business,' Haston said.

'Well, maybe you like to know anyway there's more than just us here. Few hours drive back we got a Bonanza, a back-up truck, a load more of us. No way they going to let you through. Also we got a sked with them in twenty minutes — '

Haston looked quickly at the truck's cabin. Through the open window he could see the blue-grey metal grille and the row of control knobs of a transmitter.

'If we don't keep that sked they're going to be over here like greased lightning. You figured on that?'

Haston didn't answer. A sked – a fixed air-wave contact time – with a back-up force a few hours' drive away. A force that included a Bonanza spotter plane. It could be all bluff, all truth or a mixture of the two. There was no way of telling and nothing he could do about it anyway.

'Listen,' Ginger-hair went on. 'You're lost, man, know that? You're truly lost. Whatever you do, whether the sked's kept or missed, that little Bonanza, she's going be up there circling for you. You're not going to lose her. So why not be sensible now. Save all that time and trouble. Give us the woman and piss off—'

'Listen you creep — ' Haston started but stopped as he heard the sound of the Toyota's engine. Moments afterwards, out of the corner of his eye, he saw it emerge cautiously from the trees and stop with the engine still running. Ben climbed down from behind the wheel, came back and took up his position with the Schmeisser beside Haston.

'Stores too, Ben?'

Ben nodded. 'All inside, sir.'

'Right. Hands on your heads,' Haston called at the group. 'If you get killed in the next couple of minutes, don't worry – it won't be deliberate, it'll be a ricochet.'

He shot the tyres out first, pumping bullets through the Urtzi breech as he moved round the truck, then the radiator, finally the main, reserve and supplementary fuel tanks. After the firing the only sounds were the hiss of expelled air, and the gush of water and gasolene. The vehicle heaved, lurched and settled helplessly on the sand like a broken-legged camel.

'Back off, Ben — '

Haston was round the front of the truck again. Ben stepped backwards until he was halfway between the two vehicles. Then Haston turned towards the ginger-haired man again.

'We're shifting now,' he said. 'It's like before – anyone tries to follow and they stop a gutful. And if you do have a sked, you tell your friends this. We're inside the central game reserve. A day maybe and I'll find a ranger post. They're on permanent radio stand-by. Five minutes later you'll have all Botswana looking for you. You get them and your little pile of shit here out of the country fast as you can make it. Okay?'

'Look, I got something to say first — '

The man slowly got to his feet. Haston took a pace backwards, tightened his finger round the trigger, then relaxed it again. There was nothing Ginger-hair could do and the rest of them were covered.

'Well, I got nothing to listen to,' Haston answered.

As he spoke Ginger-hair said something quickly in Afri-kaans. Haston listened uncomprehending, started to tell him to shut up – and then, even before it happened, suddenly realized he'd made a terrible mistake.

There were twelve rounds in the Urtzi's magazine. Unthink-ingly, he'd fired them all into the Chevvy and forgotten to replace the magazine with a new one. The South African had counted the shots, watched him and noticed.

As Haston reached for another magazine the man shouted 'Now!' and leapt for him.

Haston reeled back under his charge and fought for the rifle, which the man was trying to wrestle away. At the same instant he saw, horrified, another of the group rip off one of the Chevvy's side panels and snatch out an automatic hidden in the cavity behind. Neither Ben nor Charlie, watching him struggle with Ginger-hair but unable to shoot, had seen what was hap-pening.

He opened his mouth to warn them. Before he could shout, there was a burst of fire and Ben was slammed backwards, the Schmeisser flying from his hands as he clutched at his chest. Haston side-chopped at Ginger-hair's ankle, felt him stumble off-balance, jerked the rifle clear and hurled it frenziedly at the man with the automatic.

The man was swivelling to fire at Charlie. When the Urtzi struck him the automatic's muzzle was midway through the arc – pointing directly at Haston. The rifle's butt caught his mouth and he toppled against the Chevvy, letting off a final shot as he fell. Haston felt himself being whirled round, a burning sting in his shoulder, then he pitched forward, flailing, onto his face.

He knew it was all over before he hit the ground. Charlie, too late, had spotted the man with the automatic. He got off one burst seconds after Haston felled him with the Urtzi. Then a third man threw himself forward, coiled himself round Charlie's legs and knocked him down before he could fire again.

There were just two of them now against four – Charlie's single burst had almost severed the neck of the one with the automatic. Both of them unarmed, Haston helpless with a bullet through his shoulder, Charlie grappling furiously under the man who'd flattened him.

Haston lay for an instant panting as the blood from the wound seeped out onto the sand. Then, as he struggled to raise himself, he heard a shout.

'Drop that —!'

It was the woman. He heaved himself round and saw her. She was a few yards away holding his 12-gauge shotgun at her hip. In front of her Ginger-hair, with the automatic in his hands, was still on his knees – he'd crashed down after Haston tore the Urtzi away from him.

'If you don't, I'll fire.'

Ginger-hair gazed at her disbelievingly but didn't drop the gun. Instead he tried to stand, still holding onto the weapon. She waited until he was upright. Then she squeezed the trigger.

There was the deep bark of a cartridge detonating at close range, Ginger-hair's head snapped back and his face dissolved in a screen of blood. He stood there for a moment, swaying blindly from foot to foot. Then he tilted and staggered sideways, moving faster and faster out of control until he cannoned against the Chevvy and collapsed over the hood.

'The same will happen to anyone else who doesn't do what I say — '

She snapped open the breech, ejected the empty case and calmly fed in another cartridge.

'Charlie, collect your gun and this other one here,' she pointed at the automatic Ginger-hair had just dropped. 'Then come and stand by me.'

Charlie kicked away the man he'd been fighting with and did as she'd told him.

'Can you walk, Mr Haston?'

Haston managed to get to his feet and stood rocking as he examined his shoulder. The bullet had gone straight through the muscle and flesh tissue below his collar-bone and out the other side. As a wound it wasn't particularly serious, but the exit hole was large and he was losing blood fast.

He went over to where the Urtzi had dropped, bent to pick it up and sank dizzily to his knees.

'Stay there, I'll help you. Charlie, you keep your gun on the rest of them — '

There were only three now. The black, Sitavu, had slipped under the truck where he was crouching in terror. The remaining two whites were watching her, ashen-faced and immobile.

She came across, helped him up again and set off for the Toyota, Haston bumping and stumbling against her.

They reached the Toyota, Haston heaved himself over the tailgate, tripped as he tried to sit down and felt a searing pain as his shoulder hit the metal floor. Afterwards, he was vaguely aware that the truck was moving. Then he lost consciousness.

12

'Well, Lieutenant,' Schlietvan said, 'you tell this British gentleman what happened.'

His voice was hard, curt, angry.

'Yes, sir — '

Lieutenant Hannie Marais stiffened and turned towards Liddell, sitting in a low chair by the big window in Schlietvan's office. It was early evening, the last of the sunlight dazzling harlequin gold on the office blocks across the street and the room totally silent after the rush-hour traffic.

'I was second in command, sir,' he said to Liddell. 'We had been there two days. They surprised us about seven o'clock on the morning of the third, that's just after dawn — '

'They "surprised" you, did they, Lieutenant?' Schlietvan rasped. 'A young American hunter, two blacks and a woman. And they surprised you!'

Marais flushed. 'Major Hendrikks was in command, sir. I was following his orders — '

'Oh, get on, man, for Christ's sake get on!'

Marais, a bull-necked, crop-headed man in the field uniform of the security services, swallowed and continued. Liddell sat forward and listened until he'd finished.

Then he asked, 'And you've no idea where they were heading? No hint, no suggestion, nothing?'

Marais shook his head. 'No, sir.'

'And the woman, what impression did you form of her?'

Marais hesitated. 'I didn't believe it at first, sir, when she shouted and I saw her with the shotgun. Major Hendrikks didn't believe it either. That was why he stood up. I guess he thought like me, that she was after the American and the blacks. Then she fired — '

He paused again, frowning, still confused. 'I just don't know, sir. She spoke quiet, she acted calm, she wasn't trembling – not

131

even after she shot the major. But when she said she'd fire again, I reckoned she sure as hell meant it. So did Sergeant Witters; that was why we sat tight. I think maybe she didn't know what she was doing. She'd just gone crazy out there in the bush.'

Marais stopped and Liddell thought for a moment, stroking his moustache. Then he glanced across at Schlietvan and nodded.

'All right, Lieutenant,' Schlietvan said. 'That's all. You give evidence tomorrow morning at the court of inquiry on the floor below. Try not to get "surprised" on the way.'

Marais flushed again, turned back towards him, came to attention and went out.

'I am very sorry, Mr Liddell — '

Schlietvan was hunched over his desk, club-like hands shredding an envelope into tiny fragments, stone-coloured face set and bleak and furious.

'I am unused to apologizing for members of my service. I do so now. Those men were fools, idiots, incompetents. Hendrikks if he lives, as I am told there is a reasonable chance, will not hold his rank much longer. Nor will Lieutenant Marais. They were all responsible and they will all answer, that I promise you. Christ, man, to sit out there and expect this group to walk up to them like a Sunday outing!'

He broke off shaking his head in rage.

'Please, Colonel,' Liddell said placatingly. 'It was obviously an extraordinary incident, something no one could have expected. I personally find it very hard to blame them — '

He paused. 'What in your view caused it?'

Schlietvan tossed away the shredded envelope and looked up.

'I imagine it was the American, Haston,' he said. 'Somehow he spotted the men – those bloody fools – guessed who they were and realized they meant trouble for him. So he ambushed them.'

'And Miss Welborough-Smith?'

Schlietvan shrugged. 'There, Mr Liddell, your guess is as good as mine. Except maybe for one thing. I know that desert

132

and what it can do to people. I have also seen men and women after captivity by criminal *munds* like those. They lose sense of time and identity, the spirit goes, the mind starts to break up, they become zombies. I am no psychologist but I think Marais is right – she is probably at least half-crazy now.'

'So if Haston had told her your men were enemies,' Liddell mused, 'she could well have believed him?'

'Certainly,' Schlietvan nodded. 'Haston had pulled her out of a nightmare. To her he is rescuer, saviour, someone to cling to as she fights back for sanity. All he needs is to say she may be captured again and the terror comes back and she'll do anything he tells her.'

Liddell whistled softly. 'So in effect having been their hostage, she's now become his.'

Schlietvan nodded again. 'Of course. Haston knows now you must be working with my service. That makes your promise to him meaningless. In fact, he's in even worse trouble than over his hunting licence. That just gets him thrown out of Botswana. To be linked to my people sees him in prison first too. All he can do now is run – with her as his insurance.'

'Where does he run to?'

'Come here, please, Mr Liddell — '

Schlietvan stood up and Liddell went with him over to the great perspex screen on the wall. Schlietvan switched it on, tapped a selector button and a belt of southern Africa glowed inside the frame.

'The plane found their tyre tracks here —

Schlietvan touched the map somewhere to the north of the copse.

The ginger-haired Hendrikks hadn't been bluffing. There was a back-up force, another truck and a Bonanza spotter plane half a day's drive from where Haston had ambushed them. Marais contacted the others by radio when the Toyota had disappeared; the Bonanza took off and the second truck set out to find the wreckage of the first.

'The tracks were heading due north,' Schlietvan went on. 'The plane searched for an hour but couldn't locate the Toyota itself. Maybe they heard it and hid up in trees. Anyway, then it turned back. With Hendrikks badly wounded there was no question of trying to follow them. We needed the only truck left to get him back across the border and into hospital. So we have just a set of tyre tracks pointing north — '

Schlietvan paused and rubbed his jaw reflectively.

'Zambia, I think, Mr Liddell, Zambia.'

Liddell studied the map and nodded in agreement.

South and west were out of the question – once across either of those borders Haston would simply find himself in South African territory. To the east was Rhodesia but Rhodesia was in turmoil and even to get there meant crossing almost half of the Kalahari. It left only Zambia. Two hundred miles of desert, the vastness of the inland delta. Finally, if Haston was lucky, sanctuary in another black republic.

It was a desperate outside chance but the only one Haston had.

'It is still a very long way, Colonel,' Liddell said.

'And that is the only thing which makes me happy — '

For the first time that evening Schlietvan smiled, grimly, tightly.

'Out there you die without water, Mr Liddell, but you can't move without gasolene. For this American there's no difference. If he doesn't find gasolene, he dies just the same because he gets caught. The woman discovers what he's done, she talks, for him it's all over. So he has to get fuel — '

Schlietvan touched the selector button again, the image dissolved and another large-scale section of the desert flickered onto the screen.

'He has only two sources. Ghanzi here to the west or Maun. Ghanzi means a long detour. But Maun's due north, in the direction he's heading, where he has to go. He will aim for Maun, Mr Liddell.'

Liddell looked at the map again. Two tiny black dots marking the two little villages. Ghanzi, the cattle-ranch centre, on the left. Maun, at the edge of the delta, above. Schlietvan was right: if Haston was trying to reach the Zambian border, Maun was the logical place to refuel.

'And if he gets to Maun, Colonel?' Liddell asked.

Schlietvan didn't answer for a moment. He switched off the map, went back to his desk and sat down. Then he slammed his hand flat on the walnut top so the sound cracked like a pistol-shot round the room.

'He is stopped,' Schlietvan said slowly. 'Whatever may or may not happen to him that man has made himself serious trouble for all of us. For you, for me, for that wretched woman. There is only one solution for that.'

Liddell checked. It was dark now. Outside, the city's lights seemed to be drifting up to mingle with the constellations of stars in the night sky, and the second wave of traffic – heading for theatres, bars, clubs, restaurants – was rippling through the streets below.

Then he said, 'You mean you're prepared to send your men into this village of Maun to intercept him?'

'Yes, Mr Liddell, I am.'

Liddell leant back. He was thinking of a truck somewhere out in the desert, a hunter with nothing to lose now, a black and a half-crazed woman.

13

Haston stirred and opened his eyes.

Above him he could see a dark canopy of metal with spaces of white sky on either side. Below something was rocking and jolting. He frowned, tried to push himself up and fell back weakly. There'd been a sharp stab of pain as he moved and now his shoulder was aching. He turned his head to examine it, saw a criss-cross pattern of bandages, studied them for a moment, then he remembered.

It came back in a confused tangle of images. The five men having breakfast in the dawn light. The shout in Afrikaans. The confusion and violence and scything burst of repeater fire. Ben rolling across the ground and the sand in his own mouth after he'd been spun round and dropped by the last bullet. The woman's voice, the deep bark of the shotgun, the ginger-haired man, face sheeted with blood, crashing against the Chevvy. Then the stumbling walk to the Toyota, heaving himself with an immense effort of will over the tailgate, pitching forwards onto the floor and darkness.

He was still on the truck's floor although someone had put the sleeping-bag under him, presumably at the same time his wound was dressed. From the heat and the angle of the sun it was early afternoon, although he was too weary to lift his wrist and check his watch. That meant he'd been asleep or unconscious for about six hours. Part of it was just exhaustion after the march back from the pan. The rest must have been due to loss of blood.

He lay on his back, dizzy, sweating, feeling the throb at his shoulder but strangely not thirsty. The truck was moving very slowly and he could just hear Charlie's voice calling instructions from the front. Haston thought of shouting to find out what was happening. Then, as he tried to gather strength for the attempt, it suddenly didn't seem important and a few moments later he passed out again.

He slept until the temperature dropped just before dusk. When he woke then, chill in the darkening air, the truck was stationary and the tailgate down. This time he did manage to prop himself up, rolling onto his side and using only his left arm. He wriggled back against the driving cabin partition and looked out. There was no sign of the woman but Charlie was squatting over a fire a few yards away with a small tent pitched beyond.

'Charlie!'

His voice was hoarse and he was thirsty now with the same raw parched dehydration he'd felt while they were waiting for the second jerry-can of water. Charlie jumped up and came trotting over.

'How are you, *Morena?*'

'I'll be all right. Just get me a drink fast.'

Charlie unlooped a canvas water-bag hanging from the wing-mirror and held the spout to Haston's mouth. He gulped until his stomach tightened, then he pushed it away.

'You sure you're going to be okay, sir?'

Charlie's face was strained and anxious.

'Hell, I'm fine,' Haston said. 'Don't you worry about me. Just help me get somewhere I can sit.'

Charlie climbed into the truck, half-lifted Haston until he was on his feet and helped him across the floor.

'That's better,' Haston was sitting on the lowered tailgate. 'So where the hell are we?'

'Maybe twenty miles north of the pan, sir.'

'And the lady?'

'There, sir,' Charlie pointed at the tent. 'She sorting out her gear.'

'How the hell did we get that—?'

Haston stopped. There were more important things than finding out how they'd acquired her tent, far more important.

'What about Ben?' he asked.

'They got him, *Morena.*'

It was a stupid unnecessary question. Haston had known the answer from the instant he saw Ben hurled back and tumbling over, hands clenched to his chest in that last agonized response. Yet somehow vaguely, desperately in the few conscious moments since he'd clung to the hope that he might have been wrong, that Ben had only been wounded and, like him, had survived.

No longer. Ben was dead and Haston felt cold and numb. He thought of Jo, of Liddell, of himself, the woman and the terrorists – and he swore. Rhythmically, mindlessly, bitterly. Then he stopped. That part was over. Now there was the rest – and along the way someone was going to pay in blood for what had happened.

'So what did you do, Charlie?'

'We left him there, sir,' Charlie said. 'No other way we could move. Then we lit out. We go first to the pan, takes us maybe four hours. No one in the lady's camp, they skipped with most of what was there and we pick up the rest. Afterwards, we move on to the tree where the lady saw the leopard last. That animal, it's gone. But I cast and I find spoor, faint, like maybe two days' old. The lady fixes you up. Then we head north on the spoorline, the lady at the wheel, me tracking through the window.'

Haston nodded. The slow progress of the truck when he'd woken in the afternoon, Charlie quietly calling instructions. They must have been spooring the animal then.

'And now?'

'First we seen in two hours,' Charlie pointed at a clump of dead trees near the truck. 'Also we're losing light. That lady she don't know much about safari, but I tell her if she want a camp and good fire we better stop. She's not happy – she wants to go on spooring – but then she says yes.'

As he finished Alison Welborough-Smith appeared – unzipping the tent-flap, crawling out and standing up. Haston blinked and stared at her in astonishment.

When he'd last seen her she'd been in jeans, her check shirt ripped by thorn, hair matted and lank with sweat, skin grey and streaked with dust, a smoking shotgun in her hand. She'd looked like some haggard apparition from a nightmare – a gaunt scarecrow, vengeful and hideous and terrifying. Now she was wearing velvet carpet slippers, an ankle-length black skirt and a long-sleeved white blouse buttoned high to the neck. Her face was clean, her hair brushed out and she was smiling as she walked towards him.

'How does the shoulder feel, Mr Haston — ?'

She'd stopped by the tailgate. Haston gaped at her speechless. She registered his confusion, glanced down at her clothes and laughed.

'I'm sorry,' she said. 'I suppose I must look somewhat eccentric. In fact, it's all eminently practical as I've discovered by experience. The slippers relax one's ankles after a day in the bush. The skirt provides good thermal-layer insulation against the cold. And the blouse gives excellent protection against mosquitoes.'

'Yes — '

Haston stopped. It was all he could think of to say. That same morning, ruthlessly and deliberately, she'd almost killed a man with a charge of shot in the face – certainly if he lived he'd be blinded for life. Now, barely ten hours later, she might have been a Victorian spinster dressed for an evening of whist and madeira wine, who'd swoon at the very mention of blood.

He'd been wrong in thinking her mad, Haston realized now. She wasn't mad, she was something different – something even more dangerous and extraordinary. She was a woman haunted, possessed, driven by a demon. Nothing on earth mattered or held any value for her, neither life, death or her own survival – except the leopard. To find and follow that she'd walk through the gates of hell and unthinkingly expect anyone to follow her.

'And the shoulder?'

Haston shivered, pulled himself together and glanced down. The move from the back of the truck to the tailgate had set it aching again painfully.

'Sore,' he said, 'but I guess I'll survive.'

'I think I should change the dressing. Charlie!' She turned and called, 'Bring me some hot water, please.'

Charlie came over from the fire with the billy-can, she pulled out a medicine chest from the truck – it must have come from her own camp as Haston hadn't had time to find one in Gaborone – and started unwrapping the bandages.

The South African's repeater must have been loaded with soft-nosed bullets, because the wound was much larger than he'd thought when he glanced at it by the Chevvy – an ugly gaping hole from which blood started pumping as soon as she removed the gauze pad. Haston was lucky that the shell had passed straight through: if it had touched bone it would have spread out and blown most of his shoulder off.

She rubbed fluid on both sides, put on new gauze pads, and then bandaged him up again tightly.

Haston levered himself off the tailgate, stood up, flexed his arm gingerly, felt another surge of pain, and swayed.

'You'd better sit down by the fire — '

She helped him over to the mound of flame and Haston slumped down on a canvas-topped stool – something else they must have collected from her camp.

'I'm afraid you're still losing blood,' she said. 'Until that stops you'll have to take it very easy indeed. You won't be able to use the shoulder, of course, for at least ten days. But providing there's no infection, within forty-eight hours it shouldn't be more than unpleasantly bruised and stiff. Meantime, Charlie and I can manage.'

'Yes, ma'am.'

Haston sat there hunched and drained and weary with the wound throbbing.

'Wait a moment — '

She disappeared into the tent and came back with a silver screw-top flask.

'According to modern medical theory it's quite incorrect,' she unscrewed the top and poured a measure of liquid into it. 'However my grandmother was Scottish and I have considerable faith in the old-fashioned remedies. Try it.'

Haston took the silver top, sniffed and drank. It was malt whisky and he could feel the warmth burning down his throat and into his stomach. He drained the top and within seconds the ache in his shoulder seemed to have dulled. Then he looked up, amazed again, and grinned.

'Thank you, miss. That's better than antibiotics.'

'I've got those too,' she smiled back, 'but I keep the whisky

140

for real emergencies. And, please, I believe we could do with a little less formality, don't you? I much prefer to be called Alison.'

'Jerry,' Haston said.

She held out her hand and he shook it solemnly as the last of the light faded from the sky and the Southern Cross, icy and brilliant, lifted over the horizon.

'Excellent. Now let's consider our plans,' she said briskly. 'First, I trust we can forget the unfortunate relationship we've had so far. I was somewhat blunt about the consequences for you of those men waiting by your truck. For that I apologize. However, while the facts remain as I outlined them, the situation has changed. We have lost Ben, Charlie cannot drive, nor for the immediate future can you. That leaves only me, correct?'

Haston nodded. He might conceivably have been able to handle the Toyota with one arm on the metalled roads of Gaborone. Out here in the desert it was impossible.

'So,' she went on, 'we have to modify my original idea. You can no longer leave me once we've located the leopard – you will have to stay until you're fit enough to take over the truck. In fact, everything has been turned upside down. I'd imagined I would be dependent on you. That's not the case now. You are totally dependent on me.'

There was no challenge or threat in the statement – simply a straightforward assessment of the facts.

'In which case,' she added, 'we shall continue as we did today. Charlie no doubt told you what happened. As I guessed, the animal is moving north again. I would have preferred to have followed its spoor for another hour, but Charlie prevailed on me to make camp. Tomorrow we shall go on. Where we find ourselves when you're ready to drive remains to be seen. For the moment I will check what Charlie is preparing for dinner.'

She walked across to where Charlie was rummaging in a crate by the truck, and Haston held out his hands to the flames.

They ate half an hour later, a thick vegetable stew which also came from her own provisions. Alison said little during the meal. Afterwards, she got out a thick notebook and started to write by the light of a small butane lamp. Haston, drowsy from the food and the warmth of the fire, watched her. She scribbled intently, oblivious of everything else – the night calls of the bush, the whirring moths, the myriads of mosquitoes that haloed her – pausing occasionally only to brush back a strand of hair from her face or chew for a moment in frowning concentration on the end of her pen.

Then she finished. She read through what she'd written and snapped the notebook shut.

'That'll do for tonight,' she said. 'I also think it's time for your bed, Jerry. With that shoulder you need all the sleep you can get.'

'I'll get Charlie to fix up my sleeping-bag by the truck — '

Haston started to rise but she shook her head firmly and cut him off.

'There's absolutely no question of your sleeping outside. The risk of infection's great enough as it is. We're not going to compound that by exposing you unnecessarily in the open. Until you're properly healed you'll use my tent.'

Haston opened his mouth to argue, realized it was pointless and sat down again.

'What about you?' He asked.

'I'm going to sleep out. I'm more used to roughing it than you might imagine. Also,' she smiled, 'if that animal pays us a visit, at least I won't miss it.'

She picked up the lamp, Haston heaved himself to his feet and followed her over to the tent.

One of the flaps was pulled back and as she shone the light inside he saw that his sleeping-bag had already been laid out on a canvas and metal-frame camp bed. There was an extra blanket on top, a glass of water by the head-rest and a torch beside it.

'Hell!' Haston said. Then he added quickly, 'I'm sorry, miss, but — '

'Alison, please.'

'Sure – Alison. Listen, I took a slug through the shoulder. Right, that's the way it goes. But forty-eight hours and like you said, I'll be fine. Only, I don't need coddling, for Christ's sake.

I'm not a goddam baby – I'm a hunter.'

'No one's treating you like a baby, Jerry. I'm merely taking sensible precautions. You happen to be very valuable to me. Furthermore,' she smiled again, 'you seem to be forgetting that for the moment I'm running this safari – not you. Sleep well!'

She handed him the lamp and walked away, skirt rustling softly in the sand.

Haston hesitated. Then he ducked into the tent, zipped down the flap, eased himself into the sleeping-bag and blew out the light.

He lay very still on his back with his arm crossed over his chest – each time he moved the wound churned raw and burning. It was nine o'clock. At the same time the night before Ben had been carrying Alison, trussed and wrapped like an ancient suitcase, through the bush. Now Ben was dead, so was at least one other man, Haston himself was immobilized, and the woman had taken over. Somewhere behind them were both the black terrorists and the BOSS agents. In front, linking them all, an animal – a black leopard – padding northwards across the desert.

Haston tried to swear. He couldn't. His teeth were chattering in the cold, his body shaking and his head, dizzy, aching like his shoulder, revolving in circles. He reached for the glass of water, knocked it over and fumbled for the torch. His fingers touched the rubber covering, found the switch and pushed it down. There was a sudden shocking glare of light – the beam angled at his eyes.

He gazed at it for a moment. Then he tumbled off the bed unconscious.

Blackness. A terrible immense vault of blackness, by turns either bitterly cold or scorchingly hot – so hot that he had to struggle frantically not to drown in sweat.

Sometimes he'd be running, hurling himself blindly forwards in terror. There was a beast behind him then, an animal he'd never seen – hidden, prowling, fanged, hunting him with a deadly single-minded purpose. He'd hear it closing on him, smell its stench, feel its breath on his neck. Then his legs would fail and he'd collapse screaming. At other times he'd be lying bound and helpless at the base of the vault. Ben had gone and Charlie had gone but the animal was still there, menacing, circling just out of sight in the dark, readying itself to strike.

Often he could hear himself talking. There were some people standing quite close to him but somehow his words didn't seem to reach them. He'd raise his voice and shout louder and louder until the whole vault was an echoing chamber of sound. They still didn't hear him and in the end they'd walk away, leaving him alone and exhausted.

Once he woke. It was daylight, he was shivering uncontrollably and a hand was placing something damp on his forehead which felt as if it was on fire.

'Where am I?'

Before anyone could answer the blackness rolled over him once more and he was running again, racing, panting, choking as the creature gathered itself to spring.

Afterwards, the horror went on. Shouts, screams, chilling cold, waves of sweat, the animal's talons scratching unseen on stone. Jo came to visit him, golden and clean in a crisp white dress. He pleaded with her, begged her for help – he was bound again then – reminded her of everything they'd done together. She looked at him blankly, bent down, lashed him across his face with her riding whip and disappeared. After Jo there were others – even Vasha came once with the boy – but they all behaved the same. They examined him dispassionately then vanished, leaving him with the creature and the darkness.

Then suddenly it was dawn. Haston opened his eyes and saw he was lying on the camp bed in the tent. The flaps were open and the last stars were fading in the paling sky outside. He felt weaker than he'd ever felt in his life before, lightheaded, disembodied, every muscle limp and useless. But he was conscious again. He could smell the morning air and hear a distant goshawk mewing.

'*Morena?*'

Charlie's voice. Haston tried to turn his head but even that

144

effort was too much. Charlie appeared squatting by the bed-side.

'You better, sir?'

His face was furrowed with worry.

'I guess so. What happened?'

Haston's own voice sounded faint and thin. He glanced at the glass of water, Charlie picked it up and trickled some carefully into Haston's mouth.

'You been sick, sir,' Charlie said. 'Three days now you been real bad. That lady stay with you almost all the time. Without her I don't know if you make it. She's resting now but she tells me for to get her if anything happens.'

Haston opened his mouth to stop him but Charlie had already gone. Five minutes later Alison appeared at the entrance to the tent. Her face was white and drawn with exhaustion and there were dark rings under her eyes, but she was smiling. She came in and knelt down.

'How are you feeling, Jerry?'

'Like I came back from somewhere a long way off where they gave me a hell of a working over. Charlie says it's been three days?'

She nodded. 'Your shoulder must have become infected before I treated it. You had high fever and delirium. It's over now but you've been lucky, Jerry, very lucky.'

'Charlie said it wasn't so much luck as you.'

'Well,' she smiled again, 'when the whisky didn't work I was honour-bound to find another solution. I had to fall back on antibiotics.'

'Nothing wrong with the whisky – the dosage just wasn't high enough. Anyway, thank Christ for well-equipped ladies!'

Alison laughed. 'Take these — '

She produced a couple of pills, lifted his head and he swallowed them with some more water.

'You still need a lot more rest. They should put you out until this evening. Then you'll be ready to eat.'

She went out and moments afterwards Haston was drifting into sleep again, the call of the goshawk still ringing softly in his ears.

He woke at dusk, still very weak but just strong enough now to push himself up on the bed and look out. Charlie was cooking over a fire with Alison sitting on a stool beside him. The conformation of the bush was different from where they'd stopped before and Haston realized they must have moved camp while he was unconscious.

He watched them for a while as the smoke spiralled upwards and the stars came out. Then Alison stood up and walked over to the tent with a steaming pan in her hand.

'How are you feeling now?'

Haston sniffed the pan and said, 'Like food.'

It was three days since he'd eaten and he was suddenly ravenously hungry. She gave him the pan, collected another for herself and sat with him while he ate – spooning the hot stew quickly into his mouth.

'Can you find me a cigarette?'

He'd finished and put the pan down. Alison reached into the pocket of his shirt, lying over the end of the bed, pulled out a crumpled pack and his lighter, and handed them to him. Haston lit a cigarette and inhaled slowly. He felt better now, much better: the light-headedness had gone and his strength was coming back fast.

'Where are we?' he asked.

'About eighty miles further north than where you probably remember last.'

Haston whistled. 'So as well as looking after me, you've been spooring too?'

'That's right,' she said. 'In fact, it worked out rather well. For some reason you were relatively calm by day. The nights were the worst times. So when we were travelling we put you in the back of the truck strapped to this—'

She touched the bed. 'It was fairly comfortable and meant you didn't roll out. At night we put you in the tent. That was usually when the trouble started.'

'Trouble?'

'You're extremely active, Jerry. Sometimes it was all Charlie and I could do to hold you down,' she smiled. 'You've also got a very powerful voice and either a remarkable imagination, or you've known an extraordinarily large number of women.'

Haston reddened. 'Jesus, what did I say?'

She laughed. 'I'm certainly not going to repeat it. However there were occasions when you almost shocked the lions into silence. Among many others there's someone called Jo, isn't there?'

He flushed even deeper, feeling his cheeks burn scarlet. 'Sure, I knew a girl called Jo.'

'She sounds a very athletic young lady.'

'Christ! I'm sorry. I mean I'm sorry for —'

He stopped and Alison laughed again. 'Don't be sorry for anything. At least while you were holding forth I knew we were in there with a chance. It was the silences that worried me. Also zoologists tend to be a lot less shockable than lions.'

Haston looked at her perched on the stool with the night sky behind. The butane lamp was between them. Her eyes were sparkling in the small pool of light and her mouth had the wide humorous smile he remembered from the photograph. Then he laughed too.

'So now you've got my life story?'

'I seem to have acquired some interesting chapters from it. It was quite an education.'

'And the leopard?'

Alison frowned. 'It's still moving north, much faster than before. A hundred miles in the last five or six days. Charlie thinks we're almost up with it again. But late this afternoon, just before we stopped, we came across limestone. There wasn't time to check properly after we'd made camp but there seems to be a lot more of it ahead.'

Limestone. The porous rock base that lay often only feet, even inches, below the Kalahari sand. Where it surfaced in great pale sheets of stone spooring became impossible. Haston had lost countless trophies because of it. If there was limestone in front of them, there was every chance they'd lose the leopard too.

'Anyway,' Alison stood up, 'we'll find out in the morning. Meantime, I think both of us could do with some more sleep.

147

Take another of these — '

She gave him another pill.

'And if you have any further dreams about your friend Jo – or any of the others come to that – try to keep them to yourself.'

Haston swallowed the pill. Then, as she lowered her head to step outside, he said, 'You stayed up all of those three nights alongside of me?'

She glanced back. 'Most of them, yes.'

'Why?'

'What do you mean?' Alison looked at him puzzled.

'You were spooring all day,' Haston said. 'In this country however you do it that's rough, you get tired. I had a fever, a bad one. But once you fill me up with antibiotics there's damn all more you can do. If I was on the way out, I'd go whether you were watching or not. And I hadn't exactly given you cause for the extra tender loving care bit. So why bother to burn yourself out sitting up with me?'

She hesitated, frowning again. Then she said, 'We're both involved in this now, Jerry. When something like that happens you look after the other person as best you can. I suppose it's as simple as that. Goodnight.'

She went out. Haston watched her silhouette against the fire-light. Then she disappeared and he lay back gazing at the crescent moon rising over the bush.

Charlie woke him in the morning with a mug of coffee and squatted by the bed while Haston drank.

'How are we fixed for water?' Haston said.

'Good, *Morena*. The lady, she got two big jerry-cans in her camp. We filled them up at the pan. I guess going careful we got enough for a week maybe.'

'Food?'

'Same, sir. She had an awful lot of stuff there. We picked up most all of it.'

'And what about those fellows we tackled, either bunch?'

'Any time we pass a big tree I climb up. I don't see nothing yet — ' Charlie paused and frowned unhappily. 'We're moving

148

slow, *Morena*, and we're leaving big spoor behind.'

Haston nodded grimly. It would be a week at least before the action of the wind on the sand obliterated their tyre tracks. Until then the tracks would be visible even from the air. If either BOSS or Mlanda's men made another attempt to seize them, there would be a perfect spoor to follow and every incentive too. Instead of heading back for the safety of Gaborone, the tracks would show that, however inexplicably, they were moving deeper into the emptiness of the desert.

Haston wondered briefly what both BOSS and Mlanda would make of that. Then he dismissed the speculation. All that mattered now was to find the leopard and, as soon as he could drive, get out. He glanced at his shoulder. Alison had put a sling round his arm while he was unconscious and the gauze pad was still stained rusty-red. But the blood was dry now and the wound had stopped throbbing.

'Give me a hand, Charlie — '

He swung his legs off the bed and Charlie helped him to his feet. For an instant he felt his head swim giddily and his knees almost buckled. Then, leaning heavily on Charlie with his left arm round his neck, Haston walked outside, stumbling but becoming surer with every step.

'So let's take a look at this crazy animal,' he said. 'Where's the nearest spoor?'

'Over there, *Morena*, maybe fifty yards away—'

They were standing on a sheet of limestone. Charlie lifted his hand and pointed at a trough of sand behind the tent.

'You sure you can make it, sir?'

'Hell, yes. I want to see it.'

Swaying, tripping, clinging tight to Charlie, Haston crossed the stone, stopped on the edge of the sand and looked down. Then he whistled slowly.

There was a row of pug-marks printed in the ground, their rims blurred slightly by the night's frost but still fresh and deep and strong. They were the largest Haston had ever seen – bigger even than Alison had described them. From the distance between the fore and rear legs the animal must have been over nine feet in length.

'Jesus Christ!' Haston said. 'That's one big cat, Charlie.'

'I go tracking since I was a boy, sir, thirty years now. I never hit spoor like that before.'

Haston uncoiled his arm from Charlie's neck and knelt down. The pug-marks were firm and even, the print of an immense mature leopard moving quickly and resolutely. There was no hesitation, no scuff in the sand when it might have checked and tested the air for scent. Instead the unbroken pattern of taloned feet travelling northwards.

'Show those to any client,' Haston heaved himself up again, 'and he'd go crazy just looking at them. Okay, let's get some breakfast.'

Alison was up when they got back to the truck. She changed the dressing on his wound. Then they ate together by the fire.

'So what are today's plans?' Haston asked.

'I think that's up to Charlie,' Alison said.

Charlie was stacking the dishes away in the back of the truck. He finished, came over and squatted down.

'We got a good site here,' he said. 'Good fire-wood, good cover. No point in striking camp until we find the spoor again. I take a look early, there's plenty of stone around and I don't see nothing. I think best if I go ahead on foot and start casting. If I pick it up, then we move. But could be one day, could be two, could be I still don't find nothing, like I told the lady.'

Alison nodded. 'I'll go with you, Charlie. Fill the flasks, make up pack lunches and we'll move as soon as you're ready. Jerry, you'll have to stay here in camp.'

Haston shrugged. Even with the fever gone and his shoulder healing now, it would still be several days before he was strong enough to move in the bush. But there was no point in Alison going out too – there was nothing she could do to help Charlie and spooring any big animal, let alone a leopard, the most unpredictable of all, was invariably dangerous.

Haston tried to convince her but she shook her head adamantly.

'No, Jerry,' she said. 'I've followed that animal for three months. I'm not going to leave it to someone else now.'

Twenty minutes later she and Charlie left. Haston spent

a couple of hours tidying up the camp. Then, already exhausted from the effort of moving again, he went back to the tent and lay down on the bed with the Urtzi beside him to wait out the day.

They returned in the early evening. Haston was up by then, building the fire and heating water. He knew before either of them spoke that they'd had no success. Charlie's usually smiling face was blank and Alison looked tired and dispirited.

'Rock, *Morena*,' Charlie unslung the Schmeisser he'd taken with them for protection. 'Spreads out four or five miles all round. Many patches of sand in between but they full of bush. That animal, no way she's going to cut through thorn. So she stays to the stone. We don't see one track all day.'

'What's it like where the stone ends?' Haston said.

'More thorn, sir, thick acacia. Somewhere that leopard's got to go into that. But it's so thick takes me one hour to check out thirty yards of earth.'

Haston nodded. He'd come across similar areas of the desert many times before. The limestone surfaced in a low island patterned with runnels of sand and scrub. The leopard had avoided the scrub and picked an invisible zig-zag course over the bare rock. Somewhere along the island's perimeter the animal must have left the rock and continued north over the desert sand, where its spoor would show up once more. But the sand was screened by thick thorn and it had taken Charlie an hour to check just a single thirty-yard section.

At that rate, without a pointer on the rock itself, he'd need a week to comb the whole perimeter – and by then the pug-marks would have long since disappeared.

'The lady says to try again tomorrow,' Charlie added. 'North, there's maybe ten, twelve open lanes out from the stones to the sand. But like I tell her I'm not sure for hoping. Those animals, on rock they don't pick the straight lines. They go any which way. This one, maybe it's crossed east or west. If it done that, it's dropped us.'

'Okay, Charlie,' Haston said. 'Give it another go in the morning. Wash now, then fix us some food.'

Alison, without saying anything, had already ladled out a

can of hot water while they were talking and vanished into the bush round the camp site with a towel and her evening clothes. Charlie headed in the opposite direction with another can and Haston sat down by the fire. A few minutes later Alison – dressed in her long skirt and white blouse again – joined him.

'Charlie says you're going out again tomorrow,' Haston said.

She nodded. 'Tomorrow and the day after and the day after that. For as long as it takes.'

'We only got water for a week.'

'Then we'll have to re-supply. We're mobile and there must be wells to the west.'

'Gasolene's another problem.'

'Both Ghanzi and Maun are within a couple of days' drive. We've got enough fuel to reach either of them, I know because I've checked the tank and the map. They'll have water too. No, Jerry —'

She glanced at him and shook her head. 'Don't try to create obstacles now. I'll keep my promise. You can go when we've found the animal again, I've got a properly-equipped camp and you're capable of driving. Until then we stay together.'

'How did you figure I was going to re-equip your camp even when I could drive?'

'Just like before. You leave me Charlie, take the truck into Ghanzi or Maun, radio the High Commission and they'll organize it all.'

'Then I'd better tell you something —'

Haston had been thinking about it all day, the implications he'd ignored before slowly accumulating and taking shape in his mind as he lay on the bed in the tent.

'You thought first I'd been paid to get you out, then I'd been set up. You were right about being set up, not about being paid. I wasn't getting a goddam cent. I was in trouble and this guy from your Foreign Office offered me a phoney deal —'

Haston told her about his hunter's licence, Liddell's approach and the proposal. Alison listened in silence, thoughtful, frowning, hunched forwards over the flames as darkness filled the sky and the evening chill settled round them.

Then she said, 'What difference does all that make?'

'A whole bundle. Liddell knows now I've tumbled him, that I'll get kicked out anyway. He probably reckons I'm running scared for the border with you as my insurance. But he also knows that sooner or later I'll have to surface – for fuel, supplies, water, whatever. That's the moment for him to grab me and get his hands on you. He can't grab me directly but he doesn't need to. With that report in the Game Department I'll already have been declared a prohibited immigrant – he'll have gone into reverse on his promise and seen to that. Aside from the desert, Botswana's a very small place. The moment I show – Maun, Ghanzi, anywhere else – I get bounced — '

Haston paused. 'I'm sorry, Alison. We got it wrong, the both of us. I because I wasn't figuring straight, you because you didn't know the story. As far as you're concerned I'm a damn great albatross. They get me and they get you. Sure, you won't get bounced like I will. But they'll take a week unscrambling it all and you'll lose your leopard.'

She didn't say anything for several minutes. Then she stood up.

'Why did you tell me that, Jerry?'

It was fully dark now. The glow of the fire, tugged and plucked by the night wind, rippled over her blouse, turning the white lace at her wrists and throat from rose to gold and then back to rose again.

'Hell,' Haston shrugged, 'I've been given the chop whatever happens. No reason to include the animal in the whole goddam mess.'

'And what do you propose to do?'

'Stick with you a few days until I'm fit – I've got no choice there. Then I'll fade. You've got to make a re-stocking trip anyway. We'll drive to Maun or Ghanzi and stop outside. The word may be out for the truck as well as me, so we'll send Charlie in on foot to pick up supplies. Then you can head back with him. I'll lie up a couple of days, then I'll surface in the village. You'll be well clear and there's no connection between us. Somehow I'll get word to your High Commission about where you are without involving me as a link. They can take it from there.'

153

'Are you really saying you're doing all that because of the leopard?'

'Sure. Give me another reason.'

Alison said nothing. There was another reason, one Haston had been trying to work out throughout the day as he analysed the consequences of what had happened. They both knew it and it had nothing to do with the leopard.

It was Alison herself. At the start she'd attacked him, kicked him agonizingly in the groin, forced him to bind her and carry her sweating across the desert. Haston had simply thought she was insane then. Later, seeing her for the first time dressed in her extraordinary clothes, laughing, talking in that clear high-pitched voice, he'd half-changed his mind. She wasn't so much insane as obsessed, driven by an irresistible overwhelming compulsion that smashed down everything in her way. Somehow that had made her even more frightening and unpredictable.

Only now he'd changed his mind again. He wasn't any closer to understanding her, she might well be half-mad, she was certainly still obsessed by the leopard. But he knew something else. To her he was a hunter, a killer, the wrecker of her camp, everything she detested. Yet for three successive nights as he'd raved and thrashed in delirium, she'd watched sleepless by his side. Exhausting herself as she tried to calm him, fight the fever with him. Charlie said she'd probably saved his life and Haston guessed he was right.

There'd been no reason for that – except her quiet statement when she tried to explain why. *You look after the other person as best you can.* Haston still wasn't sure what she'd meant, but no one – no woman – had ever behaved like that towards him before. It had shaken and unsettled him and finally, as the day ended, left him with no choice.

'Okay,' he said eventually. 'Let's not kid about the animal. I'm a hunter, right? Or at least I was one. So to me it's just another cat – a monster maybe, a weirdie, but still a pussy-cat. But what you did, that was different. I guess I owe you so — '

Haston thought he could say it gracefully, without embarassment but the words stuck in his mouth and he came to a fumbling halt.

154

'I wonder — '

Alison didn't seem to have been listening to him. Now she started circling the fire, frowning again with her eyes narrowed in thought.

'If we can find that leopard again, establish where it's going, what it is, whether, as I believe, it's searching for a mate, then we'll have a very big story indeed. Did you know I am what is called a "television personality", Jerry?'

Haston shook his head. Liddell hadn't told him that but he was prepared to believe anything about her now.

'Well, I am. Oh, it's a frippery, a nonsense,' she waved her hand scornfully. 'I just use it to waken public interest in what I'm doing. But television's a very powerful medium – it can have many other uses.'

'What the hell do you mean?'

She stopped, sat down again and gazed at him intently, eyes brilliant in the firelight.

'If we were lucky, Jerry, and you were with me when we announced it, there'd be such a blaze of publicity they'd have to forget everything. They can't have a prohibited immigrant sharing in the discovery of a new species of the great carnivora – they've got to make you a hero instead.'

Haston gazed back at her. It had happened again and once more it was several seconds before he took it in.

Then he said slowly, 'Are you suggesting you take me with you?'

She nodded. 'Yes, only this time right to the end.'

Haston sat quite still listening to the hiss of the flames and the far-off trumpeting of a young bull elephant.

The next two days were the most frustrating Haston had ever spent.

Alison and Charlie set out each morning after breakfast and returned as the light faded. In the long hours between, still not strong enough to go with them, there was nothing for him to do except roam the camp exercising his legs, gently revolve his shoulder to ease out the stiffness as the wound healed, rest in

155

the tent or the shadow of the truck, turning impatiently as he watched the high vultures and eagles.

Twice a day he'd walk over and examine the line of spoor Charlie had shown him in the trough of sand – the last tracks of the animal they'd found. The immense pug-marks were still there but each time they'd be softer, shallower, the rims crumbling and blurring under the action of the wind and frost. By the third evening – when Alison and Charlie had spent three days in the bush without success – he knew that if they hadn't picked up the spoor again within forty-eight hours they would have lost it for good.

Alison's confidence never faltered. She might return weary after the day's search but as soon as she'd washed and changed all the conviction and certainty came pouring back. She'd sit with him by the fire talking animatedly, questioning him about leopards he'd hunted, telling him about others she had studied, always returning again and again to this one – the great black creature still loping steadily northwards, if she was right, somewhere in the desert ahead.

Then, face flushed in the warmth, eyes bright and laughing, long dark hair swirling round her shoulders, Haston found it impossible to believe she was the same person as the grotesque and terrifying apparition cold-bloodedly firing the shotgun in the South Africans' camp. She was still strange, eccentric, bewildering. She was also now a strikingly beautiful woman.

Only her implacable determination to stay with the animal linked the two – and that never wavered.

On the fourth morning the pattern abruptly changed. She left with Charlie as usual in the early morning but two hours later, while Haston was checking the tyre pressures of the truck, they suddenly reappeared. For an instant Haston thought they must have struck lucky at last. Then Charlie came straight over to him.

'Men, *Morena*,' Charlie said.

Haston froze and got to his feet beside the wheel.

'Which group?'

'No, sir,' Charlie shook his head. 'Neither of them bunches. The little yellow fellows, bushmen.'

Haston breathed out slowly, relief welling over him.

'Where did you find them?'

'Maybe a mile and a half west.' Charlie pointed. 'We figure today we try a different cast. So we head that way. We walk into a clearing and we see two little shelters. No one there – they heard us coming and all gone running. But there's gourds, skins, four, five sets of spoor. They're there, *Morena*.'

Haston thought for a moment. Then he went round to the back of the truck, pulled out a couple of bags of sugar and some cigarettes, and gave them to Charlie.

'See if you can persuade them to come in,' he said. 'Tell them we've got more.'

Charlie nodded and disappeared again.

'What are you going to do?' Alison had come up and was standing beside him.

Haston glanced at her. 'How much do you know about bushmen?'

'A little. I've never seen any but they're nomads, aren't they, a relict population of what was once an enormous tribe? I thought they were virtually extinct.'

'They're not a tribe, they're a race, a people or what's left of them — '

Haston told her. The tiny child-sized men and women with their apricot skins and high-cheeked mongoloid features who for centuries before the arrival of the black man or the white had inhabited the entire southern half of the African continent. Living in little nomadic groups, sharing everything, supporting each other, gentle, peaceful, travelling with rain and season and sun and moon. Hunting to survive but existing in a relationship with the animals, their prey but also their friends and brothers, so close and intimate that it had never been paralleled in any other human society.

Originally, there had been hundreds of thousands, perhaps more than a million of them. Then the land-hungry *Bantu*, the black tribes, had swept down from the north and the new white settlers, more ruthless, more land-hungry still, had driven up from the south – and the bushmen had been caught inexorably in the vice between the two. They'd been treated as vermin, pests, animals themselves. They were hunted and shot for sport. Their land, their territory – measureless, borderless to them – had been staked and claimed and cleared. In the process they were almost exterminated.

Finally, the last few bands had retreated deep into the Kalahari, into a desert so fierce and wild that it provided sanctuary – neither black nor white had the stomach to follow them there. And somehow they'd managed to survive as before. Shrinking in numbers every year until now only a few thousand were left. Their lovely pale-skinned daughters bought for wives by the Swana tribesmen; the last of their hunting grounds parcelled out to the safari concession companies; even the edges of the desert itself seized, irrigated and used for grazing land.

But still the last of them held on – a shadowy fugitive remnant of a race that had been systematically and mercilessly destroyed like the animals which were vanishing with them.

'Sure, it's a bad story,' Haston finished. 'Only it's over now. Nothing anyone can do is going to turn that clock back. They're not like your leopards. They mix with the Swana. Fifteen, twenty years of interbreeding and there's not going to be a single pure-blood bushman left. They'll all be in shanty-towns outside Gabs or Serowe. Meantime, there are still a few – and it looks like you hit on a group.'

'But what does that mean to us now?'

'Charlie's a tracker, a good one, among the best I ever saw. But these people, they're different. Jesus, they're almost animal, they live with game. They see tracks, smell scent, feel things in the air, from the cloud, on the wind like you'd never believe possible. If Charlie can get them in, they'll say where that creature is.'

He sat down with Alison by the truck and they waited. Three hours passed. Then Charlie came into sight again. He threaded his way through the low bush round the camp, stopped and sat down too – not beside them in the truck's shadow but several yards away on an open space of sand glaring white under the midday sun.

'I'll take the centre,' Haston said quietly. 'You put yourself on my right.'

158

They walked forwards and joined Charlie, the three of them sitting side by side in the open. For a while there was nothing except the heat and the grey thorn and the pale sky above. Yet Haston knew they were being watched. Somewhere, unseen in the thickets, small feral eyes, as unblinking and wary as a desert fox's, were examining them, studying the truck, deciding whether they were friendly or hostile.

Then an opening appeared in a bush across the clearing, the branches parting so silently that it was several seconds before Haston realized a figure had come through it and was squatting opposite them. A man, tiny, bird-boned, golden-skinned with a loin-cloth at his waist, a quiver of arrows across his shoulder and a short bow in his hand.

Haston reached into his pocket, pulled out a cigarette and flipped it over. The man caught it and clapped his hands, a quick staccato gesture of thanks. Then, just as silently, materializing out of the thorn, a second man appeared. Haston flipped him a cigarette too and there was the same sharp clap. He waited again but there was no one else.

'Tell them to come over, Charlie,' Haston said.

Charlie called, the two men jumped up and crossed the clearing at a rapid jogging trot. They were no taller than nine year-old boys but as they squatted down, close to them now, Haston saw that the first was about thirty and the second slightly younger.

'What have you told them so far?'

'I say we're spooring, *Morena*,' Charlie said. 'I tell them they come with us a time and maybe they get more things.'

'Okay, well let's show them what we're spooring first.'

Charlie spoke again and they all stood up, Haston, Alison and Charlie towering over the two bushmen. Then they went over to the trough of sand, the bushmen moving at the same jogging trot. They reached the pug-marks, the bushmen bent down and instantly started talking to each other in a series of excited clicks, grunts and whistles.

'They've got their own language,' Haston explained to Alison. 'It's different from anything anyone else speaks anywhere in the world. I don't understand one damn word, nor do most people. But most of them know a bit of Setswana too. Somehow Charlie can get through to them—'

He glanced at Charlie. 'What do they figure?'

Charlie questioned them, and said, 'Big, big animal, sir. She leopard. Went by here early evening four nights' ago. They say she's hungry – she hasn't killed two, maybe three days.'

'They can tell that from four-day-old tracks?' Alison asked incredulously.

Haston nodded. 'And a whole load more too. Its size, its age, what it's thinking, whether it's tired or angry or nervous. Jesus, if it had a name they could read that off as well. But right now all we want to know is where that animal is — '

He swung back towards Charlie. 'Tell them if they can take us to the leopard they get more cigarettes, a bag of stores and I'll shoot them a big buck.'

Charlie explained again. There were more clicks and grunts as the two little men conferred, then nods, beaming smiles and the crack of hands in agreement. A moment later, trotting, weaving through the clumps of thorn, jogging parallel never more than three paces apart, they were combing the surface of the limestone.

Fifteen minutes went by. Then there was a high fluting whistle and the two converged – distant flitting shapes now a hundred yards away behind the winding screens of bush. They crouched, chattered, the voices snapping like quarrelsome birds, bounded up and came back. One of them, the elder, was holding something cupped in his palm. He lifted his hand towards Haston and opened it.

Haston looked down. Lying on the skin was a single hair, short, fine, silky – and totally black. He studied it for a moment. Then he looked up.

'We've a hell of a way to go yet, lady,' he said, 'but I figure we're going to find your animal.'

Then to his amazement Alison threw her arms round his shoulders and kissed him hard on the cheek.

14

Mlanda clenched his fist and smashed it against the wall, feeling the skin on his knuckles tearing, the blood trickling down, the pain coursing through his hand, but not caring. Not caring because more than pain there was anger – at B'Volu, at the others, at their terrible crass stupidity, most of all at himself.

He should have known they would try something like this. The British projected themselves as cold, rigid, supremely confident, willing prisoners of their imperial protocol and their own mindless arrogance. They'd always done so in all their dealings with Africa, fostering the image, believing in it, making the rest of the world believe in it too. But when they met trouble, when they were confronted with a situation like the one he'd created, they hit back with a cunning, with a ruthlessness and ferocity so unexpected that time and again they'd retrieved the irretrievable.

Not a parachute raid, not a cordon, not an armoured ground force, none of the options he'd considered and discarded because he knew they'd discard them too. Instead a white man and a couple of hired blacks launching a surprise raid out of the darkness. Even then they'd have failed if B'Volu had been alert, if the camp had been properly guarded, if he'd stayed there himself to see the operation through to its end. But B'Volu had relaxed, there'd been no guards out, Mlanda had returned to the township to organize the drop-sites for the weapons – and the calculated gamble, the lethally unorthodox strike, had paid off.

Mlanda sucked at the broken skin, spat the blood onto the ground and swore furiously. Then he turned.

Flies were swarming in the dusky light under the corrugated iron roof. The stench of stale urine and rotting garbage filtered in through the cracks in the brickwork. A rat nuzzled its way over the dust and scurried into the darkness of a corner. Valdez, gin fumes rippling through the air like steam each time he wheezily breathed out, was perched on the crate behind the table. Beside him Tsala was still waiting.

Tsala, young, worried-looking, shy but as dedicated as Mlanda himself, operated the receiver in the bush outside the township, which linked Mlanda with the camp. Normally, the boy – on watch outside the door now – brought in the weekly reports radioed down from the north. But after what he'd heard that morning Tsala had come in person to give Mlanda the news.

The gamble to free the woman had succeeded. But afterwards something else must have happened – something so bewildering that Mlanda was still groping to guess what it might have been.

'You got all of this straight from B'Volu?' he asked.

'Ye–ye–yes — '

Tsala never stuttered over the air. Face-to-face under stress he stammered and fumbled.

'He b–bypassed the relays and came direct on the open line.'

'And he's sure – so damn sure that there can't be any other explanation?'

Tsala shook his head. 'He say none.'

Two men had died in the attack and two more had been wounded. But B'Volu, Mlanda's deputy, and the others had escaped. They hid in the bush for several hours after the firing stopped. Then at midday they cautiously returned to the camp.

The woman, of course, had vanished but from the tracks on the pan B'Volu worked out that three men had been involved in her rescue. Beyond the pan the tracks headed south. B'Volu considered following and decided against it: they were urban Africans, inexperienced at tracking, and although there were only three their attackers could have been heading to link up with another larger group close by. Instead, with forty-eight hours to go before his next radio call, he stripped the camp of most of its supplies and retired into the bush again, leaving a couple of men behind to watch in case anyone returned to the site.

Two days later, just before the call came through, the two

162

men raced back. A truck had appeared at the camp with the woman at the wheel and a black beside her. In the back was a white man apparently unconscious. Unseen in a clump of thorn they'd watched the woman and the black collect her tent and what remained of her supplies. Then the truck had driven off in the direction of the tree where she'd last been watching the leopard.

'All right,' Mlanda said. 'Go back to the set and tell B'Volu to stand by with the line open. I'll send over his instructions inside the hour. Meantime, tell that boy to get me Lumumbi.'

Tsala nodded and went out.

Mlanda paced round the floor thinking, guessing, mind churning as he tried to work it out. Maybe there'd been an accident or the white man had fallen sick or a snake had bitten him – he shivered as he remembered the sleepy puff adders he'd seen up there, great thick lengths of brown cable coiling slowly in the sand. But why weren't they driving for Gaborone or another of the villages on the edge of the desert?

And where was the third man in the attacking party? Perhaps they'd had two trucks and he'd taken the second back to the capital. But again, if the white man was ill, why wasn't he in that truck rather than in the one heading back into the Kalahari? It was incomprehensible and Mlanda gave up. All he knew was that B'Volu had to be right: the woman was after her leopard again.

'Show me where they are again — '

He was standing by the table. Valdez belched, unfolded the map and pointed with a mottled shaking hand.

'That's the camp,' he said. 'But odds are they're moving north behind that animal. Hell, I don't know but now maybe they're somewhere round here.'

He touched another blank grey area of the desert.

'And if they keep travelling north?' Mlanda asked.

'Couple of hundred miles and they reach Maun.'

'What's that like?'

Valdez shrugged. 'Little one-horse place on the edge of the delta. Two hundred whites, gas station, trading stores, a few bars and the headquarters of some of the concession

163

companies, the licensed hunting outfits — '

He paused. 'You figuring on trying to snatch her again?'

Mlanda didn't answer and Valdez went on, 'Well, I tell you something. Round Maun there's people, farms, dogs, cattle trucks. Afterwards, the other side, you got water and islands and real bad country. You want to stop her, you'd better do it in the desert before she gets there. She reaches the delta and you lose her, sure as hell.'

Valdez lurched down grabbing for the gin bottle, the door creaked open and Mlanda turned.

It was Lumumbi. Lumumbi, slow-moving, taciturn, bearded, squat with sullen fanatical eyes, was good – maybe the best Mlanda had ever worked with. If he'd been available when Mlanda conceived of the plan, he would have instantly picked him in place of B'Volu. But Lumumbi was away then, organizing riots in the Cape townships. Now he was back – and now he was needed.

'We got trouble, man,' Mlanda said. 'But looks like we got another chance — '

Lumumbi nodded. Mlanda had told him about the operation after he returned from the Cape and he'd learned from the boy what had happened that morning.

'How long for him to get up there?' Mlanda glanced back at Valdez.

Valdez studied the frayed and tattered map. 'If he grabs hitches on trucks, twenty-four hours maybe. But that just leaves him on the Ghanzi road. He's still got a hundred miles of desert before he finds them.'

'You can handle that,' Mlanda swung back towards Lumumbi. 'I'll radio B'Volu to split his group. Two of them meet you in Ghanzi. You get a truck, Jesus, you lift any vehicle that's there. Then they'll take you to B'Volu. He stays behind the woman. They'll be moving slow and with their tyre tracks they'll be easy to follow. Listen — '

Mlanda explained it carefully in detail.

Then, when he'd finished, he said violently, 'I want her, man. You take over from B'Volu and you get her. I don't give a damn what you do. You got one sick white and a black, that's all. You

164

cut them both but you make goddam sure you get her — '

He paused.

The hate, the anger and frustration that periodically made him tremble, was surging over him again now. Everything had suddenly changed. He saw the desert as a battle-field, a wild desolate arena in which the woman had deliberately pitted herself against him, challenged him for survival. The woman and the weapon she was using. A weapon she'd cowed, cheated, sweet-talked and blackmailed him with – the leopard.

Mlanda clenched his hands, nails cutting into his skin.

Then as the spasm of rage subsided he added, 'You kill that animal too.'

Lumumbi, head set deep in his shoulders, blinked slowly and nodded again.

15

Jo Marshall walked quickly round the side of the farmhouse and across the stable-yard.

It was bad, she knew that. Something had come off Majuliette like a smell when the old housekeeper shuffled into the room. Even before she spoke – and all Majuliette had said was that a hand from one of the outlying farms wanted to speak to her urgently – Jo realized there was trouble. Majuliette probably didn't know what it was herself. Somehow among the blacks bad news was contagious. They didn't have to say anything, they just exchanged glances and the disease was transmitted.

Now, ducking under the lintel into the darkness of the tack-room and seeing the man, Jo sensed the badness again even more strongly.

'What's your name?'

She knew all the workers on the home farm and the foremen on the further grazing lands. But the ordinary hands out there, the Africans who watered, herded and corralled the cattle, came and went seasonally, and there were so many it was impossible to remember them all. She was fairly certain she'd never seen this one before.

'Jacob, miss.'

He'd been sitting cross-legged by the back wall and he clambered to his feet as Jo spoke. She looked at him. A scrawny, barefooted man in a singlet and shorts. His face was broad, running with sweat now in the noon heat, his mouth thick-lipped, his ears small and flat.

The features were typical of any of the Swana tribes except that where normally they'd have been good-humoured and smiling, these were clouded and anxious.

'You want to say something to me?'

'I got —'

He hesitated and turned away, avoiding her eyes.

'Yes?' Jo prompted.

'They say many bad things up Ghanzi way.'

'Are you from Ghanzi?'

'Yes, miss.'

She nodded understanding now. He wasn't a seasonal helper on the distant pastures of her own farm. He worked for her father on one of the ranches to the north.

'What bad things do they say?'

'I don't know, miss, they no concern of mine. I just listen and forget. But then this boy comes and he gives me this. I think you better have it fast as I can —'

He fumbled in a leather pouch on his belt, scooped something out and held it up to her.

Jo took it and recognized it instantly – a glittering copper wrist chain identical to the one the man was wearing himself. Her father issued them to all his workers. Originally, they'd been a means of identification to distinguish his hands from cattle poachers, but they'd quickly become a status symbol – showing that the wearer was employed by the largest landowner in the country.

She went to the door so she could read the inscription in the light. Then she froze. The name carved on the metal band was Ben's.

'How did this boy get it?' Jo turned back, voice hard and urgent.

'He say from other boy, miss, and that one from more other boys —'

The man stopped and turned away again, face working painfully. Jo knew why instantly. She'd known from the moment she saw the name on the band. Only one thing could have separated Ben or any of the others from their chains.

'What happened?' She reached out, grabbed his singlet and shook him. 'You tell me everything, you hear. Everything!'

'Miss, I don't know. People, they been saying there's a big gun-fight out in the desert east of the ranches. White men and black men both. I don't know for nothing Ben's in it. Then this boy comes and I see Ben must be killed and I think you better

167

have it fast.'

'What else?' Jo was shouting at him now. 'Was anyone else killed?'

'I don't know, miss — '

He lifted his head to look at her. There were tears in his eyes and his cheeks were twitching.

'I promise you. I told you all I know. That's for truth.'

Jo hesitated for a moment. Then she let go of his singlet and stepped back.

'All right, Jacob. How did you get down here?'

'This boy, he came dinner-time yesterday. I jump straight on one of the *Morena*'s trucks and I ride all night.'

'You know where the store is?'

'Yes, miss.'

'You go there and you tell James behind the counter I said for you to have one extra week's pay. Then you wait there in case I need you again.'

He nodded and Jo turned and went out.

The morning heat, reflected off the concrete yard, was stifling but Jo didn't notice it. She felt chill and sick. Ben. She'd grown up with his children, played with them by the dam, eaten in his hut daily for years, treated him almost as a second father. Then when she'd been given the farm at sixteen and Ben to run it for her, she'd learned everything from him. About the land, cattle, the hands who worked for her, water and the desert.

Together with Charlie she trusted him more than any man she'd ever known. She checked and froze again. Charlie. She'd sent him off with Haston too.

She went into the house, filled a tumbler with neat vodka, drained it and swore – cursing Haston wildly and viciously. Then she stopped, collected herself and tried to think.

What had that crazy man done? He said he'd been given a chance to keep his licence and she believed him: it was all in the world that mattered to Jerry – that and screwing his bloody little pussy-cats, of course. Now, considering it, she realized the only person whc could help him with his licence was someone with very considerable influence – official influence. Yet there was a contradiction there too. Jerry had asked her not to mention it to anyone ever. If he was doing something official, why the hell the secrecy?

And who were these other white men involved in the gunfight? What was it about? What was Jerry doing up there in the central Kalahari?

The questions were endless and she shook her head helplessly. Only one thing was certain: whatever problems Jerry had had before, he was in far worse trouble now – and Charlie with him. She poured another glass of vodka and then, as she drank, she remembered something else. When he'd asked her for Ben and Charlie, she'd inquired, bitterly, taunting him, how many of the other girls he'd screwed was he crawling to now for help. The question had hit home, he'd flushed and she knew she'd been right.

She wasn't the only one. Everything Jerry had – his boys, his truck, his guns, his safari gear – were stuck in the camp at Tshane when he'd been kicked out. So he'd been making a circuit of the rest of the bitches, using his charm to con them out of what he wanted just as he'd used it to con them into bed in the first place. And no doubt, like her, the pathetic creatures had helped him.

Jo slammed the glass down on the table, so violently it almost shattered. The randy, lying, cheating, bastard whom she'd trusted totally and who in return had betrayed and humiliated her casually, without a second thought. If he got himself killed out in the desert now, she'd be even happier than when she heard about his licence.

She reached for the bell to summon Majuliette and order a groom to saddle her horse for the midday tour of the troughs. Then she checked.

She could pretend it was because of Ben, but it wouldn't be true. She remembered Jerry curled up with that slut when she opened his apartment door – she'd never forget that. But there were other things she'd never forget either. A thin hungry face, rumpled wheat-coloured hair, laughter, galloping side by side faster and faster through low thorn, lying naked by the river half in sun, half in shadow, hands between her thighs, a lean hard body on top of her, binding, pressing, exploding in waves of uncontrollable pleasure – and afterwards at night, with woodsmoke and stars and stories, the cycle starting again.

Jo turned from the bell, walked to the door, went outside and got into her car. Jerry would have needed many things but apart from the boys, Ben and Charlie, the most important were a truck and guns.

'May I come in?'

'Please.'

Two slender brown hands steepled briefly together, a small bow, the rustle of a sari. Jo stepped forwards and blinked in the dusk as the door closed behind her.

It was cool inside. For some reason cooler than the farm in spite of its flagstones and the trees curving overhead. Here the floor was made of worm-eaten wooden planks, there were no trees on the rutted side-street and diesel trucks constantly rumbled by. Yet somehow the heat was still less fierce, less oppressive.

'Excuse me — '

A child had started to cry in a room behind the arch at the back. The Indian girl turned and went through, sandals scuffing quietly on the boards.

Jo waited. She'd come there straight from the garage, taking half an hour to find the house in the maze of little roads on the outskirts of the capital.

The garage had been an obvious starting-point. She'd never met Mary Travers before but she'd heard the gossip just as she'd heard the stories about everyone else Jerry had laid since they stopped going together. Hating herself for listening, for asking, for wanting to know, but doing it irresistibly all the same. Mary Travers, according to the reports which reached her, had been a brief and messy three-week stand.

She'd been in the garage office when Jo arrived. A tight self-contained little woman, pale-faced and dowdy but with a certain frail prettiness and a neat slim figure. Jo introduced herself and asked bluntly if Jerry had borrowed or rented a truck from her. For a few moments Mary had been uncertain and evasive. Then Jo told her he was in trouble, serious trouble, and it was important she knew. Mary shrugged and said, yes, he'd borrowed a Toyota which she'd left for him in the copse behind Van Rhensdorf's house. That was over a week ago. Jerry hadn't said why he wanted the truck and she'd heard nothing since.

Jo thanked her and left. The whole exchange had taken less than five minutes. She didn't know whether Mary knew about her and she didn't care. The Indian girl, Vasha, was different. Jerry had told Jo all about her.

The crying stopped and Vasha came back with the child in her arms. Jo instantly looked down, half fearful, half curious. The boy's face was chubby and pleasant but essentially ordinary, the face of any good-looking little boy – all except for the eyes. They were pale and flecked with green – 'tiger's eyes' she'd called them once. They came unmistakably from Jerry.

She glanced up, suddenly aware she'd only mentioned her name at the door and hadn't even explained why she was there.

'I'm sorry,' Jo said, 'I was admiring your son. He's a lovely-looking boy — '

Vasha inclined her head acknowledging the compliment and Jo went on.

'I'm an old friend of Jerry Haston's,' she paused. 'I was wondering whether you'd seen him recently?'

'Yes.'

'When was that?'

'A week ago, maybe a little more.'

'Did he ask you for anything?'

Vasha hesitated, gazing at her steadily. Then she said, 'May I ask why you wish to know that?'

'Of course, I'm sorry. I should have told you I know about his licence and Jerry's idea he had some way of keeping it. He borrowed two African boys from me and a truck from someone else. Since then he's got himself into very bad trouble. I thought maybe he might have asked you for something, too.'

'This trouble – it is truly serious?'

Jo nodded. 'I don't yet know what it is. But one of my boys has already been killed. I'm pretty certain Jerry could be in

171

danger himself.'

Vasha thought for a moment. 'If you would please wait — '

She turned and climbed the tilting flights of stairs behind her.

Jo stood by the table. Coming to see the Indian girl had been a guess, but she remembered Jerry describing her uncle, old Gopal the merchant. If he'd needed stores, almost anything at short notice, particularly in secret, Gopal was the sort of dealer he'd have gone to.

There was the sound of a door opening above, the murmur of voices, then Vasha came back.

'Jerry asked to talk with my uncle,' she said. 'I think it best for you to speak direct with him. Please go up.'

'Thank you.'

Jo climbed the stairs.

Gopal met her on a small landing at the top of the stairs, bowed deep and ushered her obsequiously into a raftered attic. The blinds were drawn, dust swirled in the half-light, great crates of merchandise littered the floor and a tangle of scents – sweet, dense, cloying – filled the air.

'Please, miss, sit, please — '

He scurried round, found a chair and cleared a space on the floor.

'I have only the most profound regret I greet a member of your family in such humble surroundings — '

Jo sat down, Gopal made another deep bow and stood attentively opposite her – tiny, gold-capped teeth gleaming as he smiled, wrinkled sunken face servile and expectant.

'And what service can I afford you, Miss Marshall?'

Jo looked across at him concealing her contempt. It always happened when her name was mentioned – the instant fawning respect for the Marshall millions – and she always felt the same, scorn and repugnance for the barely-concealed greed that lay behind the lavish attentions. Only Jerry had been different. He hadn't given a damn for anything – money, power, possessions, nothing.

Maybe, she thought suddenly, that was part of what had drawn her to him first – and one of the reasons she was here now.

'Your niece told me Jerry Haston visited you a week ago,' she said. 'I would like to know what he wanted.'

Gopal lifted his hand and made a little gesture of mock alarm.

'My customers' affairs, they are matters of great discretion. I have, I humbly pride myself, a reputation. Yet — '

He paused. 'Because it is you, Miss Marshall, and because it was such an ordinary purchase, I do not think Mr Haston would mind.'

Gopal reached onto a bale beside him, picked up an invoice book, flicked through the pages and handed it to her. Jo glanced down. There was an entry for a dozen pairs of safari boots with Jerry's signature scrawled below.

'Twelve pairs of safari boots?' she said.

'They were excellent quality, miss,' Gopal giggled.

'And that was all?'

'Nothing else, miss. You go through the ledgers, you see I keep the best records in Botswana. There's nothing more there. Ah — '

Gopal stopped again, frowned and snapped his finger, the old bones making a thin dry click.

'I fear I am not telling you the truth, miss. Mr Haston forgot and remembered only on his way out. He wanted laces too. I put them in with the consignment but I never added them to the invoice.'

Gopal shook his head disapprovingly at his own carelessness, took the book back and made another entry on the page.

Jo watched him. It was a charade, a cover, she knew that. Jerry didn't need safari boots, least of all twelve pairs. He wanted something he couldn't acquire legally. That was why Gopal had prepared the dummy invoice. Jerry had got himself a truck and a couple of men. The stores for a safari he could probably have rounded up on his own. All he'd have needed then were guns and to buy guns one had to have a licence.

There was silence. Then Jo said slowly, 'I'm finding it more and more difficult to get good winter fodder. With ten thousand head it's a real problem. The quality's just not there any longer. Don't you find the same, Gopal?'

'Good heavens, miss, truly it is a nightmare.'

Gopal scrambled up onto the bale and sat there cross-legged like some small and ancient bird of prey. The politeness was still in his voice, but the servility had gone and his eyes had clouded over, becoming blank and distant impenetrable. What Gopal knew best in the world, what he lived for, was coming – bargaining and business.

'It applies to almost everything,' Jo went on. 'From tack to overalls for the boys. We use a great deal on the farm. A single first-class supplier, perhaps at the start on a one-year contract, would be invaluable.'

'With care, miss, with much care and supervision – they are such rascals out here – I think that can be arranged.'

'Yes, Gopal, I'm sure it can be.'

Silence again. Gopal blinked, stared vaguely at a blind flapping over her shoulder, raked his fingers softly through an open sack of maize.

'With Mr Haston, alas, I only do business over boots and laces,' he said eventually. 'But I believe, I am not sure mind you, Mr Haston has a friend. The friend wants some weapons, two Schmeisser repeaters and an Urtzi automatic rifle. I understand his friend acquires them. But these are very dangerous guns, miss, and of course I know nothing about that. Good heavens, with my business — '

Gopal broke off and shrugged, a little dismissive lift of his shoulders as if the story had been so casual and remote he had difficulty in remembering it.

Jo leant forwards. The 'friend' was Haston himself and the supplier of the arms Gopal, she had no doubt about that. The rest of the information was inexplicable. Jo had been brought up with and used guns all her life. She'd guessed Jerry might have wanted a hunting rifle for himself and maybe shotguns for Ben and Charlie. But Schmeissers and Urtzis weren't sporting guns, they were military weapons – and there was no war in the Kalahari.

'What did Mr Haston's friend want these guns for, Gopal?' she asked.

'Miss, how possibly do I know?'

174

Gopal managed to convey outraged disbelief at her question.

'This is just something I think I hear somewhere and tell you only, most privately, because I know you are a good friend of Mr Haston's. But for why I have no idea.'

'Then I think you and I have different ideas about a first-class supplier.'

Jo began to rise but Gopal, with astonishing speed, jumped off the bale, bowed in supplication and waved her down.

'There are things now that return to me — '

He circled the crates his hand to his head, a ghostly shuffling little figure in the dusty half-light. Jo watched him, sniffing the air: she could smell coriander and curry-powder and the sharp resinous tang of coated twine.

'When I heard of Mr Haston's friend, I was concerned – for him of course, you understand. I made certain inquiries. Naturally, I did not mention the weapons, good heavens, no. But I asked, very delicately, very discreetly, why on earth, where on earth such guns might be needed here in Botswana? I was surprised, miss, truly I was surprised, how quick the word come back — '

The word. It was always that. Never a source, a reply, a direct traceable answer. Simply the word.

It was the same with the boy from the Ghanzi ranches who'd brought Jo Ben's wrist-band and the story of a gun-fight out in the desert. She might have found the boy who'd told him, then the next link in the chain and so on back and back. But in the end the trail would vanish and she'd be left with that intangible elusive concept – the word.

'You have heard of George Mlanda, miss?'

Jo nodded. Like everyone in southern Africa she'd heard of Mlanda's exploits.

'A bad man, oh, a terrible man,' Gopal shivered. 'There is word in the townships to the south that he made a raid up here. He took a hostage and is holding her in the bush.'

'Her?'

'A lady, miss, who was studying animals out in the desert. And when I hear this I wonder — '

Gopal stopped in front of her, eyes remote and unfocused again as he gazed over her shoulder.

'This friend of Mr Haston's, maybe he was in trouble. Maybe someone offered to help with his troubles. In return maybe the friend tries to free the lady and so he needs those guns. I am guessing, miss. Truly, truly I do not know. But I promise you with the honour of my word I have told you all I hear.'

Gopal looked at her. He'd finished and Jo believed him when he claimed he knew nothing more. She sat for a moment thinking.

There could be endless other explanations, but Gopal's guess fitted everything she knew. An offer from someone in authority to fix his licence. The truck, Ben and Charlie, the weapons, the secrecy and just the crazy wild sort of scheme that in desperation Jerry might have gone for. There even had to be a woman involved.

The blinds rustled, mice darted across the eaves, on the street below a group of African women were talking and laughing. Then Jo glanced up.

'I need one more thing, Gopal,' she said finally. 'If your guess is right, if Mr Haston's friend was trying to free this woman, he'd need to know where she was being held. The person who made him the offer must have known that, but he's not going to tell anyone else – he's going to deny it ever happened. So how do I find out where Mr Haston's friend went?'

'Alas, miss,' Gopal spread out his hands and shrugged, 'on that there was no word at all. Except — '

He paused. 'Before all this the lady had a camp in the bush. Each month a pilot, Mr Linden, flies her out supplies. That I know because Mr Linden is a most valued customer of my company. He knows at least where her camp was, maybe he knows more. It is the best I can suggest.'

'All right — '

Jo stood up and walked to the door.

'Thank you, Gopal. I'll ask my under-manager to pass by this week and discuss the other matter we talked about.'

'It will be a pleasure and a privilege, Miss Marshall.'

Gopal giggled happily, his head shone like a raven's egg as he bowed low again, and Jo went out.

Vasha was waiting downstairs with the child still in her arms. Jo stopped in front of her.

'Thank you,' she said. 'Your uncle was very helpful.'

'I am glad.'

The small inclination of the head. Jo hesitated, awkward and embarrassed, wondering whether Vasha knew about her as she knew about the Indian girl. With the other woman, Mary, it hadn't mattered. But somehow the child, calm and silent now like his mother, seemed to create a bond between them, tying them together in an unspoken alliance.

She touched his cheek. Then, as she turned to leave, Vasha said, 'Where is Jerry?'

Jo checked and looked back. 'Somewhere out in the desert.'

'Are you going to him?'

'I —'

She broke off. Until that moment she hadn't really known what she was doing, apart from trying to find out what had happened. Now suddenly she knew beyond any doubt.

'Yes,' she said, 'I'll try to find him.'

Vasha gazed at her, eyes dark and luminous and tranquil. Then she smiled.

'Take with you my love too.'

'I will.'

Jo turned again, walked down the steps and heard the door click shut behind her. Outside in the heat and glaring light of the street she realized she was crying. She blinked, shook her head angrily and crossed the rutted earth to her car.

It was one o'clock. If Linden was like the rest of them, he'd be drinking at the horseshoe bar in the Inn. Jo started the engine and headed back into the capital.

16

The cane, a black rod against the sky through the windscreen glass, twitched to the left, then left again and finally swung back to the centre so that it was pointing forwards over the hood.

'Now hold it straight,' Haston said.

Alison corrected the wheel and the truck crunched on through the bush.

Haston leant back, felt a sharp twinge in his shoulder as they lurched over a rock and sat upright again, moving himself away from the jolting cabin partition. They were travelling through dense thorn and dry reed. The reeds, folding in waves under the fender, were so high that without Charlie squatting on the roof and guiding them with his cane they wouldn't have known where they were going. Somewhere ahead, visible only to the African, the two little bushmen were trotting through the undergrowth.

It had taken the bushmen two hours to find where the leopard had left the outcrop of limestone and rejoined the sand. For several miles afterwards they'd moved quickly, but then they'd come on more stone, the spoor was cold and difficult, and they'd slowed again. Haston hadn't been checking the milometer but now in the late afternoon he guessed they'd covered no more than twelve miles in all since the morning.

Suddenly the reeds parted, they came into a clearing and Alison stopped. The bushmen were crouched over something a few yards ahead. Charlie jumped down from the roof and they both got out and walked forward.

'Baboon, *Morena*,' Charlie said as they came up. 'Men say it killed three nights back. The leopard ate right here, then moved straight on.'

Haston glanced down at a pile of bones on the sand, already dry and white and clean. Then he heard an alarm call, one of the bushmen pointed and he looked to the left. There was a mopane copse on the side of the clearing with a pack of about fifteen baboons clustered in the branches. As he watched they broke into a furious chorus of barking and grunting.

'Well,' he turned to Alison, 'sure as hell your animal's in a hurry. That's its favourite dinner but it didn't even bother to hide what was left.'

She nodded. 'It looks as if it's moving continuously now.'

Haston studied the spoor leading away across the sand, the great pugmarks blurred and patterned by other tracks but still unmistakable. Then he glanced up. The sun was still well clear of the horizon but the light was beginning to soften.

'Okay,' he said. 'We've got maybe another couple of hours. We'd better shift.'

He and Alison got back into the truck, Charlie climbed onto the roof, the two bushmen jogged away and they set off again.

They camped at sunset. Charlie built a fire, cooked the evening meal and they ate together in the darkness, the bushmen darting in to take a piece of food and then trotting away to eat it, hands cupped to their mouths, in the shelter of the truck.

'What's the matter, Jerry?'

Haston glanced up. Alison was gazing at him across the flames. They'd finished the meal, the bushmen were smoking just outside the rim of the firelight, and Charlie was placing pieces of rag round the camp-site. The human smell was meant to discourage lion from wandering through. Haston didn't know if it was true, but every tracker he'd ever worked with had done the same.

'Hell,' he shrugged. 'Your friends back there, I guess — '

He'd been thinking about Mlanda and he realized he must have been frowning.

'We're making ten, fifteen miles a day and leaving spoor a blind junkie couldn't miss. If he takes another crack, we'll be like wooden ducks at a fairground shooting-stall.'

'If it does happen, which I very much doubt, I'll answer for you and Charlie.'

Haston laughed. 'We knocked over three or four of his men. That's going to take some explaining, however much you've got going with him.'

179

'I have nothing going with him, whatever that may mean,' she prodded the fire with a branch and the flames leapt upwards. 'George Mlanda once spent two weeks at a camp I had in Tanzania. I think I understand him. If I'm wrong I'll accept the consequences just as you'll have to. This is his country after all.'

'His country?' Haston laughed again, quickly, harshly, 'Who are you kidding, lady? This is no one's goddam country, except maybe theirs —'

He gestured towards the bushmen.

'And they've been screwed out of it, they're finished. So who's left? Whites and blacks, that's all. Sure, those guys from BOSS are bastards. But do you figure some trigger-crazy thug like Mlanda's got any better claim on it than them? Hell, even the goddam Boers were here before his people.'

'I can think of other forms of life which were here even before the bushmen —'

She put down the branch. Then she asked quietly, 'How did you become a hunter, Jerry?'

'How — ?'

Haston glanced at her sharply, wary and defensive. He'd known that sooner or later the question would come. It always did. Mostly, from the girls he was trying to score, in awe and admiration – and he'd spin out the answer, casually hinting at the danger, the glamour, the machismo involved. But sometimes from the others, the ones who were into 'ecology' and 'wildlife' and 'conservation', the question would be provocative, loaded with bitterness and hostility.

He looked at Alison's face. She was essentially one of the others, but there was no challenge or antagonism there. Instead straightforward curiosity in the thoughtful gaze and the direct inquiring eyes.

'I guess it started with my old man,' Haston said. 'He's retired now but he used to work for the UN as an agricultural advisor. They sent him to East Africa, that's where I grew up—'

He told her of his childhood in the house outside Nairobi. The trips into the bush as early as he could remember while his father toured the farms. Then, at ten, school back home in the States living with his grandparents in Maryland. But every year the long summer holiday – winter as it was in Africa – when he'd return.

It was on one of those that he went on his first proper safari and shot his first buck, a sable. He'd stalked it down-wind in low cover for three hours and he would never forget the moment when he finally lifted his rifle and fired. He knew instantly that nothing would ever be the same again. By chance the buck had the longest horns of any sable killed in Kenya that year. But it wasn't the size of the trophy: it was the craft, the excitement, the contest, the sense of power and triumph when the butt slammed back against his shoulder and he saw the animal drop.

Haston went on safari every year after that, saving every cent he could earn in the States from jobs out of school to buy himself better and better guns. Then, high school over, he tried college to please his parents but dropped out at the end of the first year. There was only one thing Haston wanted to do – and he wasn't going to waste any of his life away from it.

'I'd never been this far south,' he went on. 'But I got an introduction to a guy called Anderson. He used to run safaris in Kenya with a partner called Mahoney. But Kenya's been getting overcrowded, overshot for years. So when Botswana became independent Anderson moved here, leased two big concession areas from the new government and set up another branch of the company. I came down and joined him — '

Haston did a year's apprenticeship, working as second gun to the other licensed professional hunters employed by Anderson to escort clients on safari. He learned the rituals of the hunting camps: the dawn rise, the day's tracking, the return at dusk with the truck's klaxon blaring if someone had shot a prize trophy, a leopard, a lion, an elephant, the conversation over dinner with the clients – South Africans up from the Cape, rich Venezuelans, Germans, Frenchmen and Spaniards.

Finally, with the necessary written endorsements from two other hunters, he'd applied to the Game Department and been granted his own licence. It had made him a member of an elite –

there were less than forty professional hunters in the entire country. An elite who could earn big money in the seven-month season, lay any girl they wanted, live the life he'd dreamed about ever since he squeezed the trigger on that first sable, smelt the cordite from the smoking barrel, watched the buck plunge and reel and collapse.

'So that's how,' he finished. 'Sure, you won't see it that way, but to me I just got lucky. For seven years I've been paid for something I'd have paid to do myself if I'd had the bread. Not many people get that. Also,' Haston grinned, 'sounds funny but I reckon I fell in love with this place. Kenya's beautiful, sure, rich and lush and green. The Kalahari isn't. Rock, sand, thorn, mosquito, tsetse, you name it and it's all here – and all trouble. But there's other things too. The air, the light, the way the wind comes up from the mountains to the south, the places you can go and know that no one, like no one, has ever been there before. Not black, not white, not even bushmen. Just animals and a bunch of eagles maybe. Hell, that's something—'

Haston shook his head and stopped.

It was the first time he'd tried to explain to anyone what he felt about the desert, and he knew the attempt was pitifully inadequate. There were no words for the Kalahari, no way you could communicate its essence to someone else unless they sensed it too. He didn't even know why he'd tried except perhaps that after watching her for the past few days, he thought she felt some of the same awareness.

Alison sat looking at him. Then she said, 'You love it and yet you spend your life killing the only creatures who really belong to it – the animals?'

There was still no hostility in her voice, only speculation and interest, but behind that she might have been speaking to him across a chasm. Whatever she felt, however much they shared and saw and sensed, in the end they'd always stand remote and irreconcilable.

Haston shrugged and tried to answer, the old stock answer he and the other hunters always used.

'You call it killing,' he said. 'I call it cropping. Any place on earth where man and cattle start moving in, and, don't kid yourself, centuries back it happened even here, the wild balance gets blown. Then you get surplus or diminished populations. Too many lion one year, too few zebra the next. Hell, as a zoologist you know that. Someone's got to keep it straight. So what are the options? Machine-gun the surplus from a helicopter? Or give out a few game licences, controlled tight as a nut, to guys who want to hunt and will pay goddam valuable foreign currency to do it — ?'

He paused. 'I know what I'd do – and it's just what they're doing here. Sound sense, good conservation, bread for the people who live in the country. What more do you want?'

As an argument it was solid, convincing, in large part true. But there were flaws in it, dimensions it didn't take into account, and Alison knew them all.

'No, Jerry,' she shook her head. 'If you were cropping naturally, you'd take the weakest and leave the best, the strongest to breed. But you don't. You reverse the process. Your clients want trophies, big skins, long horns they can hang on their walls and put into the record books. And every time you give them one, every time you pick the finest buck or buffalo in a herd, you weaken the stock, you help wind down a species until in the end at best they'll be shadows of what they were, at worst extinct — '

She stopped and Haston frowned. He wasn't thinking about what she'd said. He'd remembered something else.

He stood up, went over to the truck and rummaged with his left hand in the shelf under the dashboard. He found the map, returned to the fire and spread it out on his knees.

'What is it?' Alison asked.

Haston studied the map for a few moments in silence. Then he glanced across at her.

'Trouble,' he said. 'Or it could be if we keep heading north like this. Do you know how the hunting concession areas work?'

She shook her head.

'Come over here and I'll show you — '

She joined him on the other side of the fire and Haston explained.

Apart from the cattle ranches, the game reserves and the scattered ribbons of mining sites, the rest of the country was divided up into vast tracts of hunting territory – each of them thousands upon thousands of square miles in extent. Most could be hunted over by anyone who acquired a licence and a Game Department ranger to accompany them. But ten of the largest and richest in game, the concession areas, were leased exclusively to the five safari companies licensed to operate in Botswana.

'The ordinary ones don't matter,' Haston said. 'You get an occasional guy up from the Cape or a local white who's serious, but for the rest it's just a few trigger-happy black poachers. They get swallowed up in the desert like they never existed. But the concessions are different.'

'Why?'

'Fixed hunting camps, clients who've paid a bundle, hunters to go with them, trucks, trackers, radio, planes, the lot. And look — '

He swivelled the map round and touched a spot south of Maun.

'That's about where we are now, maybe a hundred miles from Maun itself. We re-fuel, re-supply there like we decided, fine. But from the angle that cat's taking, look where it's pitching for next.'

Alison followed as his finger moved up past Maun into a section cross-hatched with blue to the north.

'That's a concession area?' she said.

Haston nodded. 'Matsebe. It's in Ngamiland right in the heart of the delta. Run by another East African group and one of the best. We're high season now and they're fully-booked, they were even shopping around for extra hunters a couple of months back — '

Haston let the map slide off his knees onto the ground.

'Sure, the place is so damn big you could say it's odds against. But your animal's travelling fast and straight and open. It's not behaving normally. Anyone comes across its spoor and they'll drop everything, we'll have every gun in Matsebe after it. It's like you said. The guy who knocks over that

184

leopard gets Rowland Ward, Boone and Crockett, every record book in the business reprinted.'

'But we'd know if someone tried to hunt it. We could tell them what it was and they'd stop.'

'Lady,' Haston shook his head. 'Aside from the liability of me and the truck, legally you're not even allowed into the concession. And have you ever tried to stand between a hunter and a record trophy?'

'You tried to stand between me and the leopard, Jerry.'

She smiled and Haston laughed.

'Sure,' he said. 'And look where it got me. But that was somewhat different. Next time you won't have the same arguments on your side.'

'If there is a next time, I'll have others and they'll be equally convincing — '

She got to her feet and stood looking out into the darkness, no longer smiling but serious and abstracted. Charlie and the bushmen had curled up to sleep, the night's chill had come down, the sky dazzled with stars and the sounds of the bush were all round them – jackal and hyena and owl and small soft rustles in the thorn.

She wasn't feeling the cold, Haston knew that, nor hearing the desert noises or seeing the constellations – the Southern Cross was right overhead with Orion glittering below. Her mind was concentrated totally on the animal again. The dark silken gloss of its fur, the great shoulder muscles rhythmically bunching and uncoiling as it moved, the tiny stirs in the sand caused by the prints of its passage. That was all she felt and saw and heard.

He watched her, face lit by the flames, jaw stubborn, eyes grave and distant, tall thin body outlined in the glow as the night wind tugged her blouse and skirt against her. And then suddenly, briefly Haston experienced something he'd never felt before – a surge of protectiveness, almost of tenderness. Pursuing her dream, she'd unflinchingly taken on the entire Kalahari – after the fight by the pan she'd even been prepared to face the desert alone. A single woman without water or gun or provisions risking her life for the sake of an animal.

185

It was crazy and Haston would never understand why, but he also saw now there was a certain nobility in what she'd done. He stood up too, tapped her on the shoulder and grinned.

'Don't worry,' he said. 'If you start hassling with hunters I'll be on hand to give advice. At least you got yourself an expert in dealing with them.'

Alison started, glanced round and smiled again.

'Is this a zoological breakthrough – the leopard that really does change its spots?'

'Hell, no,' Haston shook his head. 'Don't ask for the impossible. I just want to be after my own cats again. If that means I got to wetnurse yours through, well, I'll go along right to the end.'

'I wonder, Jerry, I wonder — '

She paused, still smiling, head tilted to one side as she looked at him, speculative, assessing him as if for the first time.

'What would happen if I showed you what you call my animal?'

'I haven't a clue. But if I were you I'd just be grateful I haven't got a Mauser .458 and a shoulder to put its stock against—'

Haston stopped, embarrassed now by the impulsive gesture he'd made. Then he turned away. The night before, at his insistence, they'd gone back to the original sleeping arrangements – Alison in her tent, he in his sleeping-bag which Charlie had laid out in the back of the truck. He'd have to wear the sling for another few days but there was no trace of infection now and the wound was healing fast.

'If we're going to be after that cat early,' he said, 'we'd better turn in. Take care and sleep well.'

'You too, Jerry.'

Haston didn't look back but he sensed that Alison was still watching him as he walked over to the truck, climbed inside and settled himself in the bag. He shut his eyes and resolutely tried to will himself into sleep. Normally, he slept without difficulty. That night, in spite of being tired after the long slow jolting drive behind the bushmen, he remained awake, shifting uneasily, restlessly on the metal floor.

186

Finally, he sat up and looked out. Alison hadn't moved from the fire. She was still standing where he'd left her, upright, arms crossed over her chest, gazing into the darkness as the wind plucked at her lace collar and the flames patterned her skirt.

He watched her for a while. Then he swore and lay down again. Somewhere to the west a male lion was roaring, each of the deep thundering bellows tailing away into a series of grunts. The number of grunts was meant to indicate its age, one for every year of maturity.

Haston lay on his back and began to count.

They followed the spoor for three days, Alison at the wheel, Haston beside her, Charlie on the cabin roof or in the back, the bushmen trotting, wheeling, casting, pausing for long clicking conferences, then jogging on again ahead.

It was the longest hardest piece of tracking Haston had ever done. The Kalahari he knew best, the area he'd hunted for seven years round Tshane, was copses and scattered scrub and long rolling grass plains – paling through the season from gold to white after the quick fresh greenness of the spring rains. That, as the months passed, as the heat grew and the land baked dry and the dust rose, had been harsh enough. But here, deep in the central desert, it was different – and fiercer, far fiercer still. There were few trees, little scrub, almost no plain. Instead, rock, great fissured sheets of limestone serrated with gullies and studded with boulders. Between the outcrops of stone – sand. Soft and deep and fine into which even with the four-wheel drive the Toyota's tyres would sink and churn until he and Charlie, sweating, heaving, straining at the rear bumper, Haston with one arm alone, managed to heave the truck clear. And, threading, lacing and stitching both sand and rock together, the sinuous belts of thorn – springy, needle sharp, clawing savagely at metal, flesh, cloth and rubber.

Sometimes, as on the first day, they'd be held up for hours when the spoor vanished on the stone. Then they'd wait sweltering in the cabin or pacing slowly outside while the bushmen cast wider and wider circles. But always sooner or later there'd be the high birdlike whistle and the excited clicks and grunts, and Haston would go over to see what they'd found. Often it would be no more than another single hair, a tiny scratch in the rock, a faint smear on a crumbling piece of stone – signs so small and indistinct that for Haston they were difficult to see with the naked eye and impossible to interpret once he'd spotted them. Yet to the bushmen they were unmistakable: the leopard had passed that way and they'd trot on side by side again.

Twice they came on other kills, a second baboon and a warthog. The baboon was like the first, stripped clean and dry, but there were still some scraps of flesh on the warthog's bones and a black vulture flapped slowly away as the truck stopped. Charlie spoke to the bushmen and turned to Haston.

'Twenty-four hours ago, *Morena*,' he said.

Haston nodded and glanced at Alison. 'We're closing fast, lady. Keep your fingers crossed.'

She lifted her hand, crossed two fingers and laughed.

At night they'd camp wherever they found themselves when the light went. Charlie would make a fire using wood he'd chopped from the rare dead tree they came across along the spoor-line during the day. Alison would change. Then they'd eat together, talk for a while by the fire and turn in early to bed.

Alison baffled Haston, not just because of her obsession with the leopard but because of what she was herself – as a woman. Watching her on the nights before they met the bushmen when they'd been stalled on the first outcrop of rock, he'd realized suddenly to his astonishment that she was extraordinarily beautiful. Now, talking, laughing, increasingly animated as they drew closer to the creature, she was even more so.

Yet at the same time on a different level, on the gut level he knew and had responded to on countless occasions in the past, she remained as remote as when he'd trussed and toted her through the bush. He felt no sense of challenge, no hard rising of desire, nothing except bewilderment. Somehow he could no more imagine reaching out a hand to touch her cheek than he'd touch Charlie's.

At the start he thought it might have something to do with the South Africans, his licence, the wound in his shoulder and the situation he'd found himself in as a result. Everything he knew, everything he'd lived by, had been turned upside down. He wasn't in control; she was. He had to go where she wanted, do what she said, follow where she led. He couldn't even drive the truck. Christ, if it came to a showdown he'd even be dependent on her to do the shooting.

Then, slowly, Haston began to realize it wasn't the situation. Sure, that had changed things immeasurably and at times he'd rage inwardly against his own impotence, at the way he'd been hobbled, temporarily almost castrated by what had happened. But more than that there was something else – Alison herself. She wasn't frigid or lesbian – another of his early wild guesses to explain her remoteness. She was simply self-sufficient. To Alison there was no challenge, no battle, no conquest or submission. She depended on no one. For her at that moment, through the long months before, during the days, the weeks that might follow, the leopard was enough. She needed nothing else.

And if the time came when she did need something more, or she decided to offer something herself, she'd take or give it of her own accord. Openly, directly, without skirmish or bargain or contest – just as she'd given to him in sitting up for hour after hour three nights in succession while he'd raved and convulsed in fever.

Lying in the back of the truck – it was after midnight but he still couldn't sleep – Haston shivered. He'd thought he knew pussy-cats, every size and shape and form. The way you could touch them, stroke them, handle them. How to make them laugh, how their breasts felt as you lifted them, rubbing slowly and gently from below, the smell they gave off when you reached down between their thighs and explored the dampness there, how to mould and caress the opening until suddenly you were both violently binding, arching together. And afterwards the peace, the limpness, the warmth until you started again.

Not with this one. She walked her own road along her own compass bearings, distant and solitary and apart.

There were no lion grunts to count that night. Instead Haston turned to watch the stars and track the constellations

189

crossing the Milky Way.

'*Morena!*'

Charlie calling on the afternoon of their third day with the bushmen. They'd tracked the spoor since dawn, moving much faster as the sheets of limestone at last gave way to stretches of sand broken only by thickets of thorn and scrub. With each mile as the day wore on, the pug-marks had been newer, firmer, deeper. At noon, according to the bushmen, they were following tracks the leopard had left the night before.

Haston got out. The thorn they'd been winding through for the past ten minutes was thicker than usual, briefly the bushmen had disappeared, he'd asked Alison to stop and sent Charlie on ahead to find them again and tell them to wait until the truck caught up. Charlie's voice had sounded from somewhere fifty yards in front. Edging carefully between the bushes with Alison behind him Haston walked forward.

Charlie, towering over the two little men, was standing in a small clearing. Across it the spoor ran die-straight and clean like a ribbon of lace printed in the sand. As Haston stopped one of the bushmen clicked, stretched out his arm and pointed – not with his finger, the sign of bad or dangerous tracks, but with his thumb pressed down over his clenched hand.

Haston looked across the clearing following the line of the spoor. The pug-marks vanished into the thorn on the far side, but thirty yards further still, deep in the bush, he could see a single tall acacia. He looked at the tree for a moment, frowned, then he realized and swung round towards Alison – feeling laughter, delight, triumph surging up in him.

Before he could say anything he heard the hum of the plane.

The lower you flew the worse it was. The bush was like an immense blanket, riddled with holes, thrown over a fire. Where it covered the ground the heat was contained but in the gaps of open sand the hot air thermals came up like lances – rocking and buffetting anything that crossed them.

Jo was flying at four hundred feet as she'd done all day. Any higher and she wouldn't see the tyre marks below. But every few minutes the nose cowling would jerk up, the plane lurch sideways and the whole fuselage plunge and throb like a rearing horse so that she had to fight, knuckles white on the controls, to hold it on course. Sometimes the turbulence would be so violent that she'd have to swing away, turn and come in from a different angle.

It happened now. The plane tilted sickeningly and vibrated as if it was about to disintegrate. She banked, climbed to the west, made the turn and came down again, searching for the parallel tracks in the bush once more. Her shirt was wet with sweat, her arms were aching and her jeans, soaked too, grated against her thighs.

She shook her head and peered through the perspex canopy.

The plane, a scarlet Piper Aztec, was her own, an eighteenth birthday present from her father. She'd flown it up from Gaborone to one of the family ranches at Ghanzi the day before, as soon as she'd finished with the pilot, Linden.

As she'd guessed, Linden had been drinking in the bar at the Inn. At the start he was wary and evasive, denying he'd made the supply flights out to the woman's camp, and Jo realized someone must have told him not to talk about it. Then she fell back on the same gambit she'd used on the old Indian, Gopal. She offered him a contract for the monthly vaccine deliveries to the outlying farms. It was regular, guaranteed four days work each month – to a freelance charter pilot like Linden, a job he could plan his entire year round. Making her promise secrecy, Linden had given her the camp's position. He wouldn't say anything else except there had been serious trouble out there and he urged her to go nowhere near the place.

Jo didn't comment. She checked the map, saw that the camp was in the central Kalahari and flew straight to Ghanzi. From Gaborone the camp was over four hundred miles and she'd only have a few hours of daylight left after she got there. But from Ghanzi it was less than a hundred and fifty. She refuelled at the ranch, spent the night in the farmhouse and took off again at dawn.

Two hours later she landed on the strip that had been cleared for Linden in the bush.

The camp-site was a low hillock ringed by trees with the scattered ashes of a long-dead fire and a cairn of stones at the centre. She walked round it carefully. There was nothing else, not even the faintest trace of human spoor, the place might have been deserted for months. Then she began to circle the scrub that surrounded the hillock on every side.

By midday she'd covered an area of three miles round the camp and still found nothing. She stopped, thought for a moment and walked back to the plane. If Mlanda had seized the woman, it would be logical for him to move her. Not far, but at least away from the place where Linden and maybe others knew she'd been camping. Jerry had taken a truck, he must have known where she was being held, somewhere the tyre tracks had to show up in the sand.

Jo got back into the Aztec, took off and started searching from the air.

She found it at three o'clock, forty miles to the east, a mopane copse with a blurred network of tyre marks by the trees. A mile beyond she could see a small pan. She flew low over it, the surface looked level and firm, she made another circuit and touched down. Then she walked back to the copse, glanced over the open sand – and vomited.

A collection of bones littered the ground, broken, wrenched apart, gnawed and torn and cleaned by jackal, hyena, vultures, even at the last scavenging ants and beetles. Beside them, sun-dried and grey, was a human skull. It might have been anyone's but Jo knew with an instant absolute certainty it was Ben's.

She turned away, dizzy, shivering, the bile pumping up and dribbling down her chin. Then she gathered herself, wiped her face and forced herself to look back, trying to keep her eyes from the skull as she studied the tracks. They must have been almost a week old and at first, following the faded crumbling prints from the copse to the scrub and back, Jo thought they'd been made by the same vehicle.

Then she noticed something. Years of hunting trips with Charlie had left her almost as good a tracker as any of Jerry's friends among the professional hunters. She crouched down, measured the distance between one set of marks – revolving her outspread hand across the sand – and afterwards did the same with another set. There was a small but significant difference in axle width. Not one vehicle – but two.

Jo stood up. The freshest impressions of both trucks led in opposite directions, the smaller due north the larger towards the south. Did the first belong to the Toyota? The second, she guessed, were, a Chevvy's or a Ford's – she was fairly certain of that because they were the trucks she used on the farm. She followed the first tracks for a couple of hundred yards, saw them vanish still heading north into the bush, and came back.

She had no idea what had happened except that this was the site of the gun-fight that the black, Jacob, had told her about. Jerry had attacked or been attacked by another group in the other truck, Ben had been killed, then he'd set off north deeper into the desert. Presumably with Charlie. And inexplicably.

Jo couldn't even begin to guess why he'd taken that direction, whether the woman was with him, what had happened to Mlanda's terrorists. All she knew was that somewhere out there Jerry was still travelling. That crazy disloyal man whom in spite of everything, cursing herself, denying it, fighting against it, she still loved helplessly.

She walked back to the plane and took off again. Apart from the intermittent impact of the thermals the truck's spoor was easy to follow now. It became easier still as the miles passed and the twin tracks stood out more and more sharply in the sand or traced lanes of crushed thorn through the bush. Several times she spotted the tiny black dot of a dead fire and circled puzzled. If the dots marked Jerry's overnight camp-sites, he was only making fifteen or twenty miles a day. At that rate she'd catch up with him well before dark.

It was almost five when something suddenly glinted ahead and below, the metallic dazzle of light flashing off a truck hood. Jo tensed, blinked and peered down.

Then she banked steeply and prepared to run in low directly over the truck.

'The guns, Charlie, for Christ's sake — '

They'd raced back to the Toyota and Haston was standing by the tailgate. Charlie vaulted up and pulled out the Schmeissers, the Urtzi and the carton of ammunition.

'Here, fill this,' Haston thrust an empty magazine into Alison's hand. 'Watch me — '

He painfully disengaged his arm, still stiff and weak at the shoulder, from the sling and began to feed shells into another of the metal clips. Alison copied him, working fast and deftly.

'Any ideas?' she gasped.

Haston nodded grimly. 'We're way off any of the commercial routes to the north, no one from Ghanzi would be flying this far east and the Game Department hasn't got any aircraft up here. I guess that only leaves Mr bloody Liddell's South African friends — '

He glanced up. The plane was still out of sight but the roar of its engine was coming closer every second.

'No,' he waved away the Urtzi Charlie was handing him. 'Put a couple of cartridges in the 12-gauge. No way can I handle a repeater. But maybe up close I can use the shotgun with my left — '

Charlie loaded the shotgun, jumped down and took one of the Schmeissers. Haston, resting the stock against the tailgate, slammed a full magazine onto the other and gave it to Alison.

'Hold it at the hip, swing it like a yard hose and squeeze the trigger in short bursts. Figure you can manage — ?'

She nodded.

'Fine. Damn-all they can do from the air, but they could be spotting for a support truck right behind. Now get down — '

The three of them crouched side by side on the ground in the truck's shadow watching the sky. The bushmen had vanished, melting silently, instantly into the thorn as soon as they saw Haston turn and sprint from the clearing. Haston waited, shoulder throbbing, one arm hanging limply by his side, the other holding the shotgun against his ribs with his hand curled round the trigger-guard as if it had been a revolver.

The roar grew louder, the bush quivered, rustled and bent under the down-thrust of the air, then the plane swept overhead – a flash of scarlet against the sun.

'Jesus Christ — !'

Haston was on his feet gazing in the direction where it had already disappeared, hidden by the high thorn.

'Did you see that, man?'

He swung towards Charlie, open-mouthed, disbelieving, bewildered. There was only one plane like that in Botswana and he'd flown in it many times, he'd even caught the registration number as it passed.

'Yes, *Morena*,' Charlie was standing too. 'That's Miss Jo's.'

The sound had faded now, but as Haston listened he heard the aircraft bank and turn and then the noise rising again as it came back.

'What's happening?'

Alison was standing beside them now. The roar increased, the bush fluttered and flattened again, there was a second scarlet flash. Haston, eyes narrowed, concentrated on the undersides of the wings rechecking the number. It was unmistakable.

'I haven't the faintest—'

The plane had gone and the noise was fading once more.

'But it's not what I thought,' he said. 'You remember that girl called Jo you said I was talking about when I had the fever? Well, that's her kite up there.'

Alison stared at him, shaking her head. Before she could say anything else the plane passed over them again. This time it was higher. It circled twice, wiggled its wings, changed course so it was heading west, dipped its nose, then straightened and vanished behind the thorn.

'We got a pan close, Charlie?'

Haston had recognized the signals immediately. The pilot – whoever he or she was and Haston hadn't been able to make out anything behind the canopy – was preparing to land somewhere to the west.

Charlie nodded. Until they'd stopped and he went forwards to find the bushmen, he'd been riding on the cabin roof.

'Small one, sir,' he said. 'Maybe half a mile back.'

'Let's get over there fast but hang onto the guns — '

Charlie climbed on top of the cabin, Alison got in behind the wheel and Haston heaved himself up beside her.

'Don't even ask me — '

They were jolting through the bush, Charlie's cane angled down over the windscreen and guiding them as before. Haston had glanced at Alison and seen she was still shaking her head in bewilderment.

'Far as I knew aside of Liddell, Mlanda and those South African pigs no one had any fix on us at all. But sure as hell that's Jo's plane and I don't like it. Until we find out just who's inside we hold right back — '

The cane rapped twice on the glass and Alison stopped.

'Here, *Morena*—'

Charlie led the way through thick head-high scrub to the rim of a pan, another shallow oval depression, flat and bare and dusty grey-white. As they reached it the plane drummed overhead. Haston waved them down. The pilot, still invisible through the canopy, was checking the surface. The plane skimmed the ground, lifted, turned, throttled back and came in again for the landing.

Haston looked quickly at Alison, then at Charlie. They were squatting on either side of him with the Schmeissers on their knees. Beyond them the bush surrounded the pan in a wall of scrub and thorn.

He eased the shotgun forwards and said, 'Be ready for anything and don't show yourselves until I say.'

They both nodded. The plane was low and close now, almost brushing the scrub as it made its approach. It cleared the bush, the flaps went up, the nose dipped and the wheels touched the ground lifting fans of sand behind them. Seconds later, it came to a stop fifty yards away. The propeller idled, the engine cut out, then the cockpit hatch swung open.

Haston stiffened. The lowering sun was directly behind them and he could see through the passenger windows now. Unless they were lying on the floor there was no one else in the plane apart from the pilot – and the pilot was Jo.

She climbed out, jumped down and stood for a moment rubbing her legs stiffly as if she'd been cooped up in the cockpit all day. Blue jeans, white shirt sticking tight to her body with sweat, yellow hair rumpled and blowing slightly in the small late afternoon breeze.

Haston got to his feet. He opened his mouth to call to her – and suddenly there were puffs of dust round her feet, the repeated crack of rifle-fire, coils of smoke lifting from the bush on the far side of the pan.

For an instant Haston thought it was another ambush, that the shots were being fired at him and Alison. Then, as Jo whirled round, checked, swung back again and started to run for the cover of the bush, he realized he was wrong – Jo was the target.

'Here, Jo, here!' He screamed.

She heard his voice over the rifle-fire, swerved and headed towards them, head back, mouth distended, face white with terror.

'Give her cover, for Christ's sake! Charlie, Alison, into the bushes, anywhere there's smoke!'

He held the shot gun impotently as the two Schmeissers opened in quick deafening bursts. Jo was twenty, fifteen, ten yards from them, racing, swaying, feet slithering desperately on the loose soft scree that coated the hard crystalline surface below. All round her the shots from the other side pattered like rain and the ricochetting bullets whined into the thorn.

She reached the rim of the pan below them, there was a distant choking shriek of pain as one of the Schmeisser volleys hit home, then she suddenly arched her back, staggered and crumpled. Haston dropped the shotgun and hurled himself down the low shelving slope of dry grass between the bush and the sand. Jo was on her knees, one hand braced against the ground, the other clamped to the junction of her neck and shoulder. Blood was welling out between her fingers and her shirt was blotched with red.

'Get up, Jo, for God's sake get up — !'

Haston tried to grip her round the waist with his right arm, felt his own wound stretch and tear, then turned and seized her with his left.

'A few yards, that's all, and we're there — '

She was half-standing, slumped against him, blood bubbling from her mouth too. A bullet smashed into the earth beside him

197

and sprayed them with sand. Above them the grassy slope stretched upwards like the flank of a mountain.

'Move, please Jo, move —!'

He lifted her, heaved her, smelt cordite and dust and resin, saw her eyes no longer blue but dark and glazed, felt blood on his own hands, dragged her stumbling upwards, then they were lurching into the thorn between Alison and Charlie.

'Let me, Jerry —'

Alison pushed Haston aside. Jo was lying on her face. Alison knelt down beside her, ripped off Jo's shirt and started to work on the wound.

'Who are they, Charlie?'

Haston, panting, sweating, was squatting in the shelter of the bush. The occasional wild shot tore through the branches on either side but most of the firing had stopped.

'Blacks, *Morena*,' Charlie said. 'I see them two or three times. I guess they that bunch we hit first.'

Mlanda's men. They must have regrouped, followed the spoor to the copse, found the Toyota's tracks heading north and come after them again – just as Haston had guessed they would. If it hadn't been for Jo's inexplicable arrival, they'd probably have surrounded the truck and attacked them at dusk. The plane had wrecked that plan. No doubt imagining it heralded the arrival of others they'd tried to kill Jo as soon as they saw she was alone.

Haston glanced at her, closed his eyes and looked away. Alison was desperately trying to staunch the bleeding but the wound was a massive gaping hole, blood kept pumping up over her arms and a jagged splinter of broken bone stuck out from the flesh like an arrow-head.

'How many magazines we got left?'

Charlie looked down. The metal clips they'd filled at the truck were in a pouch on his belt.

'Four, sir.'

'Give me two, you take the others —'

Haston reached for the Schmeisser Alison had been using. There was nothing he could do for Jo, only Alison could help her now. But Mlanda's thugs were still there a few hundred yards away on the other side of the pan. They'd got rifles but not repeaters and one at least of them had been hit.

'I want those bastards, Charlie, every single goddam one. They won't be figuring on us coming forwards, if anything they'll guess we've dropped back. You go right, I'll handle the left, We'll meet up opposite from here. Anyone you see between, you just cut. Understand — ?'

Charlie nodded and doubled away to the right. Alison, crouched over Jo, hadn't even been listening. Haston gripped the Schmeisser, stood up and set off to the left.

The scrub was dense and tall round the entire perimeter of the pan and although he moved warily, zig-zagging from bush to bush, he could hear the tell-tale crackle of dry twigs under his feet. Haston didn't care. At that moment he didn't care about anything: his licence, the leopard, the Englishman Liddell who'd conned him, even the pulsing ache in his shoulder where the mending tissue had parted when he'd strained to lift Jo.

All he wanted to do was to strike back, to maul and savage and kill. And he knew, running, weaving through the thorn, charging with the mindless ferocity of a wounded buffalo, that he was invulnerable. They might hear the twigs snapping but they wouldn't know what had caused the brittle cracks until too late. By then he'd be on them, the Schmeisser barrel would judder, smoke would blear the air and they'd tumble helpless, sprawling, blood darkening the sand, just as Jo had reeled and fallen.

He completed the half-circuit of the rim, stopped and checked his position against the sun. As he'd calculated he was immediately opposite the point where he'd left Alison and Jo. So far, apart from some confused fresh spoor-lines of human feet, there'd been nothing. Charlie, moving more slowly, more cautiously, was somewhere to his right. Haston lifted his head and listened.

For a while there was nothing. Then he heard a moan followed by a low vibrating cough. He edged towards the sound, moving silently, delicately now, his finger still taut on the Schmeisser's trigger. There was a small opening in the thorn. At its centre a man was lying, black, bunched up like a foetus, hands scrabbling at his face.

Haston waited. Aside from the moans – they came again and again like a whimpering animal – he couldn't hear anything else. Then he stepped forward.

'Where are the others — ?' '

He'd bent over the man, gripped his tight curling hair and jerked his head back.

One of the Schmeisser bullets, probably ricochetting off a rock, had torn his nose away leaving a deep bloody fissure down the centre of his face. The man squirmed in a frenzy of pain and fear, tried to shriek. Haston kicked him savagely in the mouth, not hard enough to break his jaw but splitting both his lips.

'You tell me, understand — ?'

He lifted his foot again and the man went limp, shivering uncontrollably, eyes dilated, breath coming huskily through the blood.

'They gone back.'

The words were choked and his hand fluttered weakly in a direction east of the pan.

'How far?'

'Don't know, sir.'

'Well, I want to know.'

Haston moved his foot closer and the man cowered as if he was trying to bury himself in the sand.

'Promise, sir. When we heard that plane, we left our stores two, maybe three miles back. Maybe they gone there.'

'How many of you?'

'Nine.'

'Is Mlanda with you?'

'No, sir. He sent another fellow, Lumumbi.'

The answers were coming fast now and Haston guessed he was telling the truth. The man was too hurt, too frightened to do anything else.

'And what the hell were you told to do?'

'That lady, sir, we get her back. She been following some leopard ever since we first catch her. So Lumumbi say now we kill the animal first, then we take her.'

'You were trying to kill the animal?' Haston looked at him

200

astonished. 'What in the name of Christ for?'

'Lumumbi say it starts all the trouble we have. We kill it and that lady, she's got nothing to follow and we get her easy then. Lumumbi bring a tracker with him so we don't lose it now.'

'Jesus — !'

Haston stopped. He'd suddenly heard the bush rustling on his right. He let go of the man's hair, whirled round, crouched and lifted the Schmeisser to his waist.

'*Morena* — !'

It was Charlie's voice calling softly. Haston relaxed and stood up. Charlie must have completed his half-circuit and heard them talking.

'Over here, Charlie,' he called back.

The rustling came closer, then the bushes parted and Charlie appeared. He glanced down at the man and back at Haston.

'I figure they pulled back, sir,' he said, 'I find a big line of spoor heading east. Prints going both ways so I don't know how many. But I guess that's where they went.'

Haston nodded, indicated the man and told Charlie what he'd just learned. Then he looked at the man again. He was lying on his back, helpless, terrified, blood trickling onto his chest from his nose and mouth. There was nothing more they needed from him now. He was just one of Mlanda's mindless black thugs who'd told everything he knew. Except beside him was lying the weapon he'd been using, an old hunting rifle, the gun which could well have fired the bullet that struck Jo.

'We'll go back, Charlie,' Haston said. 'You go ahead, give me fifteen seconds and I'll catch you up.'

'Yes, sir.'

Charlie moved away. He knew what Haston was going to do, so did the man. He watched quivering, burbling incoherently, urine spreading out in a stain across his shorts as Haston put down the Schmeisser and picked up the rifle.

There were two shells left in the magazine. Haston pumped one into the breech, lifted the gun to his shoulder and sighted, bringing the slender upright blade at the tip of the barrel carefully into the centre of the V at the back. There was no need for him to do it, at the range he could simply have aimed and fired

201

from the hip. But he did it all the same, left elbow angled out, shoulder throbbing against the stock, holding himself steady and erect and calm as he'd held himself time after time when he'd given the *coup de grace* to wounded game.

The man thrashed and moaned and scrabbled at the ground. Haston waited a moment. Then, slowly, deliberately, he squeezed the trigger. Afterwards he didn't even bother to look down. He turned away, pumped through the second shell, jammed the barrel into the sand and fired again. The muzzle ballooned and disintegrated. He tossed the rifle aside, picked up the Schmeisser and pushed his way through the scrub to find Charlie.

Alison was standing when they got back to the other side of the pan. Her shirt sleeves were rolled up to her elbows and she was wiping her arms with handfuls of dry grass. Haston stopped. He could see the trampled branches at her feet, the dark patches of blood-stained earth, but there was no sign of Jo.

Alison dropped the grass and came towards him. Her face was pale and her collar wet with sweat.

'Jo's dead, Jerry,' she said quietly. 'The shot had severed the carotid artery. She died a few moments ago.'

Haston gazed at her, half understanding what she was saying, half rejecting it.

Jo wounded, grievously terribly wounded, yes, he'd seen that, he knew that was true. But not Jo dead. Not that young vital lovely presence, with her anger and her laughter and her strong firm body. That was impossible, that couldn't be true. Jo would recover from the wound. Alison must have made some appalling mistake.

'I'm sorry, Jerry.'

She put a hand on his shoulder, Haston hesitated, then he shook it off furiously, still refusing to accept what she'd said.

'Where is she?'

'Leave her, Jerry, leave her — '

'I won't bloody-well leave her,' he shouted. 'You take me to her right now — '

Alison looked at him, turned and walked a few yards into the bush.

Jo was lying on her side by a clump of thorn. From the trail of crushed grass Alison must have dragged her there from the rim of the pan. Haston knelt down. The bullet-hole in her neck was against the ground but there was blood everywhere, on her boots, her jeans, her shirt, her face, her hair. He studied her puzzled, talking to himself under his breath, talking to her, not knowing what he was saying. The form, the shape, the colours and textures were those of the Jo he knew yet somehow changed almost beyond recognition. No longer compact and graceful, charged, even sleeping, with energy and excitement, but limp, broken, empty.

Haston reached out and gently touched her cheek. The skin was still warm and damp, sun and sweat mingling, and a lock of hair trailed over his hand.

Then suddenly he rocked back on his heels, dropped his head between his knees and started to weep.

'Get up, Jerry —'

A hand under his arm, gripping him, dragging him to his feet. Haston stood up, trembling and blinded with tears.

He shook his head, cleared his eyes and glanced at the sky. He didn't know how long he'd been kneeling there, maybe only a few minutes, but the light was draining now and it was almost dusk.

'Over here —'

The hand, the voice were Alison's. Haston let her lead him through the bush to the truck. He moved like an automaton, eyes vacant, mind cold and blank, limbs weighted with an immense tiredness. The Toyota came into view, he was dimly aware of Charlie, red-eyed and keening softly, squatting by the tailgate, then he slumped over the hood and gazed unseeing at the early stars.

'Jerry —'

Alison was shaking his arm. With an immense effort of will Haston managed to turn his head and look at her.

'Listen to me,' her voice was urgent. 'You can't just give up. That's not going to help anyone, least of all Jo. We've got to go on. Charlie told me you found tracks of those men heading back east. What do you think they're likely to do now?'

Haston frowned and tried to concentrate.

The men, the bastards who'd viciously killed Jo like children stamping on some bright flower, the one through whose brain he'd put a bullet. That had helped briefly, blotting out the knowledge, the certainty he must have had even then. But now everything had gone, even anger. All he felt was a vast weary emptiness.

'Come on, Jerry —'

She tugged at his arm again and he shook his head.

'They've gone to where they left their stores, a few miles back—'

The words came out slowly, dully. What would they do next? It seemed so unimportant now, but he tried to concentrate again.

There were eight of them left with a new leader, a good one, he had to be. Mlanda must be taking it far more seriously than before. They didn't have any automatics and they'd been shaken by the intensity of the Schmeisser fire, that was why they'd fallen back to their stores. But the gang still outnumbered them heavily and they'd try again. Not at night – darkness frightened and disorientated the blacks – but next morning.

'Tomorrow,' Haston went on. 'That's when they'll come after us again —'

He paused. Something else was plucking at the back of his mind. For a moment he couldn't recall it. Then he remembered.

'That leopard. They're going to kill it too.'

Alison stared at him dumbfounded and Haston repeated what the black had told him. Afterwards she turned away, stood looking at the sky, then abruptly swung towards Charlie.

'Get in, Charlie,' she called. 'You too, Jerry —'

Haston climbed up onto the passenger seat and sat there numbly as she started the engine and set off through the thorn.

He didn't know where they were going, he didn't even ask. Like everything else it had become meaningless. He tried to think of Jo, a sun-tanned figure diving naked into some pool while he lay drowsy in the midday heat and watched, galloping with him over the farm pastures, bringing him an ice-cold vodka in the shadowy cool of her sitting-room, smiling in bed after they'd made love with the sheets tangled at the foot of the bed, the smell of sex in the air and her body glowing in the slatted light from the sun blinds.

The images came back but he couldn't hold them. For an instant they'd be so sharp and vivid he could hear the racing beat of her horse's hooves, taste the dry coldness of the vodka, feel her breasts under him and her legs wound round his thighs. Then they'd dissolve, fugitive, blurring, sliding out of vision, and all he'd be left with was the crumpled shape on the sand, the blood matting the hair, a motionless bare shoulder where the white shirt had been torn away.

The truck stopped, Alison opened her door and beckoned him to get out. Haston stepped down. They were in the clearing where they'd heard the plane and the bushmen had disappeared. There was no sign of the two little yellow men but the leopard spoor stretched out as before, crisp and straight across the sand.

Alison went round to the tailgate, spoke to Charlie and came back.

'Listen to me, Jerry — '

She was standing very close to him. The light had gone and in the greyness her eyes had the same dark intensity Haston had seen the first time he looked at her.

'If I can I'm going to show you something. I'm not offering any simple facile solutions, but I will ask you to look, to try to understand and then to make up your mind.'

She turned and walked towards the tall acacia, set back in the bush on the far side of the clearing, at which the bushman had clicked and jabbed out his thumb.

17

The leopard lifted its head, yawned, reached out with its front paws and raked them back along the branch towards its chest, the talons leaving deep white gouges in the wood.

It had slept intermittently throughout the day, a deep relaxed sleep in which its pulse rate dropped to half the level it beat at when the animal was awake. Yet even asleep its hearing remained acute and part of its brain alert. A herd of buck might pass the tree, its ear would catch the tremors rippling through the hot still air and transmit them to its brain – for sifting, scanning, monitoring.

Normally, the range of noise was familiar, its brain would filter and discard the sounds and the leopard's sleep would continue uninterrupted. Only food, competition or danger constituted triggers for waking. By day food was seldom a reason. The leopard was a nocturnal hunter. Unless game was desperately scarce after severe drought it would only take prey in darkness. A competitor in the heat – another leopard in its territory – was equally rare. Danger signals were rarer still: apart from fire, sickness or age the leopard recognized no enemies.

That day had been different. Three times its ear had picked up sounds which its brain had rejected as alien and puzzling. An approaching hum in the bush first, then a harsh roar in the sky, finally a series of sharp metallic crackles. The leopard listened, growled, once it moved higher up the tree, but on every occasion went back to sleep again – satisfied that whatever was causing the disturbances didn't warrant a response.

Now it was awake once more – not because of noise but from the sudden drop in temperature that came with nightfall. It stood up on the branch, yawned again and surveyed the bush below.

Over the past few weeks the leopard had travelled almost two hundred miles. In the process and in spite of killing every second or third night, it had lost fifteen per cent of its body weight. Within its home territory a kill twice or three times a week would have been ample to preserve the animal in prime condition. Not on the move across the desert. There the game distribution patterns were unknown, hunting took longer, prey could only be snatched at, not gorged on, before it set off again – burning up energy as it padded for hour after hour over the sand.

Strangely, the weight-loss was barely noticeable in the animal's appearance. If anything its coat was darker, sleeker, the yellow feline eyes glowed more fiercely and keenly, the tracks it left cut deeper and faster in the ground. Only a leanness round the rib-cage, a sharpening of the silhouetted leg tendons, a bunching of the massive shoulder muscles, revealed the effects of its journey.

Its eyes systematically searched the scrub, registering antelope spoor, the scuttle of small rodents, the angle of the evening wind on the branches of a thorn thicket. Then the leopard froze. There were two upright shapes thirty yards from the tree to the south. One it recognized, the other was new and unknown.

The leopard sniffed the air, caught scent and snarled – a wary tentative challenge. The two shapes neither moved nor responded. It tried again, more strongly this time, a deep threatening rumble that trailed away in a sibilant spitting hiss. Still there was no reaction. It studied the shapes once more, merged the strange silhouette with the one it knew, then it roared and climbed down the trunk to the sand.

The shapes were like the sounds it had heard that day – alien but not dangerous. There had been no submission gestures or aggressive posturing. Only the stiff passive immobility of the two figures. For the leopard that was enough to signal they didn't represent a rival or an unidentifiable threat.

On the ground it made a token urination beside the trunk where it had urinated before – sealing its claim to the tree for as long as the stain and the smell lasted. Then it moved away north through the bush.

The leopard passed very close to the two figures. By then its brain had scanned and absorbed them just as it had absorbed the earlier puzzling sounds. They were as much part of the desert winterscape now as the thorn barbs or the wheeling constellations in the sky above. The animal was utterly unaware of its own presence in that same setting: the thick feral stench it gave off; the black shadow, velvet and menacing, it printed on the bushes; the occasional flare of starlight in its eyes; the thin splintering of frost-bound sand under its paws as it padded by.

It was also unaware of the impact it made on its watchers.

All the leopard was conscious of was belly-hunger, a warm wet irritation in its groin and the irresistible pull towards the inclining plane of the pole-star ahead.

18

Haston stood at the edge of the clearing. Behind him the tent was pitched, Alison was asleep inside and Charlie, the Schmeisser in his lap, was on watch on the truck's roof.

It was ten o'clock and Haston had been standing there alone for two hours. The wind was fierce that night and from time to time the raw stinging gusts made his eyes water. At other times the tears would come of their own accord and he'd sob uncontrollably for a while, chest heaving, hands cupped to his face, as they streamed down his cheeks between his fingers.

Partly, maybe, the accumulated shock of the past few weeks: his licence, the first bitter collision with Alison, the shot-wound in his shoulder, Ben, the frustration he'd felt as she trundled him like a piece of baggage through the bush. Then Jo. The vengeance he'd taken, the meaningless vengeance against the scrabbling black – not even cleansing, only delaying for an instant his acceptance that she was dead.

Tears then and tears now. But these were different because now there was something else. The leopard.

There were moments when Haston found it difficult to believe he'd actually seen the animal, that it wasn't some image returning from the dreams he'd had in delirium. Then the smell would come back, the stench of the rotting flesh-shreds in its paws from the prey it had taken; he'd remember the immense black shadow rippling over the bush, the diamond-yellow eyes, the rustling sand, and he'd know it was real – and still he'd shake his head in disbelief.

He'd watched game all his life, he'd had clients who'd killed record lion and elephant, he'd even shot the biggest wildebeeste ever taken in the Kalahari himself. This animal was different, not merely in degree but in kind. It wasn't game: prowling out of the dusk, vast, silent, fanged and taloned, it had been a creature from a lost primeval world – a legend suddenly materializing in blood and bone and muscle before it padded away to the north.

And it was still there in front of them, travelling steadfastly under the stars towards its destination. Haston understood Alison's obsession now. It was like finding a unicorn, fugitive in the morning mist or pale against the evening light, and then, caught up in the spell it cast, having no choice but to follow it, to find out where it was going and why. Only the black leopard wasn't a myth, there was no silken mane or single ivory horn. Instead, more dangerous, more compelling, a tangible incarnation of ferocity crossing the bleak wastes of the desert.

Haston trembled and wept again.

'Jerry —'

Haston rubbed at his eyes and turned. Alison was standing behind him. She was wearing a long nightgown with a shawl round her shoulders. Her hair was blowing loose in the wind and her face was still smudged with resin and dust.

'You should be asleep —'

Haston closed his eyes and nodded wearily. They'd agreed to rest until three and then set off again, using the moonlight to follow the spoor and put as many miles as possible between themselves and the terrorists before dawn.

'Come with me —'

Haston shook his head but she took his arm and pulled him gently, firmly towards the truck where his sleeping-bag was laid out in the back. Then, vaguely, he noticed they'd passed the truck and reached the tent.

A torch was glowing inside. Alison knelt down, lifted the flaps and guided him in. Dazed and still trembling Haston ducked under the low canvas ridge and squatted on the groundsheet. She zipped the tent flaps together, edged past him and got into her own sleeping-bag, lying on her back with her hair fanned out on the pillow.

'You're cold, aren't you, Jerry?'

Haston nodded. He glanced round, saw the shawl she'd just taken off, draped it over him and managed to force a smile.

'It's not exactly standard safari gear,' he said. 'But sure as hell it helps.'

210

'That's not what I meant — '

Alison was smiling at him too, a calm relaxed smile. Haston gazed back at her uncomprehending. Then she moved to one side of the bag and raised the cover.

'Come here, Jerry, and get warm — '

He hesitated for a moment, then he started uncertainly to crawl forwards.

Alison laughed quietly. 'You could even take your boots off first. They won't provide much insulation inside.'

Haston stopped, unlaced his boots and wriggled in beside her. He lay stiff on his back for a few minutes. Then he started to weep again.

'Put your arms round me — '

Haston tried to turn away, huddling into himself, drawing his knees up against his chest. Not out of fear but from the same dizzying confusion that had taken him, shivering and crying to the rim of the clearing.

It had never been like this before. Never. He had organized and planned and plundered what he wanted. Now he was helpless. The bag was too tight, he couldn't turn, his knees wouldn't lift – they remained pinioned in the downy cocoon of warmth. Warmth that was melting the chill, dulling the ache, slowing the violent tremors of his body.

He could feel her arms round him, her cheek against his neck, and suddenly he rolled over and held her too. Fiercely at first, burying his head in her shoulder and binding her to him with his arms clenched tight round her back. Then, as the tears and the trembling passed, his grip loosened and he lay for a while quite still, his mind slack and empty, conscious only of the warmth and the glow of the torchlight.

Later, very slowly, he became aware of something else, something that seemed so strange and incongruous it was several minutes before he realized what it was – desire.

Alison was pressed against him. Haston shifted slightly, lifted his hand and tentatively touched her breast. It was firm and round beneath the flannel and the nipple hardened under his fingers. He glanced at her wonderingly, amazed at what he'd done, and then saw that she was smiling.

211

'Here —'

Alison took his hand and pulled it down into the sleeping-bag. He felt the hem of her nightgown and then her leg, the skin soft and warm.

He waited, hesitant and uncertain, but she moved his hand further up, the nightgown riding with it, over her knee, her thigh, her hip.

Before, trying to imagine what she'd be like, Haston had thought her bony and angular. He was wrong. The muscles under his fingers were strong and supple, the texture of the flesh fine and resilient, the movements of her body as he explored it lithe and pliant and graceful.

He found her groin, stroked the wedge of hair, felt dampness and smelt her scent, musky and sweet. Then her hands were at his waist, unbuckling his belt, her nightgown came off, he shrugged down his shorts, unbuttoned his shirt and they were both naked.

The cover was thrown back now and Haston looked at her for a moment. Alison was still smiling, her legs parted and the torchlight rippling over her skin, making pools of shadow at her neck, under her breasts, across her flat sloping stomach.

He touched her again, still wondering, still bemused, trying once more to reconcile his image of a prissy asexual virgin with the confident sensual figure beside him. Then the urgency, the hardness in his own groin, became unendurable and he was over her, entering her, not violently, possessively, but with an ease and gentleness he'd never known before.

Afterwards rocking faster and faster until finally the gentleness dissolved and there was nothing except the stiff heat between his legs and his back arching and her breasts moulding and moving beneath his hands, and Alison was writhing too, whispering, fingernails cutting into his skin as the explosion came and she held it, drew it out in long shuddering waves.

'Warm now?'

Haston nodded, his face against the pillow. He was lying beside her, arms tangled with hers, drowsy and spent and calm.

'Beats central heating any day,' he said.

Alison laughed. 'I'm glad.'

212

He raised himself on his elbow and looked down at her, the bewilderment returning.

On one level it seemed inevitable that they should be there together, easy and natural and happy. On another it was still inexplicable. There was no junction or link, no point of contact between them. Unless, as he'd puzzled out watching her silhouetted against the fire a week before, she'd calculated it all, given and taken what she wanted as and when it had suited her.

Yet even that wasn't adequate. She needed him no more now than she'd needed him after he stopped the bullet in his shoulder. And she looked content, too, satisfied and fulfilled and smiling. Haston shook his head. There had to be something else, but he was no closer to understanding what than he'd ever been – even with her print on him, her smell in his nostrils, her hair brushing his skin.

'Oh, Jerry — '

He must have been frowning because she reached out and touched his forehead.

'You may be fine with game, but as a hunter of pussy-cats you've still got a great deal to learn.'

Haston coloured. 'Was that something else that came out when I was sick?'

'The phrase kept cropping up. In conjunction with the activities involved, it wasn't hard to work out what you meant.'

Haston looked away.

'Don't worry. That was mild compared to the rest — '

She paused and smiled. Then she asked quietly, 'Was Jo one of the pussy-cats, Jerry?'

'No — '

He denied it instantly, vehemently, and knew as he spoke it wasn't the truth.

Carelessly, unthinkingly, in spite of everything they'd had together, he'd used her as cynically and casually as the rest – even down to the notch on the door carved in spite the day she kicked at his groin. Until that afternoon when she'd landed on the pan, climbed out of her plane and the bullets had started spitting round her feet. Then too late, far too late, it had all changed and he'd realized what he should have known long before. Jo was

213

different and had loved him and, weeping, he'd understood at the end that he loved her too.

'Did she give you this?'

Alison was holding his wrist. Haston glanced down and saw the plaited fibre bracelet Jo had woven for him that day by the river.

'Yes,' he looked at her face again. 'How did you guess?'

'You put it against her cheek when you were kneeling over her. What was it for, Jerry?'

Haston hesitated. Then he told her, tears coming again with the story. Afterwards he reached for the bracelet, worn and frayed and blood-stained now, and suddenly tried to break it.

'No,' Alison caught his hand and stopped him. 'Leave it for what she wanted — '

He struggled with her for a moment but his wound hurt and her arm was stronger and he fell back limply on the pillow, eyes blurred and chest racked with sobs.

'She was different from the others and she loved you — '

He could hear her voice, still very quiet, and he realized that she wasn't just echoing his thoughts by accident – she'd known all along. The questions about the pussy-cats and Jo and the bracelet hadn't come from curiosity. She knew the answers before she spoke and she'd only asked to draw him out, to make him acknowledge what he'd never acknowledged before.

'And you loved her as well?'

Haston nodded. 'I guess so.'

'That's good, Jerry, that's something of value – something to keep, not to break. She must have been very special.'

He nodded again, head against the pillow.

'Tell me about her, Jerry.'

Haston tried to bring back the images of Jo alive – the images which had formed in his mind and then dissolved, vanishing as soon as he caught them while he'd sat by Alison in the truck.

The words came slowly and painfully, choked with tears, but this time the freshness, the vitality, the gaiety and laughter didn't fade: they stayed printed deep and vivid on his consciousness. And he knew as he talked, even through the grief

214

and anguish, that once again what Alison had done was deliberate. She was forcing him to speak, to remember, to confront and hold the reality of what Jo had been – not to destroy it in snapping the bracelet as he'd destroyed it once before when he'd pulled out his knife and cut the mark on his door.

'Yes, she was special, wasn't she?' Alison said, as he finished, his voice trailing away into silence. 'So special that when she somehow found out something had gone wrong, she even risked everything to come up here looking for you. Have you any idea how she managed to do that?'

Haston shook his head. He didn't know how it had happened. She'd set out alone to help him. And that after everything he'd done to her, to her pride and confidence and trust. Set out and found him and been killed as a result.

Haston wept again.

'Don't, Jerry,' Alison put her arms round him. 'That part of it's past. The how doesn't matter now, but the why still does. In Jo's case most of all, but maybe in the others' too. Had you thought of that? That maybe they weren't just your pussy-cats, but in their own ways they also wanted and loved you. Even me.'

'You?'

Haston lifted himself and gazed at her astonished.

She laughed. 'Why else do you think you're here?'

Haston shrugged helplessly. 'Hell, I guess I was cold and in bad shape and you figured — '

He broke off and she said, 'I figured what? That to make someone warm you have to make love to them? Well, it helps but it isn't absolutely necessary.'

She was still laughing. Haston was silent for a moment. Then, dazed, he remembered the leopard.

'Why did you want me to see that animal?'

She hesitated, frowned and turned her head away, not avoiding him but gathering herself together as she worked out what she was going to say. When she finally answered her voice was even quieter and slower.

'I've followed it for almost four months, Jerry, as you know. And in truth I'd almost begun to believe it belonged to me – no

215

one else. It's no excuse but it can happen, I suppose, if one's lucky enough to find something so rare and extraordinary and valuable. Well, of course I was wrong. The leopard doesn't belong to me. It belongs first to itself, then to its race and afterwards to all of us equally. You and I and Jo and everyone. I realized that today and it raised another issue — '

She turned towards him and smiled, her face gentle but intent and speculative.

'Just how valuable is the animal? For me, yes, it's worth everything, it's beyond price. But I'm single and alone and I've chosen my life. You're different. You came with me first out of necessity, then out of choice – even with your shoulder you and Charlie could have found some way of leaving. You didn't, you stayed. For that alone, for the help and support you gave me, I would have loved you. But even if it was your decision, it's still no answer. Because there's also Ben and Jo, your Jo. If it hadn't been for the leopard they'd both be alive now. They're not, they're dead — '

Haston gazed at her. He could think of nothing to say.

'Is the animal worth that? Jerry, I don't know, how can anyone know? They're unanswerable, questions like that, only somehow they've got to be asked. It's a matter of what people die for, whether it's something trivial and meaningless or something of value. You could say once they're dead it makes no difference. I think it does. I believe there's an immense difference and it happened here, but that's only my private belief. For you I had to ask the question and the only way I could do that was to show you the leopard — '

She paused and Haston waited. The confusion, the bewilderment, the blurring screen of tears were still there, but through it all he at last began to see the entirety of what she'd done. And once more it was deliberate.

Deliberate – not calculated. She'd made him look at the leopard as she'd made him remember Jo. Not to justify Jo's death – nothing could do that – nor even to explain it. But to let him see what she had been killed for and to make up his own mind – Alison never once tried to answer the question for him – whether something in the animal redeemed the bullets and the

216

terror and the blood.

'Afterwards,' she continued, 'it was up to you. All I could do is what I've wanted to do for a week or so now – hold you, have you with me, make love to you. And that shocked you, didn't it? Oh, Jerry, you've got a lot to learn. I think you believe there's either screwing or a great passion but nothing in between. You're wrong. There's a huge amount between. People can make love to say thank you, to take care of someone, to seal something they've shared, so many reasons. And they're all just as real and valid, they're all a part of loving. It can even happen in a sleeping-bag out in the desert. If nothing else at least I should have proved that to you.'

She smiled again, brushed her hair from her face.

Haston reached for a cigarette and lit it. The tears had passed but his hand shook as he struck the match. He inhaled and coughed. Then he suddenly wriggled out of the sleeping-bag, went to the front of the tent, unzipped the flap and stood up outside.

He was naked and the ground was thick with hoar-frost and the night wind cut raw and chill through the scrub, but he wasn't aware of the cold. Before, alone on the edge of the clearing, he had let it seep into him, numbing, deadening his nerve-ends as his teeth chattered and his body trembled. No longer. Instead the bitter air washed round him like water, scouring and cleansing his skin but not reaching the strong hard core of warmth inside. Nothing could touch that now and, as he stood there with the desert stars raining down, the tumult and the desolation dissolved.

In their place came a stillness that was part peace and part a driving surge of anger and determination. The peace was over Jo. He could finally accept that she was dead. But her death hadn't only been the brutal futile waste which had thrown him into shock and lethargy. It was something more. Without her the leopard would have been killed, Charlie and himself too, almost certainly Alison as well. They didn't matter but the animal did – and the anger and determination started there.

Jo'd loved the desert as much as he, as much as Alison, and the animal was more than the desert's creature – it was its triumph and jewel and essence. For that, for Jo, he'd track and defend it to the final limits of the sand.

They left the clearing at three after Haston had spent fifteen minutes hunched over a map in the tent.

From the readings he'd taken off the truck's speedometer he'd been able to calculate their position almost exactly – right up on the northern edge of the central Kalahari with Maun barely sixty miles ahead. The leopard's route, which had run die-straight, would take it slightly to the west of the little town. Immediately afterwards it would reach the Matsebe concession area – another great belt of thorn and tree and rock and scrub. Then, on the far side, it would come out into the delta and safety.

Safety – but there were another hundred and sixty miles to cover first. At twenty miles a night, the distance the animal had been averaging since its speed began to increase, that meant they had just over a week to get through. The next two nights shouldn't be too difficult. By dawn they'd only be forty miles from Maun and into the inhabited farmland that surrounded the town. Once they reached Matsebe everything would change again. Apart from the hunting parties – and the danger they posed too – they'd be back in the wilderness and locked to the leopard's progress. The terrorist attack could come any dawn or dusk from then on.

Haston folded up the map, went outside and told Charlie to strike the tent. Then he checked the water and the gasolene. Water wasn't a problem. They were down to the last few pints but in the morning they'd be able to resupply from one of the tributary streams of the Ngami river which flowed out of the delta, curled past Maun and spent itself in the desert to the south. Gasolene was far more serious. They had just enough left to make Maun, but that was all. So they'd have to detour to the outskirts of the town, send Charlie in to fill the jerry-cans and track back to where they'd left the spoor.

It had sounded simple when he'd first suggested the idea to Alison. Not now. Now every mile, every movement, every necessity was encircled by a mine-field of threats. Haston swore. Then he climbed into the cabin of the truck where Alison was already sitting waiting behind the wheel.

'Look — '

He opened the map again, spread it out on his knee and switched on the cabin light.

'Daylight should find us here, that's if your creature behaves like it's done so far — '

'Mine? I thought ownership had been transferred.'

'Right,' Haston grinned. 'I never could tell ladies apart in the dark. Anyway, this is what I reckon we'll do — '

He moved his finger across the map until it touched an area of blue.

'This is Lake Ngami. You know what that is?'

She shook her head. 'I've heard of it, that's all.'

'One of the biggest lakes in the world, or it can be. Fills up when the spring rainwater pushes down through the delta. Only a few feet deep but it can cover a thousand square miles if the rains are heavy enough. Right now it should be at its highest level. I figure the leopard should tree up somewhere along its edge. We'll take a fix on the spot. Then we'll head north — '

Haston traced another line up the map.

'There's a ridge here covered with high scrub. It'll take us almost as far as Maun. We should get there round midday. We'll lie up until dusk. Then we'll send Charlie in to scrounge some gas and head back to pick up the spoor-line again. That's if we're lucky.'

'We'll be lucky.'

Alison smiled at him, reached out and briefly touched his cheek. Then there was a thump in the back. Haston glanced round and saw that Charlie had heaved the tent over the tail-gate. Charlie vaulted up, climbed onto the cabin roof and tapped twice.

'Okay,' Haston said. 'Let's go.'

Alison started the engine and they moved forwards.

Somewhere behind them, Haston guessed, the terrorists would have heard the noise – the roar of the motor carrying for miles through the night air – and realize what they were doing.

To them it wouldn't matter. They knew the truck could only travel as far and as fast as the leopard, and they could follow the tyre spoor at their leisure in the morning – they'd hardly even need the tracker they had with them now.

Haston cursed again. Then he leant forwards and gazed at the corridors of sand winding ahead.

Although the moon was down the pug-marks stood out clearly in the brilliance of the starlight even through the wind-screen glass. To Charlie on the cabin roof it must have been like tracking in full daylight. Only twice in the next three hours, when they were passing through patches of dry grass, did he tap on the metal for Alison to stop. Then he'd drop down, cast in front, find where the spoor came out onto open sand again and they'd go on once more.

At six he tapped for a third time. Alison pulled up and Haston got out. Charlie had vanished but he reappeared a few minutes later, loping through the bush with his blanket draped over his shoulders against the cold.

'Big baobab, *Morena*,' Charlie pointed into the darkness. 'Maybe hundred yards on.'

'You're sure she's up it?'

Charlie nodded. 'Sure, sir. Spoor round the trunk, then nothing. Also I see that animal two or three times in the last twenty minutes, right in front of us, going slow and sniffing. She's looking for somewhere to hide up. She found it now and—'

He shook his head whistling softly. 'That's a big cat, *Morena*, that's the biggest cat I ever see. I don't think ever there's a cat like that.'

'Why's she stopped so early, Charlie?'

Normally, the leopard went on until the sky began to pale, but dawn was still an hour off and the darkness intense.

Charlie lifted his head and sniffed. 'Cattle, *Morena*, over to the west.'

Haston smelt the air but as with the fire-smoke by the first pan he could detect nothing. Yet Charlie would be right just as he'd been right before.

To the leopard cattle alone wouldn't signal danger. But

mixed with their scent there would be others: men, machines, fire, horses, cooking smells. A strange disturbing tangle of spores travelling the night wind currents – disturbing enough to the animal, with daylight so close, for it to choose a lair now.

'You can find that tree again?'

'Yes, sir.'

'Then we'll use what's left of the dark and split for Maun. On the roof, Charlie, until we can see.'

Haston navigated by the stars for the next hour as they climbed up onto the low ridge he'd pointed out to Alison on the map, and drove north along it towards Maun. They were running beside Lake Ngami all the while but they didn't see the lake itself until dawn began to break. Then there was a glint through the bush to their left, Alison glanced across, stopped the truck and got out. Haston joined her by the hood.

She was sniffing the early morning breeze. There was water in it now unmistakably, cold and wet and clean, and distantly they could hear the occasional splash of a flight of duck. For several minutes that was all. Then the eastern sky paled, a bowl of light lifted over the horizon and suddenly the air was full of the clamour of wings as flocks of geese streamed overhead. Thousands upon thousands of them invisible at first in the dark and then, as the light spread, taking shape as an endless trumpeting aerial caravan planing down the wind.

Alison walked forwards and stood on the edge of the ridge. Ribbons of mist were rolling off the water below and gradually the lake emerged – mile after mile of lagoon and reed bank and channel stretching out of sight on every side. There were birds everywhere now, not just thousands but millions. Purple herons and black ibis, skimming terns and stilts, fish eagles mewing like cats, colonies of lumbering pelicans, duck lighting in great silvery clouds, skeins of flamingo circling rose-coloured against the rising sun.

And every minute, more, until sky and air and water were teeming, glittering, resounding with life and colour and song as the full dawn broke and the first warmth reached their faces.

Alison turned to look back at Haston, laughing and shaking her head in delight.

'You never told me it was like this,' she said. 'If I'd known I might almost have abandoned the leopard for it.'

Haston came up. 'Almost – but not quite?'

She laughed again. 'No, not quite. Although one day maybe I'll be able to have them together. Maybe we both will.'

Haston grinned, put his arm round her shoulder and stood there for a moment looking out across the lake.

Livingstone, amazed, had stood in the same place thinking he'd discovered an inland sea in the heart of the desert, and after him all the great hunting explorers of the last century, Selou, Watson, Turnville, de Jong. Everyone of them had attempted to describe Ngami and they'd all failed. Haston hadn't even tried. He'd been there many times, seen many dawns rise over the water, but always before it had been nothing more than another area of the Kalahari, an extension of the territory he fought and worked and killed in.

Not now. Now suddenly with Alison beside him, her cheeks pink in the crisp air, her face alive with excitement, her hair tugged out by the wind, he saw it differently – saw it for an instant the way she was seeing it. Everything in front of them was linked, every single bird among those millions, from the smallest lark to the soaring eagles, woven inextricably with the lives of the rest. And not just the birds but every pool of water and the fish it held, every channel and reed bank and island down to the last grass-blade.

Destroy even one clump of marsh grass and you destroyed more than an entire community of life, you began to unlink the chain of everything else that depended on it – a chain that might reach far out beyond the lake deep into the desert. So a lagoon drained here, an island cleared and cropped, an artificial channel cut, would set off ripples of change and disturbance that could eventually affect an elephant herd grazing hundreds of miles away to the south or a pride of lion hunting the eastern plains.

He'd known it before, of course. Every good hunter knew the basic principles of ecology and conservation. But to know them didn't necessarily mean to understand what they represented in reality – in terms of birth and blood and survival, the cycle of

222

living and killing and dying and the fragile balance that bound them together. Haston did understand now and with the understanding came a realization of how pitifully little he knew.

He regarded the desert as his own. He'd lived there for seven years. He could read its tracks and signs, interpret its clouds and winds to forecast its weather, survive in it through blistering heat and chilling cold, find and slaughter its game. He'd been proud of that, of his strength and skill and courage. Alison had none of his skills or experience. She'd spent a bare six months in the desert. Yet she knew more about its life and essence than he ever would. In part it was an intuitive understanding, in part an academic one – when she looked she saw with the eye of a trained naturalist.

But there was something more than either intuition or training. Passion. An invincible passion for the desert that expressed itself in strength – a strength not just greater than in anyone else he'd ever met but greater even than his own.

Haston glanced at her awed again. Then, with the growing light flaring off the water and the bird calls ringing in the air, he turned away. The moment had gone and the sudden brief insight was fading. He'd never lose it altogether now because of what remained – the leopard.

'Maun,' he said and walked towards the truck.

It was midday when they first saw the little town – a straggle of houses and shacks on either side of the Ngami river with a bridge to link them, a few miles of paved road and green water meadows all round.

'Pull up here,' Haston said.

As Alison braked he glanced at the fuel register. The needle was flickering over the empty mark which meant there was about a gallon left. They'd made it – but only just.

The vehicle came to a halt and Haston hunched himself forwards and studied the scene below.

They were still on the ridge and screened by trees. The town was half a mile away spreading out from the point where the ridge, only fifty feet high now, dropped down to meet the river. Maun didn't have a proper centre but the focus of its life was Riley's Hotel – a rambling bougainvillaea-covered building just off the main road. He could see the hotel, its car park deserted now in the morning heat, the cluster of European-owned houses beyond, the post office, the UN mission huts and finally the gas station – straddling the junction of dirt tracks that led northwards.

There were no cars on the tracks and almost no sign of human life anywhere – only the occasional black wandering aimlessly through the tree shadows showed the town wasn't entirely deserted. By night it would be different. There'd be movement and noise and laughter, light from the cooking fires in the native huts, headlamps flickering over the earth, music and echoing shouts and the tap of horses' hooves. Briefly then under the cloak of darkness Maun would appear to have substance, permanence, character. But by day it revealed itself for what it really was – a lonely dusty staging-post scratched out of a river's bank on the edge of the desert.

Haston opened his door, swung himself out and called Charlie down from the roof where he'd been travelling all morning – watching out for farms as they approached the town.

'Reckon you know anyone here?'

Charlie shrugged. 'I don't know no one in Maun, *Morena*. But Miss Jo, she sends me many times up to the Ghanzi ranches. Lots of fellows up there, they know me. Maybe one of them's on a trip up this way. I think it better to wait for dark.'

Haston nodded.

Charlie had guessed what he was thinking. There was no question of Alison or himself going in at any time, but with the town so quiet it had momentarily been tempting to send Charlie there now, collect the gasolene and get back to the lake immediately.

Yet Charlie was right. By daylight even he was noticeable, a stranger, someone who might casually be asked why he was filling heavy jerry-cans and carrying them away by hand. And if one of the African workers from Jo's father's ranches happened to see him, they'd be finished. After nightfall it would

224

be different – as different as Maun was itself. Then, in the darkness and evening bustle, he'd be able to fill the cans and bring them back without comment or question.

'Okay, Charlie,' Haston said. 'We'll leave it for dusk. Meantime, as we're going to be up all night again we'll take it in shifts. You first, then me, then the lady.'

Charlie nodded and climbed back on top of the truck.

'Listen, this is the way I figure it — '

Haston was back in the cabin. He told Alison what he'd planned. The wait until darkness. Charlie filling the two tengallon cans at the pump. Haston going forward to meet him outside the town and help tote the cans back to the truck. Then the exercise being repeated and if all went well a third time.

'Even if we only make it twice we get gas for four hundred miles,' he finished. 'That should be enough to take us anywhere that goddam animal decides to go – providing, of course, we can lose those bastards behind.'

Alison was silent for a moment. Then she said, 'I let you down there, Jerry. I'm sorry.'

'What do you mean?'

'About George Mlanda.'

'Don't worry,' he shrugged. 'I know those people, they're savages, bloody murderous savages. I never believed that bit about him anyway.'

'Well, I did believe him. I thought he wanted his share of Africa for good reasons and I'd helped him understand what some of them are. I was wrong. Now he's not just killing innocent people – out of spite he wants to kill animals too.'

'Lady, to someone like Mlanda if you're white by definition you can't be innocent.'

'And a leopard?'

She was looking at him tight-faced and angry – the anger not just about the animal but at the vicious betrayal of trust and faith.

Haston said nothing. It was another point on which they'd never meet. To him the Mlandas were the wreckers and spoilers of the continent, barbarous thugs who'd never change. Alison had been hurt by one of them now, the hurt made even worse

225

because it touched the most important thing in the world to her. But it would pass and if the leopard lived and the same circumstances were repeated, she'd trust and believe again.

'I'm sorry, Jerry — '

The anger had gone and she held his hand.

'That's for later. For now there's something much more important.

'Like what we keep doing at the most inconvenient times,' Haston grinned. 'Sleep!'

He got out the sleeping-bags and they rested in turn in the truck's shadow until dusk fell.

Then he set out with Charlie for the town. As always with the onset of darkness Maun had come to life, but the noise and light and activity were all concentrated in the area below the ridge and they walked quickly through the trees without meeting anyone until they reached the river.

'I reckon this is as far as it's safe for me, Charlie — '

They'd climbed down the ridge and were crouching in a reed-bed on the river bank. Fifty yards to their right was the bridge that took the main road into the town and beyond it the evening clamour coming to them raucously across the water.

'What time do you make it?'

Charlie glanced at his watch. 'Right on seven, *Morena*.'

'Fine, so do I. It'll take you ten minutes from the bridge to the pump. At this hour there may be a small line waiting to fill up. So let's say twenty minutes there and that should be more than enough. Ten back to the bridge and another twenty just in case of Christ knows what – like maybe they've got a power malfunction on the pump. But whatever happens you're back here by eight. Right?'

Charlie nodded and picked up the jerry-cans.

'Okay, off you go.'

Haston watched him move away along the bank, saw his silhouette appear on the bridge and vanish in the direction of the town, then he settled down to wait.

Charlie wasn't back by eight. Long before then Haston was shifting restlessly in the reeds and frowning with worry. He'd allowed an hour but half that should have been adequate.

There were only a handful of trucks in Maun and it was inconceivable they'd all be lining up at the gas station at the same time. Groups of chattering Africans came back across the bridge, the occasional car, twice some trotting horses, once a flock of goats. Each time Haston stood up and peered into the darkness but there was no sign of the tall loping figure against the stars.

His watch showed the hour, he let a further fifteen minutes pass, then another fifteen. Finally at half past eight he got to his feet and ran back up the slope to the ridge.

He had no idea what could have happened. Charlie was reliable, Haston was absolutely certain of that. Jo had given her word for him, he'd seen Jo die and afterwards when Haston had said they'd continue to follow the leopard because Jo would have wanted it, Charlie had agreed unhesitatingly. He had been given a mission, a trust, and he'd see it through to the end. It was inconceivable he'd desert them now and inexplicable that he'd failed to keep the rendezvous by eight — not even a chance recognition by a farm-hand from one of the Ghanzi ranches could have prevented that.

Haston reached the top of the ridge and raced through the trees towards the truck.

'We've got trouble, serious trouble — '

Alison was waiting by the tailgate with the cap of the gasolene tank already unscrewed and in her hand.

'Charlie's vanished.'

She listened quietly while he told her about the one-and-a-half hours he'd spent by the river.

Then she said, 'Maybe it's just a mistake. Maybe he got delayed at the pump much longer than you thought.'

Haston shook his head. 'Charlie's a tracker. He knows about schedules, he's worked with them all his life. If you're flushing a wounded buffalo and someone in the ring gets the move-time wrong, someone else is liable to find himself very dead. Charlie's not going to make that sort of mistake. I said eight and eight's when Charlie would have been there. He's been stopped—'

He looked down over the town. The lights were glimmering

in the darkness and snatches of music drifted up to them. Before, in spite of the possible problems for himself and Alison, it had seemed safe and innocuous, a tawdry but gay and defiant little outpost guarding the gateway to the delta. Now everything about it was charged with menace.

'We picked up another can at your camp, didn't we — ?'

Haston had swung back towards her. Alison nodded.

'Charlie suggested taking it that first day when you were unconscious. It's like yours, a ten-gallon container, only I was using mine for water.'

'Get it out and the shotgun too.'

His shoulder hurt whenever he moved his arm. Alison climbed into the truck, rummaged in the back and reappeared with the jerry-can and the gun.

Haston checked the can first, shaking it with the nozzle to the ground. The last of the water had evaporated and the inside was bone-dry. Then he fed a couple of cartridges into the shotgun and handed it back to her.

'We're going down to the river,' he said.

'What are you going to do?'

'Depends on what I find the other side,' Haston glanced at the town lights again, 'but I can tell you one thing for sure. Without gas we're finished. Whatever's happened to Charlie I've got to get this can filled even if it's only once. That'll take us back to the lake and that cat. There's another pump at Ngami, maybe we can fill up again there, maybe not. But at least we'll be in with a chance. As we stand now it's all over.'

He turned and Alison followed him along the ridge and back down the slope to the river-bank.

Haston stood for a moment listening. Noise was still coming from the town and from time to time the reflection of a car's headlamps wavered over the sky, but the traffic on the bridge had stopped. He studied the arches briefly, shook his head and swore. It was too dangerous. If anyone was positioned on the far side, they'd see his silhouette as soon as he came up over the bank just as he'd seen Charlie's. He'd have to use the river.

Haston tightened the screw-cap on the can and looked at his watch. It was just after nine.

'Give me until midnight,' he said. 'If I'm not back by then, forget it. Forget me, forget everything. Go in yourself by the road and try to organize whatever you can. If you're stopped, deny you've even heard of me – let alone anything else. All they can do is hold you. Somehow you've got to get out before that animal moves on. Once it passes the lake you'll lose it to the water, the concession hunters or those black bastards back there. Either which way it'll be gone. I figure your chances at half a degree above zero – but make with that half degree.'

'And this?' Alison lifted the shotgun.

'I could come back in a hurry – that's if I come back at all. If I do and I've got company, give it both barrels but in the air. We can't afford anyone else shot, and in the dark you could be an army for all they know. It might just buy us enough time to reach the truck.'

She nodded. 'Good luck, Jerry. And if you get stuck, don't worry. I'll "forget" – I can be a very convincing liar particularly when I've got so much to lie about.'

Haston turned and waded into the river, pushing the can in front of him.

The water was still warm with the stored heat of the day and all round he could hear the sounds of the night, ripples, splashes, bell-throated frogs croaking, the zig-zag churning of a snake, the calls of nightjars and owls hunting the surface for insects. There would be hippo and crocodile too, hippo that could sever a man's body with a single snap of their jaws, crocodile that could drag him under, nuzzling flesh from bone, to suffocate choking in blood and sand on the bottom.

Haston struck out strongly for the other side. He knew the dangers and they were unimportant. Adrenalin surged in his stomach – not from fear but from anger. Ben had been killed, Jo had been killed, Charlie had been taken. They, whoever they were, black or white, were gnawing away at him, shutting off every escape route, snapping and tearing like packs of wild dogs closing for a kill.

Yet they wouldn't bring him down. Nudging the can ahead, cleaving the water with firm quiet strokes, Haston was savagely furiously determined on that. The leopard was going to survive.

229

For Jo most of all, for Alison as well and everything she'd taught him, for the desert itself, the animal's home and the home he'd chosen too. But also for something more – as his private vengeance on the destroyers and mutilators and killers.

His feet touched sand, he pushed the can into the reeds, then he cautiously crawled ashore. On the bank he paused and listened intently. There was still no movement on the bridge and the sounds of the town were fading. Maun rose at dawn and went to bed early. Within half an hour only Riley's, a few other bars and the garage would still be open. Haston wrung the water out of his shirt, picked up the can and walked crouching up to the road.

For a moment it seemed to be deserted, a pale dusty track lined with trees and curving right towards the straggling houses. Then, as he raised his foot to step forwards onto the surface, he froze.

If the man hadn't moved at that instant, Haston would have missed him. But the man did move, shifting his body slightly, and the moonlight caught his belt-buckle and Haston registered the tiny sparkle. He swayed back into the bush, dropped slowly onto his haunches and gazed at the place where the light had glinted. The man was twenty yards away leaning against a tree-trunk, a blurred shadowed figure blending with the scrub behind.

Haston couldn't see his face, his clothes, the set of his arms, the angle of his legs. But he knew without the slightest doubt who the man was and what he was doing. It was like recognizing a sable from a waterbuck glimpsed for a fraction of a second at a hundred yards through a dawn mist. If you didn't know the form and texture and contours they'd both be just antelope. But if you did know, if every distinguishing feature was printed so deep on your consciousness that you could even tell them apart blindfold by smell alone, they were unmistakable.

This man was unmistakable and Haston even knew what he'd smell of – tar soap, cologne and tobacco. Over the years he'd watched, listened, talked to and drunk with too many of them to be wrong. A white South African agent of the Bureau of State Security.

The glow of headlamps appeared at the bend in the track, Haston ducked deeper into the bush, then when the car had passed he slid forward again. The man was still leaning against the tree watching the bridge. Dust was swirling round him, raised by the car's tyres, and Haston heard a short rasping cough. He crouched there for a moment concentrating.

The only explanation could be Alison. Whatever they thought had happened, whether they guessed he was running for the border with her as a hostage or he'd dropped her and continued alone, they knew that sooner or later he'd have to surface for gasolene. Maun or Ghanzi were the sole possibilities. And because they'd evidently decided she was too valuable to lose, Liddell and BOSS alike, they'd taken the one risk he'd been utterly confident they would never chance – they'd staked out the town.

There wouldn't just be this one – there'd be others all round. Guarding the approaches, the garage, the trading stores, maybe even Riley's too. Perhaps a dozen or fifteen in all sealing the place as tight as a drum, so that as soon as he showed up they could grab him – just as they must have grabbed Charlie.

Haston tensed as anger surged again. Then another set of headlamps wavered in the distance and he pressed back into the bush. This time, as the lights swept by, he glimpsed the outline of a truck half-hidden in the scrub to the left of the tree where the South African was stationed. He peered at it, heard a third car approaching and suddenly made up his mind.

There was no possibility of trying for the garage, but without gasolene they were helpless. The truck was obviously the South African's transport. If it had standard desert equipment – and as far as he knew every truck in Maun did – it would be carrying a full reserve tank bolted to the chassis and a syphoning tube.

He gripped the can, waited until the car was level with him, then stood up and raced across the track behind it – screened by the dust and the roar of its engine. He ran fifteen yards into the bush, dropped to the ground as the engine noise died away over the bridge and listened. The man was out of sight, hidden by the thorn and scrub, but Haston knew exactly where he was and there'd been no reaction, no call or movement. Haston laid

231

the can on its side, picked up a rock, got to his feet half-crouching and moved forwards.

He was on his own territory now, confident of himself, knowing as if by instinct in the dark every rustling branch, every dry twig, every clattering stone, and stepping silently over them. The anger was still there, coming again and again in waves, but it only sharpened his concentration, his determination, and he moved with the controlled implacable purpose of a hunting cat – ferocious and hungry and lethal.

He parted the last barrier of thorn and the man was in front of him, hunched casually against the tree and facing in the opposite direction towards the bridge. Haston balanced the stone in his hand, slowed his breathing so that it was inaudible and gathered himself. The South African yawned, shifted his weight to the other foot and glanced at his watch. Haston saw the dial, green and luminous in the blackness, and caught the smells he knew would be there – the soap and cigarette tobacco and cheap cologne.

Then he leapt forward and smashed the rock down at the base of the South African's neck. The man never even heard Haston cover the last few yards. There was a thud, a small sigh and he crumpled silently to the ground.

Haston listened again. Still no sound except music floating from a bar, a drunken black singing somewhere further up the river and the changeless night noises of the bush. Then, without bothering to check whether the man was still alive, he went back, collected the can and headed for the truck.

He approached it warily, circling round from the back, but the cabin was empty and there was no sign of anyone else. So he came forward, knelt down and felt under the chassis. He was right. A reserve tank was bolted between the rear wheels and his hand touched a length of coiled rubber tube, fixed to the tank by metal spring-clips.

Haston pulled out the tube, unscrewed the filler cap and suddenly checked. Something was rustling at the extreme limit of his hearing, a soft faint scuff that didn't belong to the night. He started to turn but he was too late. A torch blazed out dazzling him and a voice shouted.

232

'What the hell are you doing?'

A South African voice, nasal and harsh. The man by the tree hadn't been alone. His companion had been patrolling the track and the scuff had been the second man's boots deadened by the thick sand.

'Jesus, it's you — '

There'd been surprise when the man spoke first, probably imagining he'd stumbled on a petty thief. Now he realized who Haston was and as he did Haston launched himself forwards – blindly plunging towards the light.

It was his only chance, the last one. If the man hadn't already pulled his gun, he'd be reaching for it now. Within seconds he could drop Haston at will. There were three yards between them. Haston hurled himself over the ground, heard another shout, flailed wildly at the torch, caught it, wrenched it clear and kicked at where he thought the man's groin was.

The man hadn't drawn his gun before he shouted. He was pulling it out of his hip holster as Haston reached him. Haston's kick missed his groin but caught his hand, the gun dropped to the earth, then they collided and grappled in the darkness.

He was big, this new one, big and strong and hard, and he fought with a trained remorseless savagery – rolling, turning, blocking Haston's blows and striking back with agonizing elbow jabs to the ribs and stomach. Haston was thirty pounds lighter and he wasn't trained but he attacked with a wild vicious frenzy, not noticing the pain or his damaged shoulder or the grazed welts on his body each time the South African jolted him away. Instead coming in again and again, spitting, clawing, gouging, butting with his head, using teeth and nails until his mouth was warm with blood and his hands were dripping.

And slowly the South African began to give way, dazed, hurt, reeling back under the ferocity of Haston's assaults until he was propped against the truck. Haston waited for an instant panting. Then he sprang for the man's throat, twisting in the air to avoid the knee which he knew would be smashed up towards his own groin. The knee came, he caught it on his thigh, but Haston's hands were round the man's neck and he was battering his head against the metal strut and suddenly it was over.

The South African choked, went limp, sagged and slumped sideways. Haston let go of him and he fell forwards onto his knees. Then Haston stepped back. He put his hands to his face and shuddered. He was trembling, his chest was heaving, he could smell and taste blood everywhere. But he hadn't finished – there was still the gasolene.

He stumbled to the rear of the truck, fed the rubber tube into the tank, sucked until the fuel reached him, spat and pushed the other end of the tube into the jerry-can. Then he squatted listening to the gasolene as it trickled through.

The can was three-quarters full when he heard another car engine and a fourth pair of headlamps flickered at the bend in the track. Haston lifted his head. The driver changed down, the noise came closer, light patterned the bush, and he realized the car wasn't heading for the bridge – it had left the road and was bumping towards the truck.

Haston glanced from left to right as the darkness began to dissolve in the approaching glare. A command vehicle checking the sites where the BOSS agents had been posted, it couldn't be anything else. He hesitated, sweating and shaking. Then he ripped out the tube, spun the cap onto the can, picked it up and started to run – doubling and weaving through the clumps of thorn.

If it hadn't been for the can he'd have made it. But the gasolene was too heavy and the container, swinging leadenly against his leg, slowed him to a lurching trot. He reached the bridge, the lights flared up, two voices shouted, a bullet snapped and whined over his head.

Haston threw himself across the track. On the bridge, framed against the white dust between the arches, he'd have been a perfect target. The river was the only possibility – the river and Alison if she was still there with the shotgun. He crashed down the bank, heaved the can into the water, dived after it and began to swim – pushing the can, buoyed up by the unfilled quarter of air, in front of him.

Alison was still there. Halfway across he heard the deep bark of the shotgun twice and twice again, glass splintering, a cry of pain, then the dazzle of light on the surface cut out.

Haston's feet touched sand, he levered the can upwards, then he was climbing the far bank.

'Let me help —'

Alison's arm was round his waist and she was reaching for the handle. Haston staggered to his feet and they ran for the slope, carrying the can between them. Behind the bridge was still in darkness and the shouting had stopped.

'South African bastards —'

Haston was gasping for breath and his voice was hoarse.

'They're all over the goddam place. I had to break for it.'

Alison nodded, hair tumbling round her face. 'I fired into the air when they drove onto the bridge, but then I could see they were going to shoot at you in the water. So I fired again at the headlamps.'

'Thank Christ you did.'

They were on top of the ridge now. Alison was panting too and they said nothing more until they reached the Toyota. Haston leant against it for a few moments, head bowed in exhaustion. The water had washed away the blood but the welts from the South African's blows were stinging, and as the breathlessness passed he started to shiver in the icy air.

He forced himself away from the truck, grasped the can and poured the gasolene into the tank. Eight gallons. With the one they still had left, nine. Enough to get them back to the lake and the leopard – and that was all. There was no question of trying the Ngami pump now: like Maun and Ghanzi it would be staked out too.

Haston went round to the front of the truck. Alison was standing by the wing in the moonlight, the shotgun still in her hand. He opened his mouth to tell her, stopped, shook his head and then there were tears in his eyes again. After everything, the miles of rock and heat and thorn, the battles and deaths, the hope and belief and trust, Charlie's sacrifice, they had lost.

'What is it, Jerry?'

'We're screwed, that's what! We can make it to Ngami, then we're finished. Without gas they've got us. In fact, even if we did have gas we'd still be finished. Before there was just that bunch of blacks on our tails. Now we'd have this crew too – they'll pick up the tyre spoor in the morning. We might have slipped one lot, not both. I'm sorry, lady, but they've got it nailed down.'

Alison stood frowning for a while. Then she said, 'Tonight the leopard crosses into the hunting area, Matsebe, isn't that so?'

'Right – it should be in there now.'

'And there's water in Matsebe?'

'Sure. Matsebe's part of the delta. There's water from there all the way to the Angolan border.'

'How far's that?'

'Straight? Maybe three hundred miles. But that cat's not angling straight. It's going north. Sixty miles and it'll come out of Matsebe, out of the delta, and into the desert again. But that part of the Kalahari; it's different, it's a real wilderness. Jesus, that's where no one goes except the bushmen up to their old sacred places in the Tsodilo Hills — '

Alison wasn't frowning any longer.

'I don't think we've lost, Jerry,' she said. 'Not yet. We can get back to the leopard. Water's no problem from now on. The way the animal's travelling sixty miles is only going to take three days. We can manage that. Then you yourself said it's much harder to follow anything in the delta. For us, yes, but also for anyone behind us — '

Haston began to understand and tried to interrupt, but she went on without letting him speak.

'We've got to try, Jerry, we haven't any choice. If we don't, we're signing that animal's death warrant. Mlanda's men have been told to kill it and even if they fail there are still the hunters out there. But if we can get it safely through Matsebe we can give it back to the desert. Maybe it's headed for the Tsodilo Hills, maybe it's going there to mate and breed. I don't know. But whatever the reason I'm going to see it has the chance and Christ help anyone who tries to stop me.'

Alison tossed the gun onto the seat, got in behind the wheel and started the engine.

Haston stood for a moment longer in the darkness. The two of them alone on foot through the delta with the animal in front, the terrorists and the white South Africans behind, and the

236

hunting parties on either side. It was insane but then everything that had happened since he became involved with her had been insane, and she'd won through it all and even now at the end, surrounded, cornered, besieged, she still wouldn't even acknowledge the possibility of defeat.

He began to laugh, shaking helplessly as the night wind swept round him and the stars drifted glittering across the sky.

'Are you coming or do I do this part on my own?'

Alison calling from the cab. He got into the cab and they set off along the ridge.

There was no need for silence or caution now and Alison drove as fast as the truck could travel, jolting and rocking through the bush along the rough track where the tyre marks of their earlier journey showed clear and deep in the moonlight.

Haston sat in silence beside her, no longer laughing but gripping the safety bar and thinking furiously. It was eleven. The drive into Maun had taken them all morning but it had been daylight then and they'd moved slowly, stopping whenever Charlie spotted a farm. This time they'd cover the distance in under three hours – reaching the tree again by two o'clock.

By then two-thirds of the night would be over and the leopard would have long since moved on. Twenty miles would take it past the northern end of the lake, across the road that linked Maun with the south of the country, and into Matsebe. By dawn the animal should be treed again on the edge of the concession area.

Spooring it as far as there would be simple – the leopard would still be moving through scattered scrub across open desert. But afterwards there was Matsebe itself, the beginning of the delta, and then the problems would start, all the problems. The delta was a gigantic patchwork of channel, lagoon and bush-covered sand, raised like low islands above the level of the water. On the areas of dry land the animal's pug-marks would be as firm and distinct as before. But to reach them from time to time it would have to swim – and the only way of being sure to track it then was by sight.

Night-spooring through water by sight. It was laughable, something no hunter he'd ever heard of had attempted. Yet

Alison was right. It was their only chance and because the animal was behaving differently from any other creature he'd come across, because it was following a course as straight and undeviating as a compass-needle, they might just succeed – if they could hold off the groups around and behind them.

The hunting parties were simply a hazard they could do nothing about. The terrorists and now the white South Africans were different. The terrorists would mount another attack as soon as possible, probably the next evening. If they got the chance, the South Africans would do the same. Having committed themselves to staking out Maun, they wouldn't stop there; they'd carry the pursuit through to the end.

All he and Alison could do was to keep moving, to run and hide, to hope that somehow in that desolate sweep of heat, water, thorn, sand and reed, they could hold onto the animal and lose the others.

Three days. Three days of mosquito and tsetse fly, hippo, crocodile and elephant, blistering sun and icy cold, pain, exhaustion, damp and constant unremitting danger. For a single leopard, a cat, an animal that even if they saw to safety they'd only glimpse again as a black shadow, distant and remote on the desert beyond.

He glanced at Alison. She was hunched intently over the wheel, hair plucked back by the wind buffeting through the window, eyes bright and steady, face absorbed and determined.

Haston shook his head helplessly once more and swayed as the truck swung from side to side.

'Take it easy here — '

They were coming down off the end of the ridge and the tree was only a few miles ahead. Alison changed gear, the truck slowed and Haston looked at the fuel gauge. As he'd guessed the needle was registering on the empty mark again – another gallon left.

'We'll squeeze out every last inch,' he said. 'Then when we run out we'll just have to ditch it. Meanwhile, get ready for action any time from now on. Those whites back in Maun won't pick up our spoor until tomorrow, so we can forget about them until way after daylight. But the blacks will have used today to track us up the last section. That means they'll be sitting out somewhere ahead. I don't figure they'll try anything serious in the darkness, but they may have scouts out. Cut the headlamps and take it at this speed until I tell you.'

Alison nodded and the flare of light in front of them was extinguished. Haston had loaded both the Schmeissers and the shotgun during the drive. He leant the repeaters against the seat between them, picked up the shotgun and sat holding it with the barrel pointing out of the window.

He was right. The terrorists had posted scouts – or at least one.

The Toyota was crunching very slowly over the sand by the light of the moon alone when he glimpsed a crouching running figure in the bush ahead and to their left. The figure vanished behind a clump of thorn, reappeared still running, and vanished again.

Haston flicked off the safety catch. The man must have been told to establish beyond any doubt that it was the right truck and not another home-going farm vehicle, or he'd have taken off instantly deep into the scrub. That meant he'd have to let them pass within a few yards of him.

'We've got company,' Haston said. 'One front left at ten o'clock. Don't bother about him. Just keep going steady, expect a bang and do what I say.'

Haston peered into the dark. The figure, racing through the shadows, came into sight again, cut diagonally towards the tyre tracks, and ducked into another clump of scrub. Haston waited but the man didn't emerge.

The truck drew closer, Haston raised the gun to his shoulder, then as they passed the clump he fired a single barrel into its centre. There was a flash of flame, a roar, a scream of pain and afterwards whisps of cordite smoke were circling in the cab.

'Headlamps again and shift!'

Light blazed up, Alison stamped on the accelerator and they surged forwards.

'Okay,' Haston was feeding another cartridge into the gun. 'That's just to let them know we're hanging in tight. The bush will have taken most of the impact of the pellets, but that guy in there's going to have something to remember for a while too. Now for the tree.'

They came to the point where they'd stopped before. Charlie's footprints were still clear on the sand. Moments later they were under the baobab. They both got out, walked round to the other side of the trunk and stopped.

The pug-marks stretched out away from them across the ground in the same unfaltering line they'd followed for almost two hundred miles. Crisp, hard, cut like little bowls in the earth with even the talon ends showing, angled implacably towards the far horizon.

Alison knelt down and explored one of the prints with her fingers, gently, wonderingly, letting the form crumble and break and the sand trickle over her hand. Then she stood up shaking her head.

'You know, Jerry, there were times in that first month when I didn't believe it,' she said. 'I'd wake at night or I'd be sitting somewhere in the day, and I'd suddenly think I must be wrong, that it was a fantasy, a trick of the light, that the animal didn't exist at all. Then I'd fret and worry until I saw it again. Even then I wasn't quite sure, I had to keep pinching myself to make certain I wasn't dreaming.'

'Well, I can tell you one thing,' Haston grinned. 'Sure as hell that isn't tractor spoor.'

'And we'll see it again?'

For an instant, for the first time, there was doubt in her voice.

Haston looked at her and saw that she was frowning and her eyes were glistening. And he realized then the burden, the almost intolerable burden, of everything she'd gone through over the past three months. The nervous excitement, the sustained physical strain, the repeated shocks of violence, the constant effort to persuade first the guerrillas and then himself that her leopard, her dream, was more important than anything else in the world – and the passionate exhausting strength with which she'd carried them all on the animal's track.

She was indestructible and the uncertainty would pass. But briefly it was there and somehow it made her more real, more human and vulnerable, than at any time since Haston had known her.

He put his arm round her shoulder and nodded firmly.

'Sure, we'll see it again —'

All his own confidence came flooding back. He was a hunter once more, a professional who could follow the spoor-line even through the delta at night. This just made them equal. They were together now, totally together in a way they hadn't even been in bed, and between them they'd take the animal to safety.

'But we need to move. I'll take Charlie's role until the gas runs out – spoor from the roof. But keep it slow. With the cold and the wind my eyes are going to be watering like mad. We don't want to finish up tracking some goddam warthog by mistake.'

Haston hugged her quickly and she laughed and kissed his cheek. Then he climbed on top of the cabin and the truck crunched forwards over the sand.

19

It was bitterly cold in the township.

Mlanda paced the floor of the shack under the single naked bulb, paused, glanced contemptuously at Valdez slumped in a gin-sodden stupor over the table, drank from the open bottle of beer by the old man's hand – the frost had parched his throat – and circled the walls again.

He was shivering and he couldn't sleep, but it wasn't the cold. He'd stopped noticing that long since. For as far back as he could remember the township had always been the same at night: icy in winter, suffocatingly hot in summer. There was never any mean between the two – just the fierce harsh extremes he'd learned to live with as a child. Normally, by now he'd have been curled up on the metal bed behind the partition wall.

Not tonight. Tonight there'd been a message radioed down from the north.

Lumumbi had linked up with the others. He'd taken over from B'Volu, closed on the truck and then, just as he was about to strike, a plane had landed. There'd been a fight, they'd hit the pilot, Lumumbi had lost a man but that wasn't important. He still had seven left, the leopard was moving straight and easy, the woman and the wounded white were tucked in behind it.

Tonight they were all lying up close to some little village. But tomorrow or the day after Lumumbi would hit them. The white would go, the woman would be caught – and the animal would be killed.

Mlanda wasn't interested in the white. He was just another anonymous racist thug, who'd get a knife in his throat or a bullet in his brain. But the woman and the leopard mesmerized him – mesmerized, enraged and baffled him. Ever since he'd heard she was following the animal again, he'd thought of little else. If he slept, they filled his dreams. If he paused by day, they invaded his mind. He'd brooded over them for hours, puzzled, wondered, cursed – and still they remained an enigma.

The tall imperious woman with her implacable purpose, the great black creature she'd described to him, and the relationship that bound them together. Sometimes the two images seemed to fuse and he'd see them as a single creation – an immense and dark and threatening presence. At others he'd have sudden fantasies that somehow their lives were inextricably linked, that if one died so would the other. Once he even woke to find himself shouting for Lumumbi: in his dream he'd told Lumumbi by mistake to kill the woman and capture the leopard.

The fantasies, the fear and rage and confusion, were always worst by night. Trying to shake them off, Mlanda would stubbornly insist to himself that the animal had to die because he needed the woman as a hostage, and while it lived she was in some way inviolate. It was partly true. As Valdez had said she was a prize, a huge prize, and the guns paid for her release would be almost priceless. Not in themselves but as symbols of pride and strength, objects with which to strike back at the armed might of white South Africa and help spark the fire that one day would engulf the continent.

Partly true – but only partly. There was another reason. Private, stronger, more compelling. Mlanda wouldn't acknowledge it but he knew it was there.

Fear. The leopard had come to stand for everything in the desert which had made him afraid. The wildness, the ferocity, the loneliness of it all. The woman had had the strength and courage and will to overcome it. Mlanda hadn't; he'd retreated overwhelmed and humiliated. But with the leopard dead the fear would be destroyed, the woman's strength negated and his own pride restored. That was why the animal had to be killed.

'Here, man.'

Mlanda swung round. The door had creaked open and the boy had slipped in with something in his hand.

'What you got?'

'Message.'

243

'Message? They came through two hours back. They're not due again until tomorrow.'

'Then I guess they just changed, man — '

The boy shrugged.

'Came over just now.'

He handed Mlanda a piece of paper. Mlanda read through it once, quickly, disbelievingly, then a second time, then a third. Finally, he crumpled it into a ball and stood gazing dully at the slit of darkness by the door-frame.

He had stopped shivering but suddenly he felt colder than he'd ever felt in his life.

The message was from Lumumbi again. Half an hour earlier Lumumbi had been out waiting to check that the woman's truck returned from the direction in which it had driven off that morning – presumably in search of fuel. It was a scout's job but after everything that had gone wrong Lumumbi decided to take it on himself. The truck appeared, Lumumbi closed on it to make sure it was the right vehicle, then someone inside spotted him and fired a shotgun.

The pellets caught Lumumbi's face. He'd lost one eye entirely and half the sight in the other. Now he'd radioed down to say he couldn't go on.

B'Volu was still there but he'd proved himself useless when the camp was first raided and the woman seized. Apart from B'Volu there was nobody, not even someone Mlanda could send up from the township.

If he was going to get the woman back now, Mlanda knew that he'd have to go back into the desert and take over the operation himself.

'No patrols?'

The boy shook his head. 'They won't be by before sun-up now.'

'Right, well you listen, man. I'm going up there to handle it myself. That means I want a signal sent back, I want a truck fixed, I want the lot. But before we start working that out you get over to a shebeen and fetch me a quart of liquor, okay?'

The boy nodded and padded out.

For a moment Mlanda looked at the distant towers of light of white Johannesburg, soaring against the sky beyond the huddled smoking roofs of the township. Then he slammed the door furiously. He seldom drank, but what he wanted now more than anything else was a jug of the acid, gut-burning cane spirit.

Mlanda clenched his hands, deliberately wiped the desert, the woman and the leopard from his mind, propped himself against the wall and waited for the boy to come back.

Three miles away, in one of the buildings Mlanda had been gazing at, Liddell was undressing for bed. It was almost three, he'd slept for only a few hours each night since reaching Jo'burg and he was exhausted. That was normal: it always happened by the time any of these incidents reached their climax. What wasn't normal was that he was also angry.

It was rare for Liddell to feel any emotion. He was given assignments, difficult often dangerous assignments, and he carried them out as best he could – patiently and systematically but never becoming personally involved with the hostage at the centre of the operation. He'd known this one would be the most difficult and explosive he'd handled. He'd carefully avoided identifying with the Welborough-Smith woman, feeling any sympathy for what was happening to her – and yet he was still angry.

He turned out the light and lay in the darkness with his arms crossed behind his head.

Haston. He was the reason, the young American with the green-flecked eyes and the hard lean face. Intelligent, brave and resourceful, Schlietvan's file had described him. He'd proved all of that and more – a ruthless sadistic bastard. He'd preyed on the terrified woman, dragged her three hundred miles across the desert, used her like a puppet, shielded himself behind her, manipulated her mind – even tonight, after Schlietvan's men had so nearly seized him in Maun, he'd be distorting the truth again to explain what had happened and force her to go on. Shocked, isolated, bewildered, helpless, she'd probably agree.

If Haston had been a terrorist himself – a black revolutionary

or a young guerrilla from an Argentine slum, it made no difference – Liddell would have understood. His behaviour would
have fitted the patterns of despairing violence Liddell knew so
well. But Haston wasn't a terrorist. He was white and mature
and responsible, and yet he'd run, twisted, hidden and killed
like a callous craven coward.

Liddell ignored the fact that Haston had been due to be killed
himself. He thought only of the woman and what Haston had
done to her. That had offended Liddell's deepest values and the
anger grew out of the disgust he felt.

Well, it wouldn't last much longer. Schlietvan had assured
him of that and he believed the South African. Haston had no
more than a quarter-tank of gasolene left – enough for perhaps
eighty miles. Soon after dawn Schlietvan's men would pick up
his tyre tracks and before nightfall they'd catch up with him
somewhere out there in the remoteness of the desert. None of
them had any doubts about what they were to do then.

Liddell turned onto his side and tried to sleep.

A mile to the west Schlietvan was looking out of his office
window onto Eloff Street, deserted now under the street lamps.
Schlietvan was more than angry – he was in a cold murderous
rage.

He'd been like that ever since the first call came through four
hours earlier. Fourteen men in Maun and Haston had walked
through them all – he'd even almost killed two of them in the
process. It had been bad enough when the American had
ambushed the patrol at the copse, but there were only five waiting for him then and his arrival had taken them by surprise.
This time all fourteen were alert and prepared and in place, and
still Haston had managed to escape.

The situation, and with it Schlietvan's fury, had grown worse
when the telephone rang for the second time. That was half an
hour ago now. Once again it was Van der Byl, whom he'd put in
command of the Maun contingent, on the line. When Van der
Byl had called before he'd been apologetic, confused and embarrassed, yet he'd insisted Haston would still be found. The

246

American only had a single jerry-can of gasolene, his tyre tracks would show up in the dawn light; and whatever he did, however much he jinked and twisted and ran, they'd have all the time they needed to spoor him.

With the second call even that had changed. Just before Haston vanished they'd seized the black. At the start the man had been stubborn. Later, like all blacks, he'd begun to talk. He was still refusing to say anything about Haston or the woman, but Van der Byl had beaten a few scraps of information out of him. Most of them were worthless. One, vouchsafed in tears without persuasion, wasn't.

The black's name was Charlie. By profession he was a foreman herder and senior tracker, and his employer was called Jo Marshall. The previous day Miss Marshall had landed her private plane on a pan near where he, Haston and the woman had been waiting. The black had no idea how she'd found them or what she was doing up there in the northern desert. But as she got out of the plane Mlanda's terrorists had opened fire from the surrounding bush. There'd been a short fierce fight, the terrorists had backed off but Miss Marshall had been killed.

Jo Marshall. Van der Byl knew the name, as, of course, did Schlietvan, so for that matter would anyone else in southern Africa. The only daughter of old Gardner Marshall, the biggest landowner and one of the richest and most powerful men in the continent – apart from his ranches in Botswana, his interests stretched across the entire republic. Schlietvan had no more idea than the black what she'd been doing in the desert, let alone how her foreman herder had come to be involved with Haston.

What he did know with absolute certainty was that as soon as she was reported missing, Marshall would have every plane in the country out searching that section of the Kalahari for her. Van der Byl's men hadn't got all the time they wanted. They had a bare seventy-two hours – and then they'd be spotted themselves.

Schlietvan smashed his fist down on the window-sill, making the whole frame quiver. Then he turned abruptly and walked over to the glowing wall-map.

Brown, grey-green and blue, the section of the desert and delta surrounding Maun. On the screen it looked bland and flat and innocuous. That was his true enemy, the Kalahari, where the brown became vast barren areas of sand and rock, the grey-green razor-sharp thorn that cut and gouged and slashed, the blue endless channels of water and reed.

Haston had been cunning, skilful, lucky. But more than that it was the desert which had saved him twice. The Kalahari had folded itself round him, concealed him like it concealed its game, given him time and space and shelter. No longer. Time had run out on him, space was a liability now, shelter had gone. Within a few hours he'd have to abandon the truck and then he was finished – if Van der Byl could find him before the search for Marshall's daughter was mounted.

Schlietvan hunched himself forwards, granite-coloured face pocked with shadows cast by the sodium light, and stared at the screen.

'*Ja* — ?'

The telephone had rung for a third time, Schlietvan had gone back to the desk and picked up the receiver. He listened to the operator, told her to put the call through and waited.

It was Van der Byl once more, his voice punctuated with static on the field line from the north. As he started to speak Schlietvan guessed he'd learned something more from the black. He was wrong. The black had given nothing else away before crumpling unconscious on the floor of the hut where he was being interrogated. Instead Van der Byl had something quite different, and to Schlietvan both chilling and electrifying, to report.

Van der Byl's group was equipped with long-range radio transmitters. Scanning the frequencies one of his operators had picked up an open-line signal ten minutes earlier. The operator had tuned in, listened and overheard a crude laconic message. 'Tell the man to stay with them. He's coming up himself to handle it.' The message had been beamed from somewhere in the vicinity of Jo'burg.

That was all. Yet to Van der Byl, and now to Schlietvan, the significance was unmistakeabie. Mlanda, it could only be

Mlanda, had decided to take over the operation in person.

Schlietvan grunted an acknowledgement, depressed the receiver, hesitated briefly, then snapped on the intercom.

'*Het mir control.*'

He waited, the operational control room clerk on the floor below answered, and Schlietvan rasped out his instructions in Afrikaans. The clerk repeated them, Schlietvan flicked off the switch and stood up.

There was no choice, he knew that. Too much had been committed, too much was at stake. He'd risked everything to get the woman back – men, guns, vehicles, there were even boats ready if Haston tried to break for the delta – and it would all be on file. Now something else would be on file too – the fact that Mlanda was up there too.

Schlietvan had no illusions about the Bureau he worked for: the jealousies, the political pressures, the warring ambitions, the constant spying, the instant readiness to jump on and break anyone, however senior, who made a mistake. If the operation went wrong now, if he lost Mlanda after searching for him unsuccessfully for five years, Schlietvan's own neck would go on the block and he'd be finished.

Only one thing could justify the gamble he'd taken – Mlanda's death. He had two or three days at most in which to see it happened and to be absolutely certain it did, Schlietvan would have to go up into the desert himself and take command.

Perhaps he'd known it from the start, from the moment he sent his men in to cordon the little town, but the realization still came as a shock and for an instant his palms were sweating. Schlietvan wiped them on his trousers and glanced at his watch. Fifteen minutes past three. Four hours before the plane he'd ordered could take off.

He reached for a chair, dragged it over to the screen and straddled himself across it. Then he gazed intently at the map again as he waited for the dawn.

20

The wind keened round Haston's head, the air was thick with stinging frost that blurred and clouded his vision. But the sand was level, the pug-marks ran straight and clear in the moonlight, and the truck bumped steadily forward.

They rounded the end of the lake, crossed the main track from Maun to the south, passed a rotting wooden sign marking the start of Matsebe – and then Haston heard the sound he'd been expecting.

The engine coughed, faded, spluttered twice again and finally cut out. Alison let the vehicle coast to a stop, Haston clambered down and peered at the milometer. They were fourteen miles from the tree – almost twice as far as he'd guessed they'd make. That was good. But from now on they'd be on foot.

'Move the gear from the back and we'll sort it out.'

Alison climbed over the tailgate and began to pass him down everything inside the truck.

Haston sifted it quickly into four heaps. The first contained all the equipment that would be of no conceivable use to the terrorists when they found the Toyota in the morning. The second consisted of supplies the blacks could use – mainly tinned food. There wasn't time to dispose of it properly but Haston hurled the cans at random into the bush on either side.

In the third heap he put anything they wouldn't be able to take with them but which would be lethally dangerous to leave – the Urtzi automatic rifle, one of the Schmeissers, most of the ammunition. Those they'd have to carry until they could dump them without any chance of being found, probably when they reached the first lagoon. Finally, in the fourth heap Haston stacked the essentials they'd need for the whole journey plus as much as he reckoned they'd be able to tote through the swamp.

It looked pitifully little. The shotgun, the second Schmeisser, some ammunition, his binoculars, a few cans of food. But he knew even that amount would be taxing enough once they hit water and reed, and anything more would have been impossible.

'Pack your lot in this — '

Haston split the fourth heap into two and gave Alison one of the makeshift back-packs Charlie had cobbled together – weeks ago now it seemed.

'You can toss in whatever you want from your own gear, but keep it light. We've got sixty miles ahead of us at least and you'll be carrying it every goddam yard.'

While she filled her pack Haston did the same with a second one. He swung it over his shoulders, stood up and briefly considered what they'd got.

The Schmeisser was for defence when the inevitable attack came. He'd dearly have liked to have taken the other one too but his shoulder still wasn't strong enough. Haston would have to make do with the shotgun – for defence again at short range and for game, a sandgrouse or a guinea-fowl, if they got the chance. Food wasn't so important. It would be rough but they could survive for days on water alone if they had to – and there'd be no shortage. The rest was the bare minimum he'd have packed for an afternoon s rough-shooting in the bush, let alone a safari across the delta, but it would have to do.

'Ready — ?'

He glanced at Alison who was standing now with her pack slung over her back and the Schmeisser in her hand. She nodded and he looked up at the sky.

The moon was down and within a couple of hours dawn would begin to break, but there was still enough light from the stars to follow the spoor. By seven they should be on the edge of the water and the leopard's last tree-base before it entered the swamp. Haston went round to the front of the truck, lifted the hood, wrenched out the rotor arm, smashed it against the heavy fender and hurled the crumpled piece of metal into the scrub.

Then he handed Alison the Urtzi, hefted the spare Schmeisser and picked up the remaining cartons of ammunition.

'Right,' he said. 'We're on our way.'

251

He tramped off, bowed under the weight of the pack and the guns, along the unwavering line of the pug-marks.

Midday. The heat humid and unrelenting. Mosquitoes covering the ground in spinning whining plumes like mist. A malachite kingfisher flashing emerald and gold through the reeds. The water beyond lapping and bubbling and rustling.

Haston slapped savagely at his neck where a tsetse fly had just lighted and bitten him, the pain sharper than a wasp-sting. Then he parted the tall grass again and looked out. Still nothing on the plain that stretched away to the south. He stood up, walked back to where Alison was sleeping in the shadow of a thorn bush and squatted down beside her, wiping the sweat from his face.

They'd been there since daybreak. The leopard had behaved exactly as before, stopping in a group of tall acacia and bounding up into the branches as the sky began to pale. He and Alison had followed the spoor to the trees, heard the rustle of leaves and a challenging snarl, backed carefully away and settled down to wait.

As he'd guessed they were on the rim of the delta – in fact they'd already crossed some patches of marshy grass on the plain behind. The first real channel was immediately ahead, bordered by reed and towering feathery papyrus. That one was narrow and shallow but the water would get progressively deeper as they went on, building up into broad running streams and deep lagoons. Then the level would start to fall again and finally they'd come out into the barren desolation of the northern desert – if they got that far.

Haston reached for a cigarette, hesitated puzzled, turned his head and tensed. There'd been no sound but his eyes must have picked up a flicker of movement. Elephant. Five of them. Immense, muddy-grey, seeming to float through the grass as they came forward eighty yards to the right.

He squeezed Alison's arm, she woke instantly. He whispered, 'Sit up very slowly and give me the Schmeisser.'

She raised herself off the ground, saw the animals and passed him the automatic.

Haston knelt and waited. The elephants came on, still utterly silent in spite of their eight-thousand-pound weight. The leader was an old bull with one tusk broken and the stump splintered and jagged. He checked twenty yards from them, swung round, took a tentative step forward, then lifted his ears and trumpeted.

'Don't move!' Haston whispered again.

He lifted the Schmeisser to his shoulder and sighted. Sweat was pouring off his forehead but he could see the animal's small dark-brown eyes, rims caked with dry clay, and he kept the metal V steadily centred between them. The bull trumpeted again, tossed its head, then suddenly wheeled and moved off with the others behind it.

'Jesus Christ!' Haston lowered the gun as the elephants disappeared. 'That's all we'd have needed – an evil old jumbo on the rampage.'

'Could you have stopped him?'

Alison had been kneeling too. Now she sat back in the shadow of the bush, her face pale but not frightened.

'Sure, that's what I'm paid for,' Haston grinned. 'Well, that's what I used to get paid for. But I hadn't just got that big fellow, I'd got four others too. Know anything about elephants – outside the zoology textbooks, that is?'

She shook her head.

'Then let me tell you, lady. They're wicked. They scare me rigid, and every hunter too. Any other animal and you're in with a chance whatever goes wrong. Jesus, you can even drop a charging lion with a .12 gauge shotgun if you keep your cool and wait until he's within feet of you. Not jumbo. He's too fast and too big. He can make close on forty miles an hour, turn like a goddam ballet dancer and open a truck like it was a sardine can. One mistake and he'll have you. I could have knocked over the big boy but if his friends had joined in, that would have been fade-out.'

'What else are we likely to meet?'

'That's dangerous? Crocs mainly, hippo and maybe some buffalo. I said jumbo was wicked and that's for sure. But in their own ways they're all killers equally. You ask any hunter which is the worst and he'll just laugh and say, "a baboon – at the wrong moment". He's right, too.'

'Even about leopards?'

Haston thought for a moment. Then he shook his head and grinned again.

'No, those cats are the exception. They belong to the night, to the place where we can't see but they can. And to get them we've got to cross into their country. That makes them different from all the rest. Except —'

He got to his feet and turned towards the barrier of high grass that separated them from the plain.

'Even leopards aren't our problem right now. We've got other company to worry about.'

Haston peered between the stems again.

There were still only groups of giraffe, occasional ostrich flocks and herds of grazing lechwe, the little antelope spreading out towards the horizon dun-coloured and fragile in the shimmering haze. Those and the bateleur eagles quartering the sky, goshawks silhouetted on dead branches, high vultures soaring the midday thermals, jackal and mongoose and meercat prowling the stiff dry winter scrub.

Nothing else – and yet sooner or later the pattern, the balance, would be disrupted and broken. The blacks might have been delayed and confused by the abandoned truck. But they'd work out what had happened, salvage whatever they could from what Haston had left and come forward again – following the treble-spoor just as he and Alison had tracked the pugmarks.

'Can you handle a spell — ?'

Haston was back by the bush again. Alison nodded and stood up.

'Okay. All you've got to do is watch the buck. It's too early for lion or cheetah to be hunting, so if the herds start to break it can only be those bastards behind us. Soon as the buck moves, wake me.'

Haston lay down in the bar of shade. Mosquitoes swarmed over his face, tsetse flies stabbed at his legs and arms, ants and

254

ticks crawled across his body. He flapped his hands casually for a few moments. Then, limp, exhausted, uncaring, he closed his eyes and slept.

'Jerry —'

Alison's hand shaking his shoulder. He blinked and sat up. The light was still strong and clear but the heat had gone and a solitary star gleamed over the reeds.

'It's the lechwe,' Alison said quickly. 'The herds in the distance started to run about ten minutes ago. I thought it was late enough to be an evening predator. But I've been using your glasses and I can't see anything, and the buck are still moving.'

Haston seized the binoculars, ran forwards and dropped down in the grass.

For an instant he couldn't see anything either except, as Alison had said, that the plain was churning with movement as the antelope herds fanned out in gallop before something pushing towards them from the back. Then through the dust, over the tawny racing shapes, he saw what she'd missed. A glint of steely light, a man advancing through the scrub, black, doubled low, wearing a ragged khaki shirt, close to him another, then another and after that a third and then more – until, swinging the glasses in an arc, Haston counted seven in the line.

Seven. Less than half a mile away and all of them armed with the high velocity rifles that had cut down Jo. Haston lowered the binoculars and swore bitterly, furiously. Only one more hour and the leopard would have been on the move with the two of them behind it, and they'd have won another night – the blacks wouldn't dare cross the delta in darkness. But dusk was still that hour off, the leopard wouldn't leave the tree until the light dimmed and long before then the terrorists would reach the rippling screen of grass.

They were caught. If they backed off into the reeds, they'd lose the leopard and the animal would almost certainly be killed. If they stayed and fought, they'd probably be killed themselves, and afterwards in spite, in vengeance, in rage, the animal would die too.

Haston smashed his fist against the earth. Then he glanced over his shoulder at Alison and told her the alternatives, quickly

255

and brutally.

'We stay,' she said without hesitation. 'Maybe we can buy just enough time for the animal to get away.'

Haston surveyed the area round them. Each time before, when they'd clashed with either the blacks or the South Africans, they'd had cover – bush, scrub, sand-banks and trees. This was different, just flat open grassland without even a rocky outcrop for protection. They'd be lucky to last fifteen minutes after the first shot was fired, but he knew Alison would be immovable.

'Let's get the guns then.'

He ran back to the thorn bush, stooped to pick up the Schmeisser and then Alison suddenly called to him.

'Look, Jerry, over there!'

Haston straightened up and whirled round. She was pointing at the group of acacias. For a moment he thought the terrorists had outflanked them and they were about to be attacked from the side.

Then he saw it in the shadow of the trunks – black, crouched, yellow eyes staring over the grass. The leopard. For an instant Haston thought it was watching them both. Then he realized its eyes were fixed on Alison alone. He glanced at her and saw she was gazing at it too and suddenly something seemed to pass between them, crackling unseen across the air like a charge of electricity. Then there was a low growl, the leopard flicked its tail twice, the contact was broken and the animal vanished – heading north through the reeds.

Haston shook his head bewildered.

'Don't just stand there, Jerry. Maybe it's the water, maybe the men disturbed it, God knows what. It doesn't matter. The animal's moving — '

Alison's voice was tense with excitement and she was already heaving on the pack.

'We've got another chance. Run!'

She set off in the direction where the leopard had disappeared.

Haston swung on his own pack, snatched for the Schmeisser and raced after her. As he ran he felt a soaring buoyant surge of exhilaration and triumph. Alison was right – they'd get a second night after all.

Haston struggled out of the water and climbed the bank, hauling himself up by the bending papyrus.

On top he stood for a moment panting, sodden from the waist down, the palms of his hands raw and bleeding from a multitude of tiny cuts scratched across the skin by the razor-edges of the papyrus leaves. The shotgun was strapped over his shoulders above the pack so that it rode high and firm and dry against his neck. He lifted it off, forced his way through the reeds to the open grass beyond, crouched and began to search the ground, first right, then left, then right again – each time casting further and further from where he'd reached land.

He found what he was looking for three or four minutes later. A trail of crushed fern, sharp gouges where talons had raked the earth, then as the grass thinned the deep unmistakeable prints in the sand.

'Ready?'

He was on the bank again calling softly across the channel.

'Yes.'

Alison's voice from the reeds on the other side. Haston checked the water. It was still too shallow for hippo but deep enough for crocodile. If a croc was using the stream to pass from one lagoon to another, its eyes would have shown smokey-red in the moonlight. There was nothing except the silver-black sheen, the stir of a diving frog, the ripples from a tiger-fish snapping at a dew-laden moth.

'Take it fast but steady,' Haston called again. 'There's a bank midway over, then a dip and after that it's easy. I'll be covering you all the way. Keep the Schmeisser up and move – now!'

He panned the surface of the stream with the shotgun's muzzle as she waded over to join him, ready to fire instantly if anything else disturbed the water, but there were only the small waves lapping out from her waist. Alison reached the bank, he leant down, took the automatic, grasped her hand and pulled her up beside him.

'Are we still on course?'

Alison was wringing the water out of her jeans but her face was turned towards him, alert and anxious and inquiring.

Haston nodded. 'We're right in there, lady. The cat pitched here —'

He moved back and along the bank to the place where he'd found the trampled fern and the talon marks in the ground.

'I figure it shook itself, scratched around, then shifted on. But the spoor's clear. We can track it.'

'Give me a moment —'

Alison must have stumbled as she entered the stream, because her shirt was clinging tight and wet against her breasts and her hair was dripping. She pulled the cloth away from her body, squeezed it and shook her head, spraying out drops of water that cascaded and glittered like falling stars in the moonlight.

Then she took back the Schmeisser and said, 'All right, let's go.'

Haston turned and set off along the spoor-line.

It was insane. He'd known that right back at the start when he'd told Alison what would happen when the leopard went into the delta. He'd known it yesterday standing by the truck outside Maun. He knew it now as he walked in the darkness through the winter grass, eyes scouring the sand ahead.

Insane and impossible – you couldn't spoor an animal by night through the swamp. Even the delta bushmen wouldn't have attempted that. And yet it was after midnight and they were seven hours into the marshes and they were still on the leopard's track.

There was a reason of course, the reason that made the leopard different from any other animal he'd ever come across. Not just in colour and size and rarity and behaviour, but in the straightness of the course it was taking. Even ten days ago that had been extraordinary. But ever since the animal increased its speed it was almost unbelievable. There were times when Haston felt he could almost take a compass, chart its route for a hundred miles in front, go on ahead and wait there in the absolute certainty that sooner or later the animal would appear at the very point he'd plotted.

It was that which was allowing them to follow the animal now. Each time the spoor vanished in a stretch of marsh Haston would take a bearing from the stars, go forward to the next area of firm sand and cast to either side until he found it again – just as he'd done on the bank of the channel.

He came to the end of the island, reeds thickened round his thighs, papyrus curled overhead like foam and he stopped. There was another stream below, deeper and swifter than the last one, with more papyrus on the far side and a further low plateau of sand and grassy plain beyond.

Haston strapped the shotgun back on top of the pack and glanced round at Alison.

'Here we go again, lady. And remember – if you see a hippo, don't let him fire first.'

She smiled, came forwards with the Schmeisser to cover him and he slid down the bank into the water.

Darkness, moonlight, stars, endless incandescent stars, the dark black shadows of the thorn and reeds. Cold and warmth alternating. The icy shock of each channel, the shivering moments on the far bank, then heat slowly returning as they trudged stumbling and sweating across the islands. All round them the night sounds of the delta – different, closer, louder and more menacing than those of the desert.

The interminable chanting chorus of frogs. The roar of lion hunting the islands for buck. The grunts and snorts of grazing hippo and the sudden splintering crashes as the great animals lumbered through the bush. Water churning and gurgling where a crocodile had caught some unwary antelope and dragged it flailing below the surface. Owls hooting, hyena and jackal calling, packs of wild dogs howling over distant kills.

Hour after hour until they were both reeling with exhaustion and every muscle in Haston's body was stretched and throbbing, and he was moving only because he knew that if he stopped Alison would implacably push him forwards again. And then suddenly the sky began to lighten and a few minutes later they came out onto the edge of a lagoon.

They'd had to swim once during the night but only for a few yards at the centre of a channel. This was different, not another of the winding streams but a broad stretch of water reaching out two hundred yards in front of them. Haston's head drooped wearily onto his chest, then he felt Alison's hand grip his elbow.

He looked up, saw she was gazing intently across the lagoon, turned puzzled towards the water and then he saw it too and for an instant all the tiredness vanished.

A hundred and fifty yards away a black head was cleaving through the water like a gigantic snake – sending out ripples in its wake through the floating lilies and the reflections of the stars. The leopard was swimming. It reached the far bank, scrambled up and stood for a moment silhouetted against the dawn light. Then it disappeared into the reeds.

Haston thought it had gone but a few seconds later they saw it again. Beyond the reeds there was a cluster of dense mopane. As they watched two fish eagles suddenly rose mewing and flapping into the air. The branches shook, a dark supple shape showed briefly against a trunk clawing its way upwards, a snarl carried across the water, then the disturbance stopped and there was silence again.

'Jesus!' Haston shook his head in disbelief, 'Sometimes I almost get to feel someone up there must be pitching for us.'

Alison rubbed her hand across her face and smiled.

With the leopard treed they could rest all day. Then before dusk they'd be able to find a land route round to the mopane clump which meant they wouldn't have to swim the lagoon. Haston glanced at the water, gold now as the sun rose, thought of the hippo and crocodile they'd heard in the darkness and shuddered.

He turned back, paused and swore furiously. Each time they seemed to have won one small victory there was always another larger, more dangerous problem crowding in on them. Of course, they couldn't rest all day – they'd got the blacks behind.

'How far away do you think they are?'

Alison had guessed what he was thinking and the smile had gone. Haston shrugged.

'Depends on what they covered before darkness,' he said. 'I

reckon we made maybe twenty miles overnight. Let's give them five before they quit. So that puts them fifteen off.'

'And they'll still be able to follow?'

'Sure,' he nodded grimly. 'It won't be as easy as the desert – a kid could have done it there. But they're close, they've got a tracker, our spoor's fresh and straight, and they're moving in daylight. Unless —'

He hesitated frowning.

It had been plucking irritably at the back of his mind all the previous day and intermittently throughout the night. The white South Africans. They had men, trucks, the tyre tracks to follow – and yet there'd been no sight or sound of them since Maun.

'I don't know,' Haston shook his head again bewildered, 'I guess it's just possible those blacks got overtaken by the other bunch. If that's happened, they'll all have had a right goddam barney. But we should have heard something and we haven't. So for the moment we've got to figure it's still just Mlanda's thugs and they're fifteen miles back and in this country that means seven hours' hard —'

He looked at his watch. Full dawn came at seven o'clock and the dial showed a few minutes before. Seven hours on from then would take them to the early afternoon – but Haston wasn't even going to risk that.

'We'll cut it back to five,' he said. 'The first three for you, then two for me. Midday we'll circle round to the mopane. Once we're there close to the cat we'll take another spell each. But you get your head down now. I'll wake you when it's time for you to take over.'

Alison nodded in agreement, shrugged off the pack and lay down on the bank, curling up under the cover of the arching papyrus. Moments later she was asleep.

Haston settled himself close to her with the shotgun in his lap and the Schmeisser between them. From where he was sitting he could see the final hundred-yard stretch of bush and plain they'd crossed before reaching the lagoon. Beyond that was a wall of thorn scrub. Anyone following them would first have to break through the scrub, as they'd done earlier, and then advance across the grassy plain.

Haston gazed at the thorn. The sun lifted over the horizon, warmth spilled out across the swamp, eddies of mist wreathed and dissolved, the morning's heat began to gather. His head slumped down, he shook himself angrily blinking, stared back at the bush, felt drowsiness seep over his arms and legs, fought it off once, twice, a third time – and then suddenly collapsed, toppling slowly over onto his side.

The strain of the night had been too great. He lay sprawled beside Alison in deep dreamless sleep.

Haston never knew whether it was sound or instinct or accident. He woke, registered from the angle of the sun that it was mid-afternoon and saw the men at the same instant. Two of them, both black, one unarmed and bending down, the other carrying a rifle – the tracker and a scout advancing ahead of the main party. They were only fifteen yards away but he and Alison were hidden in the barred shadows of the papyrus and the men hadn't seen them.

Haston didn't hesitate. In a single movement he catapulted himself to his knees, grabbed the shotgun and fired both barrels from the waist. The tracker must have noticed him a fraction of a second before he squeezed the trigger, because he hurled himself sideways, leapt up and began racing back towards the thorn. The scout never saw Haston at all. One moment he was standing there open-mouthed. The next both charges slammed into his chest and stomach, he screamed and fell backwards.

'Down the bank!' Haston shouted.

Alison was struggling to sit up. He seized her wrist, caught the Schmeisser up under his arm and plunged towards the lagoon.

The first returning shots came as he moved, but they were still screened by the papyrus and the bullets slashed wildly through the reeds on either side. Seconds afterwards their feet were in the water with the bank above them.

'Take this —'

Haston fed two more cartridges into the shotgun and gave it to her.

'Wait here. I'm going to take a look and see how bad it is.'

Haston wriggled back up the bank with the Schmeisser, parted the reeds and papyrus, and looked out across the plain.

The remaining five men were moving slowly forwards, covering each other with bursts of fire as they raced from the bush. Haston switched the Schmeisser regulator to single-shot and started to fire back, aiming carefully at the bushes from which the puffs of smoke were rising until the magazine was empty. He didn't know if he'd hit anyone but briefly the advance had been stopped and the hidden figures were stationary. Then he slid down the bank again.

The situation wasn't simply bad, it was hopeless, and he explained it to Alison, swearing savagely all the while at what he'd done. With ammunition they might have held the men off until dark and then escaped across the lagoon. But the cartons of shells had been too heavy to carry and at most they'd got enough bullets left for another two or three magazines. When those were exhausted they'd be finished. It would be a shotgun against five rifles and the ending would be a matter of minutes.

'Couldn't we try to swim now?' Alison asked.

He shook his head. 'Take us fifteen minutes to cross that stretch. They'd pick us off in the water long before we made it to the other side — '

Haston paused and glanced at the reeds curving away to left and right of them.

'I guess the only chance is a channel or a land-link. You get back up where I was with the repeater. It's on single-shot. Keep it like that. Fire wherever you see smoke, take it slow and make every goddam bullet count. I'll cast along the bank.'

He gave her the Schmeisser, Alison scrambled upwards and Haston splashed through the water.

Right was useless. They were at the head of a low promontory and another wide expanse of lagoon stretched away for as far as he could see. He turned, went back and tried the left. It was equally useless – further open water reaching into the distance.

Haston began to swing back and checked. A stake was projecting just above the water in front of him with what looked like a fibre cord on the surface beside it. He waded forwards. It was

263

a cord and it was attached to something in the reeds. He pulled, the reeds stirred and rustled, then a blunt wooden object emerged floating low in the water.

Haston knew what it was instantly. The bow of a *makoro*, the dug-out canoe used by the delta bushmen. This one had probably been left there by a group away hunting. He pulled harder and the whole boat appeared and suddenly, in place of the furious despair he'd felt a moment before, there came a surge of excitement and determination.

'Here, give it to me — '

He was back on the bank beside Alison with the last of the magazines in his hand.

She passed him the Schmeisser, he flicked the regulator to automatic, changed the almost-empty magazine she'd been using for the full one, and sprayed quick drumming bursts in an arc across the plain. Smoke billowed up from the barrel and the roar was deafening.

'Now run!'

Haston had her by the hand again. They tumbled down the bank, stumbled through the water and reached the boat.

'Get into the front, kneel and use one of these — '

Haston was already kneeling in the stern with two flat wooden paddles in front of him. Alison climbed into the bows, he passed her one of the paddles, wrenched the mooring cord away from the stake and drove the *makoro* out into the lagoon.

'Those bursts should have slowed them up, given us maybe three or four minutes before they move again. By then we've got to be in the reeds on the other side. So hit it hard!'

Sweating, panting, Haston thrust his paddle into the water and pulled it back along the gunwhale. Alison dipped hers into the lagoon on the other side of the boat and they rippled forwards.

Haston had no idea how long it took. He jabbed at the water, heaved, strained and jabbed again. In front Alison was doing the same. He could see sweat darkening the back of her shirt, smell the sweet powdery scent of the lilies, feel the heat scorch down from above and bounce back off the surface, dazzling his eyes. Every second he expected to hear the crack and whine of a rifle bullet. There was nothing. Only glittering spray and the calls of eagles and the searing aching effort as they drove the boat on.

And then suddenly there were reeds and papyrus all round them, brushing lazily across their bodies, and broken shadow and *makoro*'s bow bumping against the sand. Haston swung himself out and stood thigh-deep in water, arms trembling and lungs gasping, looking back.

They were completely hidden but through the wavering green and brown screen he could make out the far bank. As he watched a figure appeared, then a second, then a third. One of them jumped down, cast left and right, hesitated obviously confused, and finally climbed back up. The tracker. There was a short conference, the voices drifting faintly across the lagoon, and the three men vanished.

Haston lashed the mooring cord to a clump of reed and waded forward to where Alison was standing on the dry sand.

'They haven't got the guts to swim – Jesus, most of them can't swim anyway. So they'll try to make a detour like we were going to —'

He stopped. Alison wasn't listening to him. Her chest was heaving like his but she was still gazing through the reeds at the other bank – concentrating all her attention on the point where the men had disappeared.

'Jerry,' she swung towards him. 'You saw those men?'

Haston nodded. 'Sure.'

'One of them was George Mlanda.'

The wave of elation Haston had felt the moment before subsided instantly.

Then he said, 'It couldn't have been. Mlanda's not out there, you said so yourself —'

'He wasn't, Jerry,' she cut him off, 'but he is now. I've spent over three weeks living very close to him and I know what he looks like beyond any possible doubt. I must be one of the very few white people who do, but to me he's unmistakable. He was the one with the beard on the right of the other two.'

Haston hadn't noticed any of the three faces. All he'd registered were the figures clustered against the sky and the oily

265

sheen of the rifles in the hands of two of them.

'What the hell does that mean?' he asked.

She shook her head. 'I don't know. But he's strong, Jerry, in his own quiet angry way he's one of the strongest men I've ever met. The others might have got discouraged, might have given up. Not George Mlanda. Once he's got his teeth into something he won't let go.'

Haston swore. Alison had just jettisoned a hope which had begun to grow ever since the *makoro* had nudged into the reeds – that confronted by the lagoon the terrorists would abandon the pursuit. As far as he could see the water stretched back for at least half a mile on either side of the island. A detour would take the blacks a couple of hours. By then dusk would be closing in and even if they managed to work their way round to this new island, they'd still have the problem of finding the spoor again.

On their own, without Mlanda to drive them on, they'd probably have given up. But they weren't on their own, Mlanda was there to push them forwards and whether they found the spoor-line tonight or after dawn tomorrow, they'd come on again.

'Well,' Haston said. 'Whatever that bastard does we're still in concession territory, we've got forty miles to the desert and maybe an hour before the animal starts tonight's run. We need to be right by the mopane when it checks out.'

He picked up the shotgun, their only weapon now that the Schmeisser ammunition was exhausted, and pushed through the papyrus towards the clump of trees into which the leopard had climbed at dawn.

Darkness came, then night – and it was like the one before. Hour upon hour of wheeling stars, moonlight, bitter air, icy channel and stream, raking thorn, crisp frosted grass-plain, reed and bush and scrub. The same menace in the shadows, the same chilling roar of prowling lion, the same desperate thrashing of water as some crocodile prey stained the surface black, the same lunge and snort and crash as hippo or buffalo smashed through the undergrowth, the same haunting calls of owl and

266

jackal and hyena.

And throughout it all, as they walked and searched and waded and swam, the leopard's spoor led inexorably onwards. Printed deep and firm on the islands, blurring fugitive, elusively, in marsh, vanishing in wind-blown ripples across water. But seen or unseen, always there in front of them, as permanent, unvarying and inflexible as the movement of the constellations above.

The night passed, dawn tugged at the horizon in building waves of grey and rose and oyster-white, the chill softened, Haston and Alison, wearier, more drained and limp and aching than the morning before, stumbled, slowed and stopped. They could see the leopard in front of them, a black sinuous shape, panting and exhausted too, against the bare winter grass. Fifty yards beyond the animal was a single knotted acacia spearing out from a litter of limestone rocks.

The leopard circled the rocks, urinated and hauled itself up the trunk.

'One more night to go,' Haston said.

Alison nodded, too tired even to speak, walked slowly over to a small bush and lay down against it. Haston followed her. Whatever had happened to the blacks he knew there was no chance of staying awake. He dropped onto the grass beside her and within minutes they were both asleep.

This time there was no question of it being accident or instinct – it was sound. They both heard it and woke at the same moment. The hum of a plane approaching low and close from the south. Haston leapt up and gazed rapidly round them. Apart from the rocks where the leopard was resting there was no proper cover within a hundred yards.

'Push yourself as far as you can in between the roots.'

He crouched against her frenziedly trying to arrange the thin branches over them. If it was a safari plane on a routine supply flight to a fixed hunting camp, they probably wouldn't be noticed. But if it was a serious search they hadn't a hope – the bush was too small and thin and they'd be spotted instantly.

Haston peered up as the noise grew louder.

It wasn't a safari plane. He knew that even before it swept

overhead only a hundred feet above them. No safari pilot would fly as low as that. It was a single-engined Cessna and the wing markings had been painted out and there were two men in the cockpit, both with their faces pressed against the canopy as they searched the ground below.

Haston buried his head in Alison's back, pressing her against the earth, but it was pointless. The engine note changed as the pilot suddenly banked, the plane flew over them twice again, then it vanished back towards the south.

'Hell!'

Haston stood up shaking his head in fury and frustation. Alison got to her feet beside him.

'The South Africans?'

He nodded. 'Can't be anyone else, not with those wing markings painted out. And it had to be them anyway. Once they'd put their men into Maun they were bound to go on. Maun was the tricky part. This is easy. You can hide a goddam army out there – trucks, planes and all – and no one's going to know.'

'What do you think they'll do now?'

Haston glanced at his watch. It was four o'clock – two hours to dusk.

'Depends on how close their back-up is and what they've got,' he said. 'There'll be radio contact between that pilot and the guys on the ground. If they figure they can make it here before dark, they'll come straight on. If they're too far back they'll wait until tomorrow.'

'Which gives us another chance?'

Haston nodded again. 'Meantime, all we can do is wait too.'

The site was like the one they'd stopped at yesterday, an open island bordered by lagoons. They knelt back to back on the grass, not speaking, not even daring to hope, simply watching the reed on either side of the plain and listening. An hour passed, the sun lowered towards the horizon, their shadows lengthened, then they heard the noise again – a distant mechanical hum only now it was on the ground and approaching them from two directions.

Haston cocked his head and frowned. Then he realized what it was and looked at Alison.

'Motor launches,' he said. 'Maybe fifteen minutes off. Two of them at least, could be more. I guess they'll send one ahead to block the other side, then they'll come in.'

He stopped. He'd long since lost count of the days, even the reasons for what he'd done were suddenly blurred and unimportant. All he knew was that it had been a war. A solitary private war of attrition and defiance. He'd been caught up in it by accident. Alison had made him her ally, reluctant at first, then filling him with her own passionate commitment, and afterwards they'd fought it together. Across the northern desert, past lake Ngami, into the heart of the delta.

And together they'd survived every assault, beaten off every attack, won every skirmish and engagement and battle. Until now. Now, at the very end, they'd been defeated, the war was over and the bitterness in his voice welled over his entire body, bleak and acid and sour.

Alison was still looking over his shoulder at the reeds. She opened her mouth to say something, suddenly hurled herself forward instead, grabbed his arm and dragged him to the ground. At the same instant a rifle cracked and a bullet whistled overhead.

'It's Mlanda's men—'

Haston was on his back with Alison sprawling across his stomach and her voice was muffled against his shirt.

'Two of them coming through the reeds.'

Haston rolled away from under her, got to his knees and peered through the grass.

'Which side?'

'Left—'

As she spoke the rifle cracked again. This time the bullet smashed into the earth a few feet in front of them, raising a spray of sand and shattered root fragments.

'Move,' Haston said urgently. 'They've marked where we dropped and they're firing blind.'

He crawled away to the right with Alison behind him. Twenty yards away he stopped, panting and sweating. Occasional bullets were still slamming into the ground round the clump of scrub, but they were well clear of it now.

Haston lifted his head slightly and listened. Between the shots he could hear the throb of the motor-launch engines – barely five minutes away across the swamp. Then the firing stopped, there were confused shouts followed by distant rustles and splashes, and the motor launches came closer still.

'What's happening?' Alison was kneeling beside him.

'I guess they're positioning themselves to meet the boats,' Haston said. 'Those blacks don't know they're up against an armed South African unit. They probably figure it's just a hunting party they can rub out and then come after us again. It's much the same for the whites.'

'But they'll have seen Mlanda's men from the air, just like they saw us — '

'They'll have seen a bunch of blacks, that's all. Most likely they thought it was a gang of poachers. Sure, they'll have heard the shots but that could still be poachers. Any minute now and both lots are going to find out different.'

The launches were less than two hundred yards away and their engines were echoing over the hidden water.

'Where does that leave us, Jerry?'

'Right goddam here,' he answered. 'There's no cover which means we can't move. So we'll sweat it out where we are, we've got no choice. We'll let them collide and when they've argued it through, whichever group ends up in front gets us for dessert.'

Alison began to speak but the firing suddenly erupted again and drowned her voice.

The noise was coming from both sides of the island and Haston realized the South Africans must have landed. Single shots mingled with drumming fusillades, there were shouts, cries of pain, the crashing of plunging bodies in the reeds, the roar of an accelerating motor-launch engine to their right, the desperate floundering of someone in the lagoon, the bark of a hand-gun and a choking scream.

Haston lay beside Alison pressed flat against the sand with the grass wavering above them. He kept the shotgun angled out in front of him with the safety-catch off, but it was useless. There was nowhere they could go now, nothing they could do

270

except wait helplessly while the battle raged a hundred yards ahead and then, when it was finished, ignominiously give themselves up to whoever had won.

'Jerry —'

Alison was tapping his shoulder, her voice raised above the uproar.

'They're coming closer, aren't they — ?'

Haston lifted his head, listened and nodded.

The blacks had had the benefit of surprise when the first shots were fired, but now the heavy automatics of the South Africans were outgunning them and the terrorists had started to fall back along the bank of reeds and papyrus towards the tip of the island. Every moment the noise of gunfire was drawing nearer to where they were lying.

'Can you get the leopard to move?'

Haston looked at her startled. 'What do you mean?'

'I've been watching the tree. The animal's still there. If you fired the shotgun, would that drive it on?'

He glanced back at the acacia. 'Probably. But I'd have to be up close and there's fifty yards between —'

'Listen, Jerry,' Alison was almost shouting now over the drum and crackle of the guns. 'In a few minutes the leopard's going to break. If it comes down the tree with one of the blacks in range, the animal's dead. They'll just blast it off the rocks. We've got to shift it.'

'Look, I told you, there's fifty open yards —'

'Then give me the shotgun.'

She reached for the gun, Haston snatched it back.

Her hair was matted with sweat and dust, her face and arms were raw from mosquito bites and the slashing thorns, her shirt and jeans were ragged and tattered and rank. She looked like a scarecrow again, blood-spattered and filthy, but her eyes, dark, unblinking, intense, were staring back at him with the same implacable purpose and defiance that he'd seen so often since he'd pulled her stumbling out of the tent.

Haston swore, gathered himself crouching on the balls of his feet and raced zig-zagging bent double through the grass towards the rocks. Dimly he knew Alison was behind him. He

271

reached the rim of the outcrop and slithered to the ground. The gunfire was still crackling over the plain but as far as he could tell no shots were being aimed at them.

'Listen — '

Haston checked the breech quickly and snapped it shut.

'When I fire there get to be two possibilities. Either the animal moves – or it charges. Most animals, they'd just shift whatever. But these cats are different. They're the wildest, the most unpredictable. If that leopard charges I shoot again – and that means shooting to kill.'

'We've taken all the other risks, Jerry,' she said quietly. 'We'll take this one.'

The balance had shifted again. Alison had been in charge on the run through the desert, he'd taken over when they reached the delta, now the leadership had reverted to her. And coolly, indomitably, ruthlessly, she'd decided to pluck from the wreckage the one thing that had driven her from the start – the leopard's life.

He raised himself up and eased his way forwards over the rocks. Five yards from the tree he squatted, lifted the gun and squeezed the trigger, aiming at the base of the trunk. As the sound of the explosion rippled away there was a furious threatening growl from inside the shadowy leaves and branches.

Haston waited. The branches crackled, the leaves stirred, but there was no sign of the leopard. He slipped another cartridge into the breech, raised the barrel slightly and fired again. This time the animal was goaded into moving. It plunged down, whirled round, balanced itself on the earth and crouched facing directly towards him.

Apart from the echoing rifles there was no sound at all – only the glittering agate-coloured eyes framed by the black fur, the great fangs showing white against the half-open mouth, the talons quivering in the sand, the massive shoulders and haunches poised to spring.

Haston held the gun steady at his shoulder. He'd had countless animals, from buck to lion to elephant, fixed at that range in his gunsights before and he knew beyond any doubt which of

272

them would charge and which would turn and run. This cat was going to charge. He saw the muscles begin to bunch, he smelt a thick feral stench on the air as the leopard exhaled, he heard the rasp of its pads on the ground as the animal gathered itself to leap.

Haston's finger started to tighten round the trigger, and then suddenly there was something else in front of him – a shadow cast across the sand and rocks by the lowering sun behind. The shadow of a figure – Alison. Haston didn't move and he couldn't see her but he knew she'd come forwards and was standing upright beside him, and the leopard's yellow eyes were no longer staring at his but fixed on a point above his shoulder.

For almost a minute the animal remained there immobile watching Alison's face. Then it snarled, threatened to attack, surging forwards a yard so that Haston's finger was tight on the trigger again, checked, snarled once more and stopped.

Afterwards, very slowly, it began to back away over the rocks into the deepening shadows on the other side of the tree.

'Get down —'

Haston lowered the gun and pulled Alison to her knees as a new wave of gunfire crashed over the plain even closer than before. Then he looked at her.

'Jesus Christ, lady, I don't know what you did or how you did it, but sure as hell you just saved yourself a cat.'

An instant later he froze, threw himself round to face the plain, tension knotting in his stomach. He fumbled to lift the gun again.

It had been a single sound under the echoing volleys, a soft smooth click, but Haston's ears had caught it and he'd recognized it instantly – a rifle's breech mechanism being worked. He scanned the grass and saw the man fifteen yards away racing towards them. Black, bearded, mouth lathered with sweat, face drawn tight with strain and anger, rifle thrust forwards at his waist.

'It's George —'

Alison was kneeling behind him. She gasped out the words in shock, but Haston barely heard her.

'Get your head down!' he shouted.

He flailed out with his arm, pushed her over, swung up the shotgun and fired wildly as Mlanda reached the edge of the rocks. There was a dull snap and that was all. Vaguely, Haston realized water must have got into the cartridge as they crossed one of the channels. He scrabbled at the breech but it was too late. Mlanda stopped, steadied himself, raised the rifle and fired.

Haston never knew whether Mlanda had aimed at him or the leopard. There was a detonation, a rolling screen of smoke, the bullet ricocheted clear off the stones, and suddenly something was soaring over them in a rippling black arch – something vast and murderous and silent. Haston smelt the raw stench again, heard an enraged growl as the animal landed, then the leopard was springing once more – talons raking Mlanda's chest and jaws tearing at his neck.

Haston stumbled to his feet. Mlanda was swaying with the two hundred pounds of the leopard enveloping him like a dark cloak. He reeled back, staggered and then just before he fell Haston saw his eyes. They were glazed with terror. The nightmare which had prowled his dreams had leapt unseen from the shadows, not a fantasy any more but a clawing, savaging, snarling presence of tooth and bone and muscle. He began to topple, his legs buckled and he pitched backwards with not just a single animal but the entire desert crushing down on him.

Alison was beside Haston now. There was nothing except a violent thrashing turbulence in the long grass, the fragmented sheen of black fur, blood tossed up in jets against the darkening sky, the terrible grunting snarls, a helpless moan that rose for an instant to a shriek of agony and then faded into silence under the canopy of the rifle fire.

Then the leopard padded out of the grass, carefully licked its dripping muzzle and stopped five yards away from them. In the dusk it was darker, more shadowy and fugitive than ever. Only its eyes glowed hard and fierce and bright in the ebony mask that was blurring now with the rustling twilight stems. It opened its mouth and roared, a long drawn-out howl of warning and threat to the coming night.

Afterwards it turned suddenly and vanished towards the north and all that was left was the print of its body fading on the winter grass.

'Haston!'

A voice shouting, a South African voice, clipped and harsh and nasal. Haston dropped to his knees and tugged Alison down beside him again. The firing had stopped and a man was walking towards them across the plain.

'That's far enough,' Haston called back.

The man was twenty yards from the rocks. He checked, a big burly silhouette against the first stars, and raised his hands to show he wasn't armed.

'We're all round you,' the man shouted. 'We got you every side. If you're thinking about the blacks, forget them – we hit them all. You come out with the lady now and we'll make it easy. But you figure on trouble and I tell you, man, you'll get burned.'

'You stay where you are,' Haston called again.

Then he glanced at Alison. 'The animal's safe but there's no way we're going to get past this lot.'

She nodded. 'I'm sorry, Jerry.'

'Sorry? For what?'

'We were going to come back in triumph with a new species and you'd keep your licence. I can't fix that now.'

'Let's stick to what matters. There's a bunch of bastards out there. They've murdered Ben and probably Charlie as well. They'll be itching to chop me into little pieces. You just see they keep their hands off and that'll do fine.'

'No one's going to lay a finger on you, Jerry, while you're with me and I'm staying with you. And if he's alive, Charlie will soon be free. I can promise that. But it's not as much as I'd hoped.'

Haston shifted the gun to his other hand and touched her cheek.

'Listen,' he said. 'Sure, I lost a licence. But I found a lady and a goddam leopard too. I'll settle for them.'

She smiled. 'That's enough?'

'Well, I could wish these creeps hadn't won out. But apart

275

from that, the hell with it, sure it's enough.'

Alison thought for a moment. Then she stood up.

'They won't win out altogether,' she said.

Haston climbed stiffly to his feet and they walked forwards.

Hoar-frost was settling on the grass and the sky was changing from pearl to green and then to evening gold as the rim of the sun dropped behind the reeds. Dimly, through the gathering trails of mist, he could see other South Africans ranged on either side of the island.

'Miss Welborough-Smith — ?'

They'd reached the tall man who'd been waiting for them. He had close-cropped grizzled hair and pale eyes in an angry stone-coloured face. Alison paused and nodded.

'My name's Colonel Schlietvan,' he said. 'I'm glad we finally got you safe back. We'd like a long talk with you later but right now I'd appreciate one thing. You knew George Mlanda?'

She nodded again.

'A couple of minutes ago,' he went on. 'One of my men found a body. I don't wish to distress you – the man has been mauled to death by a lion or a leopard – but I wish to know if you recognize him. We believe Mlanda was leading those blacks, but we have no photographs or any other means of identifying him.'

'I won't be distressed.'

'Thank you.' Then he glanced at Haston and snapped, 'You wait over there — '

'Mr Haston stays with me,' Alison interrupted quietly. 'He stays with me wherever I go.'

Schlietvan looked at her for a moment puzzled, wary, furious. Then he walked over to the stained and trampled grass near the rocks. Alison followed him with Haston behind her. She stopped, glanced down and stood for a while in silence.

'No, Colonel,' she said finally. 'That's not George Mlanda, it's nothing like him. I have no idea where Mlanda is now. What I do know is that it will be very difficult, probably impossible, for you ever to find him — '

She paused, looked up and added, 'Now I should like to go home.'

Alison turned, took Haston's hand and set off towards a motor launch whose prow was glistening white in the darkening air between the swaying papyrus.

21

The leopard stepped fastidiously through the shallow stream, bounded up the low bank on the far side and began to lick the droplets of water from its legs.

Several times earlier that night, like the night before, the animal's entire body had been submerged as it swam the rivers and lagoons between the areas of raised bush. But as the night wore on and it travelled further north, the water level had dropped, its body fur had dried through evaporation and now only its legs were wet.

The leopard was drying them with its tongue because it knew from the dawn wind there was no more water ahead. The stream the animal had just crossed marked the northern limit of the delta. In front now there was only desert – another vast expanse of rock and sand and thorn.

It licked off the last drops, its tongue rasping across the soft black fur on the underside of its haunches, lifted its head and sniffed the early morning air.

For a long while in addition to the unvarying scents of the bush the leopard's brain had become patterned to interpret and accept other alien smells. The foetid odour of human sweat, the harsh fumes of burning petrol, the mingled stench of fire-smoke and roasting meat. Now, for the first time in four months, all of those smells were absent.

Also absent was another scent and the physical presence that had accompanied it, both printed so deep by then on the animal's consciousness that they were as much part of its orientation to daybreak as the paling stars, the morning wind and the frost on the sand. The scent and presence of the woman.

Instead the wind carried only the tangled spore-vapours cast up by the desert with the approach of day. The bitter tang of the night's chill. Fresh urine from a hyena pack's lair. Resin off a thorn branch broken by fighting zebra stallions. Wildebeeste and sable excrement. The sweetness of some far-off rotting fragment of carrion. The clear clean smell of the air itself at the point of balance between cold and heat.

All those and more – and then suddenly something else.

The leopard's ears pricked, its nostrils twitched, it raised a paw, snarled uncertainly, started forwards and then drew back, crouching flat on its stomach with its tail twitching delicately from side to side.

The scent was old and faint and distant, the lingering trace of another leopard which had passed that way days or even weeks before. Yet it sent violent troubled tremors coursing over the leopard's body. The leopard snarled again, arched its head back and began licking once more – not at the few remaining drops of water but hungrily at the cleft in its groin.

Afterwards, it sprang to its feet, stood for an instant, black and tense and quivering against the sky, then it surged away towards the north.

Before the leopard had always travelled at a steady loping trot.

Now, as the stars faded and the desert light welled up, it stretched out in wild urgent gallop.